# CONFLAGRATION

MICK FARREN

# CONFLAGRATION

A TOM DOHERTY ASSOCIATES
BOOK
NEW YORK

CONFLAGRATION

Copyright © 2006 by Mick Farren

A Tor Book
Published by Tom Doherty Associates, LLC
175 Fifth Avenue
New York, NY 10010

www.tor.com

Tor® is a registered trademark of Tom Doherty Associates, LLC.

Library of Congress Cataloging-in-Publication Data

Farren, Mick.
    Conflagration / Mick Farren.—1st ed.
        p. cm.
    "A Tom Doherty Associates book."
    ISBN-13: 978-0-765-31363-8 (acid-free paper)
    ISBN-10: 0-765-31363-4 (acid-free paper)
    1. Youth—Fiction. I. Title.
    PS3556.A7727C66 2006
    813'.54—dc22

                                    2005033829

First Edition: June 2006

Printed in the United States of America

0   9   8   7   6   5   4   3   2   1

This book is for Ken Matsutani and Yukiko Akagawa,
who opened the portal to a new world for me.

# CONFLAGRATION

# ONE

## CORDELIA

Lady Cordelia Blakeney tightened her hold on the gray gelding. The horse could sense the excitement. Its ears twitched, its head nodded, and the animal snorted and dug divots from the already trampled turf with its front hooves. The reins were tautly looped between her gloved fingers, in which she also clasped her silver-mounted crop. She hardly expected to need the whip, however. Despite the gelding, the horse had spirit, and was more than ready to run, given the slightest chance. She had been particular in her selection of a mount. The lieutenant in charge of the remuda had been told to put her on a gelding for her own safety, but a bribe of folded banknotes to the groom made sure it was one with some fire remaining in its blood.

"Easy, boy, easy."

All around her, horses and men were galvanized by an abrupt departure from the routine into which both had fallen during the previous two weeks. The sun was high in the sky, but the Army of Albany had halted. The long columns of infantry and cavalry, men and munitions, machines, wagons, and heavy guns no longer moved south, as they had done for the last fifteen days. Instead, they stood and waited, as mounts grew skittish and a collective excitement mounted. Gallopers and runners came and went, while flankers and outriders moved in close. In the ranks, the swaddies and sloggers exchanged speculation and rumor, while the engines of the motorized vehicles idled, coughed, and belched exhaust. The mounted scouts had returned that mid-morning, confirming the reports already relayed by wireless from the airships. The enemy, in full retreat all the way from Richmond, had finally stopped, and looked to be turning, preparing to face their pursuers. Simultaneously, much farther to the south, reinforcements had been observed, coming at a forced march from the Mosul beachhead in Savannah where, three years earlier, the hordes of Hassan IX had first landed in the Americas, bent on invasion and conquest. The battle that both sides had been anticipating all winter appeared to be upon them.

"Easy, easy."

Cordelia did her best to gentle the restive horse, while shading her eyes from the sun and gazing with extremely mixed feeling at the low, wooded hills that formed their immediate southern horizon. The trees were green with first spring leaf. The Virginia countryside surged with unfolding life, but the Albany advance had intruded into this season of growth with khaki ranks of marching soldiers and their trucks and automobiles, the belching steam of fighting machines, and the unnatural insect-noise of the airborne biplanes that buzzed overhead on their mysterious missions. The fresh April grass had been churned under the hooves of two thousand horses, and the boots of more than ten times that number of men, and then double-gouged by rubber tires, wooden wheels, and iron caterpillar tracks. The only excuse that Cordelia could make to the Goddess for the way in which they were despoiling the newly unfolding year was that the Army of Albany was not the first to make its mark. They were only following the scars of destruction already left by the hordes of the Mosul Empire, as they pulled back after spending a grim winter under an intermittent barrage of Albany rocket bombs, starving in the bunkers and trenches they had dug in the frozen ruins of Richmond, the same city the invaders had themselves burned to the ground just two years earlier.

This trail left by the enemy was more, however, than just the imprint of boots and wheels and the hooves of war horses. The withdrawing

Mosul had marked their passage with all of the debris of desperation and defeat. Abandoned equipment, burned-out and broken-down vehicles, plus the bodies of the dead or scarcely living, who had been unable to march or even crawl any farther despite the commands of their officers, or the barks, kicks, and blows of their squad leaders. In the first days of the retreat, the Albany pursuers saw how the Mosul stragglers had been hanged, flogged, or shot; but then, as the speed of the Mosul flight quickened, they had simply been left to the mercy of Albany, if they were able to fend off the ravens and carrion crows that followed the exodus like nature's undertakers. In the first days, most of these Mosul dead and left-behind had either been executed, or simply dropped from exhaustion, but as the slow pursuit moved into its second week, increasing numbers were victims of the ceaseless nighttime raids by hit-and-run units of either the Albany Rangers or the irregular commando groups of mountain men, freebooters, and former resistance fighters from the previously occupied territories, who moved ahead of the main force to harry and harass the already demoralized foe.

These growing numbers of enemy dead and dying had the unfortunate effect of slowing the Albany advance, and they had also put considerable strain on the quality of any Albany mercy. The elaborate cruelty of the Mosul occupation and the atrocities performed in the name of Hassan IX and the hideous twin gods Ignir and Aksura were fresh in every Albany memory. As they moved deeper into liberated Virginia, the spectacle of ravaged towns and villages, the skeletal remains on roadside gibbets, and the long hummocks of earth, not yet fully grassed over, covering the mass graves of slave laborers, made sympathy extremely difficult, even for the lowest and most wretched captives. After more than three years of war, no illusions and precious little pity remained. Had the united people of Albany, highborn and low, not turned back the invaders at the Battle of the Potomac, they, too, would be suffering the same fate as all the others who had come under the domination of the Mosul Flame Banner in what had once been the Southland Alliance, the Republic of the Carolinas, or the Virginia Freestate. With the crucial, if formally neutral, help of the Norse Union, the Kingdom of Albany had prevented Hassan's vast army from crossing the wide river that marked its southernmost border, but each and every citizen knew that, if they had failed, if the Mosul's northern thrust into the Eastern Americas had continued unchecked, they would right now be under the grinding, inhuman heel of the Mosul military and the religious oppression of the feared and hated priests and agents of the Zhaithan Ministry of Virtue.

This knowledge made sympathy for Hassan's discards hard to summon, and compassion was made even harder by the numerous and deadly booby traps that the Mosul rearguard had sown in their wake. Earlier that morning, three privates of the 14th Foot had, against their sergeant's better judgment, attempted to move the body of a dead child out of the path of a column of lorries, and had been blown to pieces by a brace of concealed grenades beneath the infant's corpse. Then, just before dawn, a grazing horse, uncomfortably close to Cordelia's tent, had put its foot on a landmine. Apart from being killed instantly, it had triggered an angry and totally unwanted stand-to. An extra element of horror was added by not all of the traps being simply explosives or woodland pitfalls with sharpened stakes, dug for the unsuspecting or careless. Two days previously, a cluster of Dark Things had appeared out of nowhere and totally consumed a luckless latrine detail, and, in so doing, provided a reminder that, although Albany might be far in advance of the Mosul in science and technology, they had nothing like the same command of those other dark and unearthly realities.

When the first booby traps had been fatally sprung, and word of the first casualties spread through the army, rage had boiled over. Fifty prisoners had been massacred out of hand, and three captured Zhaithan had been doused with petroleum and burned alive by a crowd of Albany engineers who, vengeful and drunk, had surrounded them as they died, laughing and jeering at the Mosul screams, and demanding to know how they liked those sacred flames. Cordelia had herself been a prisoner of the Zhaithan, but even she thought mob reprisal was fractionally extreme. So apparently did the King himself. Carlyle II had sent word that no Mosul prisoner was to be harmed, even the hated Zhaithan priests, although all captured agents of the Ministry of Virtue were to be held under close guard for interrogation. His words were repeated to the entire army, sent in writing to the officers, and read aloud to the ranks by senior noncoms with particular emphasis given to the final sentence.

*"We treat our captured opponent with humanity, otherwise we are no better than him."*

The order had been somewhat reluctantly obeyed, although the grim joke was that, since the King's pronouncement, the Rangers and irregulars has ceased taking prisoners during their night raids. More than one junior officer had repeated the observation that "if no Mosul is taken alive, the question of our humanity doesn't really arise."

Cordelia, on the other hand, tried not to think too hard about the unpleasantness. All winter, she had trained hard for a multitude of nastiness in multiple realities, and she needed any break that the expedition south might offer. She felt she deserved an interlude of silliness and narcissism after the long winter of a seclusion of intense study and physical self-discipline. Although a military operation, the advance into Virginia was not without its compensations and diversions. By day, they pressed forward in pursuit of the Mosul but, when they camped each night, except for those officers who were out on patrol or pulling guard duty, the wine flowed, food was good and plentiful, a portable phonograph played the latest cylinders from London, New York, and Copenhagen, and the conversation was bright and flirtatious. After the sun had set, Cordelia was almost able, if she carefully ignored incidents like the horse and the boobytrapped baby, to pretend that the whole exercise was nothing more than the prewar royal court on an extended country excursion. Being a military operation, the men greatly outnumbered the available women, but Cordelia hardly saw this as a drawback. Inevitable al fresco sexual couplings occurred, and as long as they were conducted with a modicum of discretion, the high command saw no reason to notice or comment. Cordelia, always a realist at heart, was also well aware that the diversion would be highly transitory. The Mosul would eventually be compelled to turn and fight, if only by the need of their commanding general, the notorious Faysid Ab Balsol, to save face, and now, as she sat astride her gelding in the spring sunshine and waited for news, that moment appeared to have come. On the other side of the low, tree-covered hills, if the first reports were to be believed, the forces of Hassan IX were now readying themselves to take a stand. After nursing his shattered army through the long Richmond winter, Ab Balsol had gained the reputation of a master of lost causes, and, if he had turned to fight, the party was at an end, and the serious soldiering had begun.

But seriousness was not quite yet upon Cordelia. A young cavalry captain on a bay hunter cantered down the line of horses, and she temporarily put aside her thoughts of battle and her speculation about the immediate future. She saw him first and quickly checked and adjusted her uniform. She knew, without any unreasonable vanity, that she sat a horse well. Although modern warfare was becoming an increasingly drab and camouflaged business, she was also aware that her adapted Ranger uniform showed her off to her best advantage. The characteristic short jacket of the Albany Rangers—dark leaf green with twin rows of polished buttons—squared her shoulders, accentuated her breasts, and was in no way at odds with her red hair and pale skin. Her tan riding breeches were as tight as a second skin, and her high brown boots were shined by her favorite trooper to a rich mirror finish. The entire ensemble was topped off by a soft green forage cap with a maple-leaf cockade, which added just the slightest note of levity. Less amusing was the small-caliber revolver in the flap holster on her belt.

She wore her green jacket with two top buttons undone, and the front panel partially open and folded down. This was the unofficial affectation of Rangers who had seen action behind enemy lines, and, since she had done exactly that, she didn't consider her adoption of it in any way inappropriate. A few unpleasant individuals, mainly jealous courtiers, newly drafted to active service, questioned her right to wear the uniform the way she did. They split hairs over the fact that, during those hideous days and nights when she had been a prisoner of Her Grand Eminence Jeakqual-Ahrach, and when she had made her daring escape from the Mosul camp on the Potomac, she was still technically a humble lieutenant in the Royal Women's Auxiliary. The same malicious gossips also questioned how she had so quickly attained the rank of major, but Cordelia Blakeney dismissed their arguments as being without merit. The fighting Rangers accepted her, and if those hardened and implacable killers wanted to look on her as some kind of mascot and a good luck token into the bargain, the rest could simply shut their mouths. The gossips also had no idea what it meant to be one of The Four.

As the young man came closer, Cordelia made no sign, and only cast the briefest of glances in his direction. She was shorter than most of the riders around her, and he only spotted her at the last minute, but when he did, he quickly reined in his mount, and raised his peaked kepi with a flourish. "Well, well . . . Major Blakeney."

She allowed him only a short, almost curt nod. "Captain Neally."

"Top of the morning to you, ma'am."

Cordelia eased back her shoulders and straightened in the saddle. She was well aware of the effect such a move would have. "And a good morning to you, Captain."

Neally urged his horse forward, and moved up beside her. He gestured to the clear blue midday sky. "We seem to have ourselves another fine day for this adventure, Major."

She nodded for a second time, and allowed herself a faint smile. "Indeed we do, Captain, indeed we do."

The formality of their greetings belied the relationship between Lady Cordelia Blakeney and Captain Tom Neally. The casual onlooker might only have suspected there was more to it when the captain glanced round, quickly and circumspectly, as if checking that no casual onlooker was, in fact, taking note of their exchange. Only then did he permit himself a sly grin. "And how does the morning find you, Major?"

Cordelia had difficulty keeping a straight face. "It finds me . . ."

She was also hard-pressed to censor a lewd giggle that bubbled up inside her. The devilment in her wanted to respond with the unvarnished truth that she was a little hung over from the previous night's champagne, and her muscles still ached from the bone jarring, under-the-stars shaggings to which the captain had treated her just a few hours earlier. Cordelia Blakeney and Tom Neally had become what was known as an item on the third day after they crossed the river, and had remained so ever since.

Every night that their other duties permitted, they would make for the deep, spring-night shadows, pressed close, arm in arm, and, laughing drunkenly, to lose their clothes, and have intense, if maybe temporary sex. They both knew that circumstances would not allow the situation to last, and both were determined to make the absolute most of it. In the light of day, though, they observed all the spurious niceties of the Albany upper classes, and the pretense that such things didn't really happen. If Cordelia ever needed an excuse, which she rarely did, being more than able to rationalize most of her behavior, she would tell herself that it kept the new cycle of dreams away—the bad ones with the uncomfortable white flashes that refused to make any sense.

". . . as well as can be expected, Captain, and eager to see what the day might bring."

"It would seem as though Ab Balsol and his Mosul have found themselves a place to make their stand."

"So I hear. What's the latest word?"

Neally's bay charger and Cordelia's gelding were now almost touching flanks, and their riders' knees were within inches of each other.

"This may be the final battle."

Cordelia studied Neally's face before speaking. Coral Metcalfe, one of her RWA drinking companions, had described him as "a doll, but probably stupid," and Coral's judgment could not be faulted. His jaw was square, his features classically even, his light brown hair, even with an unflattering army haircut, had a definite wave. She recognized that, had she and Neally been together in the city, she almost certainly would have tired of him by now. Cordelia was under no illusions about Tom Neally. He was a lot of fun, but hardly as sharp as a razor. Coral had guessed right: he really was a little stupid, highly uncultured in anything but the sporting pursuits of upperclass young men. What he lacked, though, in finesse, subtlety, or imagination, he made up for in rough energy, stamina, and zealousness. In the urban boudoir this might not have been enough, but deep in the rural darkness, amid the smell of woods and fields, with his weight on top of her, and dew-wet grass or last winter's dead leaves under her naked back and squirming bottom, his relentless and self-sustaining crudity was atavistically apt. No question that, out in the Virginia night, Tom Neally certainly had the knack of reducing her to a shameless and enthusiastically mewing slut, legs spread wide, hair flying, and limbs flailing in abandon.

At various times during the course of the expedition, often while laying beside him, breathing heavily and feeling the cold of the ground creep into her, Cordelia had wondered if, under the circumstances, she should be less exclusive with her favors. Perhaps her taking multiple lovers might have been better for morale, but she had decided that the long-term result would be an even more scandalous reputation than the one she already enjoyed. This certainly seemed to be the case with Hermione Bracewell, another RWA captain, who worked with Coral Metcalfe in coded communications. Hermione was making herself patriotically available to a wide assortment of young officers, sometimes two in the same day, but her patriotism was also becoming the talk of the mess, and, of course, there was Jesamine, Cordelia's companion in The Four, who had taken up with aborigines. Serial monogamy with her own kind seemed to be Cordelia's most comfortable style, and, for the duration, Tom Neally was the monogamous object.

Cordelia tapped the handle of her crop thoughtfully against her chin. Neally might be unsophisticated, but even he could appreciate a woman with a whip. "I always thought one of the first principles of warfare was that he who selected the battlefield was halfway to victory?"

"I think we can concede them that and still come out ahead."

Cordelia raised an eyebrow. "Isn't that dangerously overconfident?"

Neally dismissed the question out of hand. "Ab Balsol and his flatheads are starving and short of everything. All we have to worry about is that some kind of delay allows their reinforcements to reach them."

"So a clock is ticking?"

"You could say that.

"And what is the land like beyond those hills? Is there a reason the Mosul have chosen this particular spot to make their stand?"

Neally hesitated. He once again looked around to see if any attention was being paid to their conversation. Not, this time, to conceal their romantic involvement, but because he might be revealing privileged information. "It is rather a case of need to know."

Cordelia was suddenly irritated. Just a few hours earlier she had been romping uninhibitedly with this oaf, and now he was about to make an issue of describing the disposition of the enemy. "Who the hell do you imagine I'm going to tell? I'm certainly not going to inform the Mosul. They already know where they are. And, anyway, I can order you to tell me. I bloody outrank you, don't I?"

Neally flushed. He didn't like to be reminded that she was a major while he was merely a junior captain. "They've bivouacked in a long valley and are showing no signs of moving on. Approached from the north, it opens broad and then narrows at the far end. And the brass are guessing they'll dig in and let us come to them."

Cordelia grimaced. "Straight into a valley with high ground on either side? Does that mean they'll be pouring fire on our advance from both flanks? Aren't we going into a box?"

"The Rangers and cavalry will sweep the hills."

Cordelia felt a sudden knot in her stomach. She realized that there was a chance that Tom Neally might be one of the ones doing the sweeping, and clearing the high ground in front of the main advance had to be a high-risk assignment. She eased the gelding forward slightly so their knees touched. "Be careful out there, okay? I don't want anything to happen to you."

Neally looked away, suddenly embarrassed by Cordelia's show of concern. "I'll be careful. And you do the same. Whatever you're doing."

Concern again turned to irritation. "You know damned well what I'll be doing."

Tom Neally hung his head, with the look of denial that always came over his face when the subject of her duties came up. Like so many men of Albany, Neally maintained an absolute barrier of disbelief when it came to the other realities. Even those with firsthand experience with Dark Things in the field became profoundly uncomfortable at the first suggestion of the paranormal, and totally refused to accept that Cordelia and the rest of The Four were maybe as crucial to the Albany war effort as any division of infantry. She had been through the "more things in heaven and earth" argument so many times that she was disinclined to repeat it. Overhead, a single rocket bomb inscribed a white vapor-trail trajectory across the blue of the sky, and offered Cordelia a chance to change the subject. "At least we're still pounding them from the air."

"Maybe not."

"What?"

Neally also looked up. "That's maybe another reason the Mosul have turned."

Cordelia frowned. "I don't understand."

"Watch."

The rocket bomb's engine cut out, and the projectile started to fall. It dropped faster and faster until it impacted somewhere on the far side of the wooded hills. A brief fireball rose into the air, the muffled sound of an explosion reached them, and then a column of smoke roiled up like an elongated mushroom. Cordelia attempted to gauge the distance. "It fell short?"

"They're all falling short. The Mosul must know they've moved out of effective range."

The rocket bombs, supplied under the lend-lease, Trans-Ocean treaty between the Norse Union and the Kingdom of Albany, had been a major factor in turning back the invaders. Although the Norse maintained a flimsy neutrality with the Mosul Empire, the exchange of aid with Albany was close to inevitable. Both peoples came from the same stock, they shared culture and customs, and spoke an approximation of the same language. Indeed, the Norse had founded the very first seafaring settlements in the Americas, but for their descendants to engage Hassan IX in open warfare was unthinkable in practical terms. The Norse were far fewer in number than the Mosul, and, even though alliance between the Scandinavian Vikings, the Scotts, the Eiren, and the English of the Islands had lasted a thousand years, they controlled a great deal less territory. The only thing that stopped the Mosul crossing the narrow waters of the English Channel and overrunning them was superior Norse technology and heavy industry. The Mosul, strangled by the constraining coils of their inflexibly brutal religion, had failed to progress. The Zhaithan priests refused to distinguish a scientist from a heretic, and stifled all research and progress. The foundries in Damascus and the Ruhr turned out cannon and musket twenty-four hours a day, but they produced only crude quantity; nothing to compare with the sophistication of the repeating rifles being developed in Birmingham and Stockholm, or the keels of the submarines being laid in the shipyards along the Clyde. Prefabricated parts of Norse gasoline-powered tanks were now crossing the Northern Ocean, being delivered to the Albany port of Manhattan by convoys of cargo ships, and then assembled in a huge roaring factory complex in the city of Brooklyn. Norse Air Corps instructors were training the crews of Albany's first small squadron of airships, and cadres of officers from Albany were attending advanced command schools in London and Stockholm, learning the use of these new weapons on the battlefield and on the high seas. In the final months before the offensive on the Potomac, the Norse had even given Albany their new rocket bombs, and the rest had been history.

"Can't the launching sites be moved?"

Tom Neally regarded the dense column of smoke in the distance. "That's being done, but it's a major undertaking. Building the launchers takes time."

Cordelia remembered the concrete ramps and the steel rails that guided the howling rockets, as their engines ignited and they raced up the track before rising into the air. The installations were major constructions, and there was no way they could be made portable. In theory, dirigible airships could be used to bomb the enemy from the sky, but, in practice, it was impossible. The rigid flying machines with their aluminum and fabric frames and helium-filled gasbags were too slow, too unwieldy, and vulnerable in the extreme to enemy ground fire. Cordelia had learned all about airship vulnerability at painful firsthand in the fall of the previous year, when the NU98 had crashed behind enemy lines with her on board. The Norse-built Hellhound triplane could carry a small bombload, but it was nothing compared with the devastating unmanned rocket bombs that dropped from the upper air with such deadly effect.

In this coming fight, Albany would be without one of its most efficient weapons.

"So this battle will be won or lost on the ground?"

Neally nodded. "That's pretty much the strength of it."

"So when do you and the rest of the cavalry move out?"

He shook his head. "I can't say."

Cordelia sighed with exasperation. "Oh Tom, do stop the dramatic secrecy. This is me you're talking to."

"No, I really don't know. We're waiting for orders."

"Could it be today?"

"There's a chance of that."

She was suddenly anxious. "But I'll see you tonight if you're still here?"

"Of course."

Three riders from Neally's regiment galloped past, and Neally leaned impulsively forward and kissed Cordelia. "Something's happening. I have to go."

He turned the bay, and put his heels to it. The horse started forward, lunging as though eager to be on the move. Cordelia was always amazed how the mounts of the cavalry were so eager for the fight, when the noise and carnage of the battlefield should have repelled all of their natural instincts. Neally turned in the saddle for a final wave. His saber slapped against the bay's flank. The image froze in Cordelia's mind like a still picture. His schoolboy grin, and his broad back in its khaki tunic, with scarlet shoulder boards. She swallowed hard at the sickening realization that the chance existed she would never see him again, and that would be how her memory would always see him. She wasn't in love with Tom Neally, but he was fun. A threat of tears constricted her throat. The gray gelding seemed to sense her unease and again pawed at the ground.

"Easy, damn it. We'll be on the move ourselves soon enough."

In the pocket of her uniform jacket, she had a pair of the new sunglasses from London, the ones with the round, dark blue lenses. She quickly put them on.

## ARGO

A voice called from behind him. "Major?"

Argo Weaver didn't turn. "What is it, Riordan?"

He knew the voice, and he didn't bother to look round. The question was inevitable, and it was impossible to give Riordan the slip. "Should you be all the way out here on your own, young sir?"

Argo sighed. "No, I shouldn't be all the way out here on my own, but I'm not on my own, am I? I have you following my every move."

The rotund Sergeant of Horse spurred up beside him and reigned in his mount. "If you fancy going for a gallop, boy, you only have to tell me."

There were not too many Sergeants of Horse who would address a major as "boy," even a somewhat spurious major like Argo Weaver, but Will Riordan was one of the few. The man rode with ease. It was walking that created problems for him. He had been injured at the Battle of the Potomac when a gun carriage had overturned on top of him, fracturing his hip, and that was why he was now assigned to keep an eye on Argo, and see that he stayed out of trouble. Since the Army of Albany had started south, Argo had tried many times to duck the ever-present eye of Sergeant Riordan, but he had never succeeded. The man was as tenacious as a terrier.

"What the hell do you think's going to happen to me, Will?"

"We don't know that, do we, Major? And that's why the brass have me following after you."

"I can take care of myself."

"Sure you can, but why take the chance? There's old campaigners who've fallen foul of a Mosul booby trap. The bastards are damned clever."

Each of The Four had been assigned a personal guardian, a minder for the advance into what had previously been enemy-held territory. Their strange collective command of the paranormal and their ability to penetrate and operate within other realities made them an important factor in the Albany war effort. "I mean, we can't have you running round loose and taking the risk of running into a pod of Dark Things, or some sneaky Mosul rearguard."

All of The Four found this imposed caution irksome. At first, a great deal of pressure had been brought to bear not to allow them to go south with the army at all. Many of the civilian politicians and a few of the generals had wanted them to remain in Albany, supposedly out of harm's way. After the long winter of grueling training, and the exploration of their powers that had, on occasion, proved close to mind-snapping, none of them was inclined to be left back with the baggage. They had made vocal protests to Yancey Slide and anyone else in authority who would listen. They were trained and combat-hardened. They had held the underground tunnel during the Battle of the Potomac and they had saved the King from the last ditch assault of the Mothmen during the investiture ceremony that had followed. If the war was moving south, what possible reason was there for Albany's most effective paranormal asset to stay behind under wraps? Cordelia had finally made a personal appeal to no less than Prime Minister Jack Kennedy. Cordelia had her own, slightly mysterious, direct line to the Prime Minister. Rumors had long been whispered about an ancient affair between Kennedy and Cordelia's mother. Whatever the truth behind the gossip, she seemed to have the required influence. Kennedy had instructed that they should ride with the army, and, at that point, the argument had ceased, leaving only an insistence from all sides that they should be afforded round-the-clock protection.

Cordelia had also been the first one to balk at the constant for-their-own-good surveillance. On the march down to Richmond, she had been assigned a skinny, masculine RWA corporal, who rode a rawboned, bad-tempered mare that made them two of a kind. Cordelia had, however, become so adept at giving the woman the slip that Slide had devised the ruse of putting a young cavalry captain called Tom Neally in charge of her safety and welfare. He and Cordelia had immediately become lovers, which made Neally's assignment considerably easier. The two of them had been fucking each other's brains out every night since the army had passed Richmond. Cordelia actually believed she was being the soul of discretion, and she had everyone fooled, but the truth was that most of the high command, plus a majority of their fellow officers, were well aware of what was going on. Argo knew from months of experience that

Cordelia could be totally carried away by illusions of her own excessive cleverness.

Raphael and Jesamine, the other two members of The Four, seemed less bothered by the watch that was kept on them. Very little seemed to bother Raphael. The taciturn and withdrawn Hispanian had been a Mosul conscript the previous fall, and Argo could only assume that just about anything would be acceptable after being dragged from his home when barely in his teens, beaten and bullied through Mosul boot camp, and then shipped across the Northern Ocean in an ironclad troopship to serve as cannon fodder in the American war. Through the winter, Argo and Raphael had trained together, bunked together, and even, on a couple of occasions, drunk themselves stupid together, but Argo still did not feel that he really knew his young companion. It may have been a legacy of Raphael having served in Hassan IX's Provincial Levies, or maybe just a facet of his deep and complex nature, but a part of his character seemed to be permanently concealed, even to those who were supposed to be closest to him. He drew in his sketch pad and said little, and no overtures or encouragement seemed able to change that.

Argo could hardly say that he did not know Jesamine. They had started sleeping together almost as soon as the two of them had joined the ranks of Albany, and, although he was loath to admit such a thing openly, she had been his first extended relationship and only the second woman he had ever bedded. Although she was less than a year older than him, the nightmare experience she had suffered as a Mosul prostitute and the concubine of a brutal Teuton colonel had left her with a wealth of carnal experience he might never equal. She had been his erotic mentor, teaching him lessons, and raising him to heights of pleasure that had left him awed. They had shared a hundred secrets and a thousand intimacies, and, for a time, Argo had worshiped her huge dark eyes, her lithe, honey-colored body, and long dark hair, but she, too, seemed to keep a part of her mind closed off. Argo suspected, though, that the same could be said about him. He knew that he had never revealed everything about himself to Jesamine, even at the height of their shared passion. This may well have been a result of also having lived under the harsh rule of the Mosul invaders, when so much had to be concealed just in order to survive, and it could also have been the reason that Cordelia, who had never lived that way, chaffed so hard under the current surveillance while he, Jesamine, and Raphael were more able to take it in their stride.

Jesamine had also taught Argo to drink, passing on the fruits of her long experience, when alcohol had been the easiest and most available way to provide a little insulation between herself and her innate revulsion at being a chattel of the conquerors. At first the drunken nights had been fun—high as kites, rolling and sliding together in bed or elsewhere, their bodies slick with mingled sweat—but then the training of The Four had started, and the affair had ended. Argo and Jesamine had parted on the specific orders of Yancey Slide, their inhuman mentor, but Argo and Jesamine had always known this was the way that it would be. All of The Four knew from experience that sexual energy was one of the metaphysical triggers of their power, and an exclusive romance between two of them simply could not be if they were to function as was expected of them. Knowledge, and the demands of what they had become in this world and the Other Place, did not make the separation any easier. For the first time, Argo had turned to alcohol for solace. Drinking was an after-hours refuge from the emotional pain of having to see Jesamine for most of every day, but never being able to touch except as their duties dictated, and never to feel or taste her. His drinking had caused a certain consternation on the part of Raphael, with whom he shared quarters, but it had seemed better than living with a constant hurt, and mercifully the young and less-than-outgoing young Hispanian had not made mention of it to anyone else. Yancey Slide could hardly have been unaware of Argo's newfound taste for the bottle, but he had also said nothing, and, now that they had started on the march south, Riordan, who watched him constantly, also knew his secret and attempted to ensure that Argo did not indulge to any greater extent than the other young officers who thronged the expedition's mess tents every night.

Argo glanced at Riordan and, not for the first time, wondered what kind of reports the crippled Sergeant of Horse turned in on him, to whom, and what details they might contain. Argo knew that The Four were not only watched for their own protection, but because, on a number of levels, The Four weren't totally trusted. Albany folk had deep misgivings about anything even remotely connected to the paranormal, and were uncomfortable with even talk of the Other Places. The new Americans who had settled along the eastern seaboard of the massive and barely explored continent were materialists in a material world, living in the immediate temporal reality. It was totally understandable. To the west of the settled Kingdoms, Commonwealths, and Republics was a vast interior of great rivers, deep forests, deserts, endless grasslands, and snow-capped mountains. The aboriginal confederacies, tribes, and nations were well-versed in the Other Places, ventured on other planes and in other dimensions, and had quickly recognized the paranormal dangers posed by the Mosul; the horror of the battlefield Dark Things, and all the other hideous conjurations of the Zhaithan that they used alongside their more conventional weapons. The comparative newcomers from across the Northern Ocean had, on the other hand, left their ancient knowledge and former beliefs back in the old world. The Mosul invasion had forced them to reluctantly reconsider the old ways, but they still had serious reservations about those among them who practiced the invisible arts, even if it was in the cause of Albany and the freedom of the Americas.

Argo turned his horse and faced his minder. He gestured to the fields and woods all round them. "I'm back in Virginia, Sergeant of Horse."

"I'm well aware of that, Major Weaver, but aren't we here to be setting its people free?"

"Until less than a year ago, I was one of those people. Our village was small, just a couple of hundred people, but we had our share of Zhaithan hangings, and men and women burned in the fire for no other reason than they helped the sick, and some collaborator denounced them to the Ministry of Virtue."

The Mosul had come to the Americas soon after Argo's eleventh birthday. The invasion force had landed near Savannah on July 5th '96 by the old calendar and, on that hot summer's day, the world he'd known as a child had vanished forever. The Mosul had immediately established multiple beachheads, and then fanned out to cut through the courageous but disorganized forces of the Southland Alliance in a matter of just days.

Within a month, Atlanta had fallen and, with Florida cut off and the infamous treaty concluded with George Jebb and his gang of traitors in St. Petersburg, Hassan IX had turned his attention and armed might to the north, and the rich lands between the Appalachians and the Ocean.

Riordan grunted. "I know the people in Virginia had it hard."

Two hundred years of carnage had come and gone since the Mosul, the descendants of merciless tribal nomads from an area to the east of the Black Sea, had advanced into Europe with fire and sword, and formed their unassailable alliance with the Teutons of Germany and the Mamaluke warlords in North Africa, to subjugate the Land of the Franks, the city states of Italia, and all of the Hispanic Peninsula. The immigrant peoples of the Americas should maybe have taken warning from the Mosul conquests in the old world, but the Northern Ocean was comfortingly wide, and they had believed that it would protect them in their hard-won isolation, and make them immune to the danger. They had grown too confident, however, in their geographic safety, even though many of the American settlers' parents, grandparents, and great-grandparents might have crossed the seas as a direct result of the Mosul threat. When the enemy had landed, they had been no better equipped than the Franks, the Italians, or the Hispanians to resist the murderous onslaught of the most implacable war machine the world had ever had the misfortune to see, and they had been driven down to defeat by the Mosul's iron discipline, fanatic religious motivation, and honed battle tactics.

Argo stared out across the Virginia landscape. "I knew one of the women who went to the fire. I knew her really well. She was a friend of my mother, and she'd helped nurse me when I was sick. I hid in a tall tree with some other boys and watched her burn."

Riordan said nothing, and Argo knew he was losing control in front of the older man, but he was momentarily unable to check himself. "And the drunken bastard who denounced her could well have been my stepfather. His name was Herman Kretch, and he turned her in because she refused to fuck him."

"I hope you took care of him."

Argo thought of the night when he'd stood over the sleeping man with a loaded pistol, but had been unable to pull the trigger. He bitterly shook his head. "I was too young. I just ran away." He sighed. "I think someone else did it, though."

"Just as long as the bastard got his. That's what counts."

Argo indicated the horizon to the west. "Our village was called Thakenham. It's over there somewhere, but I haven't heard a damn thing of my mother and sisters since I ran off."

Riordan looked where Argo was pointing. "That's the way of it, boy, with families divided by war. Not knowing can be a terrible thing, but you're far from being the only one."

Argo remembered how for seven bloody months of his eleventh year, battle after battle had raged, and at the height of the terrible Winter Campaign of '97 it had actually seemed as though the Mosul would be pushed back. The boys of the village had felt a mounting excitement as more and more optimistic rumors had circulated up from the front. But then an armada of troopships, under steam and sail, brought what appeared to be limitless divisions of men and horses and inexhaustible supplies of munitions, and the tide of conflict had turned against the defenders. Fighting a series of desperate rearguard actions, they had fallen back on Richmond, for the last battle. On May 10th, Richmond had fallen, and all hope for Virginia and the Carolinas along with it.

Argo shook his head. "It's getting harder and harder to remember my sisters' faces. I'm not sure I'd recognize them anymore, and I know they wouldn't recognize me."

Riordan let out a short sigh, part sympathetic and part impatient. "Maybe, after the coming fight's done, you'll be able to get yourself some leave and ride over to this Thakenham. Find out for yourself what's happened to them?"

Riordan's mention of the battle that could now be only a day or so away jerked Argo out of his wallow of boy-child self-pity and back into the immediate moment.

"You think this next fight will finish them?"

The Sergeant of Horse nodded. "If we don't fuck up."

"You mean that?"

"Aye, lad. It'll be the end of the Mosul in Virginia and the Carolinas, but it won't be half as easy as some imagine. I heard there were Mosul reinforcements coming up from the south, and it'll go hard for us if they get here in time to link up with the sons of bitches we've followed down from Richmond."

After the two long years of stalemate and occupation, towns and villages like Thakenham accustomed themselves to living under the heel of the Mosul boot, while Albany alone faced the invaders across the Potomac. As Mosul subjects, the boys and girls, like Argo Weaver, had gone through the motions of learning to worship the twin gods Ignir and Aksura, and obey the vast complexity of Zhaithan laws and regulations, as taught by the grownup collaborators, and reinforced by the threat of the punishment stool and the long cane. Times, however, had changed so swiftly and so violently once he'd escaped from Thakenham, he had managed to shut off most memories of how it had been. Caught up in such high adventures, and swimming in the actual flow of history, he had been able to put away the small boy who tried to deal with the daily terror of Mosul rule. Only this return to the lands where he had been born and raised, and the comparative inactivity of the slow advance had allowed it all to come flooding back.

Argo turned in his saddle so he was facing the older man. "Sergeant of Horse . . ."

"Major?"

"Would you happen to be carrying that bottle you usually have with you?"

Riordan glanced up at the sun. "A trifle early, young sir, to be starting on the hard stuff?" Riordan never missed a chance to remind Argo of his comparative youth and inexperience at both soldiering and drinking. "Something ailing you, boy?"

"Memories, Sergeant of Horse. Coming so close to home seems to have let them off the leash."

"Memories, huh?" The crippled sergeant must have felt a twinge of battle-hardened sympathy because he reached into his tunic, produced a half-pint pewter flask, and handed it to Argo. "Have yourself a shot, young Major. Memories can be a damned nuisance, and they can get in the way of what matters at the worst possible time."

Memories, however, were not the only damned nuisance. Argo's dreams had also been a problem. Over the last week or so, a new and sinister cycle of dreams had taken control of his sleep. Senseless and surreal, they had brought repeated, but wholly inexplicable glimpses of brilliant white figures, seeming composed of little more than near-blinding light, that had left him with an uneasy aching in his head that only strong drink seem able to cure.

## JESAMINE

Jesamine held her arms straight out in front of her. Her hands were loosely bound with a length of soft scarlet cord that was part of the ritual. The air in the wickiup was thick with the sweet, pungent smoke that curled up from the bed of hot coals in the upturned Mosul helmet. Her honey-nude skin glistened with sweat in the orange glow, as did the darker bodies of her two companions. The lodge was small and the three of them crouched close. The faces of Oonanchek and Magachee were within inches of her's, and she could feel the slow exhalations of their breathing. Oonanchek had erected the wickiup especially for the event, ensuring that the hallucinations that drifted in and out of the wreaths of smoke were harmonious and benign, and the three naked figures, one male and two female, were completely in tune one with the other. The last fifteen nights had not been without their occasional fears and moments of intensity, but they had also been one of the most pleasurable times Jesamine had ever experienced. Inevitably, though, it was an interlude that was about to end. All three of them knew that, and the ritual through which Oonanchek was currently taking them was designed to sever the temporary *takla* that had held them so intimately during the journey south. With the *takla* dissolved, Jesamine could return to The Four fully prepared for the conflicts to come.

Magachee caressed Jesamine's arms and then moved behind her to massage her shoulders. Oonanchek picked up the hunting knife from the blanket beside him, and Jesamine fancied she could see her own reflection

in the polished steel blade. She looked proud, serious, and darkly beautiful, although maybe that was also hallucination. The two Ohio chanted
softly as Magachee reached forward and cupped Jesamine's breasts with
her hands, and Oonanchek raised the knife to Jesamine's proffered wrists.
Orders were being shouted in some other part of the camp, reminding her
of the violent outside world to which she was preparing to return, and
Oonanchek, sensing the momentary distraction, paused for a moment
before inserting the point of the blade beneath the red cord that bound
her, but then, with a swift, upward stroke, he cut the cord, and Magachee
spun it quickly off Jesamine's wrist, at the same time, speaking softly in
English.

"You are free, sweet Jesamine, to return to your primary companions, to The Four, to your true *takla*."

Impulsively, she turned her head and kissed Magachee. She found
herself suddenly clinging to the young Ohio woman with the long black
hair in an unexpected display of emotional need. "But I don't want to go
back to them."

Oonanchek stroked her hair. "We all have our duty, just as we all are
subject to our destiny."

Jesamine took a deep breath and straightened her shoulders. "Oh, I'll
do what I have to do, if only because I have my pride, but I would still
rather stay here and dream with you forever."

Oonanchek's voice was kind but stern. "We, too, give up our dreams
and face the fight."

Jesamine nodded sadly. "I know."

"But the *Quodoshka* will be with you."

"The *Quodoshka*?"

"You will know."

The briefest of fleeting visions passed through the interior of the
wickiup: a vague, pale shape like that of a loping wolf. Jesamine took a
deep breath. "I will know."

Knowing she would learn no more, there and then, she concentrated on the future. Returning to The Four was not going to be easy.
The others, especially Argo and Cordelia, clearly disapproved of her
spending her nights in the camp of Chanchootok and riding by day with

the warriors of the Ohio, rather than in the ranks of Albany. She was a major in the Albany Rangers, and she wore the same uniform as Cordelia, but she rode among the fringed and beaded buckskins and the elaborate horned and feathered war bonnets of the aboriginal horseman. She could not explain to the other of The Four how she felt more comfortable among the original inhabitants of this new world, or that the other Americans, the ones whose ancestors had come from across the Northern Ocean, were a little too similar to the Teutons for her ever to be at ease with them. She could try to tell them but she doubted that even Argo and Cordelia would understand, and knew for sure that the others of the Albany elite with whom she was forced to associate never would. Their ingrained prejudices were too strong. Of course, the Americans were not cohorts of the Mosul, they chose their own leaders, they did not share the Teutons' inventive cruelty, and they did not own slaves, but, although they would invariably deny it, their inborn snobbery would never totally accept the outsider or the foreigner as an equal. The whispering about Jesamine had started almost as soon as she had arrived in Albany. Even when she had been a heroine, one of the saviors of their King, she had been aware of the strange looks and the slightly condescending way in which the courtiers and government officials spoke to her.

When the Mothmen, the formidable controllers of the Dark Things, had come out of another reality and attempted to assassinate Carlyle II, at the investiture that had followed the Battle of the Potomac, The Four had beaten off the attack. Before that all-too-public incident, the existence of The Four and their unfathomable paranormal abilities had been a closely guarded secret of the Albany High Command and the handful of individuals, like Yancey Slide, the sorceress T'saya, and the Lady Gretchen, who had helped them find each other in the first place. After being forced, however, by the conjuration of the Zhaithan high priest Quadaron-Ahrach, to battle his Mothmen in front of half the army, plus most of Albany's royal court and political aristocracy, the secret of The Four was obviously out. The only alternative was to turn them into a nine-day, morale-boosting sensation. Jesamine called this time of fame and accolades "the honeymoon." Suddenly The Four were Albany's wonderful new weapon against the paranormal iniquities of the Zhaithan. Nothing was too good for them, and they could do no wrong. Invited to parties and galas, and all but put on display, they were the temporary toast of the town, recognized and applauded in the streets of the capital, and with their pictures in *The Albany Morning Post* and *The Albany Banner*. Jesamine had been dazzled and swept along. But then *The Banner* had run those lurid headlines that showed her the unpleasant underbelly of transient acclaim. Leading with "Slave Girl Jesamine's Odyssey of Shame," the cheap and lurid tabloid had told its own highly melodramatic story of her past life. The newspaper had described with relish how, born into poverty in the mountain outlands of the Mamalukes, she had been carried off in a slave raid and sold into prostitution as a featured, house-available whore in a knocking shop on the Cadiz waterfront. *The Banner* had gone to some trouble to point out how her caramel complexion, large dark eyes, and straight silky-black hair had made her a choice prize for the barbaric horsemen who were the Mosul's staunchest ally in Northern Africa, and then salaciously noted that it was these same attributes that had caused her to catch the eye of the cruel Teuton, Colonel Helmut Phaall, who had taken her as his chattel-concubine and carried her in chains to the Americas.

The story pretended to evoke pity for the poor native girl who had been the pathetic sex-victim of the evil Mosul, but the tawdry text, and the drawings that accompanied it, served no purpose but cheap and obvious titillation. *The Banner* had even unearthed the tale of how, in the Cadiz brothel, she had received ten lashes for clipping the purse of a Mamaluke underofficer. A prominently featured artist's impression of the beating had showed her hanging shackled in a Moorish dungeon, being flogged by a subhuman Mosul brute. In actuality, she had been bent over a chair in the whorehouse parlor, with a select group of customers paying top dinar to watch the spectacle, and the thrashing had been administered by a strong-armed madam with a lethally flexible, split-tip, rattan cane, but *The Banner* preferred drama over truth, and, once the paper had gone on sale, the passersby in the street still stared, but they no longer applauded.

Jesamine had wondered often how *The Banner* had come by its information. Cordelia Blakeney had been her closest confidant, but she could hardly believe that Cordelia, even when drinking, would have blurted the gruesome details to a reporter. When they had first met, as prisoners of Her Grand Eminence Jeakqual-Ahrach, a strong affinity had existed between them. It had intensified when they had first come to Albany and, with Argo and Raphael, forged the final links that enabled them to operate as The Four. That Jesamine had been sexually drawn to Cordelia was stating it too strongly, but a degree of girlish attraction had figured in the mix.

Once, though, Cordelia was back in her own familiar environment, the relationship had gradually but inexorably changed. Cordelia was the inevitable belle of her own personal ball, and, equally inevitably, Jesamine had become an exotic accessory, a prop in the growing and deliberately cultivated legend of Lady Cordelia Blakeney, War Heroine and Woman of Mystery. Cordelia had taken to the idea of fame with an unbridled relish, and shamelessly courted the spotlight. Celebrity had caused a widening gulf between them and Jesamine might have felt totally adrift, a stranger in a strange city, had Argo not been there for her. She and Argo had become lovers almost as soon as The Four had found each other, and the relationship had been intense and passionate. They were both in an alien and unfamiliar environment, and also the center of crass and unfeeling attention. Jesamine and Argo had found they could depend on each other when the voices grew too loud and the public whirl too hectic. Argo had needed someone to nurse him back to health after being wounded during the fight with the Dark Things in the tunnel on the Potomac, while Jesamine needed someone to provide her with some sense of permanence and integrity and insulate her from Cordelia's circle of bright young party-goers, decadent aristocrats, and conniving social climbers. In their private interludes she and Argo had the much-needed mutual therapy of being able to laugh at it all, and pretend that it was them against the rest of the world.

Jesamine had brought a concubine's wisdom to the relationship and had taught Argo the tricks of the body and the boudoir. At first, she had worried that her hard-learned expertise would condemn her in his eyes as nothing more than a well-trained slut with a deep bag of tricks, but, to her relief, he had responded with an amazed and boyish delight. Argo had provided a safe midpoint between Jesamine and Albany. He knew all about the dehumanization of Mosul rule, and the shameful compromises needed to survive, but he was also from the Americas and life in Albany was not so very different from his life in Virginia before the invasion. Argo had committed some of the natural gaffes of a country-boy-come-to-town, but he adapted with alarming speed and, although gaps of class would sometimes show, he got along well with the mindless young officers who flocked to Cordelia like moths to a flame, and could hold up his end in their endless conversations about horses, dogs, guns, and women, and also with their seemingly endless drinking.

It had, in fact, been Jesamine who had introduce Argo to the refuge of alcohol, and he had taken to it like the duck in the adage, and drank increasingly more as they were caught up and carried along by the circus of notoriety. The start of their training had, of course, changed everything. They had all known it was going to be that way. They had not been taken to the City of Albany merely to become just a social sideshow. They had been tested in paranormal combat, and although they had prevailed, they knew an infinity of learning was ahead of them. What Jesamine had called the "honeymoon" had been exactly that, a brief respite of vapidity from their deep and dangerous role in the war. And Argo had been part of that honeymoon. Both T'saya and Yancey Slide had made it clear on the very first day. The vibrant sexual energy that played such a part in the linking power of The Four was not going to be put at risk by any off-duty romance. She might possibly have pined for Argo had she been allowed the time, but finishing each day physically, mentally, and emotionally exhausted left no room for lovelorn distraction.

Early in training Jesamine had learned that not even Yancey Slide totally understood exactly what The Four were, or how their powers really functioned. He, as much as any of them, was grappling with something new and unfathomable. Of course, by the same token, no one knew exactly what Slide was. T'saya was human enough, although the old woman from deep and mysterious Africa had delved deeper into the other realities than all but a few. She called herself a dream-teller and a dream-weaver, but that was not even the half of it. Slide, on the other hand, was impenetrable, incomprehensible, and supposedly inhuman. Not even T'saya was willing, and maybe not able, to explain Yancey Slide, if asked, and Slide always and absolutely refused to define himself. Just one time, the skeletally thin figure had taken the perpetual cheroot from his mouth and told her *"I am a creature with plenty of time, my dear. I'm damned for eternity."* Jesamine had then asked him if had ever been a living man. He had merely made an unworldly gesture, and laughed his most hollow and sepulchral laugh. *"Do I look like a living man?"* Some claimed that he was a demon, but Jesamine considered that word too trite and easy. Argo had seen him take a fatal bullet and rise from the dead, and all of them had witnessed the non-human lapses, when his mind seem to vacate his body and go elsewhere, and heard him speak briefly in some unrecognizable tongue, as if confused as to where or when he had returned. Maybe T'saya had come closest to the truth when she described him as a being who existed in more than one reality at once, but that had only prompted Jesamine to wonder why, when The Four went to war in the Other Place, Slide was never there with them.

During the long weeks of winter training, Jesamine had seen landscapes and encountered entities that had filled her with an awe beyond the power of words. She also had seen sights of such deep and unrelenting horror, her mind revolted at their recall. The highest point had been the trip they had all taken into the wild interior to the Secret Lodge of the Ohio. This aboriginal excursion had brought The Four to new plateaus of paranormal fear and ecstasy, and also had shown her there was far more to the Americas than just the East Coast and its invaders and immigrants from Europe and Africa. Although Jesamine was under no illusion that these original Americans were not without their own share of conflicts, she immediately sensed that the Ohio and the other tribes did not have the same ravening and all-consuming madness of the Mosul, and also didn't share the men of Albany's belief that everything in the world had been solely provided for their arrogant and unremitting exploitation. When Jesamine had first come to the Great Settlement of the Ohio, she had felt as though she was somehow coming home. The mountain village where she had spent her childhood could not have been more different from the Ohio's winter quarters. Her first home had been a place of harsh sunlight, reflected from the white walls of the conical huts, softened only by the dry, blowing dust, but Jesamine's people had also lived close to the earth, with a very basic understanding of their place in nature. In the close warmth of the Ohio's bison-hide lodges, beside the frozen lake, and against the background landscape of virgin, pine-covered hills, the chill air seemed cleaner, and the people more in touch with the unseen that constantly surrounded them.

The time that Jesamine had spent with the Ohio, especially the short day and two long nights on the glacial mountainside, with its coyote apparitions, eagle visions, and sheets of blue-white lightning flashing from other realities, had been quite enough to convince her that the aboriginal tribes were centuries in advance of anyone in Albany in their knowledge of other realities, and maybe knew more of such things than even the Mosul's High Zhaithan Quadaron-Ahrach, or his exceptionally depraved and evil sister, Her Grand Eminence Jeakqual-Ahrach. Jesamine had also felt warmed by the open generosity of the Ohio, and how they had made her welcome beside their fires, and had shared all that was theirs with her, both material and spiritual.

Thus it was, months later, when she heard that a detachment of Ohio warriors would be joining the expedition south, she had become determined to reacquaint herself with the native people, but at the time, she had never suspected just how deep that reacquaintance would go. She had met Magachee on the second day of the advance into Virginia. Jesamine had been resting her horse, leading it at a slow walk, and had stopped as a column of Ohio rode past. Out of nowhere, a voice had called to her. "Jesamine!"

Jesamine had turned, and a young woman quickly dismounted and waited for her to catch up. She was dressed in white buckskins, and her face and arms were painted with the Ohio symbols of both war and ecstasy. Jesamine had not recognized the girl, but she already seemed to know this and quickly introduced herself. "I am called Magachee. We met just once. That night when the men were sent away, and the women were together."

Jesamine remembered the night. It had been an experience too intense to forget. "I'm sorry. There were a great many of you and only one of me."

Magachee had laughed. "I don't expect you to remember me. We only spoke briefly. I was just happy to see you."

"You are traveling with the warriors?"

Magachee's smile fractionally faded. "Among the Ohio, we women fight alongside the men, if we so chose."

She saw Jesamine's confusion, and quickly continued. "I ride beside a brave named Oonanchek."

"Oonanchek?"

"You must come with me and meet him."

Jesamine hesitated, unsure of how to answer. "I . . ."

"You have duties?"

"No, not right now."

"Then come."

As they and their mounts walked side by side, some Albany infantrymen had leaned on their muskets, and regarded her with concealed smirks. Jesamine had scowled. "They never let me forget that I was previously a slave and concubine."

Magachee had halted and looked at her with a patient calm. "Our energies are needed to fight our enemy, not to deal with the complexities of our supposed friends."

In that instant, a bond of trust had been formed, but, even after they had talked a while longer about how dislocated Jesamine felt, Magachee's offer came straight out of the blue. "Would be easier for you if you traveled with us?"

The idea took her completely by surprise. "With you? With the Ohio?"

"The army of Albany has regulations against such a thing?"

"Not that I know of. They have a lot of regulations, though."

"Your uniform proclaims you a major?"

"That's right."

"And you have no commander to forbid it?"

"Not directly."

"So?"

"If I traveled with the Ohio, it would confirm everything the bastards already believe about me; that I am a former slave and probably a whore."

"If they believe that already, what do you have to lose?"

Jesamine hesitated. "But how would the Ohio react to such a thing?"

"The Ohio do not judge."

"And what would Oonanchek think about me traveling with you?"

Magachee had shrugged, but her eyes were dark and knowing. "We can only ask him."

And with that, she had swung herself back onto her pony, indicating that Jesamine do the same. When they found him, Oonanchek turned out to be a tall warrior with strong, confident features, and his long hair tied back in the beaded band of a mystic adept. Far from raising objection to Magachee taking in a stranger, he almost seemed to be expecting her. "You are Jesamine."

"And you are Oonanchek."

"And now we travel together."

That first night with her newfound Ohio companions had seemed like a cocoon of black velvet studded with fires and stars. Slow drums had been beating, and voices that sang with rich ululations helped drown out the raucous barrack ballads of the Albany soldiers. A pipe had been passed, and Jesamine had used her clout as a major to send for a bottle of Albany applejack. Perhaps Jesamine had loosened her inhibitions a fraction too much, or maybe what happened next was somehow preordained, but the conversation had become more intimate and self-revealing. Jesamine had told Oonanchek and Magachee much about her past, and the shame that she carried with her. She had told them how she missed Argo, and how it had hurt to give him up. She had told them of the strange dreams she'd been having since they had crossed the Potomac and come south, and of the two shining white figures who had walked in those dreams. She had even admitted that the figures scared her, and at that point, Magachee had placed a firm but gentle hand on Jesamine's forearm. "Dreams may be warnings, but they are to be welcomed, not feared."

A sudden electric tingle had passed from Magachee's hand to Jesamine's arm and then suffused through her whole body causing her to gasp and then stare. "Are . . . you and Oonanchek these figures?"

Magachee had smiled and shaken her head. "We are not in your dreams. We are two others."

"Others?"

Magachee had said nothing. She had simply taken Jesamine by the hand and raised her to her feet. Then Magachee's hands had gone to the fastening of her deerskins, and, in what had seemed like a single simple motion, the clothing had fallen with a whisper, so she stood naked and painted, facing Jesamine. In the instant, Jesamine had been gripped by a need greater than herself. As Oonanchek had remained seated, cross-legged on the other side of the fire, watching but expressionless, she had slowly unfastened the buttons of her Ranger tunic, and when she, too, was unveiled to the night, Magachee had taken her in her arms and, together, they had sunk down to the dew-damp grass. Jesamine had thrown back her head and groaned as Magachee had crouched over her, her lips brushing Jesamine's body. Now a second, more powerful shock of contact left her breathless, and she heard her own voice, as if from a distance, sobbing in pleasure at the touch that was so different from the rough hands of men.

"*Ooooooooh . . .*"

And that was how it had all started. At some moment in the ecstatic darkness, she had opened her eyes to see Oonanchek standing over them, then he, too, had knelt to join them. And that had been the way of it for all of the subsequent days. Jesamine had traveled with the Ohio, only joining the ranks of Albany when duty required her. She knew that many were scandalized by her behavior, but she refused to care. While the sun was up, she rode, a solitary dark green Ranger, among the deerskins, furs, and feathers, the spears and muskets, and the flowing manes of their ponies. After dark, she, Magachee, and Oonanchek communed with spirits and with each other, exploring all of the possibilities of their minds and bodies, frequently under the influence of a quite extraordinary range of aboriginal intoxicants. She had laughed and she had moaned, she had groaned and shamelessly screamed as she had been taken to places unvisited even by The Four. No doubt she was the talk of the mess; the Mosul concubine who had been given a commission and an unprecedented promotion was now spending her off-duty in a three-way liaison with two savages. What her fellow officers would never grasp, as they swilled their gin and sniggered, was that it went far beyond any excursion into the unconventional. Magachee, Jesamine, and Oonanchek were what the Ohio called a *takla,* a confluence of minds, and among all the natives of America, it was viewed as a rare and special occurrence, and a source of great power for all those involved. Obviously The Four was Jesamine's principal *takla*; serious, unbreakable, and daunting, and Magachee and Oonanchek totally respected this. What they had between the three of them was something entirely different, although, more than once, Jesamine had speculated that the two apparently separate *takla* might be related, and wondered if the interlude among the Ohio was some deliberately engineered relief from the awful responsibility of being one of The Four, or an auxiliary source of the strength to help her maintain her sanity. If it was such a seemingly fortuitous connection, how had it come about? Had it been caused to happen, and, if so, by whom or what? She had been taught by T'saya never to question what could not be explained. If it worked, one should simply accept it. Oonanchek had said the same thing. The interlude had brought all three of them a combination of both peace and ecstatic excitement, and her dreams of the white figures had completely ceased. Jesamine had been happy, and she accepted her happiness as a great if unexplainable gift.

But now the interlude was ending. The gift was spent. In the tiny tent that Oonanchek had raised for the ritual of severance, the cut cord that was the symbol of their too-brief intimacy lay on the blanket in front of Jesamine, like something that had once lived but was now dead.

"You are free, Jesamine; free to return to your companions, to The Four, to your true *takla*."

Magachee held Jesamine from behind, cradling and comforting her, stroking her hair, like a mother about to send a child out into the world. Oonanchek brought Jesamine's uniform. Still dizzy from the smoke, she shook her head, then rose, still free and naked. Magachee leaned forward and kissed her thigh one last time. She took the uniform from Oonanchek.

A small leather medicine bag lay on top of the carefully folded garments. She looked questioningly at him and he smiled. "A final gift. A part of us to take with you. And the summons for the *Quodoshka*."

Jesamine frowned. "I have nothing to give to you in return."

"You have given and continue to give."

"But . . ."

"We need speak no more of it."

Jesamine nodded and slowly started to dress. Putting on the uniform felt too much like strapping on armor for a coming and terrible fight.

## RAPHAEL

A lumbering fighting machine clanked and rumbled past, and his horse snorted and attempted to shy. Raphael Vega brought the animal under control, but with some difficulty. He had only been riding since he had arrived in Albany, and his horsemanship was still little more than rudimentary. The steam-driven mechanical monster was one of the older models, slower and less efficient than the sleeker and more compact petroleum-driven machines that had been supplied to Albany by the Norse Union. Smoke billowed from its stack, oil leaked like black blood from between its welded and riveted plates, and somewhere inside its cramped, iron-gray interior, a sweating crew included a stoker shoveling coal into a boiler. That even the antiquated should be committed to the field indicated the desperate seriousness with which the coming fight was being treated. A few days earlier, he had heard talk among some of the staff officers. Field Marshal Virgil Dunbar, the Albany supreme commander, was personally leading the push to the south, and his long-term plan was to drive the Mosul all the way back to their original beachhead. Savannah was still the hub and nerve center of the Mosul American conquest, and it was there where they would first be surrounded, then contained. Finally, ringed with hastily constructed launch sites for Norse rocket bombs, they would be blown back into the Northern Ocean. The younger officers were completely optimistic. They had held the Mosul at the Potomac, and saw the coming task one of herding them like sheep for the entire length of the Eastern Seaboard. As far as they were concerned it presented no particular problem.

The callow captains and junior lieutenants had not noticed Raphael listening or they might not have spoken so freely. Raphael knew they did not trust him. Not only was he one of The Four, and an over-publicized practitioner in the highly suspect paranormal arts, but he had also formerly been a lowly conscript in the Mosul infantry. Just to make matters worse in the eyes of these Albany aristocrats, he was a foreigner. Thus he failed on all levels; by criteria of class, occupation, history, and nationality, he was unacceptable, and yet they had to accept him, because they needed his powers, and also because, when he had been inducted into their army, he had been given the rank of major as a matter of convenience, and so, in the chain of command, he was technically their superior. Raphael also did not share the young staff officers' view of the war. He knew too much about Mosul discipline and Mosul tenacity to believe the armies of Hassan IX could simply be herded back to Savannah like so many stray sheep. He kept his own council, however, and said nothing. Since he had come to Albany, Raphael had learned the knack of keeping himself to himself.

The fighting machine was now lumbering on, laying a pall of smoke and vented steam and leaving deeply gouged tracks in its wake. Two more of the massive contraptions followed, also bothering his horse, and forcing Raphael to keep the mare on a very tight rein. A troop of lancers passed behind him at a brisk trot, their reined-in mounts tossing their heads and snorting. The army of Albany was dividing into its components, making ready for battle in a state of controlled military chaos that made no sense to those actually in the middle of it, but, Raphael devoutly hoped, was perfectly clear to the commanders with the overall view. A column of infantry formed ranks, and then marched out with slung rifles and the peaks of their caps down over their eyes. As this column of fours hit their stride, one of the chosen men struck up a song, and the whole company joined in with the lusty and reckless confidence of swaddies who had drunk their gin ration fast and early and are deliberately not thinking about what the future might have up its sleeve.

*Oh, farewell Mary, I must march*
*On and on and on and on*
*I'll miss your tits and I'll miss your arse*
*On and on and on and on*
*From Brooklyn Town to Carver's Bay*
*Over the hills and far away.*

The infantry company moved out, and their song merged into the general cacophony of mobilization; the shouts of sergeants, the noise of horses, the grind and cough of machinery. He glanced around, and then pulled out his pocket watch. Where were the others? They should have been at the assembly point by this time. He experienced a second of unease. He was in the right place, wasn't he? He checked and quickly reassured himself that this was the part of the camp specified in the orders that they had all received the previous night. It was not unusual for Raphael to be the first to arrive at any designated meeting. Since he remained so much on his own, feeling more secure in the company of his sketch pad than other people, he usually had less to delay him than Cordelia, Argo, or Jesamine. Argo might well be still curing a hangover. Jesamine had become quite unpredictable since she'd taken up with the Ohio, and Cordelia made no secret that she considered punctuality a petty bourgeois preoccupation, well below the considerations of a lady. Even during the rigors of training, she was habitually late, and when she did arrive, she could usually be counted on to complain.

Of course, during training, they had all complained, but only Raphael had been unable to air his supposed grievances with total conviction. He had been through the horrors of a Mosul boot camp, and nothing in the long winter training could compare with that nightmare. Except, maybe in one respect. The training of The Four had been a whole lot harder on the intellect. The Mosul's goal was to turn their Provincial Levies into mindless automatons, who would simply obey like brutes, without thought or question. It was made clear that the packed rank and file of the Mosul infantry were valued less than the horses of the Mamalukes. They were worth nothing and they need expect nothing, except to be a lowly component in one of the infamous "human waves" that were hurled against the enemy and expected to prevail by sheer weight of numbers, regardless of the death toll. Hadn't Gunnery Instructor Y'assir always reminded Raphael's squad when he threatened them with execution for one of the dozen or more infractions that carried the death penalty, *"You'll be hung, maggot, because you aren't worth the three fegs it costs for a bullet and the powder to shoot you."*

The Four, on the other hand, had been expected to think. They were required to use their ingenuity, to attempt new things, to record their successes in detail so they could be repeated, and to analyze their failures so other ways could be devised to reach the same goal. Since such a regime of training had never been previously attempted in known history, both trainees and trainers were essentially making it all up as they went along, and that was why such emphasis was put on originality and creative thinking. They had been under the tutelage and care of the African woman T'saya, and the inhumanly strange Yancey Slide, although other specialists had been brought in with the hope that they might be able to make a contribution. Some of what the quartet went through, although grueling, was straightforward and physical. They had run and climbed and swum and exercised, just like any other teenage recruit, all according to an only slightly adapted version of the Albany Rangers training manual. At the other extreme, they had meditated and honed their cognitive skills. They had also drunk, swallowed, and smoked strange potions and mixtures devised by T'saya, the Shaman Gray Wolf, and the Lady Gretchen. They had experienced visions and tripped to other realities, unclear as to whether the landscapes in which they found themselves were real or merely the products of their assembled imaginations.

The metaphor of flying had been used since their very first excursions into the Other Place. They "flew" over occult landscapes of both incredible beauty and measureless horror. Their paranormal workouts had become known as "training flights." Then the metaphor had been taken too far, and a trainer had been brought in from the Norse-run flying school of the Royal Albany Air Corps, to see if he could devise a way to record the "geography" of the Other Place, but, in a matter of hours, the veteran aviator had become so violently spooked that he made his stammering excuses and left. In the Other Place, they had essentially worked on refining the pattern they had instinctively fallen into when, during the battle of the Potomac, still knowing nothing, and hardly knowing each other, they had been expected to stem the paranormal assault by Quadaron-Ahrach, the High Zhaithan, and his twin sister, Her Grand Eminence Jeakqual-Ahrach. They had found through trial and error that the original approach, and playing to their basic strengths, was always the best way: Cordelia tended to surge ahead, while Argo followed like a protective, ever watchful shadow, on the lookout for unexpected danger. Jesamine would take a center position and her inclination was to function as an anchor. Raphael brought up the rear, and was constantly sensitive to what might suddenly appear behind them. An implacable caution seemed to be emerging as his strongest attribute. Plus, a remorseless and deadly resentment of any enemy that tried to blindside the *takla*.

As though acknowledging his thoughts of flying, three heavy RAAC Odin biplanes buzzed overhead, filling the clear morning air with the whine of their engines. The aircraft were either on a nuisance raid on the Mosul, flying out to drop their payloads of twenty-pound bombs on an enemy who was now halted and digging in, or else they'd been ordered up simply to enhance morale and military spectacle as Albany went to the shooting war. Their undersides were painted gray-blue so as to present a less precise target to possible ground fire, but Raphael knew the upper surfaces were bright and aggressive, and the Crowned Bear of Albany was emblazoned on top wings and tailplanes as though on the banners of ancient knights. The airplanes of the RAAC had no need of camouflage from the air. The Mosul so far possessed no aircraft, although everyone knew, sooner or later, their Teuton scientists, even hampered as they were by Zhaithan religious constrictions, would back-engineer one or more Norse flying machines. Eventually the Mosul would have a warplane of their own. But, until then, the RAAC could soar and swagger like Masters of the Air.

Raphael knew how the Odin pilots must value their ability to rise above the terrestrial slaughter. The illusion of flying at high speed that figured prominently in The Four's first forays into the Other Place was a close approximation. They dived and they skyrocketed, and the enemy had come at them out of the bizarre cloud cover of impossible skyscapes. Further practice and a deeper exploration of their powers had presented other options, but flight was still their most powerful extra-reality. They still tended to enter the other place in the flying mode, if for no other reason than the knowledge that no safe training grounds existed in the Other Place, and even while they refined their concentration and rehearsed their moves, they were constantly at risk of attack by enemy entities every time they attempted the real thing. This was no empty fear. The enemy had come upon them no less than seven times during training. The now familiar, but no less dangerous, Mothmen had materialized out of nowhere and assailed them, lethally screaming. The new and hard to describe things with the streamlined bodies and razor-sharp cutting dorsals, that Cordelia had flippantly dubbed the "sports model," had also appeared from sudden rents in the fabric, and The Four had been hard-pressed to fight them off and retreat to terrestrial safety.

Raphael might have fallen into full reverie, reliving those desperate moments of occult violence in his mind's eye, had he not noticed Yancey Slide, mounted on a tall and rawboned black stallion, wending his leisurely way through the shout and bustle of the mobilizing camp. The tall, angular figure had watched over them all through training, and his long trademark duster coat and the wide-brimmed black hat tilted forward to conceal his face instilled Raphael with a certain confidence that at least one being understood the infinite strangeness they faced. Slide's unique oriental sword was across his back in its decorative sheath, with the hilt at his left shoulder, and Raphael did not doubt Slide's brace of equally outlandish pistols was concealed under the lavish drape of his coat. The inevitable cigar was stuck in the side of his mouth, and his hands were hidden in black gloves. Raphael had long since given up speculating as to what Slide might be, or from where he might have originated. The only thing Raphael knew for sure was that neither he nor any of The Four, even after all the things they had seen in the Other Place and elsewhere, ever wanted to look directly into Yancey Slide's eyes.

A photographer from one of the Albany newspapers was taking pictures of the mobilization with a heavy, tripod-mounted, wood and brass-plate camera. The man saw Slide and made the mistake of pointing his lens at him. Slide turned slightly, as though starting to pose, but then extended the index and second finger of his right gloved hand and created a sudden tiny but brilliant spark. The photographer tottered back, cursing, and all but knocking over his camera. While the man was still stumbling, Slide rode on as though nothing had happened. The photographer recovered himself, and then pulled the now-ruined photosensitive plate out of the device. He stared after Slide in anger and frustration, then dashed the plate to the ground and stamped it into the earth. The delivered message had plainly been received. Yancey Slide was not to be photographed.

Slide reined in beside Raphael. "The first to arrive, boy?"

Raphael nodded. Yancey Slide was one of the few people he would tolerate calling him "boy."

"So it would seem."

Slide dragged on his cigar and spat out a sliver of leaf that had detached itself. He knew Raphael had a fixation about punctuality, and didn't bother to discuss it further. "Are you still having those dreams?"

"They seem to be becoming clearer by the day."

"Any ideas?"

"No ideas, but I've made drawings."

"You want to show them to me?"

Raphael leaned back in the saddle and reached in his right saddlebag. He pulled out a thick, spiral-bound sketchbook and handed it to Slide, who paged through it without removing his gloves. "Twins?"

Raphael nodded. "That's how they appear. Twin figures, lit from within by a bright white light."

"The Mosul worship twin deities."

Raphael looked bleakly at Slide. At times, the demon tended to state the obvious. "Ignir and Aksura, I know that better than most."

"Could they be what you're drawing here?"

Raphael sighed. "I'm damned if I know. You told me to draw what came to me, and that's what I did."

"But you have no ideas what these figures might be beyond what you've put down here?"

"I was on the other side of the ocean and had no idea who or what Cordelia was when I started drawing her from my dreams."

Slide handed back the drawings. "I hate blind instinct."

Raphael sullenly replaced the pad in his saddlebag. "I'm sorry I can't be more precise."

"Don't cop an attitude, boy." Slide seemed about to say more, but both he and Raphael had spotted Argo Weaver threading his way through the moving columns of men. Slide contented himself with a fast warning. "And keep all this to yourself for the moment."

A clear path opened in front of Argo to where Slide and Raphael were waiting, and he urged his horse forward. The last few times that Raphael had seen Argo, he had either been morose or drunk, and this day was no exception. He slouched in the saddle, and when he reined in beside Raphael and Slide, he looked pale and hung over. "Am I late?"

Raphael shrugged. "Not as late as the ladies."

Argo grinned despite the obvious headache. "We learn to wait on the ladies."

"You look terrible."

Argo laughed. "And so would you, Major Vega, if you weren't such a damned recluse."

Raphael didn't like to be chided about his self-imposed isolation. "I heard the racket coming from the mess."

"Nervous officer-boys facing their own mortality."

Slide, who had been staring silently, ignoring Raphael and Argo, suddenly gestured across the field. "The Lady Blakeney approaches."

Raphael and Argo both turned and peered. At first they saw nothing. This was often how it was when Slide pointed something out. After some fifteen seconds, Raphael was able to pick out Cordelia from the milling khaki. She was mounted on her gray gelding, and wearing blue sunglasses. She seemed to be in no particular hurry, and Argo glanced at Raphael. "Those glasses, are they covering her bloodshot eyes, or is she just being stylish?"

Raphael might be a recluse, but he was not completely out of touch with his companions' adventures. "Probably both. Cordelia's been expanding her legend as hard as she can while we've been marching through Virginia."

Cordelia paused to exchange smiling pleasantries with two young officers in a halted staff car. Argo eased himself in the saddle. "Her ladyship is making an art form of being fashionably late."

Slide heard this, and snorted. Even at a distance Cordelia sensed his displeasure. Her head turned, and she looked directly at where the three of them were waiting. She bid the officers a fast adieu, and then kicked her horse into a brisk trot that quickly brought her to Raphael, Argo, and Slide.

"Good morning, gentlemen."

"Good morning, Cordelia."

She looked around for Jesamine. "So, for once, I'm not the last to arrive."

Raphael sniffed. "No matter how hard you might have tried."

Cordelia ignored him. "Any sign of Jesamine . . ." she smiled bitchily, "with or without her Indians?"

Raphael was tempted to point out that Cordelia's conduct hardly gave her moral grounds to criticize Jesamine's choice of companions, but he decided it was too early in the day and too early in the adventure to start an argument. He also did not want to make this reunion of The Four any less promising than it was already, but, as it turned out, the choice of conversation wasn't his. In the next moment, perhaps working on the principle of "speak of the devil," a column of Ohio braves thundered through the camp, moving out in high aboriginal style, clearly demonstrating how they were arguably the finest light cavalry in all the ranks of Albany and its allies. As they passed close to where Raphael and the others sat on their mounts, a half-dozen riders peeled away from the main body of horsemen, and galloped straight towards them. When they were only twenty or thirty yards away, five of the six swerved to the side, but one kept coming straight at them. Raphael tensed in anticipation of attack, but then, to his surprise, he saw the rider was Jesamine. She was making the grandest of grand entrances. Hardly a skilled horsewoman, she must have been hanging on for dear life, and Raphael was quite amazed that she was trying for such theatrical impact. Had her time with the Ohio endowed her with some new and wild spirit? Only a few yards from the group, she pulled up her rearing horse, flushed and smiling. "So, my friends, are we Four off to war?"

By this point half of the surrounding camp was watching the spectacle, and, as Jesamine brought her horse under control, she acknowledged a round of applause from the onlookers.

# T W O

☙

## ARGO

Fountains of dirt and flame erupted behind the Mosul lines, and Argo fancied he saw bodies and body parts fly high in the air. The Albany artillery leapt and thundered, pouring a barrage of fiery destruction on the enemy. As the acrid smell of gunpowder permeated everything, the field guns blew away all pretense that war was a dashing and noble business as they relentlessly pounded the other end of the valley. Even rational thought became difficult against the background of the deafening explosions and the doom-shriek of the flying shells. Mosul gun positions, hidden in the trees of the wooded ridge on the Albany right, fired in response, but their shots fell short. A line of Albany fighting machines stood just out of the enemy's range with engines running and smokestacks belching, ready to roll into the fight the instant that the deadly barrage ceased. Dense ranks of infantry were crouched behind them, equally ready to advance in the mechanized wake of the hulking battle tanks, using their iron-clad armored bulk as cover. The crucial assault would shortly start, and the outcome of the engagement, indeed, the whole future of the war, would hang in the balance. Albany had committed all of its mobile strength to the fight. If they did not prevail, there would be no second chance.

While the battle remained strictly terrestrial, The Four had no function, and Slide had organized that they be stashed close to the top brass until they were needed, believing absolutely that the generals always found the safest place on the field. The theory seemed to be that no shell would dare land among the stiffly immaculate commanders, and no shrapnel would dare tear through the tailored uniforms, the medal ribbons, mirror-shined boots and belts, and the scarlet epaulets of the general staff. A ten-man detachment of light horse had also been assigned as their escort. Albany believed that The Four were their paranormal secret weapon, and were protecting them accordingly. The last thing Albany wanted was that their spooky wonder-children, their antidote to the Dark Things of the Zhaithan, should be shot down, blown up, or captured in some idiotic battlefield mishap. Argo totally agreed with Albany's view of things. If the winter training had taught him anything, it was never be in a hurry to fight. He had his part to play and he was under no illusion that his time would not come. Romantic ideas of charging with the cavalry were exactly that. They were romantic ideas and, as such, had nothing to do with the conflict at hand.

Unfortunately, the conflict at hand was not going quite as well as the Albany High Command had hoped. Around the map table, faces were grim, and Field Marshall Virgil Dunbar had not been happy since the command vehicles had first come within sight of the valley and he had seen the disposition of the enemy as it really was rather than an abstraction on a map. He had cursed for all to hear. "Goddamn him. I swear that son-of-a-bitch Balsol has had this place in his back pocket since he marched into Virginia, going the other way as a conqueror. It's too perfect for his purpose to be blind happenstance."

He had turned excitedly to one of his aides. "You see that third ridge behind him? I'll wager good money there's some backdoor there that he can take his whole army through if the day goes against him, and he feels the need to slip away. We are going to have our work cut out, and no mistake."

The Mosul, under the command of Faysid Ab Balsol, were dug in at the far end of the valley, and, as Dunbar had expected, were waiting for Albany to take the fight to them. The valley, according to Slide, was created by some prehistoric glacier or movement of ice. It was narrow at the end into which Albany was expected to advance, but then it quickly broadened out into a broad, flat, expanse of green, valley-floor meadow flanked by steeply wooded ridges on either side. The original Albany plan had been to clear the ridges before any major assault on the Mosul center. With Mosul guns on the high ground, an Albany advance into the valley would be through a withering crossfire. Unfortunately, the original Albany plan had only been half implemented. The ridge to the east had been cleared and was held by Albany Rangers, the Ohio, and various cavalry units and crews of irregulars, but the slopes on the west side of the valley were still in Mosul hands. The enemy guns were in a dominating position, and although their fire had so far fallen short, any further Albany penetration would be met with both exploding shells and solid iron cannonballs. The enemy was now deployed as an elongated crescent, with the greater mass of them on the valley floor but with a stretched, but fully intact, left flank extended along the western ridge, and this was very close to the last thing that Dunbar wanted. Instead of a fast thrust at the heart of the Mosul center, they would be attacking a double objective, half of which had the full advantage of the local geography.

Albany was not, however, without some advantages of its own, and the greatest of these was their weapons. They came at the Mosul with the edge of aircraft, flying bombs, breech-loading howitzers, and repeating Bergman guns. One on one, they enjoyed overwhelming range and firepower, but, in this battle that so far did not have a name, the balance was nothing like one-on-one. The Mosul outnumbered Albany perhaps three or four to one, despite the Mosul losses on the Potomac, and while holed up in Richmond. Faysid Ab Balsol still had reserves of men to more than counter Albany's superior ordnance. Virgil Dunbar could, of course, hold off and simply pound on the Mosul with his artillery without unduly exposing his troops. Given the time, Dunbar's guns could inflict such devastating casualties from a distance that the enemy would either mount a last-ditch attack or attempt to flee, but time was something Dunbar did not have. An army of reinforcements was on its way from Savannah, and, with the weather clear and the ground dry as a bone, there was no reason to suppose it was not coming with all speed. As soon as Balsol had lured Dunbar and his divisions out from under the protective umbrella of the

Norse rocket bombs, both commanders knew that Dunbar's best chance was to finish Balsol and his battered and hungry troops as fast as possible, then quickly pull back into the operational range of the rockets. The fresh Mosul forces coming up from Savannah would have to choose between advancing into the decimating ravages of a prolonged rocket attack, or turning back and leaving Albany in control of Virginia.

All of this must have weighed heavily on Dunbar's mind as he faced his commanders across the mobile map table, but Argo could see no signs of strain in the Field Marshal's face or posture. Dunbar had a reputation of a steely, if withdrawn, cool, and, once a decision was made, he was totally resolute. He maybe leaned forward on the map table a little heavily, but Dunbar did walk with a limp, the legacy of a Mosul sniper who had nicked him in the leg during the standoff on the Potomac. As the Albany field guns were momentarily quiet, he spoke with careful urgency. "The option is a hard one, gentlemen. To advance into this forsaken valley is going to cost us dearly, but we have no other choice, except to brace ourselves and pay the price. Without the luxury of time, we have no other alternative. We have to go, and we have to go now."

He looked round the assembly of his senior commanders as if daring them to counsel further delay. No one did. The smooth-shaven faces of the officers were grimly impassive, as the breeze fluttered the corners of maps that might have flown away if they had not been strategically weighted down with large stones. Dunbar was running the battle from a grassy knoll that overlooked the main trail into the valley and was sufficiently elevated to provide a clear view of the valley floor beyond. Although a command tent had been pitched, he was issuing his orders in the open, in full view of his men, and everyone who was able had crowded round to watch. Argo had used his rank and his position to get as close to the maps and the flow of action as he could. The soldier in the field had no grasp of any bigger picture. All the swaddie knew was shot and shell and the smoke that surrounded him, and the man next to him being suddenly cut down. Beyond that, he had little clue of what was going on, or even whether the fight was being lost or won. Argo liked to know what was happening and what was about to happen, and, the more he saw of war, the more he became convinced that knowledge was the ultimate weapon.

Dunbar raised his voice to take in all those present. He was not generally the kind of commander who made rousing speeches to his men, but he apparently considered this the day to make an exception. "I can't tell you that there won't be blood spilled this day, and I'd be a fool or a liar if I pretended the coming fight won't be bitter. The butcher is going to present us with a bill today, lads, and it'll come with a total we'll read and weep. The valley in front of us is going to be immortalized in history, and too many will find their last resting place there. Our task is to ensure that the majority of those who fall are Mosul, and only a very few are from Albany. This day will be formidable, my friends, and nothing is going to be improved by waiting. The time has come, gentlemen. We have prepared long enough, and now we must rise to the occasion. Return to your units. We'll let the ordnance pound them a while longer, and then we'll move."

## CORDELIA

Cordelia closed her eyes and concentrated, focusing to the near-exclusion of everything around her. Finally she opened them, shook her head, and replaced her blue sunglasses. "Nothing. No sign of anything. So far it's a totally terrestrial battle."

Jesamine looked around as though seeking something that wasn't there. "I feel we ought to be doing more. So many are going to sacrifice so much and we're just standing around."

Over to Jesamine's right, a column of mounted Ohio was wending its way up into the small segment of the western ridge that had been taken and held by Albany. They were following other cavalry units that had already made the ascent. While the infantry and fighting machines advanced down the valley, they were going to make one more attempt to dislodge the Mosul from the high ground. Cordelia shared Jesamine's frustration. She had friends in that desperate bid to clear the heights, but venting didn't help. She was about point that out when Argo did it for her.

"We're doing what we have to do, and, right now, we have to wait until we're needed. Ask any of the poor fucking grunts. Waiting is what war's all about."

Behind him, Raphael nodded in agreement. "It'll be our turn soon enough. No need to rush."

The Four had come to war and found that they had nothing to do, a situation that failed to improve their already shaky cohesion. The guns had stopped some fifteen minutes previously, and the fighting machines had finally ground down into the valley, lurching forward on their steel tracks and iron treads, while the exposed infantry, advancing with fixed bayonets, stayed as close as possible to their armored sides, taking advantage of all the cover offered by the rumbling juggernauts. Some regiments had even gone into the valley singing.

*Oh, Annie gal, I must away*
*On and on and on and on*
*But I'll fuck you come the break of day*
*On and on and on and on*
*Then the captain calls and I obey*
*Over the hills and far away.*

The assault force had been advancing for maybe three minutes, when the Mosul guns on the ridge opened up, breaking the infantry formations with sudden spurting geysers of flame, dirt, and black smoke. With at least a mile to go to the Mosul's forward trenches, the Albany boys would have to endure shelling from the ridge all of the way, unless the cavalry and the Ohio could take that western high ground and silence the enemy cannon. There would be no more singing. This first crash of the Mosul artillery had been like a clap of massed thunder, and thrown Cordelia into a sudden if momentary panic. She didn't want to play any more. War was no place for her. She was born for soft pretty things, not the implacable ugliness of combat. She wanted to run away from the smoke and the flame and death-dealing explosions. She wanted to hide. She didn't want to die. But then she found her strength and reestablished control, sternly reprimanding herself. "We all have to die sometime, darling."

"What?"

She thought that no one had heard her over the guns, but Argo,

Jesamine, and Raphael were all staring at her curiously. "Are you alright, Cordelia?"

She looked from face to face. They all seemed genuinely concerned, but Cordelia tried to laugh it off. They didn't need to see her weakness. "I was finding encouragement in a well-worn platitude. We lived through the Potomac, and we'll live through this."

Right at that moment, the first Albany fighting machine was hit. A triple explosion shook the ground; the exploding shell, then the machine's magazine detonating and boiler blowing in quick succession. Hot metal, dirt, and smoking debris rained from the sky. Cordelia ducked, as did everyone around her. A chunk of twisted steel buried itself in the ground just a few feet from her.

"Fuck!"

Crouching on one knee, she glanced in the direction of Dunbar, to see if he had reacted like everyone else. Apparently the Field Marshal was made of sterner stuff than his underlings. Virgil Dunbar stood straight and still while all around him sought cover. Either he believed that he would never be touched, or he didn't care if he was. Whatever the source of his strength, he ignored the danger and stared unflinching down the length of the fateful valley where hundreds of his men were going to their deaths. Cordelia knew this was probably the only way to deal with war and command, and wondered if, one day, she would be able to do the same.

Cordelia straightened up, and looked round for the others. "Is everyone okay?"

Jesamine and Argo nodded, but Raphael was tentatively touching his forehead, where a trickle of blood ran down from just above his eyebrow. Argo was the first to notice. "Hey, man, you're bleeding."

Raphael tersely shook his head. "It's nothing, just a scratch."

"You want a medic to take a look at it?"

Raphael found a handkerchief and dabbed at the cut. His expression was scathing. "Be real. There are guys being blown to pieces just over there."

Cordelia didn't want to look, but Raphael was right. The infantry and the fighting machines were advancing into a hell of shot, shell, and deafening cacophony. Within just minutes, they had been almost totally obscured by dark billowing smoke, curling in sudden eddies, and punctuated by flashes of red-orange flame. Starshells burst overhead, leaving blossoms of white cloud, and a dirigible rode the wind currents, but safely to the east, out of the reach of even the most optimistic Mosul fire. The terrible beauty of it all left Cordelia scarcely able to speak. The battlefield was a place of brutal fascination, to which all must succumb, no matter how many engagements they had seen. The aides and officers around her had all been at the Battle of the Potomac, but they still stared in awe as the main Albany assault ground deeper and deeper into the valley that so far didn't even have a name.

Dunbar observed what was happening and cleared his throat. "Yes, gentlemen. Take a good look, and tremble. You have one minute to stare in horror at what we have wrought, and then, goddamn it, get yourselves back to the task at hand."

The officers around the map table visibly pulled themselves together. Dunbar took out a pocket watch, read the time, and then snapped it closed. He turned briskly to his artillery coordinator. "Musgrave . . ."

The stocky, red-haired colonel stiffened. "Sir?"

"Move the guns into the valley. Fast as you can."

"Yes, sir."

Cordelia had once been friends with Musgrave's daughter Hyacinth but, when Hyacinth had enlisted in the Royal Nursing Volunteers, Cordelia had lost track of her. Musgrave picked up a field telephone, briskly cranked the handle, but nothing happened. He cursed all modern contraptions of wires and batteries, then quickly turned and signaled for a galloper. A young lieutenant stepped forward—little more than a boy who had yet to start shaving. He was given quick instructions, and then ran for his horse. The spell of first combat was broken, now the officers were all in motion, casting worried glances from the battle itself to the maps in front of them. The near end of the valley was now so swathed in smoke that to see whether the advance was still moving proved hard. Bursts of small-arms fire seemed to indicate that the infantry was engaging the Mosul on the ridge. One group of staff officers was peering at the high ground through field glasses. "Field Marshal, I see explosions in among the trees, near the summit line."

"Cavalry making contact?"

"That's how it looks."

"Let's hope so." Dunbar searched for Musgrave. "Where are those damned guns?"

"They're moving now, sir."

Cheers broke out from across the knoll as galloping teams of horses, a mounted rider on the leader, charged through the camp with all the show and bravado of the mobile artillery, and then plunged on, each dragging a light howitzer. Down the trail and into the valley, they maintained a reckless speed across ground already torn up by armor and infantry. The gun-carriages were making for the base of the eastern ridge, before the enemy could draw a bead on them, to set up forward firing positions from which they could rain down all hell on the Mosul in the opposite trees.

As the last caisson rattled past, Cordelia could not resist clasping her hands together in wonder and delight. The gunners had charged out so breakneck, and splendidly headlong, Albany suddenly seemed to have a chance. They were taking the fight to the Mosul at such a dashing fury, how could they not prevail?

"Oh, magnificent."

She had exclaimed louder than she had intended, and some of Dunbar's immediate staff turned and looked at her. Dunbar himself glanced up and arched an eyebrow. "You approve of my gunners, do you, Lady Blakeney?"

## RAPHAEL

"Are we connected to the airship yet?"

When Dunbar moved, his aides moved with him like chicks following an angry mother hen, except the Field Marshal was no mother hen, and right at that moment, a Colonel Ailes, the engineer responsible for communications, was the target of his ire. Raphael didn't envy the man who was shaking his head and looking decidedly unhappy.

"No, sir. We're having trouble picking up the signal."

"Damn it, Ailes, when?"

Raphael knew that the airship constituted Dunbar's eye in the sky. He turned and looked at the pall of smoke and fire in the valley. Even with field glasses it was hard to tell what was really going on and how much progress the assault troops were making. He could see the howitzers firing from their new position at the base of the eastern ridge, but little else.

"Just five to ten minutes, Field Marshal."

"You told me that five minutes ago, damn it."

"It's a brand new system, sir. It's never been used in the field before."

"You know my feeling about excuses."

Two electricians, a corporal and a private, came in laying electrical cable as they went, and temporarily removing Ailes from the hook. Two more pushed their way through the officers carrying a ticker tape machine, and began stripping wires and connecting them to shiny copper terminals. Dunbar stood over them, watching with interest. "Is this going to work for me, Corporal?"

"We'll soon find out, sir."

The corporal screwed down the final terminal and the machine commenced to clatter. A length of paper tape unspooled and was typed on by the automatic keys. When the process stopped, Dunbar ripped the tape from the machine and examined it. "This is gibberish."

The corporal was unconcerned. "Just a test, sir. But it shows that everything's working, if you know what I mean."

Dunbar indicated he knew what the corporal meant. The ticker clattered again. This time the corporal tore off the tape and handed it to Dunbar. "Your first report from the airship, Field Marshal."

Dunbar gestured to an aide, who produced a flask and handed it to the corporal, indicating that he should drink and pass it on to the three privates. Raphael reflected how, if Dunbar came out of this day the victor, the corporal would have a story to tell his grandchildren, about how he shared a drink with the great man. Dunbar was already a part of Albany folklore. He was the hero of the bloodless revolution that had brought the present King to power and deposed his autocratic and unpopular father. In the winter of '93, the poor had marched in the streets, and only the cool resolve of then-Colonel Virgil Dunbar had prevented bloodshed on Regent Square. Subsequently arrested, but then freed by popular outcry, Dunbar had later been one of those at the legendary Midnight Meeting, the historic encounter between the King, the leaders of the Commons, and the Army that had resulted in Carlyle I's abdication in favor of his son Carlyle II, while the troops of Hassan IX were already coming ashore at Savannah.

Dunbar noticed Raphael studying the ticker tape machine, and laughed. "One of the marvels of advanced technology, my boy. Strange to think that it exists in the same modern world as you and your friends."

Raphael nodded, uncomfortable that the commander had noticed him. "Strange indeed, sir."

Dunbar looked amused. He was probably accustomed to junior officers becoming tongue-tied in his presence. "I understand you Four have had very little to do as yet."

"That's right, Field Marshal. As yet."

"I wouldn't worry about it, my boy. I have a feeling you'll all see action soon enough."

Dunbar was one of the few senior officers in Albany who harbored no doubts about The Four. Many of those immediately under him simply wished they would go away, but the supreme commander accepted their powers as mysterious but infinitely useful. His backing had helped them on a number of occasions, the most notable being in the matter of them making contact with the aborigines. The visit by The Four to the land of the Ohio had almost never happened. Although the winter excursion had been organized by Slide and T'saya, the original suggestion had been made by the Reverend "Bearclaw" Manson. The small man, with his buckskins and unkempt hair, was credited with knowing more about the uncharted interior of the continent than any other individual in Albany, and also of being in closer touch with the aboriginal world of the invisible than perhaps any living American. It had been Manson's idea that The Four should spend time with the shamans, wisewomen, and windwalkers of the Ohio. Despite all his unique insights, Manson was not a religious leader, and the title "Reverend" was little more than a nickname. At the same time, though, he frequently understood more, and his thoughts were more practical and precise than most, if not all, of those who held offices in the organized worship of God or Goddess. "When you find yourself dealing with the unknown, I figure it's a real good idea to know all that you can know, before you set to messing with it."

At first, a majority of the Albany war cabinet had completely disagreed with him. They had objected strenuously to such a meeting, considering the capabilities of The Four a state secret that should be preserved at all cost, and, under no circumstances compromised, especially at the suggestion of a character like Manson, in their estimation a possible madman who spent far too much of his time communing with who-knew-what imagined devils in the deep and primal forests of the interior. They reasoned that it was bad enough that the existence of The Four had been inadvertently revealed at the King's investiture. To allow the Ohio a close look at them should be unthinkable. Those who supported Manson, primarily Dunbar and Slide, countered that what Jesamine, Argo, Cordelia, and Raphael might learn from consulting with the aborigines, and letting the tribe's advanced adepts meet with them, would totally outweigh what they might be giving away. The final decision had been taken by Prime Minister Jack Kennedy, when he sided with Dunbar, concluding that Manson was right, and gave his approval that The Four, along with Slide, T'saya, Manson, and a full military escort, should head out through the snow-blown forest, where the tall pines swayed, bending to the same Arctic north-winds that kept the Mosul shivering in the ruins of Richmond.

Memories of their time with the Ohio inevitably set Raphael thinking about Jesamine. To say that, since the end of training, Jesamine had been acting strangely was an understatement. The winter had, of course, been hard on all of them, but especially on Argo and Jesamine, who had been expected to sacrifice what seemed to be a much-needed relationship to the greater good. This painful separation had pushed Argo's drinking well beyond social intoxication, while Jesamine had progressively withdrawn from any interaction with the other three. That she had now rejected the ways of Albany and was traveling south with the Ohio was only a part of it. He could, to some degree, sympathize. The Mosul left scars, both physical and mental, on all who came under their power, and suddenly to adapt to not only freedom, but a new social order, was not easy. He looked over to where Jesamine was standing, inevitably by herself. Jesamine noticed Raphael was looking at her, and struck a pose; then she began to walk in his direction, actually swaying her hips like the angry and highly sexual woman he had first encountered on the Potomac. Two officers turned to watch her. Seemingly men could check out women even with a battle raging less than a thousand yards away.

Before she had taken up with Argo, Raphael had hoped that Jesamine would invite him to her bed. As two outsiders, he reasoned, they were the ideal comfort for each other. But it was not to be, and, for a while, he despaired of ever finding himself a girl and a relationship. He had gloomily wondered if, in Albany, he was too much of an outsider, until an RNV nurse called Hyacinth Musgrave had made it clear, in word and very explicit deed, that an outsider could also be considered exotic. Their affair, though, had been a well kept secret. Hyacinth Musgrave had feared any gossip linking her with such an outlandish young man would ruin her reputation and embarrass her father, the same Musgrave who commanded Dunbar's artillery. She was particularly anxious that Cordelia knew nothing about them. The memory caused a slightly cynical smile to cross Raphael's face. The outsider was exotic enough to shag, but too exotic to take home to Daddy, or be introduced to her friends. Hyacinth would doubtless be highly put out if she knew he had a whole folder of nude drawings of her in his portfolio.

"What are you smiling at?"

Raphael blinked. Jesamine had caught him remembering. "Nothing. Just a random thought."

"You spend too much time on your own, Raphael Vega."

"Perhaps." An explosion caused everyone to duck. Raphael's lips were suddenly dry. "Sometimes I feel it's not enough time, if this is what having company takes."

Jesamine pointed to the ticker. As reports came through from the airship, a relay of young captains tore off the tapes, scanned them, and then hurried the news to Dunbar if there was something new. "It prints the reports being sent by wireless from the airship?"

Raphael nodded. "That's right."

Jesamine looked impressed. "No shit?"

In a field to the rear, an Odin biplane came in to land. The observer scrambled from the duel cockpit and ran towards the grassy knoll, while the pilot cut the engine, but stayed where he was as a refueling crew went to work. The observer, still in vulcanized goggles and leather flying helmet, and his face black with oil, breathlessly delivered a verbal report as Dunbar listened intently. Jesamine watched it all with precise interest. "It's all down to communication, isn't it? I mean, this beats waving flags and blowing bugles."

Raphael nodded down the valley. "Communications are for the commanders safely in the rear. Out there it's some poor fucker getting himself blown all over the map. It's about fixed bayonets and death, girl."

Dunbar dismissed the Odin's observer who stepped away, pulling off his helmet and goggles, and lighting a cigarette. Dunbar faced his aides. "Gentlemen . . ."

That one word had everyone's attention.

"The reports from the air lead me to believe that we must ready the second wave. The 19th, the 3rd Foot, Englund's Irregulars, and the 2nd Armored should all make ready." With the orders issued, a number of officers hurried away, while others attempted to use the still malfunctioning field telephones. Dunbar looked at his watch. "I want my cavalry commanders here in five minutes."

Having done what he needed to do, Dunbar dropped into a folding chair and his batman poured his first whiskey of the day into a cut-glass tumbler. Jesamine moved a little closer to Raphael. "Have you sensed anything, anything at all?"

"You mean from the Other Place?"

"Like where else?"

"No."

"And Cordelia looked and saw nothing, right?"

"Right. And Cordelia knows her looking."

"On the Potomac they carried the Dark Things with them, and kept them out on the perimeter of the camp, in these huge pens with high steel fences that glowed in the night. The bodies of the dead were thrown into the damned things, and sometimes the bodies of the living. No one wanted to go near them, and even the Zhaithan fucking loathed them. If Faysid Ab Balsol has any kind of paranormals left, we'd at least see a flare flash of their presence."

"Maybe they all died or something, during the winter. Who the hell knows? Can they starve or expire from the cold? We're just guessing here."

Jesamine took a deep breath. For a moment she looked as though she wanted to slap him for the way his desperation had made him state the obvious. "Do you want to help me look again?"

One of the techniques they had developed in training was that any two of The Four, in very close physical contact, were able to raise a representation of the Other Place that superimposed itself over the prevailing reality. They couldn't enter, but they could see a simulation of Inside.

"Here?"

"Sure, no one will notice if we make it fast."

Raphael was cautious. "It could flare us to the enemy."

"If there is one."

"We can't assume there isn't?"

"You think Jeakqual-Ahrach doesn't know we're here?"

Raphael had run through all his objections. It was Jesamine's show. He went to work. "Grab my hand and go. Rapid first impression and out."

Jesamine grabbed his hand and they went. Raphael opened his eyes and looked. And totally didn't like what he saw. The Other Place was empty.

## JESAMINE

She had their attention and a measure of trust was flowing. The terrestrial battle raged all round them, but The Four were focused. "I saw nothing. You know, a void, emptiness, complete fuck-all nothing? And that isn't right, right?"

Raphael nodded. "There was so much of nothing it was excessive. The Other Place is empty in a way that it shouldn't be empty."

Jesamine pressed the point. "A billiard-table landscape and empty colorless sky. Forever."

Raphael nodded again. "Forever amen, nothing."

Argo was thoughtful. "All the death should have at least attracted some psychic scavengers. I mean, there's some bloody energy release going on."

Cordelia sighed. "Yeah, I admit it. I saw nothing and didn't think it through."

A greater measure of trust was flowing, but Jesamine could still feel the crackle of collective emotional impediments. "We're reluctant to jump in."

Argo squared his shoulders. "That's the fucking truth."

"We need to start from scratch."

"Scratch?"

"Have sex. Run the primal force."

Cordelia's suggestion was met with unanimous disbelief. "What?" She defiantly defended herself. "I know it was me that said it, and I'm supposed to be the slut of the entire officer corps, but we're out of shape, and we've all been getting drunk, acting weird, seething with resentment, making spectacles of ourselves, shacking up with Indians, and generally fucking up."

Jesamine was starting to like Cordelia again. She could blow through the accumulated garbage when needed. "Even if we wanted to, Four-play is out. Who's going to buy us organizing an orgy in the middle of a battle, and saying that it's vital to the war effort?"

"And where would we get the drugs?"

Raphael explored the cut on his forehead with his fingers. "We have to jump and just hope for the best."

"We've been trained, we're supposed to be ready."

"Close our eyes and do it now."

"Wait!"

"What?"

"We have to clear this."

"Why?"

Cordelia laid out the military requirements. "Because we *are* in the middle of a battle, goddamn it. Aside from what Dunbar might want, we need to see that our bodies are protected while we're out of them."

Much thought had gone into the preservation and disposition of The Four's vacated bodies that remained behind when they went in the Other Place. Raphael had suggested a collective coffin, and even offered to design one, but Cordelia had vetoed the idea as too freaky for Albany. Part of the problem was there was no real continuity in how the bodies behaved. Sometimes they had stood like statues, but, on other occasions, they suffered seizures and then collapsed like cut-string puppets. In the end they had adopted an arrangement in which they simply sat square, shoulders hunched, feet touching, clasping their legs to their chests. It seemed to work, but they should jump from a protected space, with an escort guarding them.

"We have to inform Dunbar."

"And tell him what?"

"That we're going on a recon patrol. He can understand that."

"So he has one more thing to worry about?"

"Then we tell Slide. He can deal with the protection and the protocols."

"Where is Slide?"

"That's a good question."

Argo signaled to the sergeant in charge of their light horse escort. "Have you seen Yancey Slide, Sergeant?"

"Not recently, sir."

"Slide is never around when you want him."

Slide's low rasp cut off the complaints. "But he can arrive with indecent suddenness."

No one had looked, so no one could say for sure that Slide had not walked up, exactly as they were complaining about his absence, and had not appeared out of thin air, but his sudden and precisely timed arrival hinted suspiciously of demonic showing off.

"You all want to jump?"

"We think we need to."

Slide's eyes narrowed. "What have you seen?"

"Nothing. Too much nothing."

Slide scowled. "Sounds like a clampdown."

"What's a clampdown?"

"A clampdown on all condition inputs; nothing is let in to shape the landscape. It is an imposed void."

Cordelia's grammar was tight-laced. "Imposed by whom?"

"We should be able to guess that easily enough, shouldn't we? Not that it really matters. Right now, if it doesn't belong to us, it's unfriendly. The real problem is that a clampdown can be a setup for a sudden blast-through."

"And then?"

"And then you don't want to be caught by it. Inside or Outside."

"But we can't find out anything if we don't go in."

Slide drew on his cheroot. "The eternal dilemma."

Jesamine brought the discussion to practicality. "We need a place to jump."

The Four and Slide were still standing beside the ticker tape machine, and, before Slide could answer, he was distracted by an exclamation from one of the captains tending the machine. He was ineffectually calling out for the corporal who had installed it. "Damn it, man. It's sending gibberish."

The captain was holding an offending length of paper tape. Slide held out a gloved hand. "Let me see that."

Slide examined the tape and shook his head. "I was afraid of that."

The characters printed on the tape suddenly caught fire. They flared briefly before Slide extinguished them by closing his fist. His face was grim. "You have to jump. Now."

Jesamine swallowed hard.

## THE FOUR

*They rose as one. The bonding was complete. The links were forged once more. The exaltation was under their command. Far beneath them, the battle raged; it existed, but it was as insubstantial as a phantom. They flew like birds in a sky without* clouds. Most times when they jumped, the Other Place was filled with bright mobile stars and planets, but now it was as empty as Jesamine had described. "A billiard-table landscape and empty colorless sky." Automatically they shifted to the rectilinear position so the parts of The Four were positioned like the points of a radically extended trapezoid. Cordelia conjured the weapons, the others simply hung.

They acted as one and also as separate individuals that were part of that one. Each was a component and yet each was free within the confines of their common purpose. They did not have to agree, they simply knew what was to be done. They brought their own personalities with them, their own intelligence and their own memories, but they shared so much more. The commonality was greater than any single one of them, greater perhaps than the sum of all four, but neither was it oppressive nor an imposition. Acting for the commonality was the same as acting in individual self-interest, and if ever it should seem confining, the freedom and power that came with it was more than sufficient compensation.

"How do we turn nothing into something?"

"We already have. We did it by entering the picture."

In such a featureless landscape, no sense of motion was possible, so they simply hung, watchful and waiting, unsure even if they were predator or prey.

"Has it occurred to anyone this might be a trap?"

"And that we might be trapped already."

"We came in but we won't come out?"

"How would we know?"

Cordelia's personality surfaced. "We'd know when we got bored."

But they were given no time for boredom. At first the ripple was imperceptible, but, as it gathered wave-strength and harmonics, it manifested as a rush of deceptive rainbow, that slowly assumed the shape of a tendril. The weapons of The Four radiated at ready, as the tendril unfurled.

"If it doesn't belong to us, it's unfriendly."

Cordelia flicked out a tentative string of spinning white-stars, of a kind that would not harm unless challenged. The tendril lashed at them in territorial fury, and was badly star-stung for its pains. It recoiled, curling into a tight resentful spiral, blowing an unaimed bubble-wash of killer plasma that The Four avoided with ease, at the same time observing the entity sent against them.

"An Other Place veteran would have given the white-stars a go-by."

"At least it's a know-nothing."

"And it's opened the bidding with a plasma wash."

Argo brought up the heavy emitter for his quadrant and let go with a stream of bad magenta that cut viciously into the tendril, all but severing it.

A painful and abrasive howling screamed across a reshaped landscape. Furious waves of scarlet rippled the spike-torn wasteland. The Four went defensive and wilded on the rectilinear.

"Bad thought."

"What?"

"We may have been used to establish location. The flare of us coming supplied the vector."

"The vector of the Albany High Command?"

"You said it."

"Shit."

"That's right. Shit."

"What were we supposed to know?"

"What are we supposed to do?"

"Make sure that nothing nasty blasts through and goes terrestrial."

The tendril was growing pseudopodia around the wound that Argo had inflicted. Some fell off wriggling.

"Split fire between the growth and the wrigglers. Either could be going for the glory."

Cordelia flash-burned wrigglers in disgusting bunches of a dozen, vaporizing them before they could go anywhere. Argo and Jesamine poured red and green threedee fire onto the outgrowth to the tendril, but it seemed able to expand as fast as they could incinerate it.

"I have a better idea."

"Cordelia, hold the wigglers; Raphael, retard the growth. Argo and Jesamine, cut the base of the tendril. Maybe it'll reveal what it really wants."

The tendril and the virtual ground-grid around it were bathed in luminous fire, but it was proving a new and tough entity—stupid and wholly reactive, though, as if it had been created for something other than combat. While not letting up on the flame, Argo and Jesamine combined cutting edges of a dazzling yellow, and hacked at the tendril's growth-foundation, but suddenly the few remaining wrigglers that Cordelia had not yet fried dropped through the floor of reality.

*"The fucking tendril was a decoy!"*
*"The wrigglers are going Outside!"*
*"Dropping on the normal!"*
*"Right on Dunbar and his people."*
The collective order flared visual.
BREAK CONTACT
*"Out! Out! Out! Out! Out! Out! Out! Out!"*
Raphael's lone voice. *"Wait!"*
The rest. *"What?"*
*"Later."*

## ARGO

Argo was neither in nor out; not part of The Four, but not wholly himself. In the real world, the things that they had dubbed "wrigglers" were dense black, light-absorbing spheres, like Dark Things, only tiny; globes of the unimaginable contained in sweating, hide-like skins, but scarcely bigger than a standard wicket ball. For anyone in the normal world, they simply appeared out of empty air, suddenly materializing between twelve and fifteen feet up and dropping fast to hit the ground and bounce. After spinning once for orientation, the first to arrive quickly attacked the nearest available human, breaking all the laws of mass and energy by snagging the unfortunate victim, grabbing on to his throat, or smothering his face, and then totally absorbing him in little less than a second of screaming. As more baby Dark Things dropped from thin air, they adopted a more tactical purpose. They bounced to a single assembly point, laying trails of black gas in their wake. Some of the Albany soldiers were ready for a gas attack, and put on their masks, taking on an inhuman look, with snout-like filters and round staring eye-pieces under helmets or caps. Others, however, lacked the presence of mind. They saw the gas and panicked. Then a single whiff had them on their knees, in the invisible grip of shrieking hallucinations.

The Things didn't have it all their own way, though. The wrigglers that Cordelia was burning in the Other Place were exploding in mirror-delay. One moment they were bouncing, the next they were nothing more than a brief gout of red flame, the color of diseased blood, and then gone. Slide was also marshaling an Outside defense. Both pistols drawn, he alternately shouted orders and encouragement, and blew the Things away, snap-shooting with inhuman accuracy. "The gas can't hurt you if you've got a mask. And the Things respond to bullets and bayonets. If one comes at you, stab it or shoot it before it can hook on to you. They can be killed!"

Slide had already established a perimeter around Dunbar's command center and had ringed the grassy knoll with a defensive circle of any soldiers, officers, and other ranks he could press into service. Behind them, Dunbar and his staff calmly went on with their task of winning the battle. Argo was now convinced that The Four had been used, presumably by Quadaron-Ahrach or one of acolytes, to vector in on the Albany commanders, but the enemy plan had slightly misfired in that The Four had not jumped from the grassy knoll itself, but had allowed Slide to find a comparatively secluded spot where they could leave their bodies under the watchful protection of their escort. The Dark Things had not fallen directly on Dunbar, and whoever was controlling them was now having to assemble them for a fast bouncing assault, a glitch that had given Albany time to react. Part of the reaction was a young officer, bareheaded but wearing a gas mask, and recklessly swinging a gleaming saber, who rushed at the bouncing carpet of tiny Dark Things, and, in so doing broke the spell of shock that had paralyzed so many of those around him. The Dark Things sprang at him, but the boy skillfully slashed and parried as though he was on the practice floor of a fencing academy, his steel blade creating a cloud of red flame and black gas around him. His action encouraged others, and more young bucks rushed to stand with him, while rankers at his back coolly bayoneted any that got past.

Argo could not help but admire the courage and adaptability of the men protecting Dunbar, but he was also very aware that the best defense was to prevent any more of the things coming through from the Other Place. The rest of The Four were reentering their bodies, but he yelled to them to turn around. "Back Inside! Fast as you can! We have to finish these fucking things!"

*They returned to find the Other Place a forest of vertical tubes with vicious* energy pumping down through them. These "tubes" had to be the source of the Dark Things in the normal world, and they didn't hesitate. Intense cutting-fire roared between the tubes, and they began to melt and collapse. The energy spilled and, where it met the flames of The Four, it exploded into white heat. Then a tube exploded before it had even collapsed. It was followed by another and another. A chain reaction was under way, The Four had done all that they could do, and this version of the Other Place was collapsing around them.

"Okay, out again! Get clear! We've stopped them."

## CORDELIA

Cordelia fully reentered her body, and was shocked to find she had gone blind. Then she realized that she was wearing a gas mask. Either Slide or some enterprising individual in their escort had taken the initiative when the Dark Things had appeared, and put gas masks on their four inert bodies, which was extremely good thinking considering she was encircled by exploding Dark Things, and black gas billowed around where she sat. The fight around the grassy knoll, where the tiny Dark Things had charged in massed assault, appeared to be over, but she still drew her sidearm as she eased out of the semi-fetal jumping position and rose carefully to her feet. A surviving Thing bounced for her throat, but training kicked in, and she shot it almost without thinking. Large areas of burnt grass gave testimony to how effective The Four's flaming in the Other Place had been. Hundreds of the little suckers must have dropped through, but The Four, and Slide's swiftly assembled men on the ground, seemed to have done an efficient job of exterminating them before they did any damage. As the breeze quickly dispersed the gas, a dozen or more young officers were pulling off their masks, leaning on their sabers, and breathing hard.

The others were also getting to their feet, and as soon as the air was clear, Argo pulled off his mask, breathed tentatively, and then indicated to the others they should do the same. The rubber made a sucking sound as Cordelia followed suit. Enough gas still lingered to cause a catch in her throat. She coughed, but decided it was better than having her head encased in rubber. "Damn."

Jesamine wiped the sweat from her face. "We really jumped into that one."

Raphael looked less than happy. "You think that's it? Was that their best shot?"

Jesamine shrugged. "It must have taken a fuck of a lot of energy to generate and deliver those things."

Cordelia's instincts agreed with Jesamine. So much energy had been expended she doubted if another attack was immediately imminent. "None of us wants to go back Inside right now."

"If they had reserves of power, they would have launched a full-scale battlefield attack. Not just used it to nail Dunbar and cut off the head of the Albany attack."

"They didn't even provide support. There were no Mothmen, and no sign of the sports model. They used us to get vector, but there was nothing to make things difficult for us."

Cordelia agreed, and not only because she didn't want to jump again. "I didn't sense the hand of Jeakqual-Ahrach in any of that. I want to believe those wrigglers were localized; that they were created by Zhaithan at the other end of the valley; that it was all the paranormal Ab Balsol had left."

Cordelia didn't have to tell the others that previous clashes with Her Grand Eminence had left her very sensitive to the presence of Jeakqual-Ahrach behind any attack, and Jesamine totally bought the logic. "So we stay on this side and watch the skies?"

Raphael looked worried. "It's a gamble, but I know I couldn't do that all over again, unless it was really life and death."

The jump into the Other Place had left them all dazed, but the terrestrial battle continued to rage on. The entire area around the grassy knoll was on the move as the second wave of infantry and fighting machines assembled at the head of the valley in preparation for entering the carnage. Although it was hard to accept, their encounter with the new variety of Dark Things was just one small, if unusual, skirmish in the full epic of the battle. If they survived, they would have a story to tell, but so would thousands of others; cavalrymen, gunners, foot soldiers, the airmen in the sky above the fray. The battle went on, with or without The

Four, and right now, in the early afternoon, it seemed to be moving into a new and crucial phase.

A lieutenant was cleaning stinking Dark Thing residue from the blade of his saber, and Cordelia decided he was as good as anyone to fill her in on any new developments. "How goes the battle, Lieutenant?"

"Lady Blakeney?"

"That's right."

"You didn't hear?"

She indicated his sword blade. "I've been dealing with those damn black things."

The lieutenant looked a little uneasy; the unease of the junior officer presented with the unexplainable. "Will we see any more of them?"

"I sincerely hope not. But what didn't I hear."

"We took the western ridge."

"We did? Well, Goddess be praised."

"And now the second half of the assault is going in."

"And will that be the end of it?"

"We surely hope so. Dunbar is making ready to move forward with the cavalry. We have our orders. Up and mounted in fifteen minutes. Maybe you should do the same if you don't want to be left behind."

Cordelia definitely wasn't going to be left behind; she turned and started for the horse lines. Then the lieutenant called after her. "Lady Blakeney?"

She turned. "Lieutenant?"

"It seems there's a village near here called Newbury. Talk is this will end up being called the Battle of Newbury Vale."

"That's as long as we win, lieutenant."

"No question we're going to win, Lady Blakeney."

"I hope you're right."

## RAPHAEL

Even though they weren't going into direct combat, the pulse-quickening excitement was infectious. Raphael was riding with the cream of the

Albany cavalry. Despite all of his reservations, he could only think of the long way he had come from the squalid ranks of the Mosul. Hardware jingled and leather creaked, mounts tossed their heads and snorted, commands were shouted, and all the time the firing went on and on, but with the repetitive bark of repeating Bergman guns predominating, which had to be a good omen. Raphael figured they needed all the good omens they could get. He hadn't told the others about the glimpse that had come to him as they exited the other place. The vision had been fleeting and less than clear, but he was sure it was the white figures from their collective dreams. The odd part was that he was left with the distinct impression that the figures were strictly observing the engagement between the Dark Things and The Four, rather than taking any part in it, but everything was so nebulous that he was not sure how to explain his suspicions to the others without causing undue alarm and distraction. In any case, no time existed for them to talk as they plunged into the valley of noise, confusion, and death that was now called Newbury Vale. He supposed he should have been frightened, but he found himself carried along by the drama and exhilarated by the spectacle.

Dunbar himself rode in an open-topped staff car towards the rear of his massed cavalry. He and his entourage were hedged around by a high-stepping thicket of protective horsemen with drawn sabers. No chances were being taken as the four cars carrying the commander and his aides bucked and bumped over the torn-up ground, and swerved to avoid the constant obstacles presented by shell craters. Now that the western ridge had fallen, the Mosul guns were no longer laying down a deadly enfilade, and the second wave of attackers took their fight to the enemy with comparative ease. The bodies of men and horses, and the burned-out hulks of fighting machines that littered the field, bore mute testimony to just how hard it had been for those in the first assault. That leading wave had approached to within two hundred yards of the Mosul forward trenches, and there they had halted, knowing it was impossible to make the final breakthrough without reinforcements. As the second wave rolled forward, gathering momentum with no Mosul fire to slow them down, the survivors of the original attack gamely held their position with their heavy, rapid-fire Bergman guns, mortars, and the cannon on the fighting machines, keeping the enemy lines pinned down in their shallow, hastily dug trenches.

As far as Raphael could see, nothing could prevent an overwhelming Albany victory. As soon as the second wave caught up with the first, they would punch a hole in the Mosul lines and the rest would be little more than a mopping-up operation. The riders around him seemed to share the same tangible sense of optimism. The Four were fairly near the rear of the massed cavalry, and surrounded by their guard of light horsemen, short-barreled carbines at the ready. As always, Cordelia rode ahead, straight-backed in the saddle and very aware of her red hair blazing in the afternoon sun. Raphael found that Lady Blakeney never ceased to amaze him. Even on the battlefield, she reveled in the admiring glances of the men around her. Jesamine and Argo rode together a short distance behind. They were actually talking to each, which seemed to Raphael, as always bringing up the rear, to be another good sign.

Dunbar had selected the same point at the base of the eastern ridge that he had picked for his mobile field guns to serve now as his new command position. The batteries had moved even further forward and turned their attention from the western ridge to the Mosul center. Intense fire was now hammering the heart of the enemy force, softening it up for the final Albany assault. The cavalry was marshaled around Dunbar, but directly a hole was opened in the Mosul lines, the charge would sound, and the horse soldiers would surge into the breach and administer the coup de grâce. A tension that was part anxiety and part anticipation gripped both men and horses. The cavalry had only played a peripheral role in the Battle of the Potomac, but here at Newbury Vale they were being given the chance to shine, to do what they had been trained for, and in some cases, what they had been born and bred for. Hands rested on the hilts of sabers and the butts of sidearms, and reins were tightly gripped in gauntlet-covered hands. Men who were keyed up but optimistic, certain the day was going to end in victory, laughed and joked nervously, and glances were constantly being cast in the direction of their commanders, waiting the order to go.

At first, the shouting was hardly audible amid the general roar of the guns, the screaming and yelling, and everything else that made up the cacophony of battle. The cadence was what initially made it noticeable. The same word repeated over and over, in unison and rhythmically intoned. Raphael couldn't quite make it out, but everyone around him paused to listen. Argo and Jesamine had reined in their mounts, and Cordelia, who had been riding beside Sergeant Teasle, the leader of The Four's escort, was now standing in her stirrups. The chant grew louder, and, as far as Raphael could tell, it was coming from the Mosul. Suddenly Jesamine turned in alarm. She had recognized the word. A second later he recognized it, too. The word was *"Mamalukes,"* and his stomach turned to ice.

The chant was now quite clear, rising to a pounding cadence. *"Mama-lukes! Ma-ma-lukes! Ma-ma-lukes! Ma-ma-lukes! Ma-ma-lukes!"*

## JESAMINE

She had heard and seen too much of the Mamalukes not to be afraid. The best of Albany's cavalry surrounded her, but the knowledge hardly helped. Fear of the Mamalukes had been conditioned into her from birth, and reinforced by long and bitter experience. Their spiked helmets, steel breastplates, flowing cloaks, and hawk-nosed bearded faces had struck fear into her heart from the cradle. Born out of a military slave class in Nile, that had risen in revolt and massacred their masters, the Mamalukes had been a violent, brutal culture for more than three hundred years, dedicated to raising generation after generation of implacable and merciless warriors.

*"Ma-ma-lukes! Ma-ma-lukes! Ma-ma-lukes! Ma-ma-lukes! Ma-ma-lukes!"*

The front ranks of the Mosul were parting. Faysid Ab Balsol was sending out his cavalry, a final play of fanatic desperation. Ranks of horsemen plunged through the gap. With the red and black flame banners of Hassan IX fluttering and streaming above them, they bore down on the front ranks of Albany. Bergmans barked and horseman after horseman went down in a wreck of thrown men and rolling, thrashing beasts, but they still managed to maintain a tight spearhead, with enough momentum to punch a temporary hole in the Albany lines, while roaring encouragement was bellowed from the Mosul trenches.

*"Ma-ma-lukes! Ma-ma-lukes! Ma-ma-lukes! Ma-ma-lukes! Ma-ma-lukes!"*

Although the Mosul mob was chanting for the Mamalukes, the cavalry racing across the battlefield was far from wholly Mamaluke. Almost as many Teuton *uhlans,* in their too-familiar plumed shakos, galloped flat out on their heavy chargers, firing long-barreled revolvers and slashing with bloody sabers. Regular Mosul horsemen, less flamboyant in drab khaki, and on shorter ponies, added their number to the wild and suicidal charge. When Ab Balsol's cavalry had streamed out of the sudden gap in the lines like greyhounds from the slips, it had appeared that no plan existed beyond doing as much damage as possible before they were cut down by superior Albany weapons, but then, after a wild and costly ride through the Albany lines, they began to wheel. At first Jesamine was amazed that any discipline could remain after so many casualties, but, when the turn ended with the thrust of the continuing charge coming straight at her, she abandoned all objectivity and wondered what the hell she was supposed to do? She might be dressed like a solider, but, unlike maybe Argo and Raphael, she was hardly trained, or even prepared for bloody and mounted combat, and, unlike Cordelia, she had not ridden horses almost from birth. The Mamaluke breakout had plunged the Albany horsemen into an instant of milling confusion, but they were rapidly sorting themselves, coming back under the control of their officers, and, with the exception of Dunbar's escort, deploying to counter the Mosul cavalry assault.

As the personal escort backed up to shield Dunbar and his people, The Four and their light horsemen moved back with them. Dunbar was standing in the open staff car, observing the Mosul and encouraging the men around him. "Stand firm, gentlemen, they won't reach us. Our lads will stop them."

The Albany horse soldiers were moving forward at an orderly walk. Slide had moved protectively up to The Four, and watched with them as their cavalry broke into a trot and slowly gathered speed, heading for the inevitable clash with Mamaluke and Teuton. Jesamine eased closer to Slide, finding an irrational comfort by the way he always smelled of oiled leather, cigars, and gunpowder. "Will our boys hold them?"

"You want truth or patriotism?"

"Truth."

"They'll be hard-pressed."

"What are the Mosul trying to achieve by this?"

"Balsol has a sense of history."

"What?"

"He's emulating Alexander the Conqueror at Abban."

The Albany cavalry was running at a full gallop. Sabers flashed, pennants fluttered, and the drumming of hooves was deafening. Jesamine fancied she felt the ground shake, and she had to shout so Slide could hear her. "I don't understand."

"The Macedonian used his cavalry to break through the Persian lines and go after their King Darius."

The rattle of small-arms fire was added to the awesome din as the two sides came within range of each other, and cavalrymen fired from the saddle.

"Does Balsol think killing Dunbar will end it?"

"I figure . . ." His eyes became narrow and disbelieving. "Holy shit!"

Jesamine followed his gaze as Slide actually pushed back his hat and stared. The Mosul front line was dissolving and what appeared to be the entire compliment of Mosul infantry was charging at a run in one of their notorious human waves. Slide grimly shook his head. "Balsol's going for Armageddon."

"What's Armageddon?"

The answer was uniquely Slide. "In other realities, it's what they called The End."

## CORDELIA

The sound of two charging armies colliding head on was like nothing Cordelia had heard before. It was louder and more terrible than she might ever have imagined; a death-spawned symphony of collective momentum, muscle on bone, striking each other a thousand times over, the scream of men and horses likewise multiplied, the explosion of guns as though heard from inside the cannons' mouth, the amplified crash of endless steel on endless steel, all the way to hell and beyond, as the impact went on and on. From where she sat the sound was all she had, the entire field was blanketed in an impenetrable maelstrom of dust and smoke in which dark figures grappled, and explosions flashed a lurid orange. Cordelia knew, inside the dreadful cloud, the Mosul human wave was being massacred by the Albany Bergman guns, and crushed under the treads of the Albany fighting machines. The crucial question was whether Albany could kill enough of the enemy before they were overrun and drowned by the weight of numbers.

A riderless horse plunged out of the smoke, and the small force around Dunbar raised their weapons. The frightening truth was that, if even a small squadron of Mamalukes overran the Albany cavalry, visibility was so poor that those around the commander would not know about it until the very last moment. His staff and escort sat their mounts or stood to beside automobiles, with weapons in their hands, vainly trying to make out any detail of the booming but hidden combat. The wireless and ticker tape machine had been reinstalled, but the airship, even from its vantage point in the sky, could only report what they already knew. The Mosul had thrown in their cavalry and an entire human wave, but beyond that, all was smoke and confusion and nothing was clear. Some of Dunbar's staff were urging the Field Marshal to withdraw to some safer place, but, as Cordelia expected, he dismissed the idea out of hand. "If I leave now, I will concede the field. If our arms cannot prevail and hold their assault, then I have lost the Army of Albany."

Another horse galloped out of the smoke and dust, this time with a rider. Cordelia saw him clearly, a gaunt Mamaluke on a tall but ill-fed black horse. His cloak was filthy, his breastplate and helmet were dull, but the edge of his scimitar gleamed. He was all but upon Dunbar and the Albany command before they knew it. Cordelia fancied he looked surprised as he reined in his horse, causing it to rear and paw the air. Turning in his saddle, the man let out an ululating roar that could only be a signal to others. Three officers fired and three bullets hit the Mamaluke, knocking him out of the saddle. Cordelia felt her life go into slow motion. Was this the end? Had the Mosul broken through? Would this first one be followed by a thousand, or was he merely a stray? She clutched her revolver and waited for an answer.

The wait was not long. Six riders came at them; two Teutons, leading on their heavy chargers, and four Mamalukes behind. Again Albany guns barked and chattered, and more riderless horses ran loose. Perhaps these were only dislocated outriders from the original charge. Certainly the distinctive Bergman guns could still be heard. Dunbar stood up, as though filled with a sudden resolve. "Mr. Fletcher."

A young captain on a bay responded. "Sir."

"I need your horse, boy. I'm not waiting here for them to come for me."

"Sir?"

"Your horse, boy. I need your horse."

"Yes sir."

Fletcher's face betrayed that the last thing he wanted was to give up his mount, but he was not about to argue with a Field Marshal. He dismounted, and Dunbar climbed into the saddle. He turned the horse, apparently relieved to be in motion. For a moment, he studied the faces of those around him. "Well, boys, shall we go and find the enemy?" He glanced down at the now unseated captain. "Don't worry, Fletcher. You can catch yourself a runaway."

No sooner had Dunbar spoken than at least a dozen riders, maybe as many as twenty, all Mamalukes, boiled from the reek of battle, and as many Albany horsemen leapt forward to counter them. Cordelia found herself part of a confusion of dirty sweating faces, pistols and sabers, flashes and smoke, bucking horses, and men fighting hand to hand. She was in the middle of unfocused, dangerous chaos. More Mamalukes seemed to be coming at them, but, in the immediate dust and smoke, it was hard to tell who was friend and who was foe. Yancey Slide was easy to spot. The reins of his horse were gripped between his bared teeth, and he had his oriental sword in one hand and one of his strange square-sided pistols in the other. He was hacking and shooting with a vengeance, but, at the same time, along with the light horsemen of their escort, attempting to herd The Four out and away from the mounted mêlée to some safer place. This was easier said than accomplished. The combatants were packed so tight that it was hard to go anywhere in the ebb and flow. Then Sergeant Teasle went down, and a Mamaluke, with gold teeth and a raised scimitar was on Cordelia. She did not hesitate. She brandished her revolver at the smoke-blackened face and wild bloodshot eyes, and pulled the trigger. The pistol bucked in her hand and the Mamaluke was knocked backward. Her gelding reared and Cordelia desperately fought him down, while still holding on to her gun. To be thrown and find oneself on the ground among so many stamping, frightened horses would amount to a death sentence.

Cordelia calmed the horse, and was surprised to see feathers and buckskins amid the cavalry uniforms. Warriors of the Ohio were in among them, bringing down Mamalukes left and right with lances and tomahawks. A fighting machine came lumbering towards them, guns stammering and flashing, but it initially created even more confusion as Mamalukes spun away from the fire of its heavy, side-mounted repeaters. The gunfire, grinding machinery, and belching exhaust was too much for Cordelia's gelding. The gray bucked and plunged. Cordelia hung on for dear life, but then the horse collided with a riderless charger. The gelding stumbled, and she found herself pitched from the saddle, down amid the cruel stamping hooves.

## ARGO

Slide had swung down from his saddle and was standing over Cordelia, blazing away with his twin pistols at anything that threatened them. Cordelia's gelding had collided with a runaway and she had been thrown. Slide was the first to react. Straddling her body, he thrust his sword into the ground, and drew his second pistol. Argo spurred his horse forward in an attempt to cover both Slide and Cordelia from at least one side, but even as he moved to help, it became clear that the Mamalukes were turning. The fighting machine was too much for them. They might be insane fanatics, but they were not immortal. They wheeled and hightailed it into the smoke. Ohio warriors and Albany officers gathered around Dunbar, still watchful and protective. Slide pulled Cordelia to her feet and dusted her off, checking that no bones were broken, and that she did not have a concussion. Argo managed to grab the reins of the spooked gelding, and, when it had calmed a little, he led it to where Cordelia was standing and handed her the reins. She took them and spent some time stroking the animal's muzzle before she attempted to remount. The fighting machine ground to a halt and a crewman popped the dorsal hatch. Dunbar saw him and pushed his commandeered horse through those packed around him.

"How goes the day, Captain?"

The crewman's battle suit was so stained with sweat, oil, and soot, Argo was surprised that Dunbar could tell the man's rank. The tank captain pulled off his goggles, and they left circles of pale skin around his eyes. "The enemy charge has been contained, sir."

"That's extremely good news."

"The Mosul are falling back, but falling back in good order."

"Are we pressing them?"

"A lot of units are catching their breath, Field Marshal. Turning them back was hard."

"I understand, but we can't wait too long, Captain. We can't wait too long."

"The lads all know that, Field Marshal. They won't wait."

"I'm glad to hear it, Captain."

The captain mopped his face with a rag. "If you'll excuse me, sir, I have to find a fuel lorry before I get back into it."

"Carry on, Captain. You are all making me proud."

The captain dropped into the body of the machine, and pulled the hatch closed. The engine started, and the cavalrymen tightened their grip on their mounts as it clanked away. Dunbar turned in his saddle and met the eyes of his staff. "We have to get Albany moving again, gentlemen. We need one last effort before the sun goes down. I can't allow Balsol the generosity of night."

## RAPHAEL

Mosul dead were everywhere. They carpeted the valley all the way back to their own forward trenches where the survivors were now bracing themselves for the next Albany attack. Some lay slumped, and others hideously contorted, mouths silently screaming, clawed hands frozen by death in the act of clutching for dear life. Others only remained as pieces of sundered flesh, severed legs, or unrecognizable torsos in the rags of blood-soaked uniforms. But for the strangest and most elaborately twisted fate, Raphael might have been among them, and not following Virgil Dunbar as he rallied his weary troops to make one final effort to finish Faysid Ab Balsol. Dunbar himself had seemed shocked when he saw the terrible extent of the carnage, and Raphael was one of the few who heard him utter what would later be his best known observation. "Next to a battle lost, the greatest misery is a battle gained."

But the battle was not yet gained, and Dunbar rode among his men, with his staff, and the wider retinue that included Slide, Raphael, Argo, Jesamine, and Cordelia, behind him. Morale was high, but the men were tired. They would do their duty, but with a grim determination, giving all of their final reserves. Make or break, this would be the last push, or they would know the reason why. While a front line of riflemen and Bergman nests kept the remaining Mosul either pinned down or jumping, scattered units were being reassembled, and, where the casualties had been high, new ones formed from survivors. Ammunition was being resupplied, and the motor vehicles rearmed and refueled. Some men were eating and others avoided food, believing that it was bad to take a bullet on a full stomach, and depending for sustenance on their gin ration. Gin had been issued in most regiments, and, where it hadn't, men had broken out the final stashed bottles from their kit. Even Argo had found a bottle of sipping whiskey, and ridden up beside Raphael and offered him a drink. The bottle was already a third empty and Argo's voice was slurred.

"We've come one fuck of a long way, Major Vega."

Raphael accepted the bottle and took a serious swallow. "We have indeed, Major Weaver. And I hope we still have a long way to go."

Argo laughed and clapped him on the shoulder. "You should be drawing all this, partner. Preserving it for posterity."

Although Argo didn't know it, Raphael had stopped once and attempted to sketch what he was seeing, but Slide had chided him, patting him on the shoulder and moving him along. "The battle isn't over, young Vega. There will be plenty of time to sketch the dead later."

Argo cantered ahead and Raphael followed. All round them Albany was making its move. The engines of the fighting machines were in gear, and some were already moving forward. Infantrymen fixed their bayonets. Few orders were being shouted. The entire force was advancing as if by organic mutual agreement, and the Mosul trenches were the only objective. The cavalry streamed ahead; Albany regulars with lance and saber, the proud and furious war bands of the Ohio, and irregulars like the Appalachian partisans, the mountain men, and trappers out of the interior, and former bandits like English John and his boys, and the Presley Brothers with their mad old patriarch, who had started to fight the Mosul because there was nothing left to steal. The horsemen, however, did not have it all their way. The infantry ran hard on their heels, with the lumbering fighting machines bringing up the rear. As his entire force proceeded with a will, Dunbar sat on his horse among his aides and said nothing. He was not about to interfere with the process.

The army moved as a surge of men, a rising tide building to high water. No reserves were being held back, everyone was going to the show. No man wanted to be left out of the fall of the Mosul in Virginia. Scattered fire came from the Mosul front line. A handful of cannon had been assembled and half-hearted and poorly-aimed shells burst in front of the Albany advance, but the pace only quickened. Some units had broken into double time, and a strange wordless roar came from the men of Albany. The first cavalry units were almost at the Mosul trenches. Mosul officers were screaming at their men to repel the attackers, but something seemed to have snapped. At first the Mosul ranks merely stood mute and seemingly paralyzed, but then one or two climbed the crumbling walls of their trenches and began to run. A few at first, but then in increasing number, the Mosul broke ranks like a great dam bursting until a flood of men was pouring down the valley, fleeing from Albany, looking for any way to escape.

A great cry of jubilation went up. "*The Mosul have broken!* They are running!"

Some men halted and embraced each other. Other pressed on, caught up in the fury of the moment, charging after the bolting Mosul, looking to exact fatal revenge.

"*The Mosul have broken!*"

## JESAMINE

Dunbar and all of those around him rode in dour silence towards the tattered flame banner that hung from a broken flagstaff. With the onset of the evening, the earlier breeze had dropped, and the once-feared flag hardly moved, drooping like a torn and smoke-stained rag. Faysid Ab Balsol waited beneath it with a handful of his surviving officers. The dead lay piled and contorted all around them as though the standard was the focus of a desperate final stand. These last remnants of their foes were silhouetted against a setting sun that had been made a blood red orb by the smoke that hung in the air, and they cast grim and elongated shadows. The Mosul general was tall. Even stooped in defeat and leaning heavily on his scimitar, he towered over the others around him. He must have been all of six-feet-five or -six, and his elaborate helmet with its flowing chain mail and plumed spike added even more inches. Jesamine, who was riding a few horses' length behind Dunbar, as close as she was able to maneuver herself, calculated that Ab Balsol had to be of equal parts high-born Mamaluke and blood Mosul, the perfect symbolic scion of Hassan's empire, and she wondered how the man could be feeling at that moment. For two centuries, the invading armies of the Mosul Empire had experienced precious few reverses. Their only real setback had been the ill-fated expedition into the snows of the Northern Plains, when they had ridden against the Saami and the Russe, only to be forced back by Joseph the Terrible into that legendary retreat through the deadly Russland winter. Now, in the space of a single year, they had twice been soundly beaten in the Americas. Jesamine was surprised the Mosul general was allowing himself to be taken at all, and had not killed himself when all was so obviously lost. The banner was slowly lowered, and Faysid Ab Balsol pulled his sword from the ground. Dunbar reined in his borrowed mount and spoke for all to hear. "Faysid Ab Balsol, I demand your unconditional surrender."

"Virgil Dunbar, you have my surrender."

Dunbar swung down from the bay and limped towards the Mosul leader. As he approached, Ab Balsol reversed his sword and offered it hilt first with a stiff bow. The tall Mosul's left arm hung limply by his side, and the sleeve of his uniform tunic was torn and dark with blood. Seemingly the general had not come through the fight unscathed. Dunbar shook his head. "Keep your sword, sir. I don't require it."

As a military escort surrounded Balsol and his commanders, ready to march them away, Jesamine suddenly found it hard to believe that the contest of armies was all over and that she had survived. Here at Newbury Vale, the forces of Hassan IX had been brought to the field and utterly routed. The news would resonate through Hispania and the Land of the Franks, and all the other slave nations across the ocean. The Zhaithan and the Ministry of Virtue could never shut down the underground grapevine, no matter how many unfortunates were publicly flogged for negativism, or tortured and hung as seditionists, defeatists, heretics, or Norse agents. She could imagine the unrestrained joy she would have felt had she learned that the Mosul were not invincible while she had been slaving for Mamaluke and Teuton, on her back or on her knees. Right there and then, Jesamine could hardly contain herself from shouting with angry and triumphant delight. Only the supremely sobering effect of the battle's ghastly aftermath stopped her. The men of Albany and their allies had paid a terrible price for their victory. Although their casualties in no way approached the fearsome death toll of the Mosul, Jesamine bleakly wondered how many previously familiar faces she would never see again.

And then a familiar face appeared in her field of vision. At first she thought that she was dreaming or facing a newly created ghost. "Oonanchek?"

He moved stiffly. "It is I."

"Are you hurt?"

Oonanchek shook his head. "I am fine. Just a little battered. There are many who are worse."

Oonanchek's face was streaked and smeared with war paint, and grimed with smoke and powder, but he was clearly alive. He was also alone. Jesamine was suddenly alarmed. "Magachee?"

"She is alive."

"Wounded?"

Oonanchek smiled reassuringly. "Do not concern yourself. She is unhurt."

"Thank the Goddess for that. Where is she?"

"At the new camp that is being made. I go there myself now. I just wanted to see Balsol surrender."

"You're going to the camp right now?"

"No one should stay in this place where the Mosul made their stand. Too many confused spirits continue to linger."

"I just want to convince myself they're really dead."

"But now you have seen it, you should depart."

Faysid Ab Balsol was being marched away under heavy guard. He was being taken to the Albany camp that was in the process of being established at the other end of the valley. He would very aptly have to traverse the full length of his chosen battlefield as the daylight faded, and the night closed in. If he had managed to hold out until the darkness, he might have saved his army and slipped away, but now he would have to pass the piles of bodies, the great funeral pyres that were being built for the Mosul dead, and witness his own men being organized into disposal squads. The piles of wood and debris were being liberally doused with petroleum, and would soon blaze in the night, ready for the Mosul bodies to be pitched onto them by these detachments of prisoners. The Mosul had used the flame as their symbol, but now it was going to consume them, proving, Jesamine supposed, that the fire belonged only to the victor. She was well aware that thousands of the enemy dead were only unfortunate conscripts, no better than slaves to their Mosul masters, but she was not yet ready to be forgiving, or provide excuses for fallen foes. She could only take the attitude of, fuck them, they deserved it. Somewhere in the gathering dust, a lone Albany voice was singing, accompanied by a weeping harmonica.

> In the valley below, lads
> In the valley below
> I coughed out my young life,
> In the valley below.

She and Oonanchek fell in behind the guard party, and followed it towards the mouth of the valley, the point where Dunbar had launched his first attack. Jesamine glanced at Oonanchek. For a moment their eyes met, but then both of them looked quickly away. After the fear and anxiety, and all the excitement and adrenalin of the day, she had suddenly, in an unchecked, animal moment, wanted Oonanchek, in the most wanton and shameless way she could imagine; not with Magachee, not as the mystic threesome of their now severed *takla,* but as strong, all enclosing, hard-driving, penetrating man. For a wild instant, she craved a clawing, writhing release from the impossible weight of carnage and tension. She wanted to be held, and fucked, and to let it all out with wordless keening and sobbing screams, and she knew that in the same second he had felt the same, but then the moment was passed and propriety prevailed, and also the realization that, afterwards, life would have to go on. After catharsis, reality would still remain. Magachee would be betrayed. The *takla* would be compromised, and the two of them would rise from their rut unable to face each other. Jesamine let out a long sigh, not caring what it revealed. Argo, Raphael, and Cordelia were riding a little way off. "I think it would be best if I went to join them."

Oonanchek nodded. "You should do that."


## ARGO

The aftermath was strange. Argo wasn't sure how he had expected the victory would be celebrated. He knew the civilians would be dancing and drinking, and cheering crowds would throng the streets when the word reached Albany, but there on the battlefield, where reality had happened and was still happening, triumph was a very different matter. He supposed that once upon a time, his farm-boy fantasy would have been storybook excess like the old-time Vikings; a lavishly pagan victors' feast at which oxen were roasted, naked women danced, and entire barrels of beer consumed by sweating warriors—but he already knew too much and had seen too much to believe such myths. In the officers' mess, no one danced, few sang, and even when they did, it was a rising chorus of melancholy that quickly faded. A valley night-mist clung to the ground, mixed with the black gasoline smoke, and the stench from the fires at the other end of the valley where the enemy dead were being burned. If he walked out of the mess tent, the pyres were plainly visible, and, accordingly, he had decided not to walk outside the mess tent. Not that inside was much better. The men and women were shocked and exhausted. Some drank to heal the shock, and kill the very real physical pain. Others simply stared at a bottle in front of them, processing the ghastly chaos of the day. Many were bandaged, or limped with the help of canes or improvised crutches. Most had not bothered to change from their blood- and smoke-stained battle dress. The fight had been hard won, and the real moment of exultation had been back on the field, when the Mosul broke and ran. As the tide of combat had so precipitately turned, amid the hand-to-hand confusion of the late afternoon, they had, all together, yelled their shout of victory from the bottom of their lungs and from the primal depths of their beings. Now, hours later, in the dark of that first night, jubilation had been replaced by disbelief and disgust at the terrible toll of destruction, as the cost was now being tallied.

New arrivals brought fresh names to add to the roll call of the lost, and these were met by dour stares, groans, and curses, and the mood grew increasing morose and drunk. News came that an entire gun crew had been wiped out by a Mosul direct hit, one of the first guns into the valley, one of those who had pounded the western ridge. As the names of the dead were repeated, the artillery colonel who had been their commander rose to his feet, and, with great deliberation and precision, hurled an almost full bottle of good Norse scotch, from his private store, hard at the nearest support pole with enough force to smash it. Then he took a deep breath and, with a strained and shaking control, requested a replacement from the mess orderly. "I seem to have destroyed the last in a fit of rage, I believe, at the random nature of death."

An RAAC flying officer, an observer from one of the Odins, walked in and was immediately barraged with questions. "How now, young Flying Officer? What of the enemy?"

"What are the Mosul reinforcements doing? Are they still coming on?"

The flying officer dropped into a chair at an empty table, threw down his helmet, goggles, and gloves. He unstrapped his sidearm and laid it beside them, holding up a hand as if to ward off all the impatient demands for news. "A moment, gentleman." He turned to the orderly. "A whiskey, if you please, Jeeves."

The glass was placed in front of him and the flying officer drank it down in one. "You had better give me another."

This was too much for a stout, red-faced infantry major. "Damn it, man. Don't tease us like some coy fucking virgin. Are the Mosul coming or not? Will we have to go through the whole bloody business again in the morning?"

A certain resentfulness existed between the infantry and the airmen. The infantry viewed the Air Corps as privileged glamour boys who sailed way above the muck and bullets, while the infantry bled and died, and fought the war the hard way. For their part, the RAAC considered the very act of taking a piece of imperfect machinery thousands of feet into the air to be more than enough proof of their courage and endurance, let alone swooping low over the Mosul lines to drop their bombs or gather information on enemy positions. As the orderly poured the airman his second drink, he looked slowly round at the anxious, assembled faces and smiled. "It seems to be good news, my friends."

"So tell us."

"The relief column has stopped. They've been halted since before sunset. They could have just stopped for the night, but they could be stopped in preparation to get the fuck out of Virginia. It's impossible to tell. All I know was that whoever was leading the column was in no hurry to bail out Faysid Ab Balsol. They weren't exactly marching to the sound of his guns. Quite the reverse. As soon as Balsol made his stand, they noticeably slowed down."

The news that the relief column was not coming at them in double time caused a measure of relief and orders for fresh drinks, but the mention of Faysid Ab Balsol prompted the flying officer to question to the room. "What became of that bastard?"

"What bastard?"

"Faysid Ab fucking Balsol. What happened to him after he offered his sword to Dunbar?"

A youthful lieutenant who had lost most of his platoon in the first advance snorted angrily. "He's probably hung up by his thumbs someplace, before they hang him properly."

But he was corrected by a more experienced, long-serving captain of cavalry. "Quite the reverse, dear boy. He is most likely being formally wined and dined by the generals."

The young lieutenant was shocked. "I don't understand."

"They don't hang or torture supreme commanders, lad. It would set a dangerous precedent." The cynical observation elicited a fresh snippet of news from another newcomer. "On the subject of hanging and torturing, the intelligence boys have a dragnet out for surviving Zhaithan. Seems like they've been trying to slip away disguised as Mosul grunts."

One bit of scuttlebutt coaxed out another. "I heard some irregulars brought a bunch of Zhaithan in a while ago, and handed them over to Slide."

This produced some knowing and decidedly evil smiles. "Slide will know what to do with the Zhaithan. At least Hassan's butcher boys won't be dining with any generals."

## CORDELIA

The prisoner sat on a straight-backed folding chair with his hands lashed behind his back. When Slide had roused Cordelia, he had told her that the man "believes that he'll be tortured, and I've done nothing to set him straight." Now Slide walked round him with the studied deliberation of the practiced interrogator. "I'll speak very slowly so I don't have to repeat myself. I am not of this world, Zhaithan, and if I feel like it, I can fuse your fucking cortex, and have you contorting on the floor until your spine snaps. You want to put it to the test?"

The prisoner's eye was blackened and his lip was cut. He had been captured by irregular guerrillas, hard men with flowing hair and necklaces of bear teeth. He'd been trying to slip away, disguised in the greatcoat of an infantry private, but he had made the mistake of hanging on to his expensive, handmade Krupp sidearm, and it had betrayed him. The guerrillas had slapped him around for a while, as punishment for his deceit and noncooperation, but had held off from shooting him out of hand. Since the invasion, the guerrillas had lost a lot of comrades to the gallows and torture chambers of the Zhaithan and the Mosul Ministry of Virtue, and no one would have blamed them if they had exacted a measure of swift revenge, but these mountain men knew enough to realize that a high-placed Zhaithan could provide a wealth of information if a way could be found to pry it out of him. Thus they had beat the man a little more, and then brought him to Yancey Slide, working on the principle that, if anyone could crack a Zhaithan, it was Slide.

Cordelia was not quite sure why Slide had decided to rouse her from her sleep to come and look at this prisoner. She had been deep asleep. Her body was bruised and aching after her fall from the gelding, and she was exhausted from the turmoil of the day. Her first reaction on being shaken awake was a string of obscenities. Her second was to demand to know what the hell was going on. Slide had handed her his flask.

"We have a prisoner. A high Zhaithan."

The information and the offer of a drink had cut through Cordelia's bleary fury. She took a pull from the flask and coughed. "We do?"

"It has fallen to me to interrogate him. Dunbar thinks that I might be able to wring some nuggets of truth out of him."

Cordelia took a second drink. The liquor tasted strange, probably some outlandish concoction of Slide's. "And where do I come into this wringing?"

"I want you to put on a fresh uniform and come with me."

"You want me to help you interrogate this bastard?"

Slide produced a flame from the tip of his index finger and lit a cheroot. "I suspect you may have a talent for extracting truth."

Cordelia had seen the flaming finger trick too many times before to be impressed. She also wasn't sure how she felt about his last statement, but she climbed stiffly from her bed, crossed the tent to the washstand. Slide sat down on her vacated bed with the cheroot in the corner of his mouth, and watched as she splashed water on her face. She had no problem being naked in front of Slide. He wasn't human, so it didn't count. "How highly placed?"

"What?"

"This Zhaithan, how highly placed?"

"He's a Fourth Adept."

"How do you know that?"

"By the tattoos just under his armpit. They all have them, and they're updated every time they're promoted. He could well have been one of Balsol's top Zhaithan."

"In that case, he won't crack easily."

"That's why I need your help. You can sniff the metaphysics coming off him."

Slide could put things oddly, but Cordelia always understood, as she did when he continued. "I'm fairly sure you won't be impeded by any moral complexities."

"You mean you won't hear me complain that doing unto the Zhaithan as they'd do unto others would make us as bad as they are?"

"Something of that order."

"Unlike my three companions, who still retain a few scruples?"

"Exactly. So make yourself as formidable as you can. We are playing the Zhaithan at his own game."

She selected a crisp new riding habit and dressed quickly. After she had pulled on her boots, Slide nodded approvingly, and offered a final suggestion. "Wear your riding gloves, and bring your crop."

Cordelia could feel herself warming to this new and unexpected task. She was far from sure that it was a healthy warmth, but she went with it. If nothing else, being present at an interrogation would be a kind of payback for what she had suffered at the hands of Her Grand Eminence Jeakqual-Ahrach. "I have the perfect thing."

She had put on her blue glasses, even though it was dark, and Slide had nodded.

The night seemed less about blue sunglasses once Slide had led her into the isolated tent where the Zhaithan was tied to the straight-backed folding chair. The bound prisoner's bruised face was dirty and glistened with sweat, his eyes were bloodshot. He was stripped to the waist and, in addition to his face, his body showed marks of where he had been punched and kicked immediately after his capture. Two of his captors stood on either side of him. The irregulars were big, weatherbeaten mountain men in boots and buckskins, with aborigine tattoos, and rifles held in the crooks of their arms. They looked eager to use the butts of those rifles on the Zhaithan, but Slide dismissed them. "I think Lady Blakeney and I can take it from here."

"You cutting us out of the fun, Yancey?"

"Go get yourselves drunk, boys, and maybe I'll give him to you later if he's difficult."

For a long minute after the mountain men exited the tent, Slide simply stared at the Zhaithan. Somewhere across the camp, a lone voice was singing.

*In the valley below, lads*
*In the valley below*
*I'll never be leaving,*
*The valley below.*

"Understand me, Zhaithan, I can fuse your cortex and have you contorting on the floor."

A spotlight, hooked up to an outside generator, had been placed over the seated prisoner, positioned to cause him the optimum discomfort. The Zhaithan slowly raised his head and, squinting against the harsh electric glare, looked first at Cordelia, and then at Slide. "This is a charade. You won't harm me."

During this opening exchange, Cordelia had stood stiffly in the shadows, unsure as to what to do. She experimentally flexed her crop, and discovered that she liked the feeling. The smoke of Slide's cheroot drifted into the cone of light, and Cordelia decided to join the drama. She took a measured step forward. "You don't think so?"

"Your monarch, your Carlyle, issued an edict. What was it he said? *'We treat our captured opponent with humanity, otherwise we are no better than him.'*"

"You are very well informed."

The prisoner smiled unpleasantly. "We have agents all through your capital."

Cordelia tapped her crop on her gloved palm. "Then, by the time we've finished, I guarantee you will have told the name of every last one of them."

"You are wasting your time with this posturing."

"Perhaps, but let's start with your name."

The Zhaithan had no trouble with that. "Borat Omar."

"And what is your rank, Borat Omar?"

"Fourth Adept."

"What was your function in Faysid Ab Balsol's command?"

"I'm not required to tell you that. Name and rank is all you'll get from me."

Slide sighed. "Borat Omar, I think I should tell you something. My name is Yancey Slide, I have no rank, and, as I already told you, I am not of this world. Some would call me a demon out of the most evil legends, and you should know I pay little heed to the dictates of any human monarch. Does the name Slide mean anything to you, Borat Omar?"

Borat Omar betrayed himself with the just the slightest flicker of fear, but then he set his jaw and made his face expressionless. "My name is Borat Omar, and my rank is . . ."

The prisoner suddenly gasped, his spine stiffened and then his body twisted, almost upsetting the chair. At the same time, Cordelia experienced what she could only describe as a vision. It only lasted for a split second, but, in that brief instant, she saw them with great clarity. A boy and a girl, but otherwise identical; albino twins with an apparent age of eight or nine years, who stared at her with wide-eyed, knowing expressions that seemed beyond their years. Cordelia did her best to deal with the glimpse without betraying herself to the bound Zhaithan. Slide had said sniff the metaphysics, but this was more than a mere whiff of the paranormal. The Zhaithan sagged forward in the chair, almost toppling, seemingly in a swoon. She took a couple of steps back, out of the prisoner's hearing and, when Slide joined her, she whispered urgently. "What the hell did you do?"

Slide dragged deeply on his cheroot. "I just ruffled the surface of his mind a little. A taste of what he could expect if he continued to resist me."

"Your ruffling cut loose a full-flown vision."

"A vision of what?"

"The white twins we've all been dreaming about."

Slide's eyes narrowed, and he glanced thoughtfully at the captive Zhaithan. "And what did these twins look like?"

Cordelia shook her head. "It was very fast. I saw two children, a boy and a girl, identical twins with white hair, but then they were gone."

"So we have to find out what the subject of your dreams is doing in the mind of Borat Omar?"

Cordelia stared thoughtfully at the prisoner who still hung limp, supported by his bonds. "Can I take a crack at him?"

Slide extended the hand of interrogator generosity. "Be my guest."

Cordelia again approached the prisoner. "Do we have your attention now?"

The Zhaithan made no move, remaining bent forward, apparently staring at the ground. Cordelia placed the tip of her riding crop under his chin, and raised his head. "I asked if we had your attention."

"What was that? What did he do to me?"

"Are you scared, Zhaithan? That was just a tiny taste of what Slide can do to you. If I was you, I would be very afraid."

"I am Zhaithan. I am not afraid."

"I know exactly what you are. And you will be afraid."

The prisoner regained a little of his previous truculence. "I doubt that."

Without the slightest warning, Cordelia lashed him hard across the face. "That shows how little you know."

The Zhaithan gasped and closed his eyes. A livid welt flared on his cheek, and she suddenly laughed. "You thought we wouldn't harm you?"

"You can beat me all you want, woman. I won't talk."

"Right now, I don't care if you talk or not."

"I am Borat Omar. I am a Fourth Adept."

She lashed him again, backhanded, across the other cheek. "You are whatever I want you to be."

The Zhaithan gasped a second time. "I heard there were women like you in Albany."

"Women of infinite and inventive cruelty? Women who rule and punish their men? Is that what you heard?"

"I heard . . ."

Cordelia cut him off. "For your information, I was once where you are. I was a prisoner of the Zhaithan. Indeed, I was interrogated by no less than Her Grand Eminence Jeakqual-Ahrach herself. What do you think of that, Borat Omar?"

The prisoner recovered somewhat from his shock and his eyes turned sullen. "You lie."

"I what?"

"If you had been interrogated by Her Grand Eminence, you would not be standing here now."

"You think not?" She struck a third time, creating another welt a half inch below the first. "You underestimate an Albany woman's powers of survival."

She raised the crop as if to deliver another stroke, and Borat Omar flinched. Now Cordelia was smiling. "Two of your kind wanted to push an electric phallus into me."

She realized she was giving free rein to a previously unsuspected side of her nature, but made no effort to check herself. "They would have fucked me with it for a full hour of constant electrical shock, if my rescuer hadn't shot them dead."

Borat Omar looked up at her and Cordelia raised a fourth welt on his face. "They started by stripping me naked."

The man twisted his head away, so this time Cordelia hit him across his bare chest. "And then they hung me up by my wrists."

She laid the whip on his nipples.

"So my toes barely touched the floor. I can still remember how it felt as they scraped the concrete floor."

Cordelia moved behind the prisoner, flexed the crop, getting a better feel for it, and then lashed him twice across his bowed shoulders. "What are you thinking, Borat Omar?"

She struck him twice more. "Isn't it humiliating for a Zhaithan to be thrashed by a mere woman?"

Cordelia found that using the crop on the man was a source of a deep, if angry satisfaction. "Or do you hope that a whipping from me will spare you from Yancey Slide here doing much worse to you?"

She must have been hurting him because he squirmed away from the next three cuts of the whip. "Nothing is going to save you from Slide, Zhaithan. I'm beating you because I enjoy beating you. I'm beating you because it pleases me, because it's fun, because I like the feel of the crop in my hand."

She made as though to walk away from him, but quickly turned on impulse and deftly kicked the chair over. The man fell backward, and landed on his back with his legs spread. Cordelia brought the crop hard down between them. The man screamed and Slide took the cheroot from his mouth. "Easy, Cordelia."

Cordelia stood for a moment, breathing fast. The power to inflict pain was unexpectedly intoxicating. She felt her blood flowing, and a malicious excitement rising inside her. She placed a booted foot on the prisoner's chest and looked down at him. Slide, apparently conceding the questioning to Cordelia, eased back into the shadows. Cordelia spoke slowly and distinctly. "So tell me, Borat Omar, what do you know about the white twins?"

To her complete amazement, the Zhaithan's eyes widened in surprise. "The twins?"

"That's right, you fucking worm. You think we do not know about the twins?"

Borat Omar was still gasping from the blow to his genitals. "I know very little about them. It has been a long time since I was in the Holy City."

"But you've heard?"

"Everyone has heard something."

"Even here in the Americas?"

The Zhaithan nodded. "Even here in the Americas."

"So even Jeakqual-Ahrach can't totally keep the secret of her creations."

Cordelia had been guessing in the dark, jumping from step to step on pure intuition, but now, it seemed, she had stepped too far. Borat Omar's eyes flickered from side to side. "No!"

Cordelia raised the whip. "You dare to say no to me?"

"My name is Borat Omar, and . . ."

Cordelia turned to Slide. "Take him. He knows more than he's saying. Go inside the worm's mind and see what he's hiding."

Slide stepped into the light. "You've finished with him?"

"For the moment."

Without any apparent effort, Slide righted the chair with the Zhaithan still bound to it. Slide gripped the man by the neck, and a look of terror came over the Zhaithan's face. "Wait!"

"What?"

"You don't understand."

"I don't understand what?"

"They are hers, they are Jeakqual-Ahrach's creation. I can't . . ."

"What do you mean you can't? You can't what?"

"I already told you. I've been here with the army. I only know what I hear."

"And what do you hear?"

"I can't . . ."

Cordelia gestured impatiently to Slide. "Go into his mind. He's playing with us."

The Zhaithan suddenly looked desperate. "Wait!"

Slide took the cheroot from his mouth. "So?"

"I tell you."

"So tell me."

Omar sighed. "The White Twins are the creation of Her Grand Eminence."

"We already know that."

"No, you don't understand. The story is that they are the Twin Gods made flesh. That they are Ignir and Aksura come to earth, but that is not the real story."

"And what is the real story?"

"No one knows for sure. No one. They were created in the Flame. . . ."

On the word "Flame" his voice choked off, if he had been strangled by unseen hands. His spine arched, his mouth opened wide, his eyes bulged and goggled and, after holding the expression for seconds, he pitched sideways with blood pouring from his eyes and ears. Cordelia jumped back to avoid the splatter. "What the hell?"

Slide actually looked impressed as what had previously been Borat Omar twitched and shuddered at their feet with fluid running from the hollows where his eyes had once been. Slide leaned down and let out a low whistle. "That was some sophisticated mindfuck."

"Did you do that?"

"Not me."

"So what happened?"

"Looks like a complete brainmelt."

"Brainmelt?"

"The entire contents of his skull pureed."

Cordelia gazed at the body with shocked revulsion. "How the fuck did that happen."

"Some very smart post-hypnotics coupled, I'd guess, with equally advanced destruct conjuration. And all triggered if he ever talked about these White Twins beyond a certain point."

"Is that even possible?"

"Who knows what a Zhaithan may have planted inside him."

Cordelia looked quickly around, suddenly nervous, as if something might be lurking in the darkness of the tent. Slide put a reassuring hand on her arm. "There's nothing present here."

"Are you sure?"

"I'm sure."

"He was about to tell us."

Slide flicked the ash from his cheroot. "He told us a lot. We know that your dreams have a substance behind them."

"Created in the Flame?"

Slide shrugged. "That must have been the big secret."

"What can be created in flame?"

"There are many stories of unholy creatures forged in fire."

"You believe such stories?"

"I neither believe nor disbelieve."

"But we did learn something?"

"We learned something about your dreams, and you learned something about yourself."

Cordelia avoided Slide's gaze. "I was a little carried away."

"We all meet the darkness. The trick now is to meet it, control it, and use it."

"Suppose I don't want to use it."

"You will. You have no choice. On one level, we are all just equations. We cannot function without the right and left of the equivalency. The dark side will use you if you don't use it. You know that, don't you?"

Cordelia's voice was very small. "Yes." She suddenly felt an urgent desire rising inside her. "Slide?"

"What?"

"Do you ever make love with human women?"

"Never, my dear. Not if I can avoid it."

# T H R E E

𝕧

## ARGO

Argo leaned on the bow rail of the Norse destroyer *Ragnar,* almost hypnotized by the rise and fall of the great body of water, while the slipstream of the ship's passage ruffled his hair and plucked at his clothes. This was his first time on a seagoing ship of any size, but he took to the experience as though born to it. His ancestors had left Europe and crossed the Northern Ocean to settle in the Americas, and now he was returning. Indeed, when he turned and looked back at the *Ragnar*'s forward-pointing fourteen-inch guns, he could feel that, along with the rest of The Four, he was returning in style. Just weeks earlier, he would have dismissed as impossible the idea that he, Cordelia, Raphael, and Jesamine should be on board a ship, on their way to the lands of the Norse Union. Yet here he was, on the Norse warship, the pale blue flag with its white North Star flying overhead, heading east into the morning sun. If nothing else, it was a testimony to the power of politics, and what could be achieved when sufficient incentives were in place.

Through five tense days after the victory at Newbury Vale, all of Albany had waited for the relief column that had been marching to the aid of Faysid Ab Balsol to make its next move, and, when it had finally broken camp and started back towards the south, a great jubilation had broken out. The Mosul were out of Virginia and again in retreat. For a second time in a week, church bells had pealed and cheering crowds had thronged the streets. Some had thought that Dunbar and his army should have commenced an immediate pursuit, but Dunbar had vetoed that idea. He had already pushed his forces to the limit, and he had no intention of taking the fight to the enemy for a second time with regiments still battered from the first encounter. The best that he could do was to deploy against any surprise counterattack, bring in replacements, and let the veterans of Newbury Vale bury their dead, heal their wounds, and regain their strength.

With the military marking time, the politicians had gone into high gear. From the cabinet on down, Newbury Vale was seen as maybe the beginning of the end. This optimism was, however, tempered with caution. The total expulsion of the Mosul would only be achieved as long as the Norse continued to supply the irreplaceable rocket bombs, and their ships and submarines harried and impeded the enemy supply convoys from Cadiz and Lisbon. That the Norse would assist Albany in meeting their military needs was already a matter of treaty and agreement, but the extra munitions that would be needed for an all-out assault on the Mosul base and nerve center in Savannah were still a matter of debate and negotiation. A faction within the Norse elite was less than certain that a complete Mosul defeat in the Americas was altogether in the Norse Union's best interests. The concern was that the Mosul Empire, with its crude slash and burn economy, sustained itself on continual conquest. Like a shark, it moved forward to survive, and if Hassan IX found himself shut out of the Americas, he might start looking to Northern Europe. More than a few in Stockholm, London, and Oslo saw the continuing conflict in the Americas as a useful safety valve for an enemy that was only just across the English Channel from the Union homeland, and the great provincial capital of London.

Fortunately Prime Minister Kennedy had been negotiating with the Norse since the very start of the Mosul invasion. Vice President Ingmar Ericksen was a close friend, and he could always expect a sympathetic hearing from President Inga Sundquist, but, despite this, Albany still needed popular Norse support for "little Albany, standing alone against the horror of Hassan IX," while the munitions deals were done, and deliveries made, in secret if need be. Kennedy and Ericksen had decided, after some high priority discussion, that the most efficient way to accomplish this was a state visit with all possible pomp and circumstance. As the details were refined, a plan had evolved whereby Kennedy would pay an initial visit to London and then go on to Stockholm and Oslo, where he would be joined by King Carlyle for a full scale royal address to the full Norse Union Senate. While possible opponents were dazzled and largely kept quiet by the flags, the uniforms, and the parades, the hard bargaining could be conducted behind closed doors.

"A drink, Major Weaver?"

Argo turned. He realized he had been standing transfixed somewhere between strategy and the sea. Stanley, the wardroom steward, was standing beside him with a gin and lime juice on a tray. Argo blinked and looked a little puzzled. "Thank you, Stanley, but I didn't order that, did I?"

Stanley shook his head. "No sir, but Major Vega thought you might need it."

Argo took the drink from the tray. "That was very thoughtful of Major Vega."

"He seemed to think so, sir."

"And what is Major Vega up to?"

"He's back amidships, working on his drawings."

The process by which The Four became involved in Jack Kennedy's visit to London, and found themselves sailing to Europe, was slightly more complex. Their going with Kennedy on this visit to London had originally been Yancey Slide's idea. They had all been having their individual dreams about the twin white figures for some time, but it was only after Newbury Vale and the interrogation and death of the Zhaithan Borat Omar that the dreams became a matter of group planning. Argo suspected that he, Raphael, and Jesamine had not been told the whole truth about Borat Omar, and why he had died. Slide had made it broadly clear that some kind of implanted or conjured trigger had killed the man, and this was enough for him to start treating what he was now calling "The White Twins" with extreme urgency, but Argo could not shake the feeling that there was more to the story than either Slide or Cordelia was willing to reveal. When pressed, Cordelia would become oddly with-drawn, although, at times, the memory would cause a strange gleam to briefly appear in her eyes.

Using all of their collective resources, The Four, with Slide and T'saya supervising, had attempted to learn more about the White Twins, but their efforts consistently proved to be of no avail, and they repeatedly came to the same conclusion. The White Twins were too far away. Even when fully linked and partway into the Other Place, the White Twins could only be seen fleetingly and with a hazy sense of distance. The solu-tion, as Slide saw it, was for The Four to move closer to the Holy City of Byzantium and see if that improved their perception of this new mystery and possible threat. Slide's suggestion was that, with all quiet on the west-ern front, The Four should join Jack Kennedy's entourage both as a public relations exercise, and a protection against any paranormal attack. That would at least take them to Europe where more might be learned.

Both Jesamine and Raphael had responded to the idea with some seri-ous trepidation. Neither wanted to be any closer than necessary to the realm of Hassan IX. Cordelia, on the other hand, had viewed it as nothing less than a marvelous chance for adventure, while Argo initially sat on the fence, sharing some of Jesamine and Raphael's fears, but also fully under-standing Cordelia's excitement, especially her passion to go to London, a city with a worldwide reputation for shameless hedonism and a wild and unparalleled nightlife. As the days passed, he had increasing tilted towards Cordelia's positive position, and had even done his bit to convince the more reluctant pair that the potential for fun wholly outweighed the dan-gers. It wasn't as though they were actually risking an excursion into enemy-held territory. Then the cabinet in Albany had accepted Slide's proposal without any serious dissent, and The Four officially became part of the Kennedy delegation. They were all under orders, and Jesamine and Raphael had no choice but to make the best of it.

## RAPHAEL

Raphael lit a cigarette, carefully cupping the lucifer against the sea breeze, then, with the ball of his right thumb, he softened the pencil line of the horizon in the latest addition to his newest sketchbook. Sailing in the other direction in a Mosul troopship all those months ago, he had despaired of ever being able to draw the ocean in all its power and grandeur. He was better at it now, but it was still lacking in true marine majesty. Even as a background to his sketches of the cruisers *Loki* and *Rob Roy,* his rendering was weak and facile, leaving so much to be desired. He could capture the iron invincibility of the escort ships but not the power of the waves themselves. One wet afternoon, during the course of his secret affair with Hyacinth Musgrave, she had showed him a reproduction by an English artist called Turner. The man was able to paint the sea exactly as Raphael saw it, and when he heard he was being taken to London, he had resolved to try and see the originals, provided, of course, they arrived safely in London, but Raphael didn't consider that too much of a problem. No chances were being taken on this ocean crossing. The *Loki* and the *Rob Roy* flanked the *Ragnar* port and starboard. A Norse dirigible kept pace with the destroyer overhead, and, for all Raphael knew, submarines lurked protectively beneath the surface. A flight of Odin biplanes had escorted the ships out of Baltimore and stayed with them until the aircraft had reached the limit of their range, and Raphael understood that more flying machines would meet them when they approached the English coast. Normal protocol would have dictated that the Prime Minister of Albany sail in a ship of the Albany Royal Navy, but this was a circumstance where protocol was abandoned in the interests of security. The odds that the Mosul would mount a naval action against them were low, but risks were still being kept to an absolute minimum. Thus Kennedy and his delegation had boarded the *Ragnar,* rather than the Albany ironclad *HMS Constellation,* that had sailed forty-eight hours earlier as a decoy. A odd story was, however, circulating that Slide had sailed alone on the *Constellation.*

On the terrible first crossing, he had found a niche on the troopship where he could draw; a hiding place close to the stern, in a deck space between two gray-painted pieces of winding gear where he squatted out of sight. Even now he was doing much the same, although he was supposed to be returning from the New World in style. He was drawing on his own, although this time he wasn't keeping clear of seasick conscripts and the stench of vomit, or hiding from brutal NCOs, and trying not to think of the Norse submarines that he had visualized as man-made steel sharks, cruising invisibly beneath the surface of the waves.

He noticed a signal light was flashing from the bridge on the *Rob Roy,* the long and short pulses of the Standard Hamilton Code. Both the cruisers kept in almost continuous contact with the *Ragnar,* and so did the dirigible. "What does that light mean?"

Raphael turned and saw that Jesamine had emerged from one of the companionways that led below. He shrugged. "I don't know. I never learned to read Standard Hamilton."

"Could it be anything serious?"

Raphael shook his head. "I don't think so. They do it all the time."

This was the first time that Raphael had seen Jesamine on the deck of the *Ragnar.* She had been seasick since they had sailed out of Baltimore, and although she was finally up on her feet, she still walked unsteadily. She tried to time her steps between the roll of the mild swell, but only succeeded in stumbling to the rail and looking sorry for herself. "I hate the sea and I hate boats."

Raphael attempted to be placating. "This has to be better than your journey to the Americas."

"That's some kind of recommendation?"

"I could call Stanley and have him bring you breakfast, or a drink or something."

"Who's Stanley?"

Raphael had momentarily forgotten that Jesamine had so far spent the entire voyage confined in the cabin she shared with Cordelia, groaning and throwing up. "He's the wardroom steward. The Norse Navy is looking after us pretty well."

Jesamine shook her head. "I don't think I'm ready to be looked after."

"There's nothing you want?"

Jesamine straightened up, and stared out across the waves. "Yes, I want off this fucking ocean."

"You'll feel better in a while."

"How I feel doesn't alter the fact that we're being press-ganged to

London as part of the sideshow to get Albany its precious rocket bombs."

"The Norse are our allies."

Jesamine seemed to be in a particularly foul frame of mind. "Frigid blondes sitting up on top of the world in their ice and snow?"

"London isn't Oslo."

"How would you know?"

"I heard there was a lot going on in London."

"Like what? Like bigger, better, more drunken parties and fancy fucking? No wonder Cordelia's so damned hot to get there. I joined in this thing to fight the Mosul, not to be put on display like a circus freak."

Raphael had been humoring Jesamine up to that point, figuring that three days of seasickness merited a little slack, but her negativity was becoming irritating. "You know as well as I do, girl, that there's more than one way of fighting the Mosul."

The wind was freshening and the *Ragnar* rolled a little more than before. Jesamine tightened her grip on the rail. "And you think this is one of them?"

That was as far as Raphael was prepared to go. "What the hell is the matter with you?"

Jesamine may have been weak from her ordeal, but she had the strength to snarl back at him. "What the hell do you think is the matter with me? I've been sick as a half dead dog. I'm in the middle of the fucking ocean on a fucking metal boat, that's taking me to another fucking city filled with people that I can hardly tell apart from the fucking Teutons. Holy shit, Raphael, I don't even know how this fucking thing stays afloat. I mean, wood floats, iron doesn't."

Raphael folded up his sketch pad and slid it into his bag. He wanted to be understanding, but he'd had about as much as he was willing to take of Jesamine in her current mood. "If you think the Norse and the Teutons are at all similar, you're out of your damned mind."

"Am I? I've been to Albany, and now I've met the Norse close up, and I've also ridden with the Ohio, and I know which I'd rather be with."

Raphael fastened the flap of his sketching bag with a curt finality designed to show Jesamine that he was not going to pursue the argument any further. "That's what all this is about? You'd rather be back in the wickiup with your aboriginal threesome? Cordelia can be a spoiled brat, but right now you have her beaten hands down."

Jesamine pushed herself angrily away from the rail, but then the *Ragnar* rolled again and she had once again to grab for it. "Don't you dare talk to me like that!"

Raphael slung his bag over his shoulder. "I don't think I want to talk to you at all, right now. We're in a war, and we don't get to do just what might suit our personal desires."

A slight pleading came into Jesamine's voice. "It's not that I have anything against the Norse or Albany. I'd just like to get away from their cities and . . ." She looked round helplessly. "all these horrible gray machines."

But Raphael had already started walking away. He figured he would walk across the width of the destroyer's deck and go below via one of the companionways on the other side. He heard Jesamine call after him. "Wait, Raphael, don't leave me out here on my own."

But he deliberately ignored her.

## JESAMINE

Jesamine realized she had made a complete fool of herself, and she swallowed hard, fearing she was about to throw up. For what seemed like an eternity, her entire universe had swayed from side to side and been pounded by the vibrations of huge mechanisms. Her stomach had convulsed, and her body had revolted against the rolling sea and the throbbing machinery, and the combination of salt spray, ozone, and hot oil had pushed her to nausea and beyond. She couldn't claim that it was the worst thing that had ever happened to her. The original voyage from Cadiz to Savannah had been infinitely worse. She had been confined and shackled, with two dozen other half-dressed and seasick concubines, in a section of a troopship's fetid hold like so much cargo; all the time fearing the attack of a Norse submarine, and knowing that, if the timbers split, and the sea poured in, their chains would drown them in the dark. The rest of the hold was filled with sweating, stamping, terrified horses, and Jesamine saw plainly that the horses were treated better than the women. Now she was supposedly liberated, a free citizen with free will, yet she still had no choice but to cross the terrible ocean again on someone else's say so.

She shouldn't, of course, have taken out the way she felt on Raphael. He was no more responsible than she was for the fact that The Four were aboard the *Ragnar* and bound for the English port of Bristol. Their arrival in England would generate enough tension, without her adding to it. She wished she hadn't pissed Raphael off badly. She wanted to apologize and change the subject, but it was now too late. That always seemed to be the way of it with emotional outbursts. By the time the poison had been vented, it was too late to take it back and claim that you hadn't really meant the things you'd said. Raphael would forgive her, of course, and agree, on the surface at least, that it had been the stress and the seasickness talking, but deeper down, a part of him would be slightly more cautious in their future dealings. Jesamine was uncomfortably aware that the others depended on her to cover details they might have overlooked. For her to indulge herself with tantrums could only erode that very essential trust.

The wind was blowing more briskly, and the troughs in the ocean swell seemed to be growing ominously deeper. The deck beneath her feet pitched and her stomach flipped in response. She managed to stop herself from actually vomiting, but she moaned aloud into the wind. "Why do I always have to be responsible?"

"A sentiment I have, more than once, voiced myself."

Jesamine spun round, momentarily forgetting how bad she felt, and found herself facing The Right Honorable John Fitzgerald Kennedy, the Prime Minister of Albany. This was not, of course, her first encounter with Kennedy. He had been there when The Four had first fled the Mosul and crossed the Potomac, and, right before the battle, he had intervened to extricate Cordelia from being arrested as a deserter. Cordelia, naturally, knew him well, and stories were even whispered that Cordelia's mother was among the impressive if scandalous roll call of women who had graced Jack Kennedy's bed. Despite all the previous contact, however, the venerable Kennedy still inspired a certain awe, with his broad shoulders, carefully shaped mane of white hair, and the habitual and truculent cigar jutting from the corner of his mouth. Kennedy was in his seventies, but, dressed in a white linen suit with a long frock coat, and leaning on his ever-present silver-mounted cane, he still radiated a dogged and unrelenting energy. "I'm sorry, my dear. Did I startle you?"

Jesamine took a step back to the rail and gripped it hard. "I didn't hear you approach."

"You're Jesamine, and you're the one who's been seasick?"

Jesamine unconsciously pushed her hair back from her face. "I must look dreadful."

The Prime Minister's eyes twinkled. He was an old man, but somehow he could still exert a powerful physical attraction. Jesamine recalled how, in addition to the tale about Cordelia's mother, T'saya had also admitted to being one of Jack Kennedy's many lovers, and also to having been hopelessly in love with him. As he faced Jesamine, his voice was kindly and comforting. "No one looks their best in the middle of an ocean voyage. Are you feeling any better?"

At previous meetings with Kennedy, Cordelia had done the talking and Jesamine had remained mostly in the background. Now she was on her own with him, she did her best to keep the nervousness out of her voice. "I thought I was, but then I came on deck and the ship started to roll."

"And now you're not so sure?"

"It's not as bad as when I came to the Americas."

Kennedy smiled gently, as though he could guess the details of that ordeal but was too tactful to inquire further. "The first time I crossed the ocean I was as sick as a dog."

"Really?"

"I hated everyone and prayed for death."

Jesamine laughed despite herself. "You know exactly how I feel."

"Stand up straight and take a deep breath."

"It'll help?"

"Trust me."

Jesamine straightened her back, and breathed as instructed. It was only as she filled her lungs that she realized that she was also showing off her figure to its best advantage, and Kennedy had removed the large

Caribbean cigar from his mouth and was regarding her with an unconcealed admiration. "You are very beautiful, my dear."

Jesamine laughed. "You say that to all the seasick women you meet?"

Kennedy's smile broadened. "Only when it's true, or when the lady badly needs to hear it."

"And which category do I fall into?"

"I'd hope you'd not need to fall at all."

Jesamine was starting to enjoy the flirtation with this man who was old enough to be her grandfather. "But am I beautiful, or just in need?"

"You know you're beautiful, my dear. Although I do also sense some degree of need. Am I right in thinking you're not that taken with our so-called civilization and have been spending as much time as possible with the Ohio?"

Jesamine was taken completely by surprise. "You're very well informed, Prime Minister."

Now Kennedy laughed. "That's how I remain Prime Minister." He moved so he was leaning against the rail beside her. "When I was young I lived for almost an entire summer with the Ohio. Chanchootok is a good friend of mine."

"Really?"

"Don't look so surprised. When I was a young man I spent a lot of time in the interior. On one trip with Charlie Bearclaw, we made it all the way to the Western Desert."

"So you understand how I feel about the aboriginal tribes? Before I was taken by the Mamalukes, I lived in a small village."

"I understand perfectly."

Kennedy's voice was soft and sympathetic, and Jesamine understood that she was perhaps being seduced for real. In the instant of realization, she experienced a brief flush of confusion as she wondered exactly how she felt about it. She had been forced to have sex with all manner of men, but the ones she had chosen for herself had always been young. Kennedy was far from young, but he was one of the most powerful men in the world, and that, at the very least, was flattering. Also he did not appear to be using his power to coerce her, and that, too, meant a lot. He seemed to sense that she was uncertain, and covered the ensuing silence by relighting his cigar with a lucifer that he struck on the side of a small silver pocket case. As he put the matchbox back in the jacket of his frock coat, he held up a spare Caribbean. "Would you like one of these? I know some ladies do."

In the bad old days, she had stolen cheroots from the humidor of Phaall the Teuton colonel and enjoyed them greatly, but she shook her head. "Not right now. I still feel a little queasy."

"Possibly later?"

Jesamine nodded. "Possibly. I like a good cigar."

Kennedy puffed thoughtfully, and the smoke was whipped away by the ocean breeze. "There might be another reason why you felt so at home with the Ohio."

"There might?"

"Your trade is now the paranormal, and the aboriginal peoples are much more comfortable with the unseen arts and crafts. They more easily accept things that make city folk nervous and uneasy."

Jesamine looked curiously at Kennedy. "Why is that?"

"Why is what?"

"Why does what I do frighten all these smart sophisticated city people?"

Kennedy stared at Jesamine. Their eyes met. "You really don't like city people, do you, my dear?"

"What do you expect? Albany was the first city I wasn't brought to by force."

"You should maybe give cities more of a chance."

"You would say that."

"I would?"

"You may be the Prime Minister, but you're a city boy."

Kennedy chuckled. "It's been a long time since a beautiful young woman called me a boy."

He was flirting again, but Jesamine wasn't quite ready to let the topic go. "But you are, aren't you?"

"A city boy? That, pretty lady, shows how little you know. My daddy, Whiskey Joe Kennedy, ran moonshine down the Taconic, and across the

Catskills, and the woods were my home until I was all of fifteen and I was shipped off to Boston for my education. Even after that, the interior was where the adventures waited to be had and the fortunes to be made, and I spent more of my time under the stars than under a roof."

Jesamine was impressed by the way the phrase about adventures and fortunes rolled from his tongue. Old Jack Kennedy was smooth. No wonder his people so willingly followed him. "You must have been something when you were young."

Kennedy sighed. "Ah girl, you'd better believe it."

For a while they both stared across the water, at the escort ships and the far horizon, then Jesamine put the story back on track. "You must have gone back to the city, though, when you went into politics."

"Well, that was unavoidable. Things needed doing and people seemed to think that I was the one to do them."

"Things?"

"Albany hasn't always been like it is now. The old King thought he could keep all the power to himself, and it was a long hard fight to change his mind."

"You still haven't answered my original question."

Kennedy frowned. "Which was?"

"I wanted to know why the powers I have . . . that we Four have . . . scare all those educated city people?"

The Prime Minister thought for a moment. "I have to suppose it's because city people have to believe they're right; that they know all there is to know. How would they ride their trolley cars or take their elevators up and down, or turn on their electric lights, if they had any doubts? How would they sail in metal boats."

"But they must know that the Other Side is there. They can't pretend that it doesn't exist."

Kennedy shook his head. "But they do."

Jesamine frowned. "But why? There are ghosts in the city, just like in the forest."

"There's a difference."

She leaned back against the ship's rail, aware that by arching her spine just enough she showed off her breasts to their maximum advantage.

Jesamine saw no reason why seduction and discussion should not go hand in hand. "A difference?"

Jack Kennedy nodded. He must have noticed her move, but gave no indication. "The tribes of the interior live in much closer contact with the invisible. They have the thunderbird that rules skies, the trickster coyote that is the friend to man. On the plains, the *tetonka* is revered as the provider of all things. In the north, the raven preserves the light. Among so-called primitive peoples, the mundane and the invisible frequently walk hand in hand, and preserve the equilibrium." Kennedy paused. For a few seconds, he looked at Jesamine with unconcealed appreciation, but then went on to make his point. "Cities, on the other hand, are something else. They construct their equilibrium with the plumb line and the square. Supposedly civilized peoples are hemmed in by their own walls, and constrained by their progress and their structures. When civilized man is confronted by the invisible, or that which he doesn't understand, he is presented with a choice. He must decide if it exists outside of the laws of the universe, or if laws of the universe are more complicated and extensive than he previously believed. Since civilization tends to make it easier to disbelieve than believe, he will attempt to dismiss the invisible and the mysterious, and pretend that they don't really exist. Do you follow me?"

Jesamine took a deep breath. "I think so."

"The reason, my dear Jesamine, that your knowledge and skills upset the city people is that you force them to change their beliefs and they don't like that. Too often, the educated get the idea that their education is complete and hate to learn anything new." Again he paused. Now he looked her up and down with deliberate candor. "You really are quite lovely. With that honey skin you will be a sensation in Oslo, among all those so very white people."

Jesamine pouted with complete calculation. "I think I was a sensation for a while in Albany, and I didn't like it all."

"To be a sensation is a gift only given to a few. You must learn to enjoy it."

"Is that what you did?"

"I was never a sensation, girl. I had to teach myself to be a force."

Jesamine and Kennedy were suddenly in complete eye contact. Their two faces were close together, and the gulf of their ages was ceasing to matter. He was potentially a great mentor and how better could she show her appreciation of that than by giving herself to him. If the moment had held for seconds longer, he would have kissed her and she would have responded. It was not to be, however. The voice interrupted, demanding his attention. "Prime Minister?"

Kennedy half laughed and half sighed. "Observe the curse of power and the penalty of becoming a force." He turned. "What is it, Dawson?"

Dawson was the burly civilian in the dark suit who seemed to double as the Prime Minister's valet and bodyguard. "Cable, sir. Relayed from the NU380, and requiring your acknowledgment."

Kennedy looked back at Jesamine. "I fear I have to go."

Jesamine half reached towards him, intending to touch him, but not doing it. She suddenly felt so safe in the older man's company. "That's too bad. I would have liked to have talked some more."

Kennedy smiled, polite but knowing. "Perhaps later. The ocean is very wide."

Jesamine matched his smile. "Maybe I can smoke the excellent cigar you offered me."

Kennedy nodded. "Indeed you may." He turned and followed Dawson back to the business of nations. Jesamine sagged a little and felt quite breathless. She had made what amounted to an assignation with no less than the Prime Minister of Albany, and, if she read matters correctly, the assignation was serious. She had spent so much time and energy yearning for the simple life, and yet, the instant the chance presented itself, she plunged into the great game of the high and the mighty with more blind abandon than Cordelia. She looked up at the streamlined silver airship floating against the sky and clouds. A tiny light flashed coded signals from its gondola, and the designation NU380 was displayed clearly on its side.

## CORDELIA

The upper bunk smelled of a healthy young man; tobacco, machine oil, and the slightest hint of yesterday's gin. Cordelia lay by herself, but not sleeping. She had spent two nights with First Lieutenant Bjorn Hawkins, and through that time, privacy had been a constant problem. A destroyer on a mission, even a mission that was not overly dangerous, offered little chance for two people to be alone together. Thus it was not without a sense of irony that Cordelia found herself the sole occupant of the cabin in the small hours of the third morning, with not only Bjorn on watch, but also Frampton, the other First Lieutenant with whom he shared the cramped cabin. Had all other things been equal, she and Hawkins might have had their sex in the somewhat larger quarters that had been assigned to her and Jesamine, since she again outranked her lover, but a serious inequality had presented itself in the form of Jesamine's chronic seasickness. Perhaps, had Cordelia not wanted to escape being cooped up in a cabin with Jesamine's groaning and vomiting, she might not even have organized this brief maritime fling to while away the ocean crossing. Such a thing had not been her intention when she had boarded the *Ragnar*. After a fond, if somewhat insincere night of farewell to Tom Neally, who had been shot in the arm during the final charge at Newbury Vale, but was otherwise fully functional, she was on her way to London, and she knew that notorious city could not help but yield its share of assignations. She had no immediate craving for excitement, and had planned to keep herself to herself, hoping to repair the bonds with Jesamine that had somehow become so frayed since their winter training.

Cordelia had also contemplated using the ocean voyage to spend time on her own doing some unaccustomed private thinking. The side of herself—what Slide had called the factor in the equation—that she had discovered during the interrogation of the captive Zhaithan continued to distract and disturb her. The whip had felt good in her hands, as had the grip of unholy delight she had experienced as she thrashed him. Up to the moment of self-revelation with the Zhaithan, she had always believed that, when certain girlfriends had boasted about candlelit boudoir games of dominance and submission, or of visits in closed carriages to the purple confines of a few private and specially established clubs, they were merely playing charades, just extending the titillating preambles to the serious business of orgasm, but now she was uncomfortably aware that such desires might go considerably deeper, and be a possible end in themselves.

She threw back the blankets, and sat up, moving with some care, so as not to crack her head on the steel ceiling, or whatever they called a ceiling on a battleship. She eased her legs over the side of the bunk and swung down to the floor. One step took her across the narrow cabin to the small mirror that was positioned above the two men's washbasin. She may have started off with the objective of keeping herself to herself, but, yet again, it had not worked out that way. Jesamine had become seasick and that had driven her out of the cabin. In the wardroom, she had fallen into gin and conversation with the young but personable Bjorn Hawkins, and one thing had led to another, which in turn had led to the two of them sneaking off to his cabin together. Bjorn Hawkins had proved capable, enthusiastic, and wholly normal, which, at any other time would have been quite enough to keep Cordelia amused, but she found herself dissatisfied, even irritated by him. Normality now left much to be desired.

She stared with stern concern at her own reflection. "What are you becoming, Cordelia Blakeney? Do you have any idea?"

Her second night with Bjorn was still very clear in her memory. She had pushed him down on the bunk and literally ridden him, arms stiff, pinning his wrists to the mattress like a prone crucifixion. He had seemed to find this perfectly acceptable at the time, but afterwards, after they had caught their breath and drunk a little gin, he had made an odd remark.

"There was a moment back then when I wondered where you had gone."

Cordelia had blinked with some surprise and not a little annoyance. "Gone? What do you mean, gone?"

"As though—I don't know how to put it—as though you'd disappeared behind your own eyes."

Now Cordelia was simply annoyed. "You seemed to be having a good time, wherever my eyes might have been."

Bjorn had made the mistake of defending himself. "I wasn't saying . . ."

And Cordelia had cut him off huffily. "So don't."

She inspected her face in the mirror above the washbasin, looking, as best she could, for any telltale signs of change. Dark circles ringed her eyes, but she wasn't sure if they signified anything other than routine dissolution. Freckles, the curse of all those with red hair and pale skin, lightly dusted her nose. She was spending far more time in the sun and air, first on the march south with the army and now on the ocean with the Norse. Men claimed to like freckles, but she'd rather her complexion was clear and porcelain white. She frowned disapprovingly, but was also relieved that she still retained her innate and uncomplicated vanity. She cursed Slide and his damned equations, but in the moment of cursing, she also recalled how, after the interrogation, she had propositioned Yancey Slide. He had, of course, turned her down, but suppose he hadn't. To what place would that have taken her?

"Really, what *are* you becoming?"

The cabin was a little chill for Cordelia to be standing around stark naked, so she located her knickers and started to dress. Night had fallen and the temperature had dropped considerably, so she helped herself to one of Bjorn's rollneck sweaters, let herself out of the cabin, and made her way up to the deck. The sky overhead was cloudless, and filled with a million stars, far more than were ever visible on land. For a long minute she stood and stared in unself-conscious awe. For all her supposed corruption, Cordelia still found the capacity for moments of childlike wonder. She made her way to the destroyer's stern where another marvel awaited her. The wake of the *Ragnar* was a glowing path of green luminescence across the dark water. She leaned on the stern rail, impressed and a little breathless. Somewhere a seaman was singing softly.

*Oh Maggie, oh Maggie, for love of a sailor*
*You packed up your pride and went down to the shore*
*And looked all in vain for the sails of his brigantine*
*Until you were sure he'd be coming no more.*

Then the voice stopped and spoke to a third person who Cordelia was unable to see.

"Goodnight, miss. Just watch your step along there. Don't want you coming a cropper."

This immediately distracted Cordelia from the wonder of the night-time sea. *Miss?* As far as Cordelia was aware, the only two passengers on the *Ragnar* eligible to be addressed as "Miss" were Jesamine and herself. Cordelia stood very still. Had Jesamine recovered enough to be out and about, and, if so, what was she up to in the middle of the night? She had a brief glimpse of a female figure hurrying down to a lower deck. It was definitely Jesamine, but where the hell had she been? To the best of Cordelia's knowledge, the only living quarters so far back on the ship were those of the captain, and the stateroom and cabin that had been as-signed to Jack Kennedy and his bodyguard. Although Cordelia knew all things were possible, she hardly thought that Jesamine was visiting the captain. Had she arranged an assignation with Dawson? The only alterna-tive was a tryst with the Prime Minister. The high-lonesome singing sailor started a second verse.

> *Oh Maggie, oh Maggie, for love of a sailor*
> *You stiffened your back and signed up as whore*
> *Disrespected, deserted, with no consolation*
> *For love of a sailor who's coming no more.*

Jesamine was coming from a private visit with Jack Kennedy? Was such a thing possible? Cordelia knew all too well it was all too possible. Given the correct circumstances and a sufficient quantity of gin, she could do the same herself; forget the difference in their ages, and fall for his elderly but still powerful charms. Cordelia took a deep breath. "Jesamine is fucking Jack Kennedy? Well damn me."

## JESAMINE

Jesamine ducked into the cabin she shared with Cordelia. She wasn't sure why she felt the need to be so furtive, but she was relieved that Cordelia was not there, probably bunked-up with the sailor who was keeping her amused through the voyage. Jesamine closed the door behind her, dogged it shut, and flopped on her bunk, remaining absolutely still as her body continued to tingle. He had been an old man, physically slow, with an old man's body, but with the ease of confident experience, and possessed of a elemental power from which she still trembled. No wonder his people adored him and trusted him implicitly. He was like no other man that Jesamine had ever encountered; an ancient lion with a mane of white hair, who had taken her to him without self-consciousness, compromise, or effort. At one point she had straddled him, knees bent, with him deep inside her, rolling her hips against his thrusts, cupping her own breasts and moaning deep in her throat, brazenly eager to please and impress him. In her previous life, she had faked and fabricated so much passion, so many times, in so many ways, she wanted to push every wanton limit to give him something genuine, honest, and wholly of herself. Maybe Jack Kennedy would have enjoyed her just as much as a slut, but she wanted to be much more for him. He must have somehow sensed a part of what she was feeling, because, as she had dropped to her already trembling knees, and taken him in her unconstrained eager mouth, working her hard-won whore-skills, he had first groaned, but then whispered. "Easy, my dear, easy. Just take your own pleasure and relish it. You have nothing to prove to me."

She had gone to Kennedy under no illusion about how the encounter might end, but with the attitude that she was bestowing the gift of her youth on the elderly hero. She'd had no idea that she would receive a gift far more intense than her youth and willingness. He had been waiting, in a smoking jacket and silk pyjamas. He had offered her cognac and she had accepted. He been in no apparent hurry to touch her, and he had again talked about the American interior, and how much he loved the vast undiscovered continent. He had told jokes about his moonshiner father, and tales of his youthful brushes with the American city gangs, like the Booze Fighters, the Roman Bloods, Blind Rebels, and the Richmond Shamrocks. Kennedy told stories of the internal struggles in Albany during the reign of Carlyle's autocratic father, and how they had pulled him into the business of power and politics that had taken up the remainder of his life. He had not, however, concentrated exclusively on himself. So many of the so-called powerful men that Jesamine had met believed they need only boast about their exploits to impress a woman, but Kennedy was mindful to ask her about her own life and experiences. He had asked probing questions about the desert village of her childhood, and congratulated her on her ability to survive all the horrors and degradations that had been thrown at her. He had inquired about the other lands of Africa, especially those of the Zulu Hegemony, but had deftly exited the topic when he discovered just how little she knew beyond what might be expected of a Mosul camp follower. Even though Kennedy had handled the revelation of her ill-informed ignorance with the utmost grace and tact, she had spent some minutes feeling inadequate and stupid, but then Kennedy had handed her the promised Caribbean cigar, and lit it for her with meticulous care. They had sat facing each other in silence as the stateroom filled with rich blue smoke. Kennedy had stared at Jesamine with a calm intensity. Had another done such a thing, she might have been irritated or uncomfortable, but, with Kennedy, she simply met his gaze and basked in the attention. When he finally spoke, his voice was soft, amused at his own sense of awe. "Jesamine . . ." He had rolled the name as though saying it for the first time. ". . . you are very beautiful."

Jesamine had finally felt on much safer ground. Slowly and sensuously she rose to her feet. She hadn't spoken, just smoothly unbuttoned the back of her best blue dress, the one from New York, and allowed it to fall to the floor so she stood naked, but for her jewelry, her high heels, and the velvet choker around her throat. A slow smile had spread across Jack Kennedy's face, and he had stretched out a hand to her. "Come here, my dear."

Jesamine realized that, as she remembered what had just come to pass, she was unconsciously hugging herself. She knew that she must still smell of him. Her hand moved surreptitiously to touch herself, but at that moment someone started hammering on the cabin door.

## CORDELIA

The too-familiar voice had come out of the cold thin air on the stern on the *Ragnar,* and whispered sickeningly, as always, maintaining the hollow ring of the torture chamber where Cordelia and Jeakqual-Ahrach had first come face to face with each other. *"So Cordelia Blakeney, I understand you have been asking questions about my new creations."*

Cordelia's blood turned to ice. "What?"

She could see nothing, but she knew for certain the disembodied voice was neither madness nor hallucination. A split second earlier, Cordelia had been leaning on the destroyer's stern rail, trying to resolve her feelings about a possible liaison between Jesamine and Jack Kennedy, but now she was a coiled spring, poised for fight or flight. A tense silence ensued for almost a minute before the voice came again. *"Did you think that I couldn't find you, even in the middle of this great ocean?"*

"Get away from me you old and twisted bitch!"

*"Anger won't protect you, Cordelia Blakeney. When will you accept that, whatever you do, and whatever powers you might believe you have acquired, you will always be vulnerable to me?"*

"You haven't been able to get near me in months."

*"I'm with you now, aren't I?"*

Cordelia could not deny this. Behind her, the wake of the *Ragnar* still created its strange luminescence, but she could no longer appreciate it. "I order you to get away from me."

*"Do you recall the first time we met, Cordelia Blakeney?"*

"How could I forget it, Jeakqual-Ahrach?"

*"You were strung up before me, naked. You and the coffee-colored whore."*

Cordelia was frightened. She had never imagined that Jeakqual-Ahrach could find her and communicate with her here on the deck of the Norse warship in the dark of night. The knowledge was nothing less than a profound shock, but she did her best not to reveal her fear. "The coffee-colored whore has a name. She is Jesamine."

*"My black Zhaithan had the two of you hanging from a bar, straining on tiptoe, arms stretched above your heads by the silk ropes around your wrists."*

"But we escaped you. And now your army has gone down in defeat."

*"My concern is not with armies."*

"It was at the time."

*"Even you should be aware that circumstances change."*

In that respect, Jeakqual-Ahrach was right. Circumstances had changed. When the Mosul invaders had stood at the borders of Albany, poised to attack and subjugate the kingdom, Jeakqual-Ahrach and her brother, Quadaron-Ahrach, had wielded almost as much power in the Mosul Empire as Hassan IX himself. It was a different kind of power, however. While Hassan might measure his might in military divisions and conquered territories, Jeakqual-Ahrach and Quadaron-Ahrach held sway over the dark forces and nameless menaces of the Other Place, and, through their command and manipulation of the Mosul religion and Quadaron-Ahrach's control of the Zhaithan, they maintained a vicelike and unrelenting grip on the hearts and minds of enslaved millions.

Cordelia realized that she was holding on to the rail so hard that her hands hurt. Using all of her breeding and all of her training, she forced herself to relax. She wanted to run, to hide, to find the other three if a fight was to be fought. She was not going to expose her terror to a voice from empty air. "I notice that you don't show yourself."

"You want to see me, Cordelia Blakeney?"

"Not particularly, Jeakqual-Ahrach. I'm just wondering if you could stretch your power that far." Cordelia had few doubts that Jeakqual-Ahrach could manifest herself if she so desired. She would never make the mistake of underestimating the power of either Her Grand Eminence or her equally sinister brother, the High Zhaithan. Since the Mosul defeat on the Potomac, much time had been spent assessing the dangerous siblings' real position within the hierarchy of Hassan's empire. In Albany, one school of thought reasoned that the military reversals in the Americas could only have brought about an eclipse of their power. Both the High Zhaithan and his sister had visited the Mosul army right before the push across the river, and surely they must have been saddled with some of the responsibility for its failure. This theory was, to a degree, born out by Cordelia's own experience. In the first weeks The Four had been together, Jeakqual-Ahrach had harassed and harried Cordelia, not only with unbidden voices in her mind, but with actual hallucinations and, on one unpleasant occasion, a startlingly demoralizing sense memory of the brush of silver needles, to which Cordelia's body had been subjected in the Zhaithan torture chamber. Through the winter and spring, though, a diminishment had occurred. Jeakqual-Ahrach's last invasion of Cordelia's mind had been during the early days of their winter training, and Cordelia, weary, but toughened by the rigors of the relentless regimen, had, in a moment of fury, found the angry strength to cast Jeakqual-Ahrach from her with enough force that, up to this present and unwelcome moment, the woman's manifest, wind-walking presence had not returned. The paranormal attack at Newbury Vale, while seeming intense at the time, had been comparatively ineffective and weakly peripheral to the terrestrial battle. Had it not been for the common dreams about the strange White Twins, Cordelia might have come to believe that Jeakqual-Ahrach and her brother were a spent force, but now, here she was again, seemingly as effective as ever.

"I'm also wondering why you always choose me for these importunate contacts. Do you believe I'll be the first to crack?"

*"Quite the reverse, Cordelia Blakeney. I play with you because you are the boldest, the most headstrong. You see yourself as the tip of the spear, and that makes you vulnerable."*

"You believe I'm vulnerable?"

Although most of the attention and analysis in Albany had always focused on Quadaron-Ahrach, and even Slide and T'saya paid him the most attention, Cordelia suspected that Jeakqual-Ahrach was, in fact, the stronger and more intriguing of the two. History was filled with males who had used religion to scale the more obscene heights of power as pontiffs or high priests. The High Zhaithan was not especially unique, but his sister was one of a kind, in that she survived, functioned, and enjoyed unquestioning obedience in the violently misogynist world of the Mosul.

*"Entertain your illusions of power, girl. It can all seem very easy, after your first taste of playing the torturer, but, in the end, I will break you. And when you break, your Four will be no more."*

"You are very confident for one who can't even show herself."

The air in front of Cordelia shimmered. *"My voice is not enough?"*

The outline of a human figure appeared, waning for a moment, but then strengthening, until a dream-image of Jeakqual-Ahrach, with a faint background of leaping flames, stood between Cordelia and the ocean. She was, as always, dressed in a black robe, but, as if to assert her femininity, it was lavishly trimmed with red and gold. An embroidered representation of the sacred flame of Ignir and Aksura curled around the entire vertical length of the garment, which was synched at the waist by a gold, ruby-encrusted belt that displayed the curves of her breasts and hips beneath the soft fabric. Cordelia had always found Jeakqual-Ahrach's age hard to assess. Superficially she seemed to be no older than her early forties, but if she was truly the full sister of Quadaron-Ahrach, that was hardly possible. She had to be far older. History recorded the brother as being in his eighties at the very least. Cordelia had, on more than one occasion, wondered if the knives of skilled surgeons had played a part in the staving off of the ravages of mortality, perhaps along with the ministrations of apothecaries, necromancers, and other specialists whose function should not be imagined or guessed at, not in the dark of night.

*"Now you see me, Cordelia Blakeney."*

"These are still parlor tricks."

*"You believe so?"*

"You think your disembodied form can hurt me?"

*"I'm just making you aware that I can always find you, wherever you might try to hide."*

"I'm not hiding."

*"What do you think you're doing on this iron ship of the Norsemen?"*

"I'm hardly going to tell you, am I?"

*"The truth is that this ship is bringing you and your three companions nearer to me."*

"Maybe that's something that you should be worrying about."

*"As much as you worry about my new creations?"*

"What new creations, Jeakqual-Ahrach?"

*"You used your whip on the Fourth Adept to find out more about them."*

Cordelia struck a pose, doing her best to appear cold and cruelly capricious. "Just an amusement, Jeakqual-Ahrach. As you said, a taste of playing the torturer."

*"And that's why you gave him to the demon, to Slide?"*

Cordelia did her best not to falter at how much Jeakqual-Ahrach seemed to know. "I will admit I was curious as to why you might be forcing these half-formed images into my dreams. It seemed a little pathetic for one who once fancied herself so powerful."

*"I have something to show you."*

Cordelia said nothing.

*"You're not curious?"*

"What could you show me? You may be very clever at conjuring hollow, insubstantial pictures in the air, but anything you might show me would be nothing more than that."

*"Observe for yourself, and then tell me."*

Two smaller and far from distinct figures materialized beside Jeakqual-Ahrach, and then, they, too, grew more substantial. A white-faced boy and an equally pallid girl, identical, and possibly albino, and with huge, unnerving eyes, stood close to Jeakqual-Ahrach. The boy had his arm raised, gripping her robe. He and the girl were dressed in tiny, child-sized versions of Jeakqual-Ahrach's black Zhaithan cowl. At first, their infant gaze was downcast, but then the White Twins slowly raised their pale blue, inhuman eyes, and stared directly at her. A malign hatred washed over Cordelia. She could not look away from their loathsome infantile gaze. The Twins' corpse-white lips drew back in baby snarls, baring tiny, but pointed, porcelain teeth, and suddenly Cordelia was scared. In the baleful waves of dire emotion, the children seemed to be growing from just a gossamer vision, taking solid form, and moving into her reality as if they meant to harm her. Cordelia felt paralyzed, and had to summon all of her strength to stop herself screaming.

## ARGO

Argo woke from a dream. The White Twins had been a part of the dream, and yet they had not actually been in it. Even as he regained the waking world, the memory started to fragment but was replaced by very conscious unease. Near at hand, someone was in grave danger. In the cabin Argo shared with Raphael, he had the top bunk and Raphael had the lower one, but when he swung down to the floor, he found that Raphael's bunk was empty. Had something happened to him? The dream faded, but the unfocused menace grew stronger. Argo fumbled into his pants and pulled on his boots. His hand went to the handle of the cabin door, but then, acting on a sudden afterthought, he reached for the revolver that hung in its holster from the belt of his dress uniform. On a mission such as they were on, the sidearm was little more than a prop, like the formal swords worn by the Norse naval officers, but that did not mean that it was not loaded and fully functional.

In pants and shirt, and holding the pistol down by his side, Argo made his way quietly and quickly up to the nearest open deck. He could sense no located emanations that might give him an idea of the threat's direction, and he hoped that he would be able to see and feel more once he was no longer enclosed in a cabin, corridor, or companionway. A part of him felt that he ought to raise the alarm, but he hesitated while he still had nothing but a bad feeling and the final fragments of monochrome dream. He doubted that the *Ragnar*'s officers would see either as sufficient reason to place the destroyer and its crew at action stations, and recognized the irony in this. He was only aboard the *Ragnar,* only being taken to the Norse Union, because he had an ability to sense things that others couldn't, and yet he would almost certainly find himself ridiculed if he acted on that ability. On deck, the air was clear and chill, and the fear diminished slightly. If he stayed there too long in just his pants and undershirt, he would soon be shivering. He was still wondering what to do next, when a familiar voice with an Hispanian accent cause him quickly to turn.

"Are you planning an assassination?" Raphael was regarding him with a expression that was both puzzled and amused. Argo shook his head, feeling decidedly awkward. "No, I . . ."

"Then why the gun?"

"Didn't you feel something?"

"What kind of something?"

"I don't know. It was intense, but kind of vague, like something bad was happening in another part of the ship."

Raphael shook his head. "Nothing like that. I just had this need to get out of the cabin. You were sleeping and I'd been reading a book, and then suddenly I felt kinda . . ." He searched for the right word. ". . . claustrophobic, and had this overwhelming desire to get out on deck."

"So you did feel something?"

"I suppose you could call it that."

They both looked carefully around. Everything about the destroyer was perfectly normal. They could see officers moving in the dim light of the *Ragnar*'s bridge, and a crewman came out of the wireless shack and went below. Raphael frowned. "You think we should tell someone?"

"What could we tell them?"

"Maybe we should check on the girls?"

Argo nodded. That was a workable idea, in that it was something to do, and would counter the sense of unformed disquiet. "Why don't we?"

They hurried through the night interior of the destroyer and knocked discreetly on the door of Cordelia and Jesamine's quarters. At first they received no reply, and then Jesamine's cautious voice responded to a second, slightly louder rapping. "Who is it?"

"Argo and Raphael."

"What do you want?"

"Open the door. It's nothing we need to shout about."

"Hold on."

Bolts snapped back and Jesamine peered cautiously out at them. She was wrapped in a sheet as though she had been sleeping, except she had a certain dreamy sated look in her eyes that Argo knew a little too well from the time they had been together. Was someone in the cabin with her? "What's up?"

Argo glanced at Raphael before answering her. "I don't know, but something."

Jesamine didn't seem impressed. "What are you talking about? And what's the gun for?"

Argo couldn't understand why she couldn't just open the door. "Let us in and we'll tell you."

"Cordelia isn't here."

"Where is she?"

Jesamine looked annoyed. "How the fuck should I know? Probably with her sailor boy."

"Are you alone."

Jesamine's annoyance grew. "If course I'm alone. What's this all about?"

"I have a feeling . . ."

"What?"

"I have a feeling that something is wrong."

After an instant of reluctance, Jesamine visibly pulled herself together. "What kind of wrong?"

"I don't know. Not tangible, but definitely wrong."

Jesamine looked to Raphael. "Do you feel the same?"

"Not as strongly, but I couldn't sleep."

She glared at Argo. "This had better not be bullshit."

"It's not."

"Well, since we're all here, we'd better assume it has something to do with Cordelia."

"So where do we find this sailor of hers?"

"I don't know?"

"You've never been to his cabin."

"I was sick as a dog up until today."

"Right."

Raphael glanced up and down the corridor outside the cabin, but it was empty. "We're going to have to find out. Do you know his name?"

"Bjorn something, I think." Jesamine thought hard. "A lieutenant. Bjorn . . . Hawkins . . ."

"We'll have to find an officer and ask."

Jesamine looked hard at Argo. "You'd better be right about this feeling, because otherwise Cordelia is going to have a shit fit."


## CORDELIA

*"Observe the Holy Twins, Cordelia Blakeney. Observe the Gods made flesh. Meet Ignir and Aksura."*

Cordelia wrenched her eyes away from the baleful hallucination of the Twins, and they retreated a little from her reality. "These abominations are not gods."

All of Cordelia's instincts told her that Jeakqual-Ahrach was lying. Whatever the White Twins might be, they were not gods incarnate, but that didn't exclude their being potentially very evil, very powerful, and very dangerous.

*"You don't believe that gods can journey to the human plane?"*

"It's something I've never given much thought to, but, if they did, I doubt they'd be clinging to the skirts of an evil crone like you."

*"You'll believe it when you feel their power."*

A wave of hate struck Cordelia like a fist, and it was all she could do to stop from reeling. Mercifully, her own fury kept her on her feet. "I can believe they might have the power of some vile monstrosity that was conceived in iniquity and grown in some loathsome vat. Or could it be that your unholy brother somehow mated and begat these spawn?"

*"You will suffer!"*

Even allowing for the excesses of propaganda, Jeakqual-Ahrach and Quadaron-Ahrach were reputed to enjoy a particularly unique relationship, even in the perverse annals of human depravity. Maybe she had guessed close enough to the truth for Jeakqual-Ahrach's comfort. Again the White Twins seemed to be taking on solid form, as though they were about to move into her reality and hurt her. The malign energy of the Twins and the force of Jeakqual-Ahrach's rage threatened to overwhelm her. All Cordelia could do was to take a step back and scream to the full extent of her lungs. "GET AWAY FROM ME!"

And, in that exact moment, Jeakqual-Ahrach and the White Twins vanished, as though snuffed like a candle. Cordelia couldn't believe that she had driven them off so easily, and then the voice came from behind her. "Cordelia!"

## RAPHAEL

Cordelia staggered back from the stern rail of the *Ragnar* screaming at the top of her lungs, "GET AWAY FROM ME."

Argo raised his pistol and raced towards her. "Cordelia!"

No target presented itself, and he was at a total loss. Cordelia stumbled and almost fell, but Argo was quickly beside her, supporting her with one arm while he still looked for an attacker. Raphael and Jesamine were quickly there, taking her from him.

"What happened?"

Cordelia let out a long sigh that ended in a sob. "Jeakqual-Ahrach found me. The blackwitch bitch from hell knows we're on this ship."

Argo whistled under his breath. He had hoped that Cordelia's visits from the blackwitch were a thing of the past. Seemingly this wasn't so. "On the wind?"

"She windwalked to a battleship in the middle of the ocean."

"Damn."

Argo lowered his pistol. "Where is she now?"

"She vanished. It was either me screaming, or all of you showing up. Maybe she didn't want to take on all four of us." She took a deep gulp of air. "How did you all get here?"

Raphael and Argo looked at each other. "We felt something."

"Felt what?"

"We're not sure. Some kind of threat. Something indistinct but intimidating. That's how it was for me."

Raphael joined in. "For me it was more like a sudden claustrophobia, a need to get out in the air."

Argo concentrated on Cordelia. "You heard her voice in your head?"

Cordelia nodded. "Yes, I heard her voice in my head. But that was only for openers. She quickly showed me that she could be a full-scale, full-color, life-size, virtual fucking vision."

Argo rolled his eyes. "Damn."

At which Jesamine snapped, "Can't you say anything else?"

Argo treated her to a bleak look. "Maybe not right now. I'm processing the information."

Raphael decided it was time to intervene. "I think the information would be better processed after we get Cordelia back to her cabin and, at the very least, get her something to drink."

Cordelia nodded weakly. "I think that's a very good idea."

Raphael supported her on one side and Jesamine on the other, while Argo brought up the rear, watchful and with his pistol still in his hand. Once they'd reached the girls' cabin and settled Cordelia in her bunk, Raphael looked around. "Do you girls have anything to drink?"

"We have some gin."

"And this Norse soda pop called Vimto."

"Forget the Vimto."

Jesamine passed Raphael the gin bottle. He found glasses, poured four stiff shots, and handed them round. Cordelia swallowed half her gin in one gulp. "She brought the White Twins with her." If Cordelia was looking to create an effect, she had no need to be disappointed. Raphael was rendered speechless, and Cordelia managed a smile. "That got your attention, didn't it?"

He asked the obvious question. Someone had to. "So what did they look like?"

Cordelia took a slow breath, considerably recovered and clearly relishing the melodrama. "They looked like two horrid little baby vampires, all white and disgusting like they had crawled out from under a rock, and with these huge pale blue eyes that stare right through you."

Raphael looked hard at Cordelia. "Vampires don't *exist*."

Cordelia looked up at him with a flash of her more normal impatience. "I didn't say they *were* vampires. I said they *looked like* vampires; like seven year-old vampires with sharp little teeth and these evil eyes."

"You thought they were going to hurt you?"

"That was my distinct impression."

"I thought they were a windwalking vision."

"It was like they were going to come through to this side."

"So how did you get away from them?"

"That was the weird part. Jeakqual-Ahrach was clearly showing off. The blackwitch expended a whole lot of energy, just to impress me, but then you all came on the scene and she vanished, like she fled, rather than risk facing us all together."

Argo frowned and reviewed the facts. "So Cordelia was confronted by an apparition of Jeakqual-Ahrach, I felt an unformed threat, and Raphael became claustrophobic. It's like Cordelia was the primary target and the rest of us caught the backwash. Does that sound logical?"

Cordelia and Raphael nodded. Argo looked at Jesamine. She avoided his eyes, but Cordelia supplied an answer. "She didn't feel anything. She was fucking Jack Kennedy at the time."

Jesamine's eyes flashed. "Fuck you, Cordelia."

Raphael looked up at her in mild surprise. "Is that true?"

"And what if it is?"

Argo refilled his glass and poured another for Cordelia. He offered the bottle to Jesamine, who angrily shook her head. "Will you all stop looking at me?" When nobody said anything, she changed her mind and grabbed the bottle from Argo. "Okay, so it's true. Who wants to comment?"

Raphael sat down on Jesamine's bunk. "The fact that you were fucking would not necessarily have stopped you being aware that some bad stuff was happening to another of us."

Jesamine pouted. "Well, pardon me for not paying attention."

Argo let out a long breath. "Having it off with Jack Kennedy is flying pretty high."

"I was hardly the first."

Cordelia raised a cynical eyebrow. "Maybe the sexual energy of Jack Kennedy knocks out all other wavelengths."

"You might be more right than you know, girl."

Raphael gestured to Argo to pass him the gin. "Do you think we could forget the Prime Minister and Jesamine, and concentrate on what happened to Cordelia?"

## ARGO

Argo took a deep breath of clean sea air. He'd drunk a lot of gin, but he wasn't drunk. He was tired, but he didn't want to sleep. Grit was under his eyelids and a hundred thoughts and feelings had his head spinning. The Four had talked through the night. At one point Cordelia had burst into tears, and, at another, she and Jesamine had almost come to blows. In a moment of perplexed frustration, they had clasped hands, and attempted to share visual memories, but, like all the times they had tried it in training, they were unable to forge the link. Cordelia's description of the children was graphic, but it took them no further forward than what she already knew. It was agreed that they could only be some weapon or force, but beyond that, the sinister children's true nature was anyone's guess. Equally problematic was their origin. Cordelia, in her confrontation with Jeakqual-Ahrach, had accused the Zhaithan witch of growing the things in a vat, or that they were the product of some twisted relationship between her and her brother. One of these spur-of-the-moment guesses seemed to have goaded the woman into a fury, so maybe one or the other had been uncomfortably close to the truth. The Zhaithan knowledge of sorcery, conjuration, and necromancy was so advanced that the creation of artificial living entities might be possible. Jesamine had voiced the one major objection to the idea that the Twins might be the product of some strange Ahrach-sibling incest. "Can you really see Jeakqual-Ahrach going through the pain and inconvenience of childbirth?"

To which Cordelia had posed the counter argument that "She wouldn't carry the damn things herself. She'd have them implanted in the womb of some poor fucking slave girl and then ripped out when the time was right."

At the words "poor fucking slave girl," Jesamine's face had hardened. All through the night the knife edge of some conflict over the matter of Jesamine and Jack Kennedy had been a petty but tense subtext to the discussion, and both were ready to offer or take offense far too easily. Argo quickly steered the discussion in another direction. "Maybe we should ask ourselves why she should want to reveal the twins to us?"

Cordelia had obviously been shocked and frightened by Jeakqual-Ahrach's paranormal visitation, and the shock and fear were now manifesting themselves as a growing belligerence. "In case nobody noticed, she revealed them to me."

Raphael reminded Cordelia "We've all seen them in our dreams."

Cordelia mouth was a tight, down-turned scowl. The combination of post-trauma and gin was making her mean. "They didn't try to come through from the Other Side, and try to bite any of you."

Raphael took a deep breath. "They were also observing the attack of the small dark things on the battlefield."

The others all looked at him in surprise. "What?"

"At the very end, I had the briefest glimpse of them watching the action."

Jesamine voiced what all of the others were thinking. "Why the fuck didn't you tell us?"

"It was so fleeting, I didn't want to make a big deal of it."

"Fuck you, Raphael. We all need to know everything."

Argo though about this. "There are two obvious options. The first is that, for some reason of her own that we don't yet know, Jeakqual-Ahrach wants to frighten us with the Twins, maybe to keep us off balance."

"Or?"

"Or she doesn't totally control them."

Silence reigned for a moment as everyone digested this thought. Finally Cordelia spoke. "Whether she made them, and whether she controls them, it seems to me that they could very well be a direct answer to us. A countermeasure, if you like."

"The Two against The Four?"

"Something like that. I mean, although we have Slide and T'saya and all of the others advising and helping and training us, we do, to a great degree, operate according to our own free will."

Argo rubbed his chin. He was starting to need a shave. "That may only be because no one understands what we are."

"And maybe it's the same with the Twins. Maybe Jeakqual-Ahrach no more really controls the Twins than Slide controls us."

Jesamine looked up sharply. "Has anyone asked themselves why Slide decided that he'd sail alone on the *Constellation* rather than cross the ocean with us on the *Ragnar?*"

Cordelia held up a hand, at the same time, shaking her head. "No. Let's not even go there. I really don't want to get into a discussion about Slide and what he gets up to. You all know as well as I do that what Slide does is so totally his own affair that we shouldn't even guess at it."

Raphael, however, was still thinking. "Maybe if Slide had been around, Jeakqual-Ahrach wouldn't have been able or prepared to risk doing what she did?"

"Didn't you hear me? I said I wasn't going to start getting into a whole lot of speculation about Yancey Slide. It's the path of total fucking madness and I've had enough madness for one day."

Argo shrugged. "Okay. Forget what Slide might be up to. There is a way that we could find out more about these Twins for ourselves."

The others stared at him with a measure of suspicion. "How?"

"We could jump into the Other Place and try to look for them? Maybe even try to link minds while we were in there."

Cordelia was already shaking her head, and Raphael right along with her. "Not a fucking chance. Linking minds and trying to suss out those nasty-looking beasts could be nothing short of a suicide mission. While we were looking, it could leave us blind to every kind of strangeness. The Other Place is the combat zone, and to go into it with any other intention is just plain crazy."

"We've scouted there before."

"Not hoping to find an enemy with totally unknown powers. I've seen those things close up. They're dangerous. Very dangerous."

Raphael was in total agreement. "Cordelia's right. It would be foolhardy to say the least. To go in wide open, looking for something we can't even make an informed guess about, could just leave us sitting ducks for Dark Things, Mothmen, and any fresh paranormal enemy unpleasantness that might come at us."

Argo admitted defeat. "Okay, so it was a bad idea. There might be another way to go about it."

Now all of the others were shaking their heads. "No."

"Enough."

"It's been a long day."

Jesamine sighed. "It's been a long day and I want my bed."

For a moment, Argo though Cordelia was going to make some feline remark about Jack Kennedy, but mercifully she didn't. The two boys got to their feet, and made their exits. Outside in the corridor, Raphael looked at Argo. "Bed?"

Argo shook his head. "I think I'll take a walk around the deck and clear my brain."

"Suit yourself."

Up on the deck the daylight watch was taking over the running of the ship, and the smell of breakfast wafted from ventilators, reminding Raphael that, despite the gin, he was hungry. A few sailors nodded, but most ignored him and went about their duties. The general bustle seemed to indicate that the destroyer was being prepared for something, but, being unversed in the ways of warships, he had no clue what that something might be. After standing in the bows for a great deal of time, simply staring at the gray ocean dawn, he asked a passing deckhand, who paused and looked at him in surprise. "Why bless you, sir. Didn't no one tell you? We're nearing land."

"We are?"

The man pointed directly ahead. "Those clouds . . ."

"Yes."

"That's the Eiren coast. We'll be in the Bristol Channel by this afternoon."

# F O U R

𝕧

## CORDELIA

Half of England seemed to have turned out to greet them. Or, to be
more precise, to meet Jack Kennedy and those who might be with him.
Kennedy was more popular with the Norse than the King of Albany. Although some of the Norse states had retained their monarchies, most no-
tably the English, the Swedes, and the Danes, they kept them under strict
constitutional control, and were not impressed by royalty for its own
sake. Kennedy, on the other hand, had earned the respect of the Norse
people for the historic stand that he had taken against the old autocrat,
Carlyle I, and the former King's attempts to terminate democracy in the
Kingdom of Albany; then, much more recently, it was reinforced and
magnified by how he had faced down and ultimately turned back the Mosul invaders in the Americas. The *Ragnar* was proceeding up the Bristol
Channel, to the city of Bristol, the most westerly of the Norse Union's
great English naval ports, and the reception had begun while they were
still well out to sea. The destroyer's two escorts, the *Loki* and the *Rob Roy*,
had fallen back and taken up line astern positions, then the three ships
had proceeded at a slow and stately speed, while a flotilla of other Norse
vessels moved into position to escort them to safety. Overhead, the single
dirigible that had escorted them across the Northern Ocean was joined
by three more of the big cylindrical balloons and numerous biplanes.

These other Norse vessels were bringing the *Ragnar* home with sirens blaring and flags flying, but Cordelia knew that there was more than just ceremony to all this stately naval display. Neither the Prime Minister's visit nor the means by which he had crossed the Northern Ocean could any longer be a secret, and although it was highly unlikely that the Mosul would be crazy enough to attempt any last ditch suicide attack, no chances were being taken. This major concern for security was also why their destination was Bristol, and they were not proceeding on up the English Channel and then making the turn into the Thames estuary and docking in the Port of London, in the shadow of the ancient Elizabeth Tower, and the landmark dome of the Cathedral of Mithras. To do so would have involved the *Ragnar* in steering a course that was only a matter of ten miles or less from the Mosul defenses on the Frankish coast, making the destroyer too tempting a target for enemy guns should the Mosul have decided that killing Kennedy was worth an international incident. Thus Kennedy and his party would disembark at Bristol, and then travel on to London in a special railway train. Although it might have been nice to sail into the historic provincial capital of London, Cordelia was hardly disappointed. She liked trains almost as much as she liked boats, and she did not doubt that they would be fêted all the way, and, even better than boats and trains, Cordelia liked attention. In addition, it also appeared to be a lovely day to be welcomed to another country as a visiting celebrity.

Although Cordelia had no actual firsthand experience, she could only imagine that this was a perfect spring day in Southern England. All too often, in saga and storybook, the English territories of the Norse Union were pictured as a damp and overcast island, a place of fog and drizzle when it wasn't actually raining, but on this day a blue-green sea was canopied by a blue sky garnished with fluffy white clouds, scudding from the southwest on a light breeze. As many of the *Ragnar*'s crew who could find an excuse were either on the deck or clinging to some part of the superstructure, and Cordelia had made sure she was among them. She had slept too late to stake out a vantage point but had used all of her charm and wiles to ease her way to the bow rail, at what she had taken to referring in innocent and disarmingly childlike terms as "the sharp end." Obviously Cordelia knew the correct terminology for the basic parts of a warship, but a pose of airheaded naïveté was regrettably guaranteed to get her what she wanted. She tended to view such silliness as a kind of therapy after all that she had been forced confront and endure. She was well aware that all of the pomp, circumstance, and attention of their coming reception in England was not designed solely for her, but that wouldn't stop her pretending that it was. She had played crucial roles in two major battles against the Mosul, and if the Norse in general and the English in particular wanted to greet her like a heroine she would totally permit them to do so. She smiled to herself as a phrase came into her head. "I am Major, the Lady Cordelia Blakeney, look on my charms and adore me."

## ARGO

Argo craned to stare up as five Norse biplanes roared overhead in a tight V formation with even more flamboyant and heraldic designs in their wings and fuselage than the ones that had bombed and strafed the Mosul at Newbury Vale. As the *Ragnar* steamed slowly up the Bristol Channel, passing under the intricate span of a towering suspension bridge, small boats, flying both the North Star flag of the NU, and the Crowned Bear of Albany, and packed with waving, cheering people, crowded the water ahead, behind, and on either side of them. He could see Cordelia, in her tightest dress uniform, had somehow managed to find herself a place at the rail, close to the destroyer's bow, and she was actually waving back. Jack Kennedy's arrival in the Norse Union was being treated with an enthusiastic anticipation that was close to hero worship, but Argo knew the hero was being carefully guarded. All the way up the Bristol Channel, the defensive gun emplacements were fully manned, and a number of small, fast gunboats had moved purposefully in among the boats of the floating spectators. He was also aware that not everyone in the Norse Union was as ecstatic at the arrival of Jack Kennedy or the coming visit of the King. Argo may have been drinking heavily in the time between training and when the army had moved out on the advance into Virginia and Newbury Vale, but that did not mean he had been completely inattentive at the various gatherings, functions, and whiskey-soaked nights in the officers mess, or oblivious to the gossip, rumor, and given intelligence that constantly circulated. He knew that some factions did not share the support for Albany of NU President Inga Sundquist and her Vice President Ingmar Ericksen for the Albany cause. Among them were the Latvian bankers, too heavily influenced by their need to deal with the Swiss, who, in turn, sat in their alpine national fortress with their money, their chocolate, and their cuckoo clocks, maintaining their own unsteady and always mutable neutrality by acting as unofficial economic mentors to Hassan and the Zhaithan. Then there were those who favored the Hindi Raj over Albany. In the Americas, few ever looked to the east of the Mosul Empire and considered the Hindi Raj, who also had the military weight of Hassan IX and his murderous hordes hard against their frontiers. To the Rajahs in Jaipur and Calcutta, the Mosul invasion of the Americas was seen as a much-needed second front, and, should the Mosul be driven out of the New World, the pressure of Hassan's need for conquest would fall squarely on them.

A few nights before The Four had boarded the *Ragnar* for their ocean crossing, T'saya had served her famous gumbo to Argo and Raphael, the two girls being elsewhere on prior engagement, and while the three of them ate highly spiced shrimp and drank Baltimore beer, she had filled them in on the various groups who would cause trouble for Albany inside the Norse Union, lest they make the mistake of believing that all of the Norse unquestioningly loved them. She had told them of the political extremists in the far north of the NU, who had publicly called Ingmar Ericksen a traitor for having such a close relationship with Jack Kennedy; fringe groups of jackbooted absolutists like the Slaves of the Serpent, the Thulists, the Brownshirts, who, according to T'saya's geopolitical view, "sat up there in Oslo and Helsinki dreaming masturbation dreams of Crom and the Old Gods, and growing wistful for what they imagine are the politics of the war axe."

He recalled her words very clearly. "They're nothing but emotionally stunted schoolboys at heart. They envy the Zhaithan for the treatment of women, but would run a mile from a real Viking saga. They're petty but they're still dangerous, and they're almost as much our enemy as the Mosul. They, too, have their nasty, little-boy dreams of conquest, and power. That's why they are so opposed to President Sundquist's tacit alliance with Albany, and why they would happily shoot Ingmar Ericksen if they thought they could get away with it. As always, my Raphael and my Argo, mark me very careful, and take nothing at face value."

He recalled T'saya's words as the *Ragnar*'s Bristol pilot steered the destroyer close to the pier where they would dock and a military band struck up the Albany national anthem. The elaborate reception that awaited them made it hard to believe that Kennedy and all those with him were not universally adored. Flags and bunting decked the pier, and, in addition to the brass band, a company of Norse Marines, in full dress, blue tunics and white kepis, stood at rigid attention. A line of almost a dozen large black automobiles were waiting to take them to their next destination, and a reception committee of Norse leaders, dignitaries, and diplomats were grouped where the first gangplank would run out, ready to greet Kennedy and his party. Farther down the pier, a double line of police held back a crowd of sightseers and well-wishers who had brought more flags and banners of their own, creating a fluttering sea of red, white, gold, and pale blue. Less impressive, but also a vital part of the process, was the small throng of reporters and cameramen, with the notebooks and microphones, tripods and flash trays, all waiting to relay word and image of the Albany arrival to the rest of the country.

Once the gangway had been wheeled into place, and secured by a detail of sailors, the marine band struck up a reprise of "Hail Albany" and Kennedy started down it, closely followed by the ever-present and watchful Dawson. Bareheaded and waving, hat in hand, acknowledging the cheers from the other end of the pier, he posed for the big bulky cameras of the newsmen, looking a little dazzled by their exploding flash powder. At the bottom of the gangway, as protocol dictated, he was met by England's Provincial Governor, Sir Richard Branson. Kennedy would have to wait until he reached Stockholm before his public audience with President Inga Sundquist. As the two men shook hands, the band segued into "Hammer of the North," and the rest of the Kennedy party began to descend. The Four were among the last to go ashore, but the cheering had hardly diminished, and as they negotiated the gangway, Argo could not help feeling that he, too, was something special; in his own way a minor hero, if only by association. He also resolved to make every possible use of this notoriety and adoration.

Once he had both feet on dry land, Argo, hero or not, would willingly have just stood and stared, taking in all of the Norse military circumstance. The band, the honor guard, the reporters, and the crowds of well-managed spectators, the airships, even the endless Bristol Naval Yard, with its moored lines of huge and immaculate gray warships, all combined to overwhelm him. Argo had seen a lot since he had left his village in Virginia, but he suddenly felt like a child in an entirely new and wondrous land, and knew he would need to operate on a fresh scale of values and assumptions. He was suddenly aware how, in comparison to these old nations of Northern Europe, Albany was little more than a pioneer settlement, despite its castle, and its pretensions to tradition. Even Jack Kennedy, the focus of all this ceremony, was nothing more than the first-generation son of a backwoods moonshiner.

## JESAMINE

"This way!"

"Jesamine! Major Jesamine!"

"Jesamine! Jesamine!"

"Look this way, Jesamine!"

"Major Jesamine!"

The reporters were actually shouting at her, and, even before she set foot on the dock she found herself half blinded by a blaze of exploding flash powder.

"Look this way."

"Major Jesamine, can you tell us why Prime Minister Kennedy picked you to accompany him?"

She had been warned that Norse had their tabloid press, and some of those newspapers were infinitely rougher and more sensational than *The Albany Banner,* but she had expected nothing like the baying mob that confronted her. It was as though they knew about her already. And then she realized that, in all probability, they did. These reporters did their research and had informants all over. They had almost certainly checked the lists of who was in the Kennedy party, and it would have been no great stretch for them to find the exposé of "Slave Girl Jesamine" in *The Banner*. Horrified that her dubious history and reputation might have preceded her across the Northern Ocean, she managed to make her way down the gangway and onto the hard flagstones of the dock in her New York high heels, but after that she hesitated, dazed and totally unsure of what to do next, frightened that she was going to stumble, until a firm hand grasped her by the arm, and a calm voice spoke with an authoritative urgency. "Just say nothing. Ignore them. Once we get to London, we'll do our best to keep them away from you, but for now just keep your head down and get in the car."

"What?"

"Just come with me to your car, Major. As fast as you can."

"Who are you?"

"Tennyson. Commander Jane Tennyson." Commander Tennyson was a thinly officious blonde woman dressed in the stylishly tailored uniform of an officer in the Norse Navy.

Jesamine was bemused, but survival instinct and Tennyson's official air stopped her from pulling away. "I don't understand."

"I'm your NU liaison for the duration of your visit, and I'm also responsible for your safety."

"These reporters . . ."

"I'm afraid they rather go with the territory. But I would have thought you'd be accustomed to all the attention by now."

Jesamine said nothing. So the story from *The Banner* had preceded her. Even her liaison officer knew about it, although, to know things had to be part of a liaison officer's job. Tennyson gestured to a line of large, black, square-sided automobiles that waited with their engines running on the other side of the dock. "Shall we? . . ."

As Jesamine allowed herself to be propelled towards the cars. She saw that Cordelia, Raphael, and Argo were being likewise herded along by a male officer. As she and Tennyson took off at a semi-run, the men and women of the press started up again with their loud and idiotic questions. "Major Jesamine, how did it feel to cross the ocean with Prime

Minister Kennedy? Is his reputation as a ladies' man all it's made out to be?"

At this, Jesamine again almost tripped. The English press might have read up on her past in back issues of *The Banner,* but how the hell could they know anything about her and Jack Kennedy? She could imagine a sailor or servant not being averse to picking up a few extra shillings by feeding tidbits to the newspapers, but no one on the *Ragnar* could have used the destroyer's wireless communications to spread that kind of gossip. It was only then that she realized they actually knew nothing, and were just wildly adding two and two, not knowing that, by blind luck, they were actually making four. She only hoped Jack Kennedy would not blame her for all the cheap speculation, and have nothing more to do with her.

## RAPHAEL

Clearly Jesamine had to be moved away from the howling mob of loud and uncouth reporters who seemed close to obsessive about her, doubtless as a result of all the nonsense printed about her in *The Albany Banner.* Raphael pushed to get to her and hustle her away, but, before he could reach her, a slim but determined naval officer took care of her. The line of cars was discreetly guarded by a squad of more Norse marines in camouflage battledress, armed with Bergman rapid-fire rifles. The fact was again not being overlooked that their enemies were only a relative stone's throw away, across the narrow waters of the English Channel. These grim men in combat drab were infinitely closer to Raphael's reality than the ceremonial honor guard, in their crisp blue and white and gold, shouldering their polished but extremely antique muskets. Kennedy and the English Provincial Governor were now heading for the first and most luxurious car in line, the one that flew pennants of the NU and Albany. The Four were being directed to the next to last in line, which seemed somehow apt. Jesamine's commander pushed her into the car, and out of sight of the photographers, but then Cordelia, who, for reasons known only to herself, had taken on some frivolous, airhead persona, managed to thwart the smooth getaway by actually stopping and posing for the press, and then asking a totally fatuous question. "Why are we going by car? I thought we were taking a train to London."

Commander Tennyson dragged Cordelia into the car, snapping tersely. "The cars are just to take us to Temple Meads railway station. From there we go on by special train."

An entire platform had been closed off at Bristol's Temple Meads station, and a red carpet laid. Raphael expected another crowd scene with reporters and milling onlookers, but mercifully the only welcoming committee was the station master and some official from what was called Amalgamated Western Railway, although more heavily armed soldiers in full battle dress stood guard. The Kennedy motorcade drove straight up to the most splendid train Raphael had ever seen. The gleaming steam locomotive was freshly painted, green livery with red trim, and four carriages the same, except in turquoise and gold. The sour note was the flatcar behind the guard's van on which a rotating, twin-barreled light field gun was mounted for the protection of the train and its passengers. The moment the car came to a stop, Commander Tennyson indicated that The Four should sit tight. "Let the bigwigs and the brass shake hands with the station master, and then get aboard before we make our move. The security detail wants the least number of people on the platform at any one time."

She watched carefully for maybe two minutes and then swung the car's door open so it was only a matter of a few steps to the train. "That's it, people, let's go."

The Four scrambled out of the car and, guided by Tennyson, walked quickly to the last carriage, nodding to the two stewards who were waiting to assist them. The locomotive noisily let off steam, and blew a double blast on its whistle. The next stop was London.

## ARGO

The English countryside rolled by outside the window. In many ways it was a lot like Virginia, only smaller and neater, more compact and organized. The Kennedy train rattled through towns and villages, through tunnels and over bridges, and past spring-green hedgerows, woods in freshly budding leaf, and well-tended handkerchief fields. Argo could see how, when the first settlers had landed in the new world, on the East Coast of the Americas, they must have thought themselves in a kind of rough and ready, unkempt and uncultivated paradise. Virginia and Albany were a vastly more lush, unfenced, and uncontrolled version of the lands that they had left. Cars and horse-drawn wagons waited at level crossings, and on the platforms of the stations that they passed without stopping, English commuters stared curiously at the clearly unusual train as it sped by. The interior of the train was quite as lavish as the outside. The apartment into which they were first ushered by the stewards was paneled in richly polished chestnut and upholstered in dark leather. As they settled themselves, and the train pulled out of the station, clattering over multiple sets of points, drink orders were taken. Raphael and Jesamine played it sensible and requested coffee. Cordelia went native and asked for tea, but when Argo threw caution to the winds and demanded a large scotch, she did the same. They remained in the compartment as the train made its way out of the port city, past the famous Exchange Building, the Bristol Rovers' football ground, the buttressed bulk of the Cathedral of Odin, with its soaring gothic spire, and the much smaller Tabernacle of Jesu Ben Joseph.

As the train rolled out of Bristol, Tennyson filled them in on their itinerary once they arrived in London. "We will first go to the Asquith Hotel where you will all be staying. Once you get there, you'll have a little more than an hour to freshen up before we leave for the official reception at the Palace of Westminster."

Raphael had sighed. "Reception?"

Tennyson nodded. "Members of the Government and foreign dignitaries will formally welcome Prime Minister Kennedy to London."

"And we'll be expected to go?"

"Of course."

Jesamine shook her head. "Exhibits in the zoo again."

Tennyson ignored Jesamine and looked down at her clipboard. "The next thing after that will be tomorrow afternoon when you are expected to accompany Prime Minister Kennedy in the procession to the Hall of the Provincial Parliament."

Jesamine's point seemed to be made for her. "Like I said, exhibits again."

Tennyson folded her clipboard shut but said nothing. At that point, Argo had turned and looked out of the window again. He did not want to think about an official reception. They were passing rolling fields between wooded hills, with placid cows grazing contentedly. Earlier, however, Argo had seen something else from the window that had not been quite as pleasing as unfolding rural England. They had gone by a large billboard obviously positioned so it could be easily read from passing trains. The image was a crude and ugly cartoon of Jack Kennedy, armed to the teeth, dressed like a stereotyped hillbilly complete with coonskin cap, driving a broken-down cart drawn by a donkey. The slogan was in huge, blood-red letters . . .

DRIVIN' THE NORSE TO WAR!

On the car ride to Temple Meads, they had also passed a small group of demonstrators with placards that had read, *"Go Home Warmonger!"* and *"Hassan Is Not The Enemy!"* Argo had noticed that a number of them were wearing the double axe symbol of the followers of Crom. At the time, no one had said anything, but the billboard had caused the eyes of The Four to turn to Tennyson, who could only purse her lips and look a little embarrassed. "What can I say? You can't please everyone. Especially the Crom nutters."

"The Crom nutters?"

"Groups like the Iron Thulists. We're always having trouble with them. Up in Norway, they took to burning down Jesu Tabernacles. They think that down here in the south we're soft and decadent. I suppose, one of these days, we're going to have to show them how wrong they are."

Argo glanced round the apartment. "Do you think Kennedy saw the billboard?"

Raphael shrugged. "It was pretty much impossible to miss."

Tennyson's face tightened with embarrassment. "I hope he doesn't think we all feel that way."

A moment later, a steward slid back the door of the compartment and announced that a late lunch was being served in the restaurant car. Argo was quickly on his feet, defusing the moment. "I don't know about the rest of you, but I'm starving, and if I go on drinking on an empty stomach, I'll probably disgrace us all." They others agreed, and with the steward in the lead, they made their way down the train to where they found that the entire Kennedy party, plus the Norse reception committee, were already assembling.

## CORDELIA

Lunch was as about as traditional as it could be. The hors d'oeuvre was a pâté of Norwegian smoked salmon on thinly sliced triangles of toast, then a main course of roast beef, green vegetables, and a strange, bread-like substance called Yorkshire pudding. The china and silverware was about as fine and expensive as one could expect to find on a moving train. A salad was also offered as an alternative for those who might not eat meat, either out of health or humanitarian considerations. This was not the case with any of The Four. Cordelia knew that Jesamine had once attempted to become a vegetarian, but had abandoned the idea sometime during her stay with the Ohio. The Four had been seated at a table that appeared as far from the Prime Minister and the Governor of England as was possible. Cordelia decided that it was pointless to feel demeaned or insulted. The Four had no diplomatic function, and certainly no training in international relations. They were part of the party and that would have to be enough. They had to be content to be sidelined until their yet undefined function was made clear to them. Cordelia had assumed that, as their liaison officer, Tennyson would eat with the four of them, but their place settings were for four only, and Tennyson seemed required to circulate. She moved from table to table, bracing herself with some style and panache while standing and conducting conversations on a swaying train. Cordelia watched her progress for a while, and noticed that heads turned in their direction, indicating The Four must have been a topic of conversation.

Jesamine spent most of the meal staring down the length of the restaurant car as she ate, almost certainly obsessing about Jack Kennedy, and probably fuming that they had not been seated closer to the man who, as far as Cordelia could judge, was the current object of Jesamine's affection. Damn, but the old lion must have had something going for him to have such an effect on a girl like Jesamine. Cordelia would have bet good money that her companion's history was too long and scandalous for her to succumb to any girlish crush. Of course, old Jack Kennedy was the Prime Minister of Albany, and, as such, one of the leaders of the free world, but was that the whole of it? While wholly unwilling to admit that her reactions might be colored by an element of jealousy, Cordelia had definite reservations about the relationship between Jesamine and Kennedy. Maybe it was the stories about the Prime Minister and her mother, or maybe because she was the complete little aristocratic Albany snob, she felt somehow proprietorial about Jack Kennedy and resented that Jesamine had aced her out of a connection that she had previously considered her own exclusive domain.

The dessert came and Cordelia, ever the sensualist, turned all of her attention to a fluffy chocolate confection that she would later describe as heavenly. Once finished, she noted that the Norse really did themselves proud. From what little she had so far been able to observe, life in the Norse Union looked easy and affluent, and she was reminded that Albany, even though on the apparent ascendant, was still very much a country at war, with shortages, rationing, and a general austerity, which tended to become the norm when one had nothing else with which to compare it. Sure they had a good time, but, in the consumer sense, it was poverty compared to what the NU offered. The number of automobiles, even in the small towns they hammered through in their private train, exceeded the density of traffic in the city center of Albany on a Friday afternoon. Every available space seemed to be covered in garish, brightly colored advertising. Even their view of the countryside was interrupted by lurid and erotic billboards, suggesting the English had nothing on their minds but sex and fashion. This was, to a degree, confirmed by the young women on the platforms of the stations through which they passed. To Cordelia's Albany eye, the English girls made themselves decidedly more provocative, and tended towards a high level of what they obviously considered to be either glamorous or torrid. Very short skirts, very high heels, tight trousers, and low-cut tops aspired to a level of flamboyance beyond even that of a thirty-shilling doxie on Castle Street. The young men equally flaunted their sense of style. Coming from an environment in which most of the eligible boys were in uniform, she enjoyed the fact that these young English men wore their trousers as tight as the women, but with flounced shirts, capes, and flowing scarves, that created an effect that was, at one and the same time, both swashbuckling and effeminate. And these were only the provincial towns. How would things be when they reached the capital? Cordelia was fascinated, but simultaneously a little shocked. Then she caught herself. Shocked? Lady Cordelia Blakeney, the dangerous vamp of Newbury Vale and beyond? You, my dear, are being wholly provincial. Stop it immediately or these damned Norse will think you're a hick from the hills.

## JESAMINE

Jesamine had to stop herself from wanting to simply stare at Jack Kennedy. It was absurd. He was at the opposite end of the restaurant car, but he might as well have been a hundred miles away. She knew how stupid she was being, but if only he would look or nod, or in some way acknowledge she existed . . . But Jack Kennedy could not possibly acknowledge her without starting tongues wagging. The damned reporters at the dock had been bad enough. If he singled her out for public attention they might as well rent one of the billboards—that kept flashing past the windows of the train—to announce that they were lovers. That was if they were lovers at all. Jesamine had no confirmation of that. Maybe she had been nothing more than a shipboard interlude. She needed to ease back on a possibly fictional romance and look for some other diversion. The dessert helped a little. She could truthfully say that she had never in her life tasted anything like the dark chocolate that had been somehow whipped to a fine froth. When she had first escaped to Albany, it had seemed as though the people there had everything, but Albany was positively austere in comparison to how the Norse lived. She remembered how she had previously likened the Norse to the Teutons, and knew she had been completely wrong. The Norse, or at least the English, were nothing like the Teutons.

They liked their comfort too much. Then the dessert was finished, and Jesamine wondered what would happen if she asked for more. She decided that it was probably not the done thing. The stewards were serving coffee, and Jack Kennedy had lit a cigar. She noticed Cordelia looking at her speculatively but then becoming distracted by the tall Englishman that Jane Tennyson brought to their table.

"I like to introduce you all to Colonel Gideon Windermere."

Colonel Gideon Windermere was the most unlikely soldier Jesamine had ever encountered, or, to be more precise, he was the most unlikely soldier to obtain the rank of colonel that she had ever encountered. His uniform was tailored, but he wore it with a kind of studied and sloppy disregard. His collar was loose, his posture was casual, and his sandy-blonde hair was considerably longer that the military average. He seem to be very aware of the paradox he presented because his first gesture was one of self-deprecation. "Please, forget the rank. It's just an honorary title. They didn't know what to do with me so they made me a colonel."

Argo grinned. "They made us all majors, but we did very little to deserve it."

Colonel Gideon Windermere laughed. "I think, in my case, it's just so they can calculate how much to pay me."

Cordelia treated Windermere to one of her most dazzling smiles. "And do they pay you a lot, Colonel Windermere?"

"They like me to be comfortable. I work better that way."

"And what work do you do?"

"I'm part of what's laughingly called Military Intelligence."

Cordelia fluttered her eyelashes. Jesamine was a little stunned. She had already decided to make this man one of her conquests? "Does that mean you're a spy?"

Tennyson, who seemed uncomfortable with this highly unmilitary humor, moved to clarify the situation. "Colonel Windermere is head of what's called the ES Section. The work that you all do is, in some respects, parallel."

"We'd ask Colonel Windermere to sit down," Cordelia gestured to the four places at the table, "but we don't seem to have the room."

Tennyson took matters in hand. "It would be best if we all returned to your compartment so you and the colonel can talk in private."

Raphael shrugged. "Whatever you say."

Windermere treated the suggestion as though it was purely a social matter. "We can ask the steward to bring us drinks, and do the best we can to get to know each other before we pull into Sloane Square station, and the social carousel starts up again."

Argo was first on his feet. "Shall we make a move?"

All round them, the party in the restaurant car was starting to break up. The stewards were clearing tables and those who lingered had broken up into conversational or even conspiratorial groups. Jack Kennedy and Governor Branson were already on their way out. With a single backward glance at Kennedy, and a reluctant sigh, Jesamine followed Argo, Windermere, and the others back into the corridor that led to the rear coaches. At the door of their compartment, Windermere stepped to one side, and allowed The Four to go in first, but then politely waylaid Jane Tennyson. "I think I can take it from here, Commander."

Tennyson obviously didn't like being excluded, but stiffened to attention as though receiving an order from a superior. "As you wish, Colonel."

"Thank you, Commander. If you could send a steward along to take our orders, I'd be extremely grateful."

With that, Windermere stepped into the compartment and closed the door behind him. The deftness with which Windermere had moved Tennyson out of play led Jesamine to believe there was a lot more to this man than met the eye, and she was far from sure that she trusted him.


## RAPHAEL

"It takes all kinds to make a war. One man's freedom fighter is another's gangster."

Raphael raised an eyebrow. He was far from sure if he trusted this strange English colonel. "The enemy of my enemy is my friend?"

Windermere nodded. "As long as one accepts the limitations."

Jesamine's expression was bleak. "Phaall, the Teuton, liked to use the expression."

"It's the classic Teuton justification."

"Except he never accepted the limitations."

Windermere sipped his gin. "And that will be the Teutons' ultimate downfall."

When the colonel had first sat down opposite them, he had lowered himself stiffly into the seat. "An interlude with the Zhaithan rather messed up my leg."

Cordelia had blinked. "With the Zhaithan?"

"They caught me somewhere where I wasn't supposed to be."

"So you are a spy?"

"Perhaps. Although hardly of the common or garden variety."

"Jesamine and I were once prisoners of the Zhaithan."

Windermere had nodded. "I know."

"You know?"

"It probably seems like an intrusion, but I've read your dossiers."

The Four exchanged glances. Then Cordelia turned on her smile again. "So how did the Zhaithan get you?"

"It was my own fault. I lingered too long in this saloon of especially ill-repute, showing card tricks to the harlots."

He glanced at Jesamine. "It was in Cadiz, incidentally. A joint called the El Matador. Maybe you knew it?"

Jesamine colored and her jaw clenched hard. Windermere knew what she was in Cadiz and it made her angry. "I've heard of the El Matador. Damp sheets, bad booze, and cheap tricks. I never went there."

Windermere shrugged. "Whorehouses are part of the territory. The most effective placement of agents can be in the brothels. Invisibility is built in, and a lot of secrets get spilled on the damp sheets after the bad booze."

Raphael wondered why Windermere was going to such lengths to demonstrate that he knew their histories. Did he think it gave him some kind of control over them? He did not like the way the English colonel was treating Jesamine, and was about to say something, but Argo beat him to it. "You seem to know all about us, Colonel. Perhaps you'd like to tell us something about yourself and this ES Section."

Windermere nodded. "That seems only fair."

"So?"

At that moment, the steward arrived with drinks, and Windermere waited until he was through before answering. Windermere's drink was a clear, colorless liquid in a conical glass with an olive on a toothpick in it. Cordelia stared at it curiously. She didn't seem to share the others' distrust of the man. In fact she seemed quite enamored of him. "What's that?"

"It's a martini."

"What's a martini?"

"A new invention. A lot of gin, a lot of refrigeration, and very little else."

Cordelia looked down at her own aquavit as though regretting its lack of sophistication, but Raphael had no more time for pleasantries and chat. "You were about to explain the ES Section."

Windermere nodded. "The ES Section is one of those units that the rest of Military Intelligence wishes didn't exist. We deal in the metaphysical, the stuff you can't see until it suddenly appears. We make the regular soldiers very uncomfortable. You've probably run into the same kind of discomfort yourselves. Am I right?"

Raphael and the others nodded. At least this Windermere could be direct when he so desired. "The regular Norse army wishes it didn't have to come to terms with the possibility of big balls of paranormal gelatin bouncing around the battlefield, eating whole companies of infantry."

Raphael scowled. "We've seen big balls of paranormal gelatin bouncing around the battlefield. Also little ones."

Argo nodded. "Whole formations of them."

Jesamine pursed her lips and Raphael saw she took some pleasure in reminding Windermere that they were hardly novices in paranormal combat. "We have also faced them down and destroyed them."

Windermere looked down at his boots. Raphael reflected that he probably had a batman or servant who shined them to their deep chestnut gloss. Maybe the Norse were not all that different from the Teutons. A lock of hair fell in Windermere's face and he brushed it back as he looked up. "I'm sorry. Forgive me. I've offended you with my flippancy."

Maybe there was a difference. Teutons did not ask to be forgiven.

Cordelia stopped treating Colonel Windermere to her sultry look for long enough to be serious for a moment. "The NU are not actually at war with the Mosul Empire."

Jesamine backed her up. "That's right. We've been in the shit, close up, and very personal, Colonel."

Windermere continued to be placating. "Exactly. And that's why I was so anxious to meet you. We may not be in a shooting war with desperate Mamalukes, but it is a war all the same."

Windermere paused, waiting for any of The Four to speak. They didn't, so he continued. "It's a war that being fought with wraiths in the dark of night, apparitions in back alleys, and the murderous emanations of Quadaron-Ahrach, and Her Grand Eminence, his loathsome sister."

Cordelia raised an eyebrow, but allowed Windermere to continue. "It's a war being fought all over Europe and the Middle East. It's fought by the continual resistance in the occupied territories. This resistance can take many forms. Everyone has heard the stories of soldiers starving while food rots in the boxcars of trains that have been directed to the wrong railway line or parked in the wrong siding. Sometimes it's just Mosul inefficiency. Stuff fucks up naturally, all the time, in a totalitarian theocracy, but the fuck-ups can be eased along and made more destructive. Paperwork can be misplaced, supplies can be wrongly routed, and private secrets accidentally revealed. Sometimes these actions are more bold; a poisoning, an assassination, a High Zhaithan dies in his sleep and his concubine is nowhere to be found." He glanced briefly at Jesamine. "It's a war that produces strange alliances; Hispanian streetwalkers, Turkish opium runners, and the Romany underground; washer women who are clandestine witches, and who hide the tattoo of Morgana's Web. It's the Secret Mandrakes, the Carpathian Legion, the Black Hand, and Il Syndicato . . ."

Jesamine leaned forward. "In Cadiz we had Il Syndicato, but they were just thieves and pimps and smugglers."

Raphael agreed with her. "I heard about Il Syndicato in Madrid. They were supposed to be degenerates and cutthroats."

Windermere smiled. "Like I said earlier, one man's freedom fighter is another's gangster." Then his face turned serious. "There are a lot of people, in the lands across the English Channel, risking their lives and worse to bring the Mosul Empire to ruin, and it falls to units like ES Section to give them what help and support we can. That includes balancing all the idiosyncrasies."

"Hence the devil-may-care attitude."

"It's sometimes the only way when you're making deals with devils."

## ARGO

The thought hardly made any sense, but, although he had no doubt that Colonel Gideon Windermere was wholly and totally human, something about him reminded Argo of Yancey Slide: the lazy posture that occasionally verged on insolence, the uncertainty about what he took seriously and what he treated as a joke, a strange and languid distance in the way he talked. Argo also did not know how much of this was good and how much of it was bad. "Are we more of the devils with whom you have to deal?"

Windermere laughed, seemingly not offended by Argo's tone. "Quite the reverse. I've been very anxious to meet to you. As Jesamine said, you all have been in the shit close up. You have put Jeakqual-Ahrach to flight. I and my people have a lot to learn from you."

"Is Jane Tennyson one of your people?"

Windermere blinked. "Good grief, her? Heavens no. She's from naval public relations. Stiff and martial as they come. Don't let the uniform fool you. The boys and girls of ES Section are neither of those things."

During the exchange, Argo had been thinking. "You said you had a lot to learn from us."

Windermere nodded. "That's right."

"I was wondering what we get in return."

"In return?"

"You learn from us. What do we get from you?"

Windermere looked at Argo as though properly assessing him for the first time. "I though we were all in this for the overthrow of Hassan IX."

Argo took a sip of his scotch. "It's been my experience that, in war, even among allies, things are frequently transactional."

"You want to know what's in it for you and your friends? Is that what you're saying, Major Weaver?"

"That's what I'm saying, Colonel Windermere."

"Well now . . ." Windermere pondered for a moment. "I imagine what I would do for you is to assist you however I can with your mission."

Argo looked sideways at the Englishman. "Our mission?"

"We all know that you have an objective over and above just being here as part of Jack Kennedy's goodwill visit, don't we?"

"We do?"

Windermere eyes twinkled with a sly illusion. "That's what Yancey Slide led me to understand."

If Windermere's objective was to take The Four totally by surprise, he more than achieved it. They looked at each other in amazement and then back at him. "Slide? He was here? When?"

"Just two days ago. He arrived on the *HMS Constellation*."

"And you spoke to him?"

"Of course I spoke to him. Slide wouldn't come to the NU without getting in touch. He and I go back a very long way. He claims it was in multiple timestreams."

Argo knew he would be a whole lot happier if Slide was with them. "He's here now?"

Windermere shook his head. "No, he stayed long enough to meet up with me and fill me in, and then he moved on. I assume he went to Oslo, but you never quite know with Slide."

Argo was disappointed but found himself more ready to accept Gideon Windermere. He did resemble Slide. He had that same world-weary look, old beyond his years from too much premature experience; the air of someone who has been there and done that, maybe too much and maybe too often. And was perhaps only surviving or, at least, re-maining, by keeping up an amused detachment. Raphael, on the other hand, was still mistrustful. "He filled you in?"

"That's what I said."

Jesamine also held on to her suspicions. "What exactly did he fill you in on?"

"He filled me in on your urgent need to know as much as possible about these White Twins, these apparent new creations of Jeakqual-Ahrach."

This statement stopped all conversation. Even Cordelia was staring at Windermere in disbelief. "You know about the Twins?"

Raphael held up a hand. "I think we should stop this talk right now. We don't know what he knows, and we don't know what we might be giving away."

Windermere finally seemed to be running out of patience with Raphael and Jesamine's skepticism. "There has to be a point when we start marginally trusting one another."

Jesamine scowled. "We're the ones with the most to lose."

"Would it help if I told you the decision I should work with you was made days before Slide embarked on the *Constellation*? Or that the plan was approved by T'saya, Miramichi, The Lady Gretchen, and Magachee?"

Jesamine swallowed hard. "Magachee was never in on this. She would have told me."

"Would she?"

Jesamine sighed. It was war and she had to be realistic. "No, probably not."

"So don't you think that you should either grant me a measure of trust, or at least admit one thing?"

"What one thing?"

"That if I'm the enemy, and I know as much as I do, then you, my dears, are wholly and totally fucked."

## CORDELIA

Cordelia was using all of her considerable powers of self-control to contain herself. Gideon Windermere was adorable. After he had stopped Jesamine in her tracks, the lock of hair had again fallen in his face, and as he had casually blown it out of his eyes she had almost groaned out loud.

"If I'm the enemy and I know as much as I do, then you, my dears,

are wholly and totally fucked." No only was Colonel Gideon Windermere adorable, but his logic was irrefutable. They had to trust this bizarre
character from the NU intelligence community, or they were basically
going nowhere. Cordelia wanted the mystery of the White Twins resolved, and she wanted Windermere. She had no reason to think that the
two objectives could not be combined. The Twins liquidated and Windermere possessed; the goals were in no way mutually exclusive. The
others might start giving her the look if she took up with Windermere,
but she really didn't care. There was a war on and she wanted him. Jesamine was fucking Jack Kennedy, so she was without even a foot on the
moral high ground, and the boys were only boys, and therefore didn't
count. Gideon Windermere made Cordelia think of a swashbuckler pretending to be a college professor, but one who had done enough swashbuckling to know what lay behind and beneath the romance.

"What is Morgana's Web?"

Windermere looked at her a little curiously. "Why do you ask?"

Cordelia shook her head. "I'm not sure. When you said it, it just
kind of resonated."

"It's a network of sensitives and windwalkers inside the Mosul occupation. Their communications are invaluable. They also cause their own
havoc, and their poisons are legendary."

"And they're named for Morgana . . . *the* Morgana?"

Windermere nodded. "The symbolism is pretty obvious."

Jesamine bit her lip and looked excluded. "I've never heard of Morgana. Is she some Norse thing?"

"Fifteen hundred years ago, Morgana was the renegade priestess at
the court of Utha the Dragon King. It's one of the Common Sagas."

Jesamine had clearly never read the Common Sagas, but Argo covered her annoyed confusion. "When the Mosul marched into Virginia,
some of the first books they burned were the Common Sagas."

Jesamine sat stiffly. "I have never read the Common Sagas. I was not
raised as a . . . Northern European."

"Utha Pendragon was the legendary English king. He was supposed
to have forged the first links that led to the thousand-year alliance between the Scandinavian Vikings and English of the Islands."

Jesamine stopped pouting and half smiled. "Anyone who beats Teutons gets my approval."

"His wife was Gwyneth and his mistress was the witch Morgana, who was both his salvation and his downfall. Morgana was the classic practitioner of shadow power and invisible manipulation. She held even Augustine in check. Or so the story goes." Windermere turned his attention back to Cordelia, which was exactly the way she wanted it. "I'm still interested in why Morgana's Web resonated for you."

Cordelia shook her head. "Nothing I can put into words. Just one of the prods that we learn not to ignore."

"Some of the first reports to the Section came from Morgana's Web."

"Could we be put in contact with them?"

"It would seem like a good idea. But the final approval would have to come from Madame de Wynter."

"Madame de Wynter?"

"Anastasia de Wynter. She is somewhat territorial about the London end of Morgana's Web."

"She's part of your ES Section?"

"If you asked her, she might tell you that ES Section was part of her."

"I don't understand."

Desire again overtook Cordelia as Windermere's eyes twinkled playfully. "Anastasia de Wynter is always hard to understand. A defrocked priestess, a notorious libertine, an ex-minister of the Frankish Government-in-Exile. You name it and Anastasia has probably done it, and even been prevented from doing it again. She is what you might call an independent operator."

"Can we meet her?"

"That's already been discussed. In fact, Madame de Wynter is having one of her parties after the official reception at the Palace of Westminster."

Cordelia's face lit up. "A party?"

"No one should live their life without having gone to one of Anastasia's parties."

"And this is after the big formal bash?"

"It is indeed."

Raphael groaned. "I'd forgotten about the reception."

Cordelia smiled at him. "It won't be as bad as you think it is. You can always get drunk."

Argo leaned back in his seat. "That's *my* plan."

Windermere glanced at Argo and Raphael. "Don't get so drunk you're not able to make it to Madame de Wynter's."

"We're all invited?"

"That's the ulterior motive of the whole event, so you Four and Anastasia can become acquainted."

Outside the train window, the day was ending in a red sunset, and they were passing through the suburbs of a big city. It could only be that they were heading into London. Windermere rose to his feet. "I have to be getting back to my compartment. We'll be pulling in to the Sloane Square station in just a few minutes." He turned and slid open the door to the corridor. "I trust I will see you all later tonight."

"Will you be at the Palace of Westminster?"

Windermere nodded. "Of course."

Cordelia beamed. "Then we will definitely see you later."

After Windermere was gone, Jesamine treated Cordelia to a look of scorn. "Why didn't you just get down on your knees and blow him in front of us?"

Cordelia returned the scorn with a smile of bland confidence. "I am much more subtle than that, my dear."

# FIVE

❧

## ARGO

Argo admired himself in the full length mirror. He had to admit that he looked pretty damned good in the black, gold, and green, full dress uniform of a Major in the Albany Rangers, with its gold braid, short swagger cloak, and tasseled boots. He liked it better still now he had his own rightfully earned campaign ribbons to wear on his chest, including the coveted Golden Order of the Bear that each of The Four had received for their part in the Battle of the Potomac. Compared to the Rangers' forest green combat kit, the dress uniform was like a costume from some frivolous light opera, but Argo had to admit something might be said in favor of cutting a dash among the elite of a foreign city with a very glamorous reputation. The realization of the full potential of this voyage across the ocean had really only sunk in after he had checked into his room in the Asquith Hotel, and opened up the trunk that contained his official uniforms. He was in England, in London, and he was a decorated and battle-hardened hero from across the seas and, he looked as sharp as a tack in the full ceremonial fig. There was no way that he was not going to have himself some excellent adventures in the city. He had been drinking in corners for too long. It was time to strut his stuff for the girls of the Norse country.

The sudden rapping on the door was authoritative and also impatient. Surely it was not time to leave already? "Who's there?"

"It's Tennyson, Major Weaver."

"I'm not quite ready to leave yet."

"I need to have a brief word with you."

Argo crossed to the door and opened it. Tennyson was flanked by two large men in civilian bowler hats and belted trench coats, who could only be policemen. Argo took a step back, looking these newcomers up and down. "I haven't been here long to be in trouble, have I?"

Tennyson ignored him and stepped through the door, looking around, as far as Argo could tell, to see if they were alone. The two supposed policemen followed her inside, the second closing the door behind him. Argo moved to the room's small complimentary bar and poured himself a scotch. "What's this all about?"

"There's been a development, and I was told to inform you."

"A development?"

"After our train left Bristol, one of the stewards who was supposed to be on the train was found dead in the gentlemen's toilet in Temple Meads Station."

Argo blinked. "Dead?"

Tennyson nodded. "He had been shot once through the back of the head and his uniform had been taken."

"But wasn't he missed when he didn't show up for his duties on the special train?"

"That's the disturbing part. According to our records, he did show up. Or at least someone masquerading as him."

Argo frowned. "But nothing happened. The impostor could have poisoned us or blown up the train, but he didn't."

"Therein would lie the mystery, Major Weaver."

"Have you told this to the others?"

"The others of your group?" She shook her head. "I can leave it to you to pass on the information?"

A hint of need-to-know in Tennyson's tone caused Argo to raise a curious eyebrow. "If I deem necessary?"

"You know the psychology of your group better than I do."

Argo nodded. "Right." He thought for a moment, looking puzzled. "Why choose me to tell them, Commander?"

Tennyson half smiled. "You seem to be the most reasonable."

Argo sighed. "I'm not sure that's saying very much."

As Tennyson had been delivering the unsettling news, the two men in trench coats had removed their hats, but were now looking round at the hotel room with a cop inquisitiveness. Argo protested to Tennyson, "Who are these guys?"

"They're Sir Harry Palmer's boys from the Metropolitan Constabulary Special Branch. You'll find we'll be working very closely with the civilian police."

The two large men nodded. "Just here to keep an eye on things, sir."

"Nothing to worry about."

One of them tapped an index finger on Argo's sidearm. The Ranger issue, double-action revolver in its polished holster lay where Argo had left it on the room's small writing desk.

"Wouldn't be thinking of wearing this to the reception tonight, would you, sir?"

Argo tried for a jocular approach. "Not tonight. With this uniform, it's a saber or nothing."

The two cops did not smile. "Or on any other night, sir?"

"I don't understand."

"Going out in public with a revolver, sir, it just won't do."

Argo did not like the sound of this. Did these Norse coppers think everyone from across the ocean was a gun-toting hick. "I don't understand."

"We have a number of regulations governing the carrying of firearms by foreign belligerents, sir."

"Belligerents? I'm a commissioned officers in the Royal Albany Rangers."

Tennyson shifted awkwardly on her feet. "But the Kingdom of Albany is in a state of war with the Empire of Hassan IX. That qualifies you as a foreign belligerent."

Argo smiled, but his face was hard. "The Rangers have a saying, Commander. 'You take my gun when you pry it from my cold dead fingers.'"

"We don't want to take your gun, sir."

"Just don't take it to the party?"

Tennyson sighed. "Or anywhere else for that matter. I'm afraid it's the law."

"You just came here to report a murder in our party, and now you're telling me I can't legally carry a weapon outside the hotel?"

"I afraid that's how it is."

The policeman removed his hand from Argo's gun. "Don't worry, sir. You'll be very well protected."

"I have your word on that?"

"Oh yes, sir. You have our word on that."

Tennyson was stiff and formal. "You'll relay this information to the others."

"You can count on it." He moved to the door and opened it, indicating he wanted Tennyson and her brace of heavies to put on their bowlers and leave. "Now if you'll excuse me, I'm expected to be at the Palace of Westminster and I need a few moments to get myself together."

Tennyson seemed happy to leave, and she ushered the two Special Branch men out in front of her. "I regret having to tell you all this."

"You don't make the rules, Commander."

"The automobiles should be here for you in a quarter of an hour."

"Thank you."


## CORDELIA

Cordelia had paused for a moment to take in the Vikings. The guests made their entrances down the wide stone steps, under the Gothic arch and the hugely ancient, hammer-beam roof of the Great Hall of the Palace of Westminster, and these steps were flanked by elite Viking infantry of the Asgard Division. Even Cordelia had to admit a degree of awe at the way these men stood motionless, huge and heraldic, in their ceremonial winged helmets, gleaming gold chain mail surcoats, and with their traditional war hammers at parade rest. The Viking regiments had a reputation for berserker ferocity that quite rivaled the Highland Scotts, and went back for centuries, all the way to the Old Alliance that predated the formation of the modern Norse Union. They were like something from another time, even another world, but the old, long-tended leather, the burnished metal, and the royal blue fabric of their loose tunics under the protective layers of their archaic armor were still intimidating and not in the least absurd. Cordelia hardly, however, had time to linger. The Master of Ceremonies, in his traditional powdered wig and gold-trimmed scarlet coat, had announced her. "Major, the Lady Cordelia Blakeney of Albany." And she had started down the grand staircase. Heads had turned and conversation had momentarily faltered among the knots of guests below her. Everything was exactly as Cordelia could ever have wanted it, and she felt justified in congratulating herself on her own cunning.

The fashions of the city were calculated, blatant, opulent beyond her wildest visualization, and at times leaning to the decadent. London couture was without any kind of standardization and certainly followed no single dictate. All the myriad of styles had in common was a provocative flamboyance, and a tendency to expose and even to flaunt. Colors ranged from dark and perverse to flagrant explosions. Soft fabrics clung to torsos, strategic slits allowed silk legs to flash, and extreme décolletage revealed flatteringly supported breasts. Waists were cinched by laced corselets, or stomachs were exposed with rings or jewels in navels. Hair might be cropped short or vast and elaborate. Had Cordelia made her debut at the party in the most stunning outfit that a combination of Albany, New York, and her own ingenuity had to offer, she would have still betrayed herself to the whole Palace of Westminster as so gauche to be almost a bumpkin, an out-of-touch rustic from the uncouth side of the ocean.

Cordelia had, however, thought her way out of the dilemma. If the Norse of London wanted extreme, she would give it to them. She had trumped style's ace with her Ranger uniform, but not just any Ranger uniform. She had bullied, cajoled, and almost seduced an old, bald Seventh Avenue military tailor in New York into making her the full dress black, gold, and green major's uniform. The only twist was that it was the uniform for a man. The ceremonial wear for women in the Rangers, of which there were precious few, was frumpy black evening dress with a small green approximation of a mess jacket. Approximation would never be good enough for Cordelia. For a while she had considered combining the short, frogged man's jacket and swagger cloak with a long skirt, but she had rejected the idea. The men's skintight cavalry breeches and the tall tasseled boots with the stacked riding heel were just too, too perfect. Cordelia might be going to the party in a man's outfit but she definitely was not going to be mistaken for a man. Onlookers might think she was a dangerous lesbian, or some red-haired valkyrie hot from the new world, but no one would take her for a long-haired boy. Regulations almost certainly prohibited what she was doing, but who was going to enforce regulations? She reported to no superior officers. The rest of The Four knew nothing about it until she came down to get into the official car, and by then it was far too late. She wore the Order of the Golden Bear on the orange ribbon, and the fates help anybody who would deny her anything. As the reception progressed she saw a number of other women wearing men's formal evening suits, but they could in no way challenge the perverse impact of her Ranger outfit.

Of course, to stage such a show and then carry it off required considerable courage, and although Cordelia hardly considered herself either shy or retiring, she was prepared to accept any help that might present itself. She had auditioned her very first martini by experimentally ordering one from room service, and sipping it as she organized her makeup and laid out her costume for the reception. As Windermere had said, it really did consist of nothing but gin, a hint of an aperitif, and extreme cold. She liked the first one a great deal, but she suspected that they might make her very drunk, very quickly, and she had mindfully refrained from ordering a second. The reception itself, on the other hand, was something else again. She was causing herself to be noticed and a little alcohol would only make the attention more exciting. As she moved across the Great Hall, skirting the couples sedately dancing to the small orchestra, she spotted a waiter with a tray of the signature conical glasses, and quickly moved in his direction to whisk one from him. She knew the speeches would start soon, and a martini, and maybe one more to follow, would be a measure of insulation against the exterior boredom of international diplomacy.

The potential speech-makers were all round her. A small crowd was gathered, paying their respects to General Giap from the South East Asian Confederacy, while Ambassador Mbandeni from King Cetshwayo's Zulu Hegemony, flanked by his shaman Credo Mutwa and three spectacular wives, held court in another part of the room. Ambassador Mbandeni was shadowed by a personal bodyguard from one of the crack Impis that, for almost a century, had held back all Mosul inroads into the southern realms of the African continent, be they Teuton prospecting teams or Mamaluke expeditions seeking slaves and ivory. Turbaned Hindi Rajahs from the Indian subcontinent rubbed shoulders with bearded Russe in white fur-trimmed evening coats, who drank something called vodka and laughed loudly. Caribbeans in ultraconventional white tie and tails still retained their spectacular hair. It seemed as though half the world had turned out to welcome Jack Kennedy to England; certainly the half of the world that felt itself threatened by the Mosul. Jack Kennedy himself was conducting a slow circuit of the area, meeting and greeting and accepting all of the respect accorded to the guest of honor.

Cordelia noticed that Jesamine was loitering somewhere on the outer edge of the circulating Kennedy party, and in Cordelia's opinion, her comrade was being too damned obvious. Jesamine clearly had a terminal crush on Jack Kennedy, and Cordelia hoped she was not riding for a fall. Her night with Kennedy might have been nothing more than that; just a night. Jack Kennedy was a notorious love-'em-and-leave-'em womanizer, and if that was the case, Jesamine would take it too hard when she found out the truth. She was dressed in the filmy blue gown that, against Cordelia's good advice, she bought in New York along with a number of others. The same one that she had put on when she went to Kennedy's cabin that recent night on the *Ragnar*. Cordelia had warned her not to spend all of her money in the Manhattan store, but Jesamine simply could not see that what might work in New York would never do for London. To be fair, the dress was short and had almost no back, and it showed off her honey skin and extraordinarily long legs to their best advantage. Cordelia did not think she was being a bitch by being of the opinion that Jesamine really did not need clothes.

By force of habit, she looked round for the others of The Four. She could not spot Raphael anywhere, but she could see Argo in the crowd. In Albany, since his enforced break with Jesamine, Argo could usually be found on his own, or perhaps in the company of some other alcoholic young officers. Cordelia had wondered if Argo was turning into something of a drunk; a quiet drunk, a reserved and well-disciplined drunk, but a drunk all the same. Here in London, though, something had changed. He looked strapping in his dress uniform, and he was already deep in conversation with a young blonde woman who could only be described as stunning. He had the body language of one who was stunned, but doing his none-too-skilled best to conceal it, while the woman, for her part, challenged him to do anything else. Her dress was black chiffon, short in front but falling to a kind of flowing train in the back. Her multistrapped platform shoes were an aggressive yellow, and had maybe the highest heels that Cordelia had ever encountered. She wondered how the woman could walk in them. The fabric of her dress was sheer, only marginally on the decent side of transparent, and Cordelia could imagine what that was doing to Argo, who, by London standards, was a naïve provincial. Cordelia finished her martini and looked for another. "I just hope the poor boy isn't in over his head."

## RAPHAEL

The Caribbean's hair was like nothing Raphael had ever seen before. It was packed into long snakelike braids, each one thicker than Raphael's thumb, and held together by the use of some adhesive preparation about which he could not even hazard a guess. The man's neck was tattooed, as were as much of his wrists that showed beneath the immaculate double cuffs of his tuxedo. Aside from the lavish mass of tropical island hair, he was so slick and spotlessly conventional in his attire that he was almost dazzling. Raphael couldn't help but stare at his cufflinks, each decorated with the head of lion, and each the size of a forty-shilling gold piece. The man noticed Raphael looking and held them up with a laugh. "No bad, hey?"

Raphael grinned. The gleeful delight in showing off wealth was refreshing after all the snobbery and pretension that Raphael felt all around him as the London elite honored Jack Kennedy. "Not bad at all."

The Caribbean gestured round the room. "You got that right. No bad for the son of a Dahomey galley girl and a Mayan sergeant major. Who'd have thought I'd end up here?"

Raphael nodded in agreement. "I never really imagined myself in a place like this."

"Americano, right?"

"Right."

"Army?"

"Albany Rangers."

"You're supposed to be hard bastards, right?"

Raphael opted for modesty. "The Rangers have a reputation."

"You in that battle they just had over in the Americas?"

"Newbury Vale?"

"That's the one?"

Raphael nodded. "I was there."

"Some shit, I hear."

"You could say that, especially for the poor bastards in our first advance."

The Caribbean looked at Raphael curiously. "Funny thing. You don't sound like no Americano."

Raphael laughed. "That's because I was in Hispania until less than a year ago."

"You kid me?"

"I swear."

"How did you get away from the Mosul."

"I almost didn't. They drafted me, put me in the infantry, and shipped me out to Savannah. If I hadn't escaped, I would have been in one of their human waves."

"Is it true the sorry fuckers in the front lines are so certain to be killed they don't even give them guns?"

"That's what the NCOs told us when they wanted us good and scared. I didn't wait around to find out firsthand."

The Caribbean slapped the table. "Man, I gotta buy you a drink."

Raphael quietly observed that the drinks at the reception were free, and the Caribbean beamed. "A figure of speech." He indicated his own drink, something dark brown with a lot of ice in a tall glass. "You ever have one of these?"

"What is it?"

"Rum and Kola-Pop. It's like the national drink where I come from. You ever taste one?"

Raphael shook his head. "I never did."

The Caribbean ordered two of the concoctions, and then regarded Raphael with an expression that hinted he wasn't all about rum, bizarre hair, and flashing cufflinks. "You must have made major pretty damned fast after you got away from the Mosul and went over to Albany."

Raphael regarded the Caribbean with a fresh watchfulness. It was not by accident that he was always the backstop and lookout when The Four went into action. Instinctively he looked for the others. He could see Argo, some distance away in the crowd, talking to a very attractive blonde in a revealing black dress and yellow shoes, but he couldn't spot either Jesamine or Cordelia. Raphael knew that he, too, ought to be checking out the London girls, but, for the moment he was content to sit and talk with the Caribbean. He was a refreshing change from all the Norse/Albany cold-weather assumptions and attitudes. His response to the overly direct observation was noncommittal. "Let's just say I had something they needed, and I also performed some services for them."

The waiter brought two tall glasses and the Caribbean urged Raphael to try it. "Rum and Kola-Pop, man. Nothing like it."

Raphael had no argument with the last statement. The Caribbean wanted his reaction. Raphael smiled and nodded. "A lot of sugar, but it has a kick."

The Caribbean tasted his own drink and then turned to survey the room. "You know something? Most everyone here is missing the crucial point."

Raphael sensed that the conversation was moving to another level, and maybe this happenstance, falling in with the Caribbean, was not as random as it had first appeared. Raphael made himself totally noncommittal. "They are?"

"Sure they are. Everyone you talk to avoids mentioning the fact that Hassan IX is getting old; very old."

"I haven't talked to very many people, so I wouldn't know."

"Take my word for it."

"I do know that, before the Battle of the Potomac, Hassan supposedly showed up to fill the Mosul troops with killer enthusiasm."

"You were there?"

"I was."

"Still a Mosul grunt?"

"That was the day I got away."

The Caribbean pushed back his hair. "No shit?"

"No shit."

"But, man, you actually saw Hassan IX?"

Raphael shook his head. "But it wasn't him. It was a double. A young man in armor. It couldn't have been him."

"That's what I mean. Sooner or later, the doubles and all the other deceptions won't work no more. Hassan is going to die, and everyone will know it."

"Will that really make all that much difference?"

"It's going to make one hell of a difference, my friend. Hassan has more than a hundred sons, right?"

Raphael nodded. "Some put it as high as three hundred."

"So they're all going to fight each other for the succession, and then some of them will reach some kind of accommodation, and the Empire will hold for a while, but history tends to prove that, in these kind of situations, there's one of the stronger heirs who's forced out, and he escapes and takes to the mountains or some stronghold in the stinking desert where he gets stronger and meaner. Bit by bit, he gathers an army around himself until he's got enough power and enough fighters and then he come down from his mountain or out of the desert and makes his play."

"And then what happens?"

"What do you think? You got civil war in the Mosul Empire, just like with the old Romans, and there goes the game."

"The Empire collapses."

"That's usually the way of it with autocracies that get too big under one leader." The Caribbean glanced round the room, and grinned ruefully. "But what are all these folks going to do without the Mosul to fight against? I mean, look at them: Kennedy, Giap, Chomsky, that humorless fucker Mbandeni. They all made their name fighting Hassan. What are they going to do without him? What but the threat of the Mosul can hold all this together? And what happens when the occupied territories ain't occupied no more? Times get complicated after the fall of empires."

Raphael frowned. "There's one thing you haven't factored in."

"What's that?"

"The Zhaithan. It's religion that holds the Mosul together. It's the fucking Zhaithan."

The Caribbean grinned enthusiastically. "You said it, brother. Religion, that's the other factor. The fucking Zhaithan." He looked hard at Raphael. "You're one of those Albany paranormal kids. Right?"

Raphael was taken by surprise. The Caribbean laughed. "Shit, man, don't be coy. Your picture's been in the paper and everything."

"I'm afraid you have the advantage of me."

"Most people call me Country Man. I'm what's known as a cultural attaché."

Raphael knew that was usually a euphemism for spy. He extended a hand. "Raphael Vega. I'm glad to meet you."

Country Man grasped it in an odd but convincingly warm handshake. "And I'm glad to know you, too, Raphael Vega. And you know something?"

"What's that?"

"You're right." Country Man leaned back and took a drink. "It is religion, man. And I know what I'm talking about. Half my family are Maya, and they know about the real Old Gods. If anyone is going to hold the Mosul Empire together, it's Quadaron-Ahrach, Her Grand Eminence, Jeakqual-Ahrach, and definitely the fucking Zhaithan. They could play the last card: eliminate the emperor, implement the full theocracy, and no problem of succession. Direct rule by the Twin Gods. Simple as that. And from what we hear, they're making their moves to do that right now, they even have the Twin Gods, or something that looks like the Twin Gods."

Raphael blinked. "What are you saying?"

"It's just a rumor, see? You gotta understand that. But out in the islands we ain't so sun-happy isolated that we don't know what's going on. We hear things, okay? The big Zulu triremes haul into port and we get the story. The Asian clippers stop over and we hear the story, and even them Mosul steam buckets come into dock and we hear what those crew gotta say when the Zhaithan ain't listening."

Now Raphael was paying rapt attention to this talk of replica Twin Gods. "And what do they say? What is the story?"

"They say there's something being built in the Frankish territories. You never heard about that up in Albany?"

Raphael's head was starting to whirl slightly. "We paranormal kids are often the last to hear."

Country Man nodded, plainly pleased with the reaction he was getting from Raphael. "Story going round is that they're building something in this Frankish valley. Lotta stone work and slave laborers and stuff. Big magick. Real big magick. The best guess is that it's going to be some kind of weapon, a power source, and you gotta know those Ahrachs are behind it."

Raphael did his best to digest this unexpected and unverified piece of news. "Why are you telling me this?"

Before Country Man could answer, he was distracted by a young woman with her hair arranged into a thick black pompadour, and semi-dressed in a short skirt, long boots, and a loose military-style evening coat over a gold brassiere. As she walked past, Country Man sighed. "Man, will you look at her." The girl had derailed the whole conversation, and Raphael could have cursed. Country Man finished his drink and rose to his feet. "We gotta to talk some more, man, but this ain't the place. Are you all going to Madame de Wynter's party later?"

"I don't know. I was invited but I hadn't made up my mind."

"You gotta, man. No one should live their life without having gone to a de Wynter party."

Raphael was bemused. "People keep telling me that."

"You be there, man, and maybe we talk some more."

## JESAMINE

Jesamine didn't want to be at this reception at the Palace of Westminster. She didn't want to be wearing the same blue dress that she had worn to her tryst with Jack on the *Ragnar*. She wished she could just leave quietly, without telling anyone she was going. Cordelia and the others—especially Cordelia—could cope with the social whirl. They hardly needed her in a situation like this. As it was, she seemed to be drifting round in the wake of Jack Kennedy like some tremulous love-starved stalker. She looked at Kennedy and the mob of dignitaries around him. Now they were in this city of the Norse, how could he possibly have a moment of time for someone like her? Okay, so there had been the night on the ship, under the moon, in the middle of the Northern Ocean. She was a woman of the world. She understood it could not go anywhere. He was the Prime Minister, damn it. She had fucked him, and it would stay with her, probably for all of her days, but, practically, that was that. Even if he did see her again, it would only be a matter of time before they were forced to go their separate ways.

She was also aware that beyond the glittering gowns and spectacular uniforms, beyond the ancient walls of the Palace of Westminster, was the whole city of London. On the drive to the reception, the automobile had passed through an area of bars and restaurants, wide pavements, and sooty urban trees. She had seen the electric façade of one of the new photoplay theatres that actually featured recorded sound that was synchronized with the flickering images. The moving picture being shown was apparently an historical epic titled *Hengist*. She wanted to see a moving picture, and walk on those streets that were softened by the mist that rose from the river Thames. She had seen warm public houses with yellow light shining from the windows, and sounds of music from within. She wanted to drink in those pubs instead of at this overbearing reception. From both the crowd at the reception, and the faces she had seen in the streets, she could tell that London was a cosmopolitan city that provided a home, in some cases a refuge, for people from all over the world. Out there were Africans and Caribbeans, Chinese and the strange, brown-skinned Maya and Aztecs from the Southern Americas. She wanted to get away from all the pomp and ceremony and mingle with the ordinary and the exotic. She suddenly realized that was what was troubling. She was a prisoner of a timetable, and every moment of her time, for as far ahead as she could possibly see, was planned out and preordained. Most of all, deep inside, she wanted to be free. For once in her life, Jesamine wanted to drift, to be free of duty and responsibility, and just go where her fancy might take her. And yet, how could she be free when she now found herself carrying this ridiculous torch for Jack Kennedy.

"From the way you are staring after Jack, I have to assume you must be Jesamine."

The voice, that was soft but commanding, and had the slightest trace of a Frankish accent, took Jesamine completely by surprise. At the same time, Jesamine felt a tingle, as though brushed by a powerful psychic presence. She turned quickly and found herself facing a tiny woman, timeless and slight, verging on an ancient transparency, but who made up for her lack of physical substance with an overstated flamboyance. Her hair was dyed an implausible shade of purple that, even partially concealed by her wide plumed hat, would have looked absurd on most other women, but, on her, it only added to her commanding intensity. A gold-embroidered black velvet cape was thrown over her shoulders with the attitude of a swashbuckler. Her dress was constructed of multiple falls of weblike black lace that seemed to best serve as a background for her considerable complement of jewelry. The emerald collar at her throat and the falls of chains and pendants, the pendant earrings, plus the mass of bracelets, rings, pins, and clips all contributed to an aura of material vehemence and a sense that she was unstoppable. The left hand was covered in a soft red leather glove, with rings on the outside, and she carried a silver falcon-topped cane, but seemingly had no need of its support.

"I . . ."

"You are Major Jesamine?"

Jesamine's mind flashed back to the conversation with Colonel Windermere on the train. Something he said resonated. *"Anastasia de Wynter is always hard to understand."* Jesamine quickly gathered her wits. "You must be . . ."

"I am Madame Anastasia de Wynter, my dear. Don't look so alarmed. If I didn't make it my business to know everything, I would never have survived this long."

Behind Madame de Wynter stood a huge man who could only have been her bodyguard. His face was flat with slanted eyes and broad cheekbones, his head was perfectly shaved, and he was built like an Ottoman wrestler with shoulders that seemed too big for his black footman's coat. Jesamine was surprised and a little awed. De Wynter gestured with a smile. "This is Garth. He looks after me."

This Garth would have looked more at home in the ranks of the Mosul than in a diplomatic hotel in central London, but, right there and then, he was the least of Jesamine's worries.

"You said 'Jack'?"

"That's right, darling. Jack."

"I don't know what you're talking about."

Madame de Wynter brushed aside Jesamine's dissembling. "Of course you do. Don't be silly. I was right where you are twenty-five years ago. Jack is old and he's been doing this for all of his life. You're not the first; you're probably not even the hundredth."

"You're taking about Jack Kennedy? The Prime Minister of Albany."

"Don't be deliberately dense, girl. You know I'm talking about Jack Kennedy."

Jesamine was starting to feel extremely uncomfortable. "But how can you know so much?"

"If for no other reason than I can read the patterns."

"You've been watching me?"

"Enough to know that right now you are completely infatuated with Jack Kennedy and his power. Just as I was all those years ago. Here you are now, all on your own and casting adoring glances in his direction when you think no one is looking. Don't get me wrong, I don't condemn you for feeling the way you do. Jack Kennedy is glorious. He is a natural force."

Jesamine noticed that a number of people were looking curiously in their direction. "Does everyone know about Jack and me? Is it public gossip?"

De Wynter shook her head. "Of course not. That's just me. I seem to have that effect on people. Aside from the ever-present Dawson, and a few of his personal bodyguard, no one knows. Jack Kennedy is too much of a gentleman, and also too secretive, to have word of his affairs bandied around. I only really know because he told me."

"He told you?"

"In fact, he gave me a message; that's why I'm coming up to you now, unannounced and without formal introduction."

"A message? You talked to him?"

"Of course I talked to him. We are very old friends. In some respects, more than very old friends." De Wynter laughed. "Be assured he likes you, Major Jesamine."

Something inside of Jesamine leaped in exultation. "He does?" She knew immediately that she had given herself away and eased back, reasserting control. "He wants to see me?"

"When this is over, he has a meeting with General Giap. He isn't sure when it will end, but he said that I should take care of you until he's free."

"I thought you were throwing a party tonight?"

"I am. It was Jack's suggestion that you should come there with me until either he arrives there himself, or sends a car for you."

Jesamine looked uncertain. "Maybe I should just go back to the hotel and wait for him?"

De Wynter shook her head. "Rushing back to the Asquith and waiting for him is the last thing you should do. Jack's a selfish bastard. You could wait there all night while he's debating philosophy and drinking cognac with his old pal Giap. Once upon a time they used to play chess, but the general was too predictably brilliant."

"He said I should go with you?"

"That was his suggestion. That's if you want to see him."

Jesamine exhaled hard. "Of course I want to see him."

"Then stick with me, my dear. I assure you that you won't regret it."

## CORDELIA

"You look like the principal boy in a pantomime."

"What's a pantomime."

"It's a comic musical play that's performed around the Winter Solstice."

"And I look like a boy?"

"The principal boy is never a boy."

Having finally found him, Cordelia would have liked nothing better than to climb all over Colonel Gideon Windermere right there and then, press herself against him, and feel him indecently instead of bandying cultural quips from a culture she knew very little about. "I don't understand a word you're saying."

"In the pantomime, the women are played by men and the men are played by women."

"More English decadence?"

"Pantomimes have been going on for hundreds of years. The principal boy is a comely, sometimes even buxom young woman playing the leading man, often costumed in a uniform not unlike yours."

"Are you calling me buxom?"

"No, but you're definitely comely."

"Finally a compliment?"

"That outfit is really something."

"I'm entitled to wear it. I'm a Major in the Royal Albany Rangers, and I hold the order of the Golden Bear."

"It's a man's uniform."

Cordelia knew that she was a little drunk, but Windermere couldn't condemn her for that. He had introduced her to the concept of the martini in the first place. "Don't be so damned conventional. What you have on is hardly regulation issue."

Windermere's dress uniform was clearly his own invention. The exquisite Rick Blaine tuxedo with small military tabs on the collar, and an assortment of medals above the breast pocket, was about as civilian as one could go without being out of the Army altogether. She had spent over an hour waiting for him to arrive at the reception, tensely consuming martinis, and now he was there, he seemed amused to hold her jokingly at arm's length when she unashamedly wanted to throw herself at him. Of course, Cordelia was not about to make a drunken spectacle of herself in the Palace of Westminster, in front of everyone who was anyone in the Norse Union. She was too much of an aristocrat for that, but that did not stop her becoming increasingly frustrated at both his attitude and the situation in which they found themselves, surrounded by people, most of whom Windermere seemed to know and who kept distracting his attention away from her. Cordelia decided she needed to get him focused on something that involved her, but was connected with his own mysterious agenda. "Is Madame de Wynter here?"

Windermere nodded. "I saw her a while ago. She was talking to Major Jesamine."

"Jesamine?"

"I think it was her. She was wearing a blue, somewhat see-through dress."

"That's her."

Windermere turned and scanned the crowd. "I think that's them over there. They seem to be leaving together."

Cordelia looked where Windermere was pointing. He was right. Jesamine was walking beside a small woman with purple hair in a black velvet cape and wide plumed hat, and they appeared to be making an exit. "Maybe we should go after them?"

Windermere shook his head. "I don't recommend running after Madame de Wynter."

"No?"

"No. And why bother? We'll see her at the party, and, in any case, your friend Jesamine seems to have everything under control."

Cordelia snorted. "Yes, Jesamine seems to have everything under control."

"If Anastasia is leaving, we might also move along in a while."

Cordelia decided that it was maybe the time to be totally brazen. She coyly lowered her eyes and deliberately made her voice soft and low. "I was hoping that you and I could slip away someplace on our own."

"Madame de Wynter's party is close to a duty. We're expected."

"I know, but . . ."

"I thought you liked parties. You seemed like the party girl."

"I am, only . . ."

Windermere leaned close and spoke quietly. His expression was both gentle and knowing. "My dear Lady Blakeney, there will be plenty of time for all the slipping away you could desire."

Cordelia pretended to look sheepish. "I'm just afraid that, after the party, I'll be too drunk. It's all your fault. You got me onto martinis. I was a martini-virgin before I met you."

Windermere straightened up and laughed. He felt in the pocket of his white tuxedo jacket, and then opened his hand with a conjurer's flourish. A capsule of yellow powder lay on the palm of his hand. "Try this."

"What is it?"

"A remedy for the cold gin. It's a benodex capsule. Everyone who strains under the cruel yoke of high society takes them to keep going."


## JESAMINE

"I don't know what I'd do without Garth. He is my constant protection."

"You need that much protection?"

Madame de Wynter moved forward. "These are desperate days, my dear."

The huge, shaved-headed Garth was now behind the wheel of Madame de Wynter's vast yellow automobile, and they were moving with rapid authority through the streets of nighttime London. Yellow gaslight bathed everything in a soft and deceptively comforting glow, and the streets were still crowded, despite the late hour, with what seemed to Jesamine like crowds of very good-looking people. The big automobile was of the kind in which the passengers sat enclosed in the back, separated from the driver by a safety glass screen, while his section of the vehicle remained open to the elements. It seemed less than egalitarian, but Jesamine had already surmised how that was probably the way of all things with Anastasia de Wynter. Jesamine, however, could not worry too much about de Wynter and how she treated her servants. She was finally feeling as though she was really in London.

Maybe it was being away from the other three, but she at last had some sense of being her own woman. Of course, she might just be de Wynter's woman. The small Frankish aristocrat needed to command everything and everyone, as she immediately proved when she asked Jesamine, "Do you mind if we talk frankly."

Jesamine had nodded. "It's usually the best way."

"You must know there's considerable interest here in you and your companions."

Again Jesamine nodded. "I wouldn't have expected otherwise."

"Without knowing all the details, we have a broad idea of your capabilities."

"The secret was out after we saved the King from Jeakqual-Ahrach's entities."

De Wynter looked sharply at Jesamine. "You hold Jeakqual-Ahrach responsible, not her brother?"

Jesamine bit her lip. "I think I may have said too much."

De Wynter lips compressed to a thin impatient line. "I thought we were talking frankly?"

"We've only just met."

"And you fear that I am an enemy? That I'm a threat to either you or your Prime Minister?"

"That wasn't what I meant."

"No?"

"No."

Madame de Wynter looked sideways at Jesamine. "I'd imagine the furtherance of your education was a large part of why Jack brought the four of you here?"

Jesamine shifted in her seat. Suddenly she felt like she was being interrogated. "That's what we were told."

"Have you noticed how things have changed?"

Jesamine frowned. De Wynter seemed to have abruptly switched direction. "Changed?"

"Once upon a time, it was the brother we feared. Quadaron-Ahrach was the High Zhaithan, and all trembled at his name. Now it's the name of the sister that casts the cold shadow, and makes the candles flicker."

Jesamine realized that de Wynter was right. "Quadaron-Ahrach would seem to have taken a back seat."

De Wynter nodded. "Jeakqual-Ahrach is now the force. She is the shark that swims forward. While her brother grows corrupt and ancient along with his emperor, and they ponder succession and how to prolong themselves, Jeakqual-Ahrach is the initiator. She is the seeker and the researcher. She has the power because she finds it and she takes it."

The car had turned onto a wide boulevard running along the perimeter of a park. The outlines of trees, fountain, and statues, and of shadowy figures moving among them, were just visible in the darkness. Jesamine thought for a moment. "Could it simply be she's so much younger than her brother?"

"You've seen the woman. How old did she look to you?"

Jesamine shrugged. "Maybe forty, a powerful middle-age. Except, when she removed her gloves, her hands seemed older."

De Wynter smiled. "It's always the hands that give you away."

"Cordelia and I did wonder if the knives of skilled surgeons had played a part."

"Even when you were about to be tortured, you wondered how she looked so young?"

"The mind protects itself any way it can."

De Wynter stared hard at Jesamine. "Our most conservative estimate makes Jeakqual-Ahrach more than ninety years old."

"If that's true, how does she do it?"

"Morgana's Web has spies clear across the Empire, but even they haven't penetrated that dark vault. Some claim that she became a vampire."

"But vampires don't exist."

"Other suggested ministrations of apothecaries, necromancers, like you said, knives of skilled surgeons, and other specialists at whose function you wouldn't even want to guess."

Jesamine glanced out of the window of the automobile. She did not relish all this talk of their sworn enemy. "Right now we're at war and we're discussing how Jeakqual-Ahrach stays looking so young."

"You think we should maybe be talking about the White Twins?"

Jesamine started, stunned, unable to conceal her surprise. "You know about them?"

De Wynter nodded. "Reports have been coming in for about six months."

Jesamine was speechless. She had hardly expected anyone in the Norse Union to have heard about the White Twins except The Four, Slide, Jack Kennedy, and maybe a few others. Now she learned, if Madame de Wynter was to be believed, word of them was all over. Before Jesamine could frame a question, however, from all of those that crowded in her, Garth made a sharp left turn and swung into a pair of imposing gates that opened in a high, spiked wall. The wheels of the yellow automobile crunched on the gravel of a wide driveway that ran through trees and flowerbeds that seemed to be a private extension of the park they had just passed, and led up to an imposing white house with multiple bay windows, pillared portico, and a somewhat incongruous turret on the farthest corner. Seeing that Jesamine was impressed, de Wynter smiled. "Welcome to Deerpark, Major."

Jesamine shook her head. "You live here? It's like a palace."

"It belonged to my late first husband, the Archduke-in-Exile. It was really too bad about Rudolph."

Before Madame de Wynter could explain what had happened to the Archduke-in-Exile Rudolph, Garth brought the car to a halt in front of the portico. He pulled on the handbrake and climbed down to open the door for his mistress. Madame de Wynter exited the car, looking around, noting that a number of other cars were parked where the driveway widened beside the house.

"I see my guests have already started to arrive."

If Madame de Wynter hadn't gestured in the direction of the parked cars, Jesamine might never have looked, but, when she did look, what she saw stopped her dead in her tracks and filled her with a horrible chill. As she pointed in alarm, her voice was little more than a choked gasp. "Zhaithan! There, by that car! Zhaithan in full uniform!" She swung round to face de Wynter. "What are the Zhaithan doing here? What are you doing to me?"

## ARGO

"What the fuck?"

"What?"

"Zhaithan. Fucking Zhaithan, in full uniform, standing around bold as brass. One of them is even smoking a fucking cigarette."

Argo leaned forward and rapped on the partition in the official car that separated the passengers from the driver. "Go. Quickly. Get us out of here!"

Raphael, meanwhile, looked at Bowden Spinrad, their ES escort, in alarm. "What the fuck is this?"

Spinrad attempted to calm the two of them. "It's nothing to be alarmed about."

Argo looked back at him in total disbelief. "What do you mean it's nothing to be alarmed about."

"They're just a chauffeur and bodyguard."

"What are a Zhaithan chauffeur and a Zhaithan fucking bodyguard doing in the middle of London?"

"They belong to the Mosul chargé d'affaires."

"The Norse and the Mosul have diplomatic relations?"

"We're not officially at war."

"And they come to de Wynter's parties?"

"Khurshid Nawaz, the chargé d'affaires of the Mosul Empire, is quite the party boy. He's a royal cousin; they had to send him someplace he couldn't do too much harm. I mean, the relationship between the NU and the Empire is so bad, there's nothing he could do to damage it."

Argo and Raphael stared at Spinrad, not wholly believing him. "Are you sure about this? We've been targets of the Zhaithan for too long to screw around with this."

Spinrad again did his best to allay their fears. "You really have no need to worry. Khurshid Nawaz isn't the kind to try anything."

Raphael glanced at Argo. "What do you think?"

Argo shrugged. "If Spinrad here says it's okay, I guess we can take him at his word."

Bowden Spinrad was young, not much older than Argo and Raphael, and a junior operative in Windermere's ES Section, although, as far as Argo could see, something of a party boy himself, unless the long lank hair, the long leather evening coat, and the androgynous eyeliner were just some kind of cover to enable him to move through London's high society without anyone taking him very seriously. He had arranged for a government car to take Argo and Raphael from the Palace of Westminster to Deerpark, the residence of Madame Anastasia de Wynter, and then come along with them for the ride. Since he seemed to know everyone, and also kept up a stream of genuinely funny banter, Argo and Raphael were pleased to have him along until the two Zhaithan appeared in the darkness beside the parked cars in front of Deerpark.

The driver was now forcing the issue by climbing down from the car to open the passenger door. Raphael treated Spinrad to a hard stare. "You're sure about this?"

"Certain."

As they cautiously exited the car, Spinrad turned to the driver. "Do you have a sidearm, Wilson?"

The driver nodded. "Of course, sir."

Spinrad gestured to the two Zhaithan, who were maybe twenty yards away, in their black cloaks, red and black tunics, spiked and turban-swathed helmets. "You see those two?"

"Indeed I do, sir."

As Argo had observed, one of them was smoking a cigarette cupped in the palm of his hand. "If either one of them makes a hostile or threatening move, shoot them."

Again Wilson nodded. "Whatever you say, sir."

Spinrad turned back to Argo and Raphael. "Shall we go inside?"

## RAPHAEL

*"Cold cruel, cold cruel, cold cruel,*
*You're a cold cruel bitch!*
*Cold cruel, cold cruel, cold cruel,*
*You're a cold cruel bitch!"*

Raphael could not believe the volume of what was only a five-piece combo. The small stage was flanked by a pair of huge conical steel horns, maybe five feet across at the open end, that came close to dwarfing the musicians with their stringed instruments—the string bass, the guitar, the hipzither. Raphael had never seen anything like the objects they were playing. Even the Mosul occupation had not been able to eradicate the guitar from Hispania, and he was familiar with the common, six-string model with the hollow wooden sound box, but these devices were a whole new development. They were carved from solid wood and came with odd electrical contacts and wires that ran back to boxes with glowing radio valves that, in turn, altered and amplified the sound and then hurled it out at the enthusiastic, dancing crowd like waves of physical force. The noise the young men created was harsh, angry, and metallic. At one and the same time, it was aggressive and all pervasive, dense with an excitement that was close to sexual. Raphael not only heard it, but was able to feel it in his skull, bones, and chest cavity. In addition to the three string players, two oriental boys hammered with mallets on huge wooden drums. Overhead, multiple beams from electric spotlights were directed at an imposing pedant chandelier, creating refracted rainbows that rotated like radiant hallucinations over the people below. At the Palace of Westminster the dancing had been formal and sedate, but at Madame de Wynter's party, the total reverse was true. The crowd in front of the stage and under the lights was wild, sensually unfettered, and wholly improvisational. Some were even flailing and violent. A number of young men and also some of the young women had stripped to the waist, sweating and shaking, in contortionist abandon. One pair of youths was costumed in formfitting bandages, with medical prostheses attached to perfectly healthy limbs. A gilded boy in shorts was being passed hand to hand. A woman in hellfire scarlet flicked her partner with a knout as they quivered together, while someone of indeterminate gender, wearing an elaborate gold mask, was prancing all on his/her own, a palsied leaping and twitching that was more akin to an affliction of the nervous system than a dance. Dancers around him/her had cleared a space, wary of the unpredictable arms and legs. Raphael pointed him out to Spinrad.

"Is this how London gained its reputation for decadence?"

Spinrad looked down and laughed. "As a matter of fact, that is none other than Khurshid Nawaz, the chargé d'affaires of the Mosul Empire. You see now why I said he was no cause for concern?"

Deerpark was large enough to have its own high-ceilinged ballroom. The place was also incredibly soundproof. He, Argo, and Spinrad had hardly heard the noise until they were actually entering. It was not until much later that he learned Madame de Wynter needed soundproofing for some of her rituals, and that Deerpark had been built with walls that, at some points, were more than three feet thick. The Archduke Rudolph, in addition to being obscenely rich, even for an exile, also had a morbid fear of being blown up by his supposed enemies, and had, before his untimely end, that ironically had nothing to do with explosive or infernal devices of any kind, endeavored to make his London home as bombproof as was scientifically possible. They had entered the ballroom by way of a mezzanine or minstrel's gallery at the opposite end from the musicians, from which they were able to look down on the squirming mass of eerily lit dancers. From there, they could descend to the main floor down a theatrically curving flight of stairs. The whole interior design of this house, that all but qualified as a palace, seemed to be designed for dramatic effect, and the fact was certainly not lost on the tall and skinny woman, in the short white dress, white lipstick, with dead straight platinum hair, who had a daisy painted in pink and magenta on her left cheek, and was climbing the stairs toward them. Raphael stood with Argo and Spinrad at the top of the stairs. The woman in white seemed in control, but nevertheless intoxicated to the point where she had to stop and focus on the three men. Assuming that they were about to descend to join the dance, she said, "You don't want to go down there, unless you really get off on your arse being groped at random by total strangers."

A new song started, slower than the previous thrash, and, instead of bellowing in English, the guitarist began to sing in a language that Raphael was at a loss to explain, but would subsequently be informed was a mixture of Carib, Zulu, and Icelandic. The seafaring ways of the Norse, and especially the English, had created some exotic cultural mixes in their cities. The woman in white with the daisy on her cheek continued to peer drunkenly at the three of them, especially Raphael and Argo. She advanced up three more steps and then stared at them as though inspecting specimens. A knowing smile spread across her face. "You're them, aren't you?"

Spinrad, talking it upon himself to act as some kind of proxy host, attempted to handle the situation. "Aren't we what?"

The girl looked at Spinrad and shook her head. "No, not you, those two." She indicated Raphael to Argo. "You're them, aren't you?"

Argo grinned. "Are we?"

"Sure you are. I saw your picture in the evening edition, getting off that battleship."

Raphael nodded and fell into the torturous sentence construction. "Then them we must be, mustn't we?"

The daisy-painted girl seemed quite excited. She inarticulately waved in the direction of the dancers below. "I have to . . ."

"I thought you didn't like it down there."

"I have to tell my friends you're here."

As the girl descended, familiar hair was coming up the staircase. Country Man's tuxedo was gone, and he was now in a flowing dashiki. He exchanged greetings with Raphael but made as if to walk on past. Raphael shouted above the band. "We must talk some more."

Country Man looked uncomfortable. "I dunno, Major Ranger. I maybe talked too much, know what I mean?"


JESAMINE

Jesamine and Madame de Wynter, followed by Garth, emerged onto a broad terrace of white flagstones that ran the entire length of the rear of the house, and was partially illuminated by flames from the stone braziers that stood at regular intervals along the balustrade. "This is where Rudolph shot the dreadful Ciccone woman and then himself."

"That must have been a terrible shock."

De Wynter dismissed the incident with a wave of her cane. "I suppose it was at the time, but it was almost certainly the best thing that could have happened to all concerned. Rudolph was not what you would call a nice man."

Beyond the terrace, an expanse of immaculate lawn stretched back
to the dark trees in which colored lanterns had been hung. Jesamine
could see dark figures moving on the lawn and in among the trees, mostly
in couples or in threes. The band playing in the ballroom was audible, but
not intrusive. She caught a snatch of the lyrics. As a musician herself, she
had yet to make up her mind about this loud and desperate Norse music.

*"They will know her by the wreckage that she leaves*
*Know her name when they feel the need to grieve."*

When they had first entered Deerpark, Jesamine had assumed the
music and dancing was the full extent of the party, but de Wynter had
walked determinedly on. "Let the young people go crazy in the ballroom.
There are some people I'd like you to meet before Jack Kennedy sends his
summons and you go flying off as fast as you can."

White wrought-iron tables and chairs were set on the terrace,
tended by waiters working from a bar and buffet at the opposite end. One
of the first tables they approached was occupied by burly men in wide-
brimmed hats, long dark overcoats, extravagantly padded shoulders, and
a conversational style that was one moment conspiratorial and the next
boisterously loud. One individual had leaned back, pointing in guffawing
triumph to a companion. "Almost fucking had you there, didn't I, Cyril?"
The move caused his pinstriped coat to fall open, and reveal that he carried an ultra-modern, nickel-plated revolver in an underarm shoulder
holster. De Wynter saw that Jesamine had noticed and laughed. "Just local wide boys."

"Wide boys."

"I maintain my ties with underworld, my dear. It's enhances my
credibility as a Woman of the People. They can also be incredibly useful
whenever the system fails, or is too limiting."

The wide boys half rose and raised their hats to Madame de Wynter. For a moment Jesamine had thought that these were the people that
de Wynter wanted her to meet, but mercifully these criminal gangsters
were not. Instead, the two of them continued towards a table that seemed
to be filled with other refugees from the reception at the Palace of

Westminster, including the same blonde women in the black chiffon and yellow high heels she had seen talking to Argo. Madame de Wynter nodded in her direction. "That's Harriet Lime. I'm going to park you with her for a little while, while I do some obligatory circulating."

"What if Jack sends a car for me?"

"Don't worry so much, my dear. If he does, you will be told immediately. Everything is arranged. In the meantime, I want to you to get acquainted with Harriet. She is not the vacuous beauty she pretends to be in public."

They reached the table and introduced Jesamine to those seated there. Harriet Lime inclined her head. Gold ringlets dropped, partially concealing her face. "You'll have to excuse me not shaking hands, the absinthe ceremony has to be done just so."

Harriet Lime had a small stemmed glass in front of her, over which was suspended a cube of white refined sugar supported in what looked to Jesamine like a tiny silver cage with a spoon-like handle. Taking the most exquisite care, Harriet Lime was pouring a clear green liquid from a chilled flask over the sugar cube and into the glass. When the glass was about half full she removed the sugar, put down the flask and picked up a jug of water. The small splash immediately turned the green liquid cloudy, which was the signal for those around the table to break into quiet applause. Harriet Lime beamed at Madame de Wynter. "Did I make this one for you, Anastasia?"

De Wynter shook her head. "Not now, my dear. I have to shake the obligatory hands and watch out for the less than obligatory knives in the back. Give that one to Jesamine. She is worrying too much and needs to relax."

Jesamine seated herself, and Harriet Lime pushed the glass of what now looked like green milk towards her. As she extended her hand, Jesamine noticed that the woman's long fingernails were lacquered in the exact same yellow as her shoes, and that she wore an ornately gothic ring, a polished yellow stone, that also matched the shoes, gripped in the eight legs of a silver-crafted spider. "Here, Major. Try this."

"I don't wish to appear rude, but what is it?"

"It is absinthe, Major. The emerald goddess."

## CORDELIA

Windermere had not been particularly taken with the band in the ball-room, and, although Cordelia had wanted to linger, he had taken her hand and led her straight on through a number of rooms in the seemingly endless house, until the two of them emerged onto a broad terrace under the night sky. Flames leapt from braziers and groups of people sat on white chairs at white tables. One entire table was filled with men who could only be part of the local criminal fraternity, but Windermere ignored them, heading instead for a table where Jesamine was sitting, looking decided bored and a little anxious, while the same blonde in the near-sheer black dress who had previously been impressing Argo appeared to be holding court. "Is that Harriet Lime?"

Windermere nodded. "That's her. Just remember what I told you."

Cordelia and Windermere had driven to the party in Windermere's dark green, two-seat Armstrong roadster. The spring night was perhaps a little chilly to have the top down, but she was delighted with the sensation of being in a foreign city with the wind making her red hair stream behind her. While halted at an intersection by a mechanical stop sign, Windermere had placed a hand on her thigh. Everything seemed to be going according to her plan and more. The smallness of the car encouraged such intimacies. Cordelia had quivered and put her own hand over his in happy validation of the unstated-but-promised objective of having him fuck her before the dawn. Gideon Windermere was going to make her night. That had been gloriously and victoriously agreed, even if the agreement was unspoken. She was also elated that the people on the crowded pavements turned and looked as though they were something special, smiling and exchanging unheard remarks as Windermere deftly threaded the car in and out of the nighttime traffic, steering his way around the slow-moving horse-drawn cabs and broughams, the trams that drew their electricity from a network of overhead cables, and the diesel-driven, open-topped, double-decker buses. She was tempted to try one more time to persuade him to forget the party and come straight back to her hotel, or else take her to whatever lair he inhabited and called home, but she knew it was a waste of time. No matter how alluring Cordelia might make herself, attendance at Anastasia de Wynter's party was nonnegotiable, and she suspected it was the kind of gathering where plots were hatched and devious deals done in dark corners. Windermere as good as confirmed this for her when, as they drove along a broad boulevard that bordered a park on one side, he spoke to her in a tone that was suddenly professional and authoritative.

"You'll almost certainly meet a woman called Harriet Lime."

"Harriet Lime?"

"That's right."

"And?"

"She maintains the pretense of being the mindless party girl, but don't let that put you off, or cause you to underestimate her. She may be very helpful. She's one of our leading authorities on Her Grand Eminence Jeakqual-Ahrach."

"A leading authority?"

"She's actually met the woman."

Cordelia's eyes hardened. "So have I, darling. I'd advise both you and her to remember that."

Windermere realized his error. "I didn't mean . . ."

"I know you didn't mean, but don't underestimate either."

"I won't. I'm sorry."

"Where did she meet her?"

"In Muscovy, before the invasion of the Americas. Back when it was still thought some kind of accommodation was possible between the Mosul and the Norse. Both of them were at a performance of the Nureyev Ballet and talked afterwards."

Cordelia pouted. "And I met the bitch naked in a Zhaithan torture chamber. I think my insight might be a little more acute."

Windermere sighed. "Harriet Lime also had a sister, Gina, who was an operative for Morgana's Web. She was captured, tortured, and buried alive. Harriet Lime isn't any more an amateur than you are, Cordelia, so don't be difficult."

Gideon Windermere was actually telling her off. Cordelia didn't know whether to be angry, or love him more, and, then, before she had a chance to decide, he spun the Armstrong, rather faster than was strictly necessary, into a hard left, and through the open gates of what would turn out to be Deerpark.

As Cordelia and Windermere approached the table on the terrace, Harriet Lime looked up, directly at Cordelia. Their eyes met, and Cordelia knew by instinct that the woman was going to be a problem.

## ARGO

"Who wants a benodex?"

Spinrad's question elicited an immediate and excited response from the three intoxicated women. Daphne, with the daisy painted on her cheek, and her two friends, Nell and Estelle, jumped up and down like gleeful four-year-olds. "We do! We do!"

Argo looked at Raphael, and then they both turned to Spinrad. "What's benodex?"

Spinrad laughed. "It's the crutch of life. It keeps you going long after you should have dropped."

He produced an ornate silver pill box from somewhere inside his evening coat, and flipped back the lid, clearly a long-practiced, one-handed gesture. Inside the box were maybe a dozen clear capsules filled with yellow powder. "Try one."

Argo hesitated. He wasn't in the habit of taking strange pills just because they were presented to him. Back during training, T'saya had given them all kinds of psychotropics to enhance the paranormal experience and help them navigate the Other Place, but this was something else. The Virginia farm boy inside him had doubts, and remembered the old-time country saying about the evils of the big city. *Don't take money from a woman and don't mess around with dope.* On the other hand, he could only suppose that the effects had to be highly desirable if the girls were prepared to become so totally infantile for one of the pills. Daphne insinuated herself between Argo and Spinrad. "Pretty please, may I have one while he's making up his mind."

Nell and Estelle joined in.

"And me?"

"And me?"

Spinrad extended the pill box as though bestowing a blessing. Three greedy hands reached for capsules "Can we take one each for later?"

"No."

"You're mean."

"And you're all freeloading she-ingrates."

Nell shrugged off his condemnation and swallowed her capsule with a sip of wine. "There're times when I think benodex is better than fucking."

"Both together's good."

"That's very true."

Spinrad again offered the pill box to Argo and Raphael. "Benodex was originally developed for the NAF, to keep the aircrews alert for longer periods as the operational range of the planes kept extending, but now about everyone just takes it for fun."

Raphael made Argo's decision for him by helping himself to a benodex and swallowing it. "What the fuck? We were only going to get drunk anyway."

Argo sighed. "What the fuck, indeed."

He took his capsule and waited to see what would happen. Estelle, who seemed to be cultivating a dark wantonness in a corset that severely nipped her waist, leaned an arm on Argo's shoulder. "You did the right thing, darling."

"I did?"

"You'll soon feel very polymorphous."

"Polymorphous?"

"You know, all flowing and flexible and ready for anything."

Just how polymorphous the party already had become was demonstrated a few moments later. The three boys and three girls were moving like an expedition down one of Deerpark's many corridors when they encountered a strange apparition coming like a wide-eyed zombie in the other direction. The man was barefoot and naked, save for a leather thong, an antique Teuton slave belt, and a black leather hood with goggle eyepieces, the lenses of which were a disconcerting red. A small sign was hung around his neck on a chain. It read . . .

IF I DISPLEASE, PUNISH ME!

To facilitate said punishment, a short but probably effective tawse dangled from a second chain attached to the belt.

Argo glanced at Spinrad. "What the hell is that?"

"There're a half dozen of them wandering about behaving like waiters."

"How the fuck did he get like that?"

"Madame de Wynter's pet perverts. Usually they're wealthy but confused young men who gravitate to her power, although one is reputed to be a member of Governor Branson's provincial cabinet. She feeds them homeopathic antipsychotics and has her fun with them."

## JESAMINE

Jesamine wondered if it was possible to be both bored and anxious at the same time. Most of her mind was on the nervous edge of her seat wondering if and when Jack Kennedy would send for her. She knew she was verging on obsession about Kennedy, although she suspected that might partially be the result of the yellow capsule she had taken without thinking, on top of the absinthe, and on top of the other drinks at the reception. One of the women at the table had smirkingly intimated that, among its other properties, the drug enhanced sexual pleasure. What was it called? Benodex? That had been quite enough to prompt Jesamine to take the first one without further question. It was probably also the benodex that was causing her to lose track of time. It did not, however, do anything to make the waiting more tolerable. Indeed, it actually made her feel more jangled than she already was, plus it created distracting wisps of hallucination at the periphery of her vision, and firmly convinced her that she was once again somewhere she did not want to be. For what seemed like an hour or more, Cordelia and Harriet Lime had been verbally sparing and drinking more and more absinthe. Gideon Windermere was in an intense conversation with a young officer in the Norse Air Force and a woman in scarlet, who seemed to be the officer's girlfriend, although relationships were hard to evaluate in what seemed to be a city that was headlong in its promiscuity. Every so often, some-one would address a remark to her, and she found it increasing hard to respond.

"Jesamine?"

She blinked at Cordelia. "I'm sorry, I was miles away."

"Did you ever hear of the Knights of the Rhine?"

Jesamine grimaced. She noticed Cordelia's speech was becoming progressively slurred. "I've heard of them."

"And?"

"That was about it. Even Phaall wouldn't talk about the Knights of the Rhine except for the odd cryptic hint that they dabbled in really deep abomination."

Now Lime was speaking to her. "They seem to be currently working with Jeakqual-Ahrach."

Jesamine frowned. "I guess abomination attracts abomination."

At that moment, she spotted a waiter moving purposely in her direc-tion. Her heart leapt. Was this the word that she had been waiting for all evening? The peripheral hallucinations glowed brighter, and she could have sworn the flames from the braziers blazed higher. The waiter kept on com-ing. Harriet Lime was saying something to her about necromancers, and how women of childbearing age were being held prisoner by Jeakqual-Ahrach. It was probably important, but Jesamine found it impossible to breathe. The waiter stopped at the table. "Major Jesamine?"

"Y . . . yes." She gathered what wits she had left. "I mean, yes."

"Your car has arrived."

"My car?"

"I believe it was sent for you, Major."

"Right. My car." She was on her feet. She smiled around at the table. "I have to go."

Harriet Lime simulated distress. "So soon? We only just got here. Things haven't even started to hum."

"Alas . . ."

Cordelia chuckled drunkenly. "The major has a very important and very secret assignation."

## RAPHAEL

Daphne pulled Raphael's head back and her tongue was in his ear. Raphael's eyes were closed, his jacket was unbuttoned, and his shirt was open to the waist. Nell leaned in and ran her hand up the inside of his thigh until she cupped his crotch. Raphael let out a groan that only he could hear, then Nell gripped harder, as if challenging him to resist their concerted advances.

His fling with Hyacinth Musgrave was a long time in the past, and half a world away, and, for once, Raphael Vega was not going to resist any damn thing. He was as elevated as a kite and two young women were eagerly pawing at him. Daphne's skirt had hiked up revealing her fine, black-stockinged legs and an expanse of white and glorious thigh. He rolled lengthways on the cushions, which was easy to do, and kissed the whiteness. The movement caused tiny stars to dance daintily on the backs of his eyes, and he exhaled happily. Daphne reached down and ran her fingers through his hair. "Our Americano is flying. He has made the acquaintance of the magic capsule."

Beside him, Estelle was starting to unbutton and undress a totally acquiescent Argo, and Raphael had felt a need at least to minimally assert himself. "I am not an Americano. I am a son of Hispania, and we are a proud people."

Nell had not relinquished her grip when Raphael moved, and now she dug her fingers harder into him. "You're a son of something, but you're dressed as an Americano, so therefore you are an Americano. Our Americano."

Raphael could only groan. Acquiescence had its rational limits, and he would be whatever they wanted. "Okay, okay, I'm an Americano."

The room in which Raphael found himself groaning and hallucinating was large, indistinct, and dimly lit, a dark cavern that had been draped in silks, satins, and tapestry; a place of shadows and sensual mystery, lit by candles and the occasional shaded electric globe, where the air was thick and scented, and many people, in varying degrees of dress and undress, sprawled on piled drifts of cushions. This was another level of Madame de Wynter's bacchanal. So far, with Nell, Daphne, and Estelle as part of their group, he, Argo, and Spinrad had passed through the ballroom, with its forceful dancers doing their sweating utmost to the loud music, to a pool house, where more guests swam and nakedly embraced to the accompaniment of a fully clothed string quartet. They had crossed the broad terrace in the rear, and seen Cordelia and Jesamine seated at a table, but they had been with Gideon Windermere and a number of other men and women, and Raphael had not been inclined to join them. He saw no reason why The Four needed to hang together like an inseparable crew during their off-duty hours, although one of those seated at the table had been the blonde called Harriet Lime, and that had caused Argo some slight consternation. He had been talking to this highly desirable, ringleted blonde earlier, and from the way she looked to be dominating the conversation at the table, even with Cordelia present, she was not only beautiful, but also had to be possessed of a forceful personality. Raphael knew that Argo had been attracted to her, but, with Daphne, Nell, and Estelle now firmly in tow, and seemingly with their own erotic designs, Argo had been forced to choose, and had apparently opted for what might be called the birds in the hand rather than the one at the table. He and Raphael had merely waved and, after collecting glasses of sparkling Frankish wine from a passing waiter, had moved on to the extensive grounds, where they encountered more varieties of coupling, and in one case a tripling, in the shadows, and also a number of men and women practicing night-time archery with luminous arrows and a burning target. Raphael considered this more dangerous than decadent, and had made to shepherd the others back inside the house.

The soft dark space where they were commencing their own coupling, appeared, as far as Raphael could tell, to be the calm but pulsing, exotic heart of an event wholly devoted to advanced and fairly complex hedonism, with clear threads of pain and power passing through it. The six of them had entered the large dark room in time to catch the end of an entertainment by a naked dancer who moved to the accompaniment of bodhran, pipe, and dulcimer, with such high authority that she commanded the room's central open space, and did not look in the slightest bit absurd when she incorporated a well-fed python into her finale. Raphael and the others had found themselves an alcove with a deep semicircular couch where they were first to sprawl and watch and then, after some moments of acclimation, to begin to take a more intimate interest in each other. In fact, Raphael did not look up at all until the music stopped, and he raised his head from Daphne to see why. As far as he could tell, some new diversion was now being prepared. Three girls in the costume of torturer's assistants, one with the lower half of her face covered by a combined mask and gag of purple leather, and the other locked in a collar with razor spikes, were erecting a tall tripod. Raphael was somewhat shocked by how it was almost identical to the tripods used in the Mosul infantry for their milder, but still often life-threatening, field punishments. The only real difference was that where the Mosul tripods were made from remorseless unfinished iron, this frame was upholstered in black velvet and blood-red leather. Raphael glanced at Daphne. "Is that thing what I think it is?"

Daphne had grinned naughtily. "That depends what you think it is."

"It looks like a whipping frame."

"That's what it is. Someone's going to be put smartly through their paces."

The someone in question turned out to be an oiled young man with the bleached curls of an adolescent god, who was brought into the room by the torturer's assistants once they had fully assured themselves that the tripod was set correctly. The young man walked naked and barefoot between the two women, his spine straight, but his eyes submissively lowered. He skin was oiled, his head was crowned with a small chaplet of what looked like oak leaves, and a locked slave collar was round his neck. Raphael blinked. "He looks like a human sacrifice."

Nell affected innocence. "There are some who believe suffering constitutes an offering to the Goddess."

Daphne laughed. "Especially if it turns you on."

She watched intently as the two assistants carefully stretched the young man on the tripod. He offered no resistance to the restraints placed on his wrists and ankles, nor to the wide belt when it was strapped around his waist. For Raphael, the ceremony continued to resemble some softer distaff version of a military flogging, but it seemed to be having a mesmerizing effect on Daphne. Her hand went to Raphael's thigh as the boy was stretched against the triangular framework. The same percussion that had previously kept time for the dancer started a soft sonorous beat, and an eerie silence settled on the room. The dulcimer picked a mournful lilt. Daphne's grip tightened, and guests who had previously been wholly engrossed in each other came up for air. The beat of the drum quickened, and became more threatening and dramatic as the assistants withdrew and two fresh figures entered the room's central pool of amber light. Two statuesque women halted beside the immobilized victim. They were stripped to the waist, save for necklaces of silver mail, and were garbed below in belted leather kilts and high-studded, over-the-knee boots with straps, buckles, silver spurs, and exceptionally high heels. Their skin seemed artificially bronzed to show off their already well-developed and decidedly unfeminine musculature. As they removed their gauntlets and ran their bare hands over the boy's body, feeling and testing, the assistants returned, each bearing a selection of implements on purple velvet pillows. Daphne leaned close and breathed in Raphael's ear. Her fingers dug into his thigh. "I would love to be a Lictoress."

"What's a Lictoress?"

"They are. Nadia and Matisse. They are famous all over the city. They also make an awful lot of money."

"I see."

"How would you like to be in that boy's place."

The statuesque women were looking over the implements. Raphael shook his head. "I don't think so."

Daphne smiled wickedly. "Wait until we take you to the Turret Room and Anastasia. You might just change your mind."

"The Turret Room?"

"That's right."

"Anastasia?"

"You'll see."


## CORDELIA

Cordelia leaned against a pillar and felt extraordinarily wonderful, although moving and even thinking coherently was something of a challenge. The tunic of her uniform was unbuttoned to reveal very unmilitary cleavage.

By her own admittedly hazy count, she had taken either two or three benodex capsules, consumed at least three shots of absinthe, and the number of martinis she had thrown back since that first experiment in the chilled glass back at the Asquith Hotel was beyond all reckoning. The new room was a luxury womb, or a velvet tomb, filled with people feeling and fondling. The two bronzed amazons had paused in their flagellation, and a half-dozen spectators were crawling slowly into the light, transfixed and slithering, completely focused in their desire to reach and touch the young man who was cuffed and belted to the whipping triangle. She wondered how so many of those present had conceived of the same move. No invitation had been issued and no permission granted. Cordelia could only think that entertainments of this kind were regular occurrences, and the crawling prostrates were an accepted part of the ritual. The amazons were plainly in control of the rite. When the first hands reached for boy and his latticework of crisscross body welts, one of them snapped. "No hands, only tongues!"

Tongues were extended, and necks craned as the prostrated licked the sweat from the victim, but then a girl in lace lingerie steadied herself while rising unsteadily from all fours by placing a hand on the inside of the boy's thigh. The plaited singletail in the hand of one of the amazons cracked, causing the miscreant to cringe and squeal, and raising a red weal that extended across the backs of both her legs.

"Oh my!" Cordelia was pleasantly shocked. Was this what happened to a culture after a thousand years? Cordelia was talking to herself, but she didn't give a damn. She appreciated the amazon's technique. She wouldn't have been able to wield a whip with even an approximation of accuracy. But she had tasted the meting out of real torture. The interrogation of the Zhaithan prisoner had left her with the unnerving realization that she had both the talent and taste for it. "But that's my little secret."

"What is?"

Cordelia was suddenly aware of a presence behind her. First she smelled the perfume, then heard the breathing, and sensed the proximity. She spun as fast she was able, and came face to face with the knowing smile of Harriet Lime. "Are you following me?"

Harriet Lime looked past her at the prostrates running their tongues over the victim, while the amazons looked on and occasionally delivered a corrective lash. "Actually I was. You left the table so abruptly."

"I was bored. This party had been very heavily promoted, and I was seeing nothing of it apart from a table on the terrace."

Harriet laughed. "And Gideon was away in his own cleverness."

Cordelia's expression became bleakly unfocused. "Colonel Gideon fucking Windermere does not know how to squire a lady."

"Many of us have learned that the hard way."

Cordelia gestured across the dark cavern of the room to where Argo and Raphael, shirtless and not caring, were laying on an elevation of cushions, with three girls and another young man. One of the girls had her skirt hiked up practically to her waist, and Raphael, uncharacteristically bold, was kissing her thighs. "I mean, there are the so-called men of my group disporting with local floozies, and I was just sitting at a table getting fictional from pills and liquor."

Harriet Lime's knowing smile broadened. "You feel shortchanged on the disporting?"

"I think I do."

"So why don't you join your friends? They probably have room for one more."

"I was hoping to be disporting with Colonel bloody Windermere by now."

Lime grinned. "Believe me. He's glorious when you can pin him down. And very inventive."

"You've had him?"

"Naturally."

"Naturally?"

Lime corrected herself. "Well . . . maybe a little unnaturally. But, like I said, the trick is pinning him down for long enough. He has this fixation that he's required to save the world."

Cordelia pouted determinedly. "I fully intend to pin him down." She was aware, however, that this was extremely bold talk. Right at the moment, she was having trouble focusing her eyes, although she would never have admitted it. Harriet Lime brought out the competitor in Cordelia.

"Although . . ."

This section of Madame de Wynter's party was progressing to random and seemingly anonymous fondling, groping, and much deep breathing. Or was the word degenerating rather than progressing? Either way, Cordelia doubted she would have resisted, or even complained, if a reasonably personable stranger had put a hand on her or worse, but the presence of Harriet Lime obliged her to remain on her feet, and at least minimally maintain the honor of Albany. If she was going to abandon herself and her identity to all the hands and mouths that moved around and below her, Lime would have to abandon herself as well. In addition to being bored, inebriated, and annoyed at being virtually ignored by Gideon Windermere, she was also irritated by the way that Lime so totally insisted that her opinions were the right ones. In the center of the room, fresh and more fiendish-looking devices were being readied by the torturer's assistants. The boy hung limply from his cuffed wrists, panting for breath, eyes closed and chest heaving. Four distinct trickles of blood ran down his back from where welts of the whipping had crossed and the skin had broken. Lime made a casual gesture that seemed to indicate that the boy's discomfort was more theatrical than real.

"His name's Crowley Vane. He's Anastasia's nephew, and the town's most notorious pain-slut. I mean he's very pretty and everything, and also disgustingly rich from the munitions business, but that's not nearly enough for young Master Vane. His need to be noticed is so intense he will suffer just about any excruciation as long as he's the center of attention." Lime turned back to the preparation for the next round of torture. "You could join in if you felt so inclined."

Cordelia blinked. "I don't think so. I think I'm a little too drunk for wielding a lash."

Lime placed an understanding hand on Cordelia's shoulder. "A whip can be a dangerous thing in the grip of the intoxicated."

Lime's hand on her shoulder was casual, companionable, or perhaps sisterly, but then her fingers started to stroke and caress, and the mood changed. Even so, Cordelia was hardly ready for the kiss. It was sudden and deep, and Harriet Lime's red lips were anything but tentative. Cordelia did not pull away, but, afterwards, she could only respond with a wide-eyed expression of surprise. "Miss Lime."

Lime drew back and looked Cordelia full in the face. "Major Blakeney?"

As drunk as she was, Cordelia no longer had any uncertainties about the woman. Harriet Lime was a mischief-maker, probably a libertine, and definitely an instigator, but an instigator who should both be accommodated and emulated. Accordingly, Cordelia twisted her fingers in Lime's hair and, with a certain authoritarian roughness, pulled the woman's mouth back to hers.

## JESAMINE

Jesamine closed the door behind her, took two paces across the thick pile of the luxury hotel carpet, and dropped to her bare knees with a deep sigh. She could do nothing else. She was helpless and enthralled. Alone in the backseat of the government automobile, she had been physically shaking, but now her body had turned to helpless, acquiescent liquid. She knew that the alcohol and the yellow benodex had opened doors to long-buried needs and desires. She wanted to worship and love him, she wanted to prostrate herself at his feet and shamelessly serve him. She wanted to use all her acquired skills and corruptions to transport the two of them to new and undiscovered sensual summits. She who, as well as any, knew the full horror of slavery, wanted Jack Kennedy to enslave her. He was her monarch; he could be her god.

"Oh, Jack . . ."

Kennedy was standing in the middle of the room, facing her. A gulf of two paces separated them. His robe of dark burgundy silk, and the fact that his mane of gray hair was still damp, indicated he had recently bathed. When he moved to her he smelled of practical unscented soap. Her hands were immediately inside the robe, running up thighs that were still muscular even though he was old enough to be her grandfather. Mouth open, tongue crawling, she kissed his body. Her lips circled him. She wanted him to stiffen in her mouth, as confirmation that she did have the power to make him notice and lust for her. She realized that this was the moment she had been waiting for all night. The one that she had craved all through the craziness of the reporters on the dock, the train journey, the reception, the interlude with Madame de Wynter, and then her party with all of the drinks and finally the capsules. But now the moment had come, and she could feel him growing and his blood rising. After all the waiting, she had his attention. She paused to sigh from deep in her breast, maybe from her soul.

"Oh, Jack . . ."

"You don't have to . . ."

"Oh yes I do. Believe me. I do have to. . . ."

Impatiently she leaned back, still on her knees, and pulled the blue dress from New York over her head, not caring if she ripped it, and flung it to one side. Now she was naked but for her scanties and shoes. He could do what he liked with her. Reaching around with both her hands, she pulled his body back to her hungry mouth as though she wanted to consume him. She felt his legs start to quiver, and then he groaned. "Slow down, my dear, I am not as young as I used to be."

She disengaged from him long enough to gasp. "I think you're immortal."

Her hands went to the fabric belt on his robe, untying the simple knot. As the robe fell open, she ripped the belt loose from its loops and held it up to him, hands extended, wrists crossed. "Tie me."

"Your hands?"

"Tie my wrists. Show me that I'm yours."

"A lover's *takla?*"

"You know?"

Kennedy smiled and quoted. " '*A lover's takla, while the night lasts.*' I have spent my time among the Ohio."

Kennedy took the belt. "It's not blood-red hemp, but we will make our own *Quodoshka.*"

Was Kennedy seeing the visions in her head? Her inner vision had flashed back to that night in the lodge of the Ohio, when Jesamine had held out her arms for a scarlet cord to be cut and another *takla* severed by Oonanchek's polished steel hunting knife. Her honey-nude skin had glistened with sweat, and the air in the wickiup had been thick and sweet with smoke and sexual magic. In the present, Jesamine did not question what Jack Kennedy saw or what he only guessed at and understood. She was creating her own sexual magic. "It will serve to bind me."

The room was turning as Kennedy looped the burgundy silk around her wrists, and the hallucinations were even more insistent than on the ride there. The car had roared through London streets that had been nothing more than gas-lit flickering stage sets for a drama that was wholly beyond her imagination and equally beyond her control. Even the leather upholstery of the automobile's dark interior had crept and crawled beneath her as though anxiously alive. Then, as she had hurried through the hotel lobby, tripping on her heels, clacking on the marble, running to Jack Kennedy, ignoring the puzzled looks of the commissionaire, the desk clerk, and the bellboys, she could have sworn that she saw Yancey Slide leaving by another exit. He had discarded his stained duster for a long and immaculate pearl gray overcoat of much the same cut and with a black velvet collar. In an instant of shock, Jack Kennedy had almost been pushed from her mind. Slide was not supposed to be in London. He had gone on to Oslo. That's what they had been told. Did his sudden presence mean something terrible had happened, something terrible maybe to Jack?

She had ridden in the creaking electric lift in a state of apprehension so extreme that it verged on dread. But then Dawson, Jack Kennedy's civilian valet/bodyguard, had let her in. Jack Kennedy had been standing there in his burgundy robe, and everything was alright. That the oriental design of the wallpaper in the Prime Minister's suite had taken on a serpentine life of its own didn't matter, nor that the ornate moldings on the ceiling would start to move if she stared at them too long. Jack Fitzgerald Kennedy, the Prime Minister of the Kingdom of Albany, with unexpected strength for a man of his advanced age, was gathering her up in his arms and carrying her to the bed, and, holding her with one arm, whisking off the top covers, and laying her on the cool white sheets. With her arms above her head, she undulated her hips, and slowly and wantonly spread her legs, showing him, with no space for error or misunderstanding, that she wanted him inside her right there and then. But, as he entered her and she let out a heartfelt groan of delight, the fingers of her bound hands accidentally discovered the cold metal barrel of the heavy revolver under Jack Kennedy's pillow, and the shock of inevitable death and danger violently invaded her ecstasy.

## ARGO

Argo's eyes were remarkably large in his head. He was drunk, and drugged, and using every last reserve of his control to stop himself swaying and stumbling. The reception at the Palace of Westminster now seemed as though it had been days ago instead of earlier the same night. His mind was reeling, not only from what he had consumed, but from the gauntlet of experience he had been running over the last few hours. Had his equilibrium been more under control, he might have asked more questions when Daphne, Estelle, and Nell announced that they were taking them to the Turret Room. He probably would have asked more questions when it became clear that Spinrad was being left behind, and whatever awaited them in the mysterious place was reserved for just him and Raphael. Estelle, Daphne, and Nell, adjusting their own clothing, had indicated that the boys should put their shirts on and come with them. Lacking any will to argue, Argo had done as he was told. Nell and Daphne had each taken one of his hands and commenced to lead him away, while Estelle brought up the rear with an equally unhesitating Raphael—past Cordelia kissing Harriet Lime, in a public display of passion that Argo did not care to contemplate.

They had ascended a broad flight of stairs that brought them to the second floor of Deerpark, and, after walking a lurching zigzag course past a number of vigorously occupied bedrooms, they reached a cast-iron spiral staircase that curved round the outside of what looked from below like a wide chimney of mortared stone work. Daphne started up the steps, but when Argo didn't immediately follow, she turned and looked back. "Is there a problem?"

Argo was walking reasonably well on flat floors, but to go after Daphne was something of a challenge. "A spiral staircase requires some consideration in my current condition."

"Just walk straight on up."

"Walking straight may be the core of the problem."

"Don't even think about it."

Argo put his foot on the first step but experienced an instant of alcohol vertigo. "Are you sure about this?"

"You could do it with your eyes shut."

"I might have to do it with my eyes shut."

As it turned out, Daphne was quite right. Negotiating the spiral was easier if he did not think. The climb worked best when he put one foot in front of the other and kept leaning to the left. He only once came close to spilling to humiliation and maybe disaster, but he was able to right himself in the nick of time, and did not crash down on top of Estelle, Nell, and Raphael, who were following closely behind. Finally they reached a small landing that confronted a heavy oak door, reinforced with medieval iron nails. As they halted, Raphael looked around curiously. "This place makes me feel like I should be a carrying a sword."

Nell laughed. "This place has seen its share of swords."

Daphne rapped on the huge door and it opened with an unexpected lack of creaking or grinding. The five of them entered a circular room of perfume and smoke, curtained and mysterious, where a hundred candles were burning. Some sections of wall were nothing more than bare masonry, while others were curtained in damask and brocade. Overhead, in the conical space formed by the eaves, a tame raven sat reflectively on a beam. Incense rose from censers and curled in the light rays from what Argo assumed was some form of camera lucida that projected dim images of the activities in the other parts of the party, only to have them distorted by the unbroken curve of the brickwork. A hunchbacked technician crouched in a narrow alcove under a faux-arrowslit window, with phones clamped to his head, and his face dimly illuminated by glowing wireless tubes. He was alternatively listening and making notes on a pad, then tapping an electric key to send messages in what sounded like Standard Hamilton Code. The effect was that they had entered some inner sanctum that was part boudoir and part fortress, and that spoke of deeper designs than just sex, absinthe, nighttime archery, and novelty masochist waiters.

The focus of the entire chamber was the vast and conveniently cir-

cular bed, where, beneath a rearing dragon headboard of dark and ancient wood, supported by a pair of carved gargoyles, Madam Anastasia de
Wynter held her most closed and intimate court, surrounded by satin
covers and silken sheets, an infinity of pillows and cushions, a litter of
books, newspapers, and loose notes and documents, as well as a half-
dozen young men and women who had all the obeisance and deference of
attendant acolytes. Although she affected a wide-brimmed hat with a veil
that almost totally concealed her face, her white and surprisingly youthful-
looking body was an exhibition of near nakedness in flowing and carelessly
open peignoir, stockings, garters, and lace gloves. A young woman was
massaging Madame de Wynter's shoulders, a young man held her wine-
glass, another lay at her feet simply staring in glazed admiration. Beside
the bed was quite the most elaborate pipe that Argo had ever seen. A small
brazier heated whatever the smoking mixture might be, and then a series
of tubes conveyed the resulting smoke through cooling devices, that included a water-filled chamber in which small fish played cross-eyed in
the bubble streams, to finally distribute it through multiple hoses and
carved bone mouthpieces that enabled a number of smokers to partake
of the pleasure at the same time. As the girls brought Raphael and Argo
to the bed, Madame de Wynter was smoking, with her veil slightly raised.
As she exhaled and placed the hose and mouthpiece to one side, the raven
in the rafters coughed. She dropped her veil, but Argo could make out that
she was smiling as she spoke.

"Majors Vega and Weaver, I presume."

"Yes, ma'am, that's us."

"I am Anastasia de Wynter."

"Yes, ma'am. We are very pleased to meet you."

Raphael bowed slightly. "We have heard a lot about you. You have an
amazing home."

"And now you've come to my Turret Room?"

Argo indicated the three girls. "The ladies were very insistent."

"They were only obeying my orders."

Nell giggled. "We always obey Madame's orders."

Daphne grinned. "If we know what's good for us."

De Wynter looked Argo and Raphael up and down with a directness that was akin to a military inspection. "You are both very handsome in your uniforms."

"Thank you, ma'am."

"But now it is time to remove them."

Argo was momentarily taken aback. He glanced at Raphael. Had he heard de Wynter correctly? Did she really expect the two of them to strip on her orders? Raphael seemed only able to shrug, and his hands went to the top button of his dress tunic. Behind them was a huge man with a perfectly shaved head, slanted eyes, and broad cheekbones, who had to be Madame de Wynter's bodyguard. His general demeanor left Argo in no doubt he could very easily and very swiftly refute any argument. Thus Argo also started to unbutton his tunic, but de Wynter had already noticed the hesitation. "Don't be shy, Major Weaver. The Turret Room is where all secrets are revealed."

The raven croaked in apparent agreement, and Argo and Raphael began removing their uniforms. The hunchback at the Hamilton key didn't even look up as they stripped. He really did have total detachment. De Wynter, on the other hand, was watching closely, and did not seem to think they were undressing quickly enough. "Daphne, Nell, help them divest. The boys still seem a little bashful."

While Estelle poured glasses of wine, Daphne and Nell made short work of the boys' remaining buckles and buttons, pulling their tunics and undershirts over their shoulders and then easing down their tight breeches. Once their boots were off, the floor was cold underfoot as he and Raphael stood naked, unsure of what was expected of them. De Wynter sensed this and beckoned. "Come to me now, lads. Without your grand Albany uniforms, you really have no ceremonies on which to stand."

Propelled forward by Daphne and Nell, Argo irrationally felt like a small child being invited to the bed of his mother, back in those so much simpler, happier days, long before the Mosul had come and when his father had still been alive, but he also had a sense of absurdity as he climbed onto the circular mattress and crawled across the covers. At a gesture from de Wynter, the girl who had been massaging her shoulders and the adoring young man withdrew to the outer shadows of the room. De Wynter patted the bed. "I want one of you on each side of me." She looked up at Nell and Daphne. "And you girls will be ready to attend us."

The girls needed no further urging. Their party dresses came over their heads and they were down to brief lingerie. Loaded as he was, Argo knew that this was hardly a usual situation, even by London standards, and he might as well relax and enjoy whatever happened. And the first thing that happened was that de Wynter offered him a mouthpiece to the pipe.

"My dear Argo, it's a blend of recreational opium and other herbal delicacies, most gathered deep in enemy territory and one, I was led to believe, actually purloined from the personal reserve of no less than Jeakqual-Ahrach."

After hearing such a provenance, Argo was not going to refuse. He took the mouthpiece and inhaled deep, but almost coughed the smoke back out of his lungs when he heard Raphael's blunt comment. "I don't believe you."

Argo looked away, not wanting to be a part of whatever happened next. Madame de Wynter was plainly unaccustomed to being disbelieved, and she initially froze, and Garth the bodyguard stiffened, but then she smiled from behind the veil. "You think I exaggerate, Major Vega?"

"How could anyone get close enough to Jeakqual-Ahrach to steal her drugs?"

"There are not many with the courage to question me like that, right here in my own bed."

Argo grinned. The effects of the smoke had him reeling. "I think she might be telling the truth, brother."

"It seems like Raphael here has inherited a laudable Hispanian scepticism." She made an odd sign to Nell. Nell slid her way up the bed and began fondling Raphael. He gasped, but de Wynter continued the conversation as though nothing was happening. "In answer to your question, there are very few who have ever stolen from Jeakqual-Ahrach, and lived to enjoy the theft."

"I can . . ." Raphael suppressed a groan. ". . . believe that."

"But Morgana's Web is almost without limits."

Daphne was now tracing unreadable symbols on Argo's stomach and her breast was against his leg, but he felt he was required to maintain his end of the conversation. "We'd never heard of it until we came here."

"And yet you were in contact with it, Major Weaver."

"I was?"

"Almost immediately after you left your home in Thakenham."

"I don't understand."

"The sadly deceased Bonnie Appleford was one of the Web's associates."

"What?" Argo's surprise at the unexpected mention of the name from the past was almost matched by his confusion at seeing that Nell had now taken Raphael in her mouth and Raphael had fallen on his side. The raven stared down at him, and he knew de Wynter was putting the two of them through some kind of test.

"Bonnie Appleford was an associate of Morgana's Web?"

Bonnie had helped him escape the Mosul, but had been killed in a fire-fight while the two of them had been running with Slide and the Rangers, before The Four had even found each other. He knew that de Wynter couldn't be lying. No way existed that she could know of Bonnie Appleford, let alone make up such a story. "It hardly seems possible."

"Believe me, it is possible. With the Web nearly everything is possible."

Daphne was now kissing Argo's thighs and rubbing him with her cheek. De Wynter observed his confusion and tousled his hair, then she patted Daphne's bobbing head. "You'd be mistaken to assume that all you have seen here, and all that is happening now, is merely empty decadence and hollow hedonism."

Argo could not stop himself groaning, and de Wynter seemed amused. "All Four of you are moving to a new stage."

"I don't understand."

"You will."

"We will?"

"It is happening already. You two are here with me. Jesamine is with Jack Kennedy." She again pointed to one of the curved images on the wall. "And if you look closely, you see Cordelia in the arms of Harriet Lime. You are all cross-connected to powerful energy sources."

Daphne took her mouth from Argo and began kissing de Wynter's stomach. De Wynter sighed. "There is, of course, one more hurdle that you to have to surmount."

"What's that?"

"I want the two of you boys to take hold of each other."

## CORDELIA

"You Americans are not quite as straitlaced as you seem on the outside."

Cordelia whipped her tongue over Harriet Lime's parted lips. "Full of surprises, darling, when our corsets are off."

And soon her metaphoric corsets would be off. Harriet Lime was unfastening the remaining buttons of her Ranger's dress tunic. Cordelia did not actually resist, but traces of doubt had managed to find their way into her mind. "Does this qualify as an orgy?"

Lime smiled. "I believe so."

It certainly seemed like an orgy, maybe with some of the properties of a ritual. The music was rhythmic and insistent, and a light projector had commenced to beam swirling patterns over the draped walls, and even across the disorder of prone and supine guests. The beating of the bodhran was relentless in its demand that all remaining reservations be abandoned. An old and basic power was unbound and would not be denied. Clothes fell away and bodies alternately tensed and relaxed.

"I'm very drunk, but I don't know if I want to do it in the middle of all these people."

"Do what my, darling?"

Harriet was kissing Cordelia's right breast, and Cordelia was enjoying the sensation immensely. She raised her arms to give Harriet Lime easier access. "You know very well what we are about to do. We are practically doing it right now."

"But you feel inhibited by the crowd?"

"Not exactly inhibited."

The benodex and absinthe had placed Cordelia at some detachment from the activities of her body. From a narcotized middistance she could watch herself moan and squirm obscenely, and very much enjoy the spectacle. She just wasn't sure that she wanted a whole lot of strangers enjoying it along with her. Cordelia was reasonably accustomed to a variety of erotic permutations. The various coupling and multiples employed by The Four to achieve a sex-energy trigger to push them into the Other Place had more than prepared her for what was now taking place, and she was also evolving a theory, in so far as mental evolution was possible in her condition, that an orgy had to be, by definition, more than just a lot of couples having sex, one on one, in the same room. Like the shark must swim to survive, the movement forward of the orgy had to be to extreme and challenging, numerically unconventional, creatively depraved, and physically innovative.

"So exactly what?"

Cordelia reached out and stroked the English girl's hair. "I don't know." But she did know. The increased sensitivity that had come with her training told Cordelia, even in her current insobriety, that a massive sexual energy was being generated right there in the room, enough to knock over a house, perhaps, if it could ever be channeled, and she was more than a little apprehensive that it might be channeled through her. Then Cordelia's back arched. As Harriet's lips moved down her body and her hand slid between Cordelia's legs, she qualified her first statement. "But I don't think I actually care."

Harriet was unbuttoning Cordelia's breeches, and Cordelia wrapped a languid leg around her. Tiny bright flashes danced in front of her eyes, and temporarily hid the identity of the figure who was suddenly standing and looking down at them. Cordelia assumed it was an interloping male looking to join their girl-play, but then he spoke. "I came to see if you wanted to leave, but you seem to be otherwise engaged."

She instantly recognized the voice. "Gideon!"

Gideon Windermere, the previous objective of her entire evening, was staring down at her as she lay sprawled and wanton, half out of the uniform, legs spread for Harriet Lime and loving it.

"When I told you to be nice to Miss Lime, I didn't have anything so extreme in mind."

For once, Cordelia was at a loss for words. "Gideon, I . . ."

"You're busy and I have to go. Doubtless we'll catch up with each other tomorrow."

Cordelia started to protest, but Windermere was already walking away. "Gideon, no . . ."

She began to hurriedly disengage herself from Harriet Lime and, at the same time, pull on her uniform. Harriet immediately began to take offense. "You're leaving me to run after *him?*"

"I'm sorry. I have to."

As Cordelia stood up, Harriet Lime rolled onto all fours. "You really are a bitch."

Cordelia couldn't worry about Harriet Lime's feelings. She was on her feet and lurching through Deerpark, trying to fix her clothing. As she emerged from the front door, Windermere was already staring the engine of his Armstrong roadster. She ran towards the car, stumbling on the gravel. "Gideon, wait! Please wait!"

But he either didn't hear her or was ignoring her. He put the car in gear and started down the drive. Cordelia halted and let out a forlorn cry. "Oh shit!"

Her distress was so great that she did not notice the figure moving up behind her until the hand holding the stinking, chemical-soaked rag was over her face, and she was already plunging into black unconscious oblivion.

# SIX

## ARGO

Argo sat in the café in the Asquith Hotel and stared dismally at his plate. It was occupied by a very large English breakfast: two sausages, two fried eggs, bacon, mushrooms, tomatoes, baked beans, fried potatoes, and something called black pudding, plus toast and black-currant jam, and the two fried eggs seemed to be staring back at him in mute reproach that he had ordered so much food and was now not eating it. He had hardly slept, but was hungover to the point of mutilation. Earlier, he had sworn an oath that he would never drink or take benodex again, but he had lately relented sufficiently to order a gin and orange juice along with his coffee, and, had anyone offered him one of the capsules of yellow powder, he probably would have taken it and asked for another, justifying his oath-breaking by claiming it was a matter of survival. He had managed to shave and dress for the day's parade, and make it down to the café for a late breakfast, but, after those efforts, he had flagged. He took a sip of gin and orange and decided he should force himself to eat. He liberally poured catsup over the eggs, and then tore off a piece of toast and stabbed the yolks with it. He ate the piece of toast with its coating of egg and tomato sauce, but felt queasy before he had even swallowed.

Argo was facing the entrance to the café, and this afforded him a clear view of the lobby. It was already busy with hotel guests from the

Kennedy party making ready for the upcoming parade. The plan was that Jack Kennedy and his retinue, of which The Four were a part, should ride with full ceremony from Jutland Square down Whitehall to, once again, the Palace of Westminster, although this time their destination would be the chamber of the Provincial Parliament, not the Great Hall. Streets would be closed to traffic for the event, and, if all went according to plan, lined with enthusiastically cheering crowds. The parade was designed to demonstrate Norse/Albany solidarity, and confound all those who opposed it, and came with the full trappings of horses, military escorts, and proudly marching brass bands. The Four were not needed at the assembly point for more than an hour, and had no part in the arrangements, but he could see Jane Tennyson holding a clipboard and conferring with a half-dozen officers from the London Metropolitan Police. The day was plainly underway, and that meant, very shortly, he would have to face Raphael. Right at that moment, Argo did not want to think about facing Raphael, or the strange culmination to the previous night. They had drunk too much, taken too many of the new Norse drugs. All of that was understandable. The bizarre and erotic encounter orchestrated by Anastasia de Wynter, on the other hand, could not be shrugged off as high spirits or boyish excess. Since they had become members of The Four, he and Raphael, and Jesamine and Cordelia, for that matter, had been subjected to a variety of strangeness, but the episode in the turret room surpassed any deviant behavior that they had engaged in during their training or after. All he could hope was that he and Raphael would both do the gentlemanly thing and pretend that what had happened had, in fact, never really occurred, and, if it had, they'd both been too messed up to remember.

As it turned out, the first of The Four to enter Argo's day was not Raphael at all, but Jesamine, who, in total contrast to his hungover misery, positively radiated a happy and beaming energy. Argo could only assume that her rumored night with Jack Kennedy had been everything that she had desired it would be. She, too, was dressed and ready for the parade, and, when she spotted him, she came directly to his table and sat down. She inspected his hunched form and grinned. "You look really terrible."

"I feel really terrible."

She pointed to his breakfast. "Are you going to eat that?"

Argo shook his head and drank a little more gin. "I don't think so."

She pulled the plate to her and grimaced. "You put catsup on your eggs?"

"You don't have to eat it."

But Jesamine had already picked up a sausage, and Argo knew from experience that she hated to waste food. She looked at him again as she chewed. "So what happened last night to put you in such a wretched state?"

Argo sighed. "Benodex and Madame de Wynter."

"That Madame de Wynter is really something."

Argo nodded. "So we discovered."

"We?"

"Raphael and me."

"Jack Kennedy thinks very highly of her."

Argo didn't say anything. The last thing he wanted to talk about was the previous night. Fortunately, Jesamine didn't notice, having news of her own to impart. "Did you know that Cordelia's gone missing?"

Argo blinked. "Missing?"

"I went to see if she was up, but her room was empty and her bed hadn't been slept in."

"Should we be concerned about that?"

Jesamine did not appear bothered. "Maybe, if it wasn't Cordelia. The odds are that she went off somewhere with that Colonel Windermere. She was totally after him."

Argo tried a piece of dry toast. "The last time I saw her, she was in a hot and heavy embrace with that Harriet Lime woman."

Jesamine raised an eyebrow. "Cordelia's gone back to girl fun?"

Argo avoided looking Jesamine directly in the eye. "I think she was close to paralytic drunk."

"Yes, well, we all know Cordelia." It seemed as though Jesamine was going to say more but then she looked across the café. "Shit. He looks as bad as you do. Maybe worse. What the hell did you two do last night?"

Raphael had come into the café and Jesamine was right. He did look awful. He hesitated for a moment, and then made his way to the table. Argo took a deep breath as Raphael sat down. Was the whole story going to come out? Raphael also seemed uncertain. He was silent for a moment and then asked, "So how are you two this morning?"

Jesamine beamed. "I feel great. More than ready for a parade."

He turned to Argo. "And you?"

"Lousy."

"Did we have too much fun last night?"

Argo half smiled. "I think we may have. I'm damned if I can remember much about the end of it."

Raphael nodded. "Me neither." Argo began to relax. The gentlemen's bond was intact. Raphael looked round the room. "Can you get a drink in here at this time of day?"

"They brought me a gin."

Raphael smiled through his obvious pain. "Good." A fresh thought occurred to him. "Have either of you seen Cordelia this morning? I ran into Windermere and a blonde called Harriet Lime. They were both looking for her."

Argo and Jesamine looked at one another. "Then who the hell did she go home with?"

## CORDELIA

The smell was the first sensation to filter through the pain; brine, with a hint of fish and wet wood that made no sense at all. Next came sounds that were other than in her head: footsteps overhead, the lapping of water, an occasional loud flapping, and a continuously repeated creaking. Cordelia did not want to open her eyes quite yet, fearing she might learn more than she needed to know, and yet crucial curiosity about where she was, and what had happened to her, could not be held at bay forever. She would have preferred to lapse back into her previous unconsciousness, but that did not seem to be possible. She was also becoming aware that, beyond the throbbing in her head, and the lurch of nausea in her stomach, something hard and cold across her ankles was making it impossible for her to move her legs. She also could feel a regular, side-to-side, rolling motion that she decided was external and not a part of her general malaise. She finally looked, very quickly and tentatively, and found to her surprise that she was in a close semidarkness. A little light leaked through what she could only identify as some kind of overhead hatch, but it was enough to show her that she was lying on a narrow bunk in an oddly shaped, asymmetrical room. She was in her underwear, and a dirty, coarse-woven blanket had been thrown over her. This first inventory of her situation was enough to convince her that she was in trouble. Just how much trouble would require further exploration.

She found that she could move her arms, and, after this discovery, Cordelia decided that she needed to sit up. The move would require effort, and she was going to make it slowly and with a great deal of care. Before attempting to rise, she reached up and felt how much headroom she had. Even at full stretch from a prone position, her extended fingers encountered nothing solid, so she eased her upper body forward. Sitting up, the rolling motion was much more noticeable, and Cordelia's subconscious must have been processing the painfully gleaned information much faster and more efficiently than her thinking mind. Realization came to her fully formed and on the half-shell. She was at sea. She was on a boat at sea. Her voice became small with the forming horror that was driving out the pain in her head.

"I've been fucking press-ganged."

The boat was not a large warship like the *Ragnar*. The roll was too pronounced and there was no all-pervading throb of engines. From the smell and the general accouterments, it also wasn't any kind of pleasure craft. Cordelia was becoming increasingly frightened. She threw the blanket to one side and moved her hands down her bare legs and found that heavy shackles had been locked around her ankles and secured to a metal ring at the foot of the bunk. Her heart sank, and she felt even more unwell than she had previously.

"I'm on a boat and I'm in irons."

Fighting down panic, she very slowly lay back down and turned on her side to think about what to do next. As things stood, her options were exceedingly limited.

## RAPHAEL

The banner on the scaffolding tower read *Biograph News,* and two men on the platform were operating a large camera of wood and brass, mounted on a sturdy tripod. One man peered through an eyepiece and adjusted the lens while the other cranked the handle that wound the celluloid film through the shutter. By the following day, flickering images would be projected on screens in moving picture theaters across the entire Norse Union. This parade was a very bold piece of diplomacy, and receiving saturation news coverage, even though it was really only the prologue. The full pomp and circumstance would be wheeled out when the King himself followed Jack Kennedy in a few days, and the two of them met with President Inga Sundquist in Stockholm to map out the final phase of the war against Hassan IX in the Americas, which they hoped would have the full popular support of the Norse people. Raphael sat stiffly in the open horse-drawn carriage as they passed the camera. The carriage in which they were traveling was either seventh or eighth in the parade. It was designed to hold six, but, in fact, it was currently only carrying five. Argo, Jesamine, and Jane Tennyson faced forward, while Raphael and a plain-clothes policeman looked back in the direction from which they had come. The empty seat was intended for Cordelia, but Cordelia had not arrived at the Asquith in time to join the parade at its start, and now appeared to be missing it altogether. Cordelia's failure to show had prompted both concern and tightlipped anger on the part of Commander Tennyson, and although the remaining three had attempted to cover for her by making light of it, they too had started to worry. Cordelia might be head-strong, thoughtless, and have her little ways, but she had also been trained from birth to turn up for official functions, and her nature was such that she would never miss a moment in the spotlight. Once there, she might behave outrageously, and say what was inappropriate, but she would never absent herself from the focus of attention.

*Biograph News* had set up their camera at the approximate halfway point on the procession route. The parade had started in Jutland Square, with its huge statue of Horatio Hamilton, the legendary poet and Sea Lord, on its tall pedestal, the famous lion fountains, and, on the East side, the Temple of the Goddess-in-the-Fields. They had proceeded into the wide street called Whitehall that ran south between imposing government buildings, as though they were passing through a manmade canyon of gray Portland stone. The procession was led by a formation of Metropolitan police motorcyclists, and then the pipes and drums of the Black Watch. The pipers and drummers were in turn followed by a detachment of Lifeguards, mounted on their large black chargers, and arrayed in plumed helmets, gleaming steel breastplates, and scarlet coats. Behind them marched a company of the Asgard Division of Viking infantry, and only then came the leading and most ornate carriage, which carried Kennedy and Governor Branson, along with their personal bodyguards. Next was a formation of Roper's Light Horse, in their khaki uniforms and wide-brimmed hats, with carbines at the ready, and horses on a tight rein. At that point the rest of the carriages followed, open landaus, one after the other, in order of their occupants' diminishing importance, with twin protective files of the Scotts Grays and 17th Lancers riding on either side of them. As everyone in the Kennedy party had hoped, Whitehall was lined with cheering crowds, with flags of the NU and Albany being waved and flourished, although lines of uniformed policemen and foot soldiers kept the public enthusiasm safely confined to the sidewalks. Those in the carriages had, however, been warned they would encounter a knot of protesters just before they reached the Palace of Westminster, but they should pay them no mind since the police had them effectively contained.

The Four's carriage was so far behind Kennedy and Branson that even those looking forward were unable to see them, and the sound of the Black Watch pipers was faint and distant, and sometimes even snatched away by the brisk spring breeze. If those who opposed the Norse/Albany alliance wanted to kick up a commotion, they would do it as the Prime Minister and the Governor passed them, and it would most likely be all over once The Four reached that spot. As far as Raphael was concerned, they were scarcely in the parade at all, except, when the first shots rang out, the sounds were wholly unmistakable as anything other than gunfire, and The Four certainly shared with the rest the sense of shock and alarm.

## CORDELIA

Footsteps thudded across what was, to Cordelia, the ceiling of her prison, but could only be the deck of what she had now firmly decided was a boat at sea. Applying a worst-case scenario, she had to assume that she had been kidnapped from the party at Deerpark, either by Zhaithan or some other Mosul operatives. It was not a happy assumption, but Cordelia was hard-pressed to think of any other reason why she should be making an ocean voyage chained to a bunk in her underwear. She might, of course, have somehow fallen victim to random white slavery, but it seemed highly unlikely, and all that remained to be seen was whether the others had also been abducted, but were being kept in isolation, or whether she alone had been singled out for kidnapping. She knew that, in due course, the details of who exactly had lifted her would probably be revealed, but she had already decided that, ultimately, only Jeakqual-Ahrach could be behind the outrage. The illogical part was the style of her capture. It seemed unlike their foremost adversary to resort to methods that were so crude and physical, and this discrepancy made Cordelia furious, and prompted her to issue an angry if maybe rash mental challenge. "What's the matter, you withered bitch? You couldn't find a way into my mind? You had to use drugs and strong-arm tactics?"

Cordelia was quite disappointed that this achieved absolutely no result. Had Jeakqual-Ahrach appeared to her in an occult vision as she had on the *Ragnar,* it would at least have forced the issue and she wouldn't have been lying in the dark, waiting to find out her fate. She tried again. "Losing your touch, bitch? You were able to find me on the *Ragnar* in the middle of the Northern Ocean, but you can't find me when I'm your prisoner? Or are you scared to face me, even when I'm helpless?"

This second outburst yielded a result, but hardly the one that Cordelia had wanted. No apparition of Jeakqual-Ahrach manifested itself, with or without the White Twins, but the footsteps above her halted, and male voices exchanged words, although Cordelia could not make out what was being said. She realized that the challenge to Jeakqual-Ahrach had not been exclusively mental. She had spoken out loud, and warned whoever was up there that their prisoner had woken from her chloroform stupor. She'd wanted to force the issue, but maybe not in the way that it was now going. The footsteps turned and moved toward what she had already concluded was a hatch in her "ceiling." Bolts squeaked as they were pulled back, and then the cover was lifted, flooding Cordelia's confinement with more light than she could, at first, handle. It took her a few seconds for her to see that the figure who crouched looking in was a skinny, barefoot, tow-haired teenager in ragged canvas trousers and a striped seaman's shirt; hardly what a Zhaithan agent was supposed to look like. She knew her only course was to play the indignant aristocrat to the hilt. "Do you have any idea what you've done?"

The boy's eyes widened, but, instead of answering her, he turned and shouted. "Hey, Skipper, she seems to have come round."

An older man's voice gruffly responded but, again, Cordelia couldn't make out the words. She decided to go on pressing the boy and see what happened. "You know you're going to pay dearly for this, don't you?"

The boy looked nervous. "I'd put a lid on that, girlie. You don't want to piss off the skipper."

"And you, lad, don't want to piss off Lady Cordelia Blakeney." Cordelia wished that she could stand, but the leg irons prevented her.

The boy shook his head. "You're cargo. I shouldn't be so much as talking with you."

"You, my boy, should be down on your scrawny knees begging my forgiveness."

The sound of heavy boots stamped across the deck, and Cordelia figured it had to be the skipper. Matters were proceeding a little swiftly, but she supposed it was better than waiting. Now a weatherbeaten, bearded face, topped off by a peaked naval officer's cap; white but filthy and battered, with the insignia stripped off. "So you're awake, are you?

Cordelia now doubly wished she was standing. "That's right, I'm awake. And you may well be looking at a hanging party when all this comes out." The slightest flicker of doubt crossed the captain's face, and Cordelia knew she had him. "Would you care to explain what exactly has been happening here? Maybe starting with what happened to my clothes?"

The captain did his best to bluster. "Lady whatever you are, I have a boat to sail. I don't have the time for explaining and, moreover, I'm not paid for explaining."

Cordelia snapped back. "And I'm not accustomed to being chained nearly naked and against my will." That the man seemed to be English also made her revise some of her original conjecture. Neither the boy nor the skipper was anything like conventional Zhaithan, or even Zhaithan operatives. If they were working for Jeakqual-Ahrach, the degrees of separation had to be numerous and very much removed. The situation appeared more complicated than she had imagined. "Do you know what kind of manhunt is being mounted for me right now?"

A third figure now joined the skipper and the boy. This one was a muscular Caribbean with wild braided hair, an eyepatch, and gold earrings. "Man, I knew the bitch wasn't no Limehouse doxie."

"So what is she?"

The boy volunteered the information. "She says she's Lady Cordelia something."

Cordelia pulled out all the stops. If her top drawer voice of authority did not do it, nothing would. "I'm Lady Cordelia Blakeney. I'm a major in the Albany Rangers on the staff of Prime Minister Kennedy of the Kingdom of Albany on a state visit to the Norse Union. The fact that I find myself in leg irons and my skivvies may well constitute, at the very least, a diplomatic incident."

The Captain jumped down into the space in which Cordelia was confined. "You'd better not be shitting me."

"I've told you my name, Captain. What's yours?"

"I'm Joe Conrad, lady. Master of the *Nancy Belle*."

Cordelia went for a logical guess. "A smuggler perhaps?"

"I prefer the term 'free trader,' ma'am. Or 'embargo runner.' Not a wholly dishonorable trade in this day and age."

"So, Captain Conrad, why don't you do the honorable thing and take these irons off me?"

## JESAMINE

Jesamine could not remember any time when she had been so happy. She had spent a thrilling and blissful night in the arms of Jack Kennedy, and now she was riding as part of his parade through the streets of London, in an open carriage with a ceremonial guard, acknowledging the cheers of the crowds packed on the pavements. Her only regret was that she was not riding beside him in the lead carriage, openly recognized as his woman. Then the shots had rung out and absolutely everything changed. In an instant she knew in her heart, beyond any doubt. "Jack! They're shooting Jack!"

Argo was the first out of his seat in the carriage, rounding angrily on Jane Tennyson. "Give me your damned sidearm, Commander."

Jane Tennyson shrunk in her seat. "I can't do that."

"You took our fucking weapons away from us, and now an attempt is being made on the life of our Prime Minister. And we're unarmed."

The plainclothes police officer raised a warning hand. "Easy, lad, we don't know . . ."

Raphael had a revolver in his hand and a grimly merciless expression. He had clearly disobeyed the order that had disarmed them. "Give him the gun."

For a moment it seemed as though the policeman was going to do something brave but stupid. Tennyson clearly decided to prevent that by giving in. She held out her gun to Argo. "Here, take it."

Raphael was already springing from the carriage. "Let's go, damn it."

Argo was a pace behind him, and Jesamine, freed from the momentarily paralysis of shock, was also galvanized into action, and jumped down with the men. Her honey skin had turned pale but her face was set. They ran forward down the length of the procession. Up ahead the ranked and orderly parade had turned into a milling chaos. Jesamine was doing her best not to come apart. "If they've hurt Jack . . ."

Argo looked quickly back at her. "We don't know anything yet."

The noise alone was a storm of deafening madness. The clatter of hooves on cobbles, the roaring of the crowd, screams and shouts, sirens somewhere in the distance; orders were being yelled by authoritative voices, but they constantly countermanded each other. The crowds on the sidewalk pushed forward, and police and soldiers struggled to hold them back. A lancer galloped past, also making for the melee at the head of the parade. Discipline had broken down as everyone followed their own idea of what to do. A man with blood on his long civilian overcoat, and cradling a light Bergman gun, was coming toward them, running with desperate speed as two of Roper's Light Horse galloped after him. Jesamine knew it had to be an attacker. The man realized he couldn't outrun the cavalry horses, and turned to fire a wild burst. A horse and rider went down, in a confusion of thrashing limbs, but then the other horseman cut the man down with a saber. The assassin fell with blood arcing from a gaping wound between his neck and shoulder. He half rose, but was kicked by the horse as it turned. He rolled and lay still. Jesamine attempted to blot out the gore that made the road surface slick underfoot. She was maintaining her sanity by holding on to a single lifeline of hope. Maybe the attack, or whatever it was, had been beaten off, and Jack was safe. But then she reached the milling crowd and could no longer run. They had to push, duck, and weave, negotiating the confusion, although their uniforms, and Raphael's and Argo's drawn pistols, did compel people to let them through.

All hope drained from Jesamine as they reached what, moments earlier, had been the head of the procession. She pushed past Black Watch pipers who milled, dazed and without orders, among the rearing, wild-eyed mounts of the Lifeguards. All around the carriage in which Jack and the Governor had been riding was a scene of carnage, bloody as an abattoir, the clear aftermath of murder.

"Jack!"

One wheel had come off the ornate landau, and it lay like a tilted ruin, bullet-ridden and surrounded by the bodies of men and horses. Governor Branson sat in the street, a few yards from it, head in his hands, and with a crude, bloodstained bandage wrapped around his left arm. Two soldiers knelt beside him, talking quietly to ease his shock. One of the police motorcycles lay on its side, in a pool of burning petroleum from its fuel tank that had mercifully not exploded, adding grim red flames and an evil pall of black smoke to the hideous tableau.

"No!"

The body of Jack Kennedy was surrounded by more soldiers and police, as it lay on its back where it had obviously fallen, sprawled half out of the wrecked carriage, legs twisted, arms out-flung, eyes staring, and with the top of the skull blown away on the left side. The Norsemen remained at a distance, unsure of what they should do, and maybe shamed by their inability to protect their distinguished guest. Dawson's bullet-riddled body lay a few feet in front of Kennedy, as though he had been vainly attempting to take the bullets. Jesamine, suddenly detached, could hear someone screaming an insane mantra.

"Jack! Jack! Oh no! No! No! No! Jack! No! No!"

Then she realized the screaming voice was her own.

## CORDELIA

"Are you telling me that you've never taken money to change loyalties in mainstream, Captain Conrad?"

Conrad shrugged and smiled. "I wouldn't say never, Lady Blakeney. No one could accuse Joe Conrad of not seizing fortune by the forelock."

Cordelia smiled. "I always thought the phrase was 'fortune by the foreskin'?"

Conrad looked rueful. "I believe you're right. I was modifying my language, seeing as we had a lady on board."

"But you won't take a higher price to turn the boat around and take me back to England?"

"The freebooter must always, first and foremost, look out for himself and his crew. I won't say the offer isn't tempting, but in your case, m'lady, such a thing would present a few too many problems. For a start, and meaning no disrespect, you don't have any actual money. Only promises to pay later."

Cordelia had to concede he had a point there. "You're saying you don't trust me?"

"It's hardly a matter of trust, now is it, m'lady? A deal has been made and we're out on the water making good on the transaction. It's a little late to be putting about on just your say-so."

"My say-so can carry a good deal of weight."

"That's as may be, but we also have to face the fact that someone has sold you out, Lady Cordelia, and someone else is willing to pay a pretty penny for your warm body. I've already trusted you enough to bring you up out of the chain locker when my orders were to not so much as speak to you, but I fear that's about the limit."

Joe Conrad was completely correct about how he had trusted Cordelia sufficiently to unfetter her, allow her to exit her cramped confinement, and join him and the crew of the *Mary Belle* up in the fresh air on deck. It had taken logic, begging, all the high-born authority she could muster, plus a garnish of mildly seductive flirtation, before Conrad had finally produced a key and freed her from her leg irons. The flirtation part had not been hard considering that Cordelia was almost naked through the conversation, to the point that, as Conrad had unlocked her shackles, he dryly advised her, "You'd do well to wrap that blanket around you, Lady Blakeney. The wind off the Channel is brisk and frisky this fine day."

Emerging onto the deck of the *Nancy Belle*, Cordelia had discovered that it was indeed a fine brisk day, and that the *Nancy Belle* was a small battered sailing vessel with patched red sails, perhaps a two-masted sloop; she was not exactly an expert at identifying types of ship. In addition to Conrad, the boy, and the Caribbean whose name, as it turned out, was Reuben, the *Nancy Belle*'s crew of five was completed by a Frank called Marcel, and Lars, a squat Swede who hardly ever spoke. Her mission had been to find out where exactly she was, why she was there, and who was behind it all. Conrad had no problem answering the first question. They were in the English Channel, marking good time, and waiting for the arrival of the small Mosul herring fleet that worked the North Sea. The fishing boats were an odd assortment of craft with which Conrad could mingle, after a minimal change of the flags, and use as enabling cover under which to slip into the port of Boulogne without attracting the attention of either Mosul patrol boats, or Imperial customs officers and Zhaithan harbor police. He had even revealed that Cordelia had been delivered to him as part of an entire cargo of contraband that had included machine parts and parabiotic medicines denied the Mosul by the Norse trade embargo: the inevitable benodex, some boxes of the brand-new Bergman parabellums, so highly prized by Teuton officers, cases of aquavit and Scotts whiskey, bundles of London pornography and other publications prohibited in the Empire, but also craved by the Zhaithan, boxes of Caribbean cigars, plus a quantity of small individual items privately ordered and sent as sealed packages. For all practical purposes, Cordelia herself fell into the latter category since Conrad professed to having no knowledge of where she had come from, or what her ultimate destination might be. Seemingly the *Nancy Belle* quite regularly transported women prisoners from England to the occupied lands of the Franks, and usually they were young, pretty, and destined for the upmarket brothels in the provincial capital at Lyon or to be some general's concubine. Conrad therefore claimed to have believed she was just another of these high-priced unfortunates when she was carried aboard unconscious, and to have thought nothing of it. "I swear, m'lady, if I'd known you were some important Americano out of Albany I would have asked a few questions and probably have upped my price."

"But you'd have taken me anyway?"

"That I would. A man's got to earn a living."

Once the *Nancy Belle* was in Boulogne and had off-loaded the cargo from England, the sloop (or whatever) would take on a new one; Frankish champagne, Hispanian vintage sherry, and cases of other wines, cognac, opium, bolts of Egyptian cotton and Damascus silk, plus three Norse agents making a covert getaway from the Mosul. Once back in Rye, with Norse customs either bribed or outwitted, Conrad would show a handsome profit. Cordelia thought about this. "From what you say, you'd be hard-pressed to turn around, even if I had a secret belt of gold sovereigns under my knickers and I offered you all of them."

"You're probably right, ma'am. But you don't, do you? The question is wholly hypothetical."

"Talking of hypothetical, do you know what happened to my hypothetical clothes?"

Conrad was a picture of innocence. "You were delivered to me just as you are, except of course for the blanket. I threw that over you."

"You seem a bright man, Joe Conrad, but this seems a highly complicated way to make a living."

"I'm a seaman, Lady Blakeney. Maybe it's my downfall, but I like the feel of a ship under me."

"So why didn't you simply enlist in the Norse Navy?"

At this Reuben and Marcel laughed out loud, and even Lars and the boy smiled. "I don't like officers, ma'am. I don't like to serve them, and I've certainly never wanted to be one. I like to master my own ship, and that's the start and finish of it. Up until about a year ago, I was privateering in the Caribbean, but since the Corsairs made their damned treaty with the Marley administration, and went legal, it hasn't been a fit place for an honest man."

Conrad was able to talk all he wanted because the *Nancy Belle* had nothing to do right there and then except mark time, hold her position, and wait for the fishing fleet to come through the Straits of Dover. The worst that could happen was that a Norse warship or customs boat should happen by and decide to board them, but there seemed little chance of that, since no example of either was anywhere in sight, and the *Nancy Belle* was still flying the flag of the Norse Merchant Marine.

"This embargo-running still seems like a very complicated business."

"That's Il Syndicato for you. They take care of every detail."

Cordelia blinked. "Il Syndicato?" Both Raphael and Jesamine had dismissed Il Syndicato as "thieves and pimps and smugglers, degenerates and cutthroats," but Gideon Windermere had indicated that, although on one level, they were an extensive criminal network, based in Naples, but operating throughout the occupied territories, they were also part of the resistance in the lands across the English Channel, whose members were risking death and worse to bring the Mosul Empire to ruin. If Jeakqual-Ahrach had organized her kidnapping, Her Grand Eminence had gone about it in a very strange way, unless Il Syndicato was playing both sides against each other and simply reaping the benefits.

Joe Conrad treated Cordelia to a very direct look. "That's another reason I wouldn't take your money, even if you had it. Only a fool crosses up Il Syndicato, because that fool is almost immediately a dead fool."

The idea that she might, for the moment, be in the remote de facto hands of Il Syndicato opened a whole new door of fear, worry, and confusion, not least in that Cordelia had no idea exactly what Il Syndicato really was, and what being their prisoner really meant. A part of her simply wanted to sink to the deck of the *Nancy Belle* and start sobbing like a child. It was all too much for her. She had never asked for any of this and now it had become so much more than she could handle. Cordelia simply wanted to give in and give up, but, of course, she couldn't. It would obviously do her no good at all, and destroy even the slight sympathetic rapport that she seemed to have established with Joe Conrad. Also, on a much deeper and more basic level, she had been schooled from birth that her greatest responsibility was to keep up appearances come what may. It didn't matter that come-what-may had turned out to be disastrous and life threatening. An upper-class upbringing accepted no excuses. Not that she was allowed any time to make excuses, or so much as to think through all the fresh information that the conversation with Conrad had provided. Two totally unrelated happenings pitched Cordelia's world into another round of upheaval and motion. While she had been talking to Conrad, the boy has been dispatched to the top of the taller of the *Nancy Belle*'s two masts to keep a lookout for the Mosul fishing fleet, and, shortly after Conrad informed Cordelia that he was freebooting for Il Syndicato, the youngster shouted a warning.

"Ship ahoy, Skipper! Sail on the starboard bow."

"Is it the fleet, boy?"

"I dunno, skipper. But it's a sail, not a motorboat or steamer, so it's not a Norse patrol."

"Well thank the gods for that."

Conrad pulled a telescopic spyglass from under his coat and looked where the boy was pointing. "Off the starboard bow? Damned if I can see a thing."

"I see two more, skipper. It's gotta be the fleet."

Cordelia suddenly felt herself struck by a burst of negative mental energy. It hit her like a thunderclap, and she was hard-pressed to stop herself from reeling across the deck. Fortunately Conrad and his small crew were too busy scanning the horizon to notice, and Cordelia gritted her teeth and righted herself. She was certain that whatever it was had emanated from England, although she was not sure how she knew that, and equally it meant something terrible was happening, possibly to the rest of The Four. Conrad hadn't known anything about any other Americano kidnap victims being spirited across the Channel, and so she had to suppose that Argo, Raphael, and Jesamine were still in London, and, as far as Cordelia could estimate time, they should have been taking part in the ceremonial procession for Jack Kennedy. She could not, however, worry about the others. She had more than enough troubles of her own, and they seemed about to enter a new phase. Those on deck could now see the same ships as the boy at the masthead, and Conrad immediately busied himself. "This is it lads. It's the herring boats. Time to mix and mingle and look innocuous. Haul down the Norse Star and hoist the bloody Mosul Flame. Jump to it, or they'll be on us before we have our disguise on." He turned quickly to Cordelia. "And you'd better get below, m'lady. No one's going to believe we're a fishing boat with a fine young woman like yourself on deck."

"Are you going to put me back in irons?"

"Not if I have your word you won't be causing any trouble."

"You have my word, Captain Conrad. I mean, what trouble could I cause in the middle of the Mosul fishing fleet?"

## ARGO

Argo did his best to restrain Jesamine while, at the same, trying to work out exactly what had happened. He had grabbed her round the waist and swung her round as she'd rushed forward plainly intending to throw herself on Kennedy's bullet-ridden body, as though, by pressing his corpse close to her, she could infuse the life back into it by an effort of will.

"They've killed Jack!"

As Argo struggled with Jesamine, he found he had nothing to say to her that could be of any effective comfort. Yes, they had killed Jack Kennedy, and Argo was also in shock. The ugly and too obvious truth could not be denied, but, right then and there, he had no idea who they were, or why they had done it. The obvious conclusion was that the killing was the work of Zhaithan assassins, but that might be too easy. Gideon Windermere, Anastasia de Wynter, and even Jane Tennyson had mentioned isolationist political groups inside the Norse Union like the Sons of Thor, the fundamentalist Crom worshipers, and even unashamed Mosul sympathizers like the Iron Thulists, who were violently opposed to the alliance between the NU and the Kingdom of Albany. Maybe some hardcore group of them might have been willing to go as far as public murder to achieve their ends. Okay, so Jesamine had just come from Kennedy's bed, and her lover was sprawled dead in front of her, but she couldn't just let go her grip. They were in the middle of a war, too much was at stake, and, now, it would seem, the stakes had been raised even higher. He needed help, and all he could do was to yell at Raphael, who was standing transfixed, his pistol held down at his side, "Get over here and help me, man! This may be the deepest shit we've been in yet."

Raphael pulled himself out of his own shock, tucked his revolver into the flap of his dress tunic, and moved quickly to Argo, taking Jesamine's hands in his, and talking to her in the kind of low and gentle tone that one might use to calm a frightened horse. "Easy, girl, easy. This is exactly the wrong time to come apart."

She snarled angrily at him. "What would you do?"

Raphael remained calm. "Probably the same, but you have to hold it together."

Raphael's technique seemed to work. Jesamine had stopped struggling and was at least talking. "I was with him just a few hours ago."

"I know, I know."

Argo tentatively put Jesamine back on her feet and let go of her, but Raphael still held her hands. She stood forlornly for a few moments, and then looked back at Jack Kennedy. "Are they just going to leave him there?"

A press photographer had eased though the confusion, and was starting to aim his bulky camera at Kennedy's body when Jesamine spotted him. She let out a shriek of fury, and, before Argo or Raphael could stop her, she threw herself on the man, alternately beating on him with her fists, and trying to claw the camera out of his hands. "Leave him alone you bastard! Leave him the fuck alone!"

Most of the police and soldiers in the immediate area were either waiting for orders, or attempting to secure the assassination scene with less than total effect. Others were trying to clear a path for the first motorized ambulances. Jesamine's sudden assault on the photographer provided something familiar for them, something with which they were able to cope. Jesamine and the unfortunate photographer were instantly surrounded by uniformed men trying to pull them apart. This was too much for Argo. He lurched towards this new mêlée, shouting angrily, "Leave her alone, dammit!"

The combination of his uniform and attitude made the confusion part, but two London coppers continued to hold Jesamine's arms while another two restrained the photographer. Argo gestured irately to the two holding Jesamine. "I said let her go. She was his girlfriend, you idiots. She needs to be sedated, not manhandled!"

"I think it would be best if you all came with us, Major."

Argo turned to see the source of this new voice, and found himself facing a grim knot of what were obviously plainclothed policemen, or the heavyweight agents of some other branch of national security. A man whom Argo identified as being the leader of the group by the more expensive cut of his trenchcoat, held out his hand. "Please give us the gun, Major Weaver. You're breaking Norse law by having it with you at all."

Argo was too furious to be intimidated. "That's our leader who's just be murdered. How does that sit with your Norse fucking law?"

"I appreciate that you're upset, sir. That's why it would be best if you came with us."

"You're arresting us? You bastards allow Jack Kennedy to be gunned down in broad daylight with half your fucking army looking on, and you're arresting *us*?"

"No sir, you're not being arrested. This tragic situation unfortunately requires a swift response, and Sir Harry Palmer would like to hear what you have to say. But first give me the pistol. Everyone is under a lot of stress, and we don't want any accidents, do we?"

The plainclothes men were backed up by ten or more of the Asgard Division, still in their winged helmets, but carrying thoroughly modern Bergman carbines. They hadn't actually raised their weapons, but they were staring intently at Argo. Argo expelled some of his more reckless anger with a sigh. He didn't want any accidents either. He turned the pistol in his hand and offered it to the plainclothes man butt first. "Here, take it. It's one of yours anyway."

He refrained from ratting out Jane Tennyson with the detail that the revolver was hers. The man took the gun and dropped it into his coat's copious pocket. Taking his cue from Argo, Raphael turned over his sidearm. The man gave a formal nod. "Thank you, sir. Now, if you want to follow us . . ."

"What about the body? You expect us to just leave him?"

"Once the injured have been taken out, we'll be sealing the entire area so our forensic teams can go to work. It's not the romantic way, Major, but we have to make accurate records of everything if we're going to nail the bastards who did this."

The first ambulance had halted by the wrecked carriage, and Governor Branson and two injured soldiers were being helped into it.

"But he was our man."

"I know, sir, but it's the modern world."

"I suppose you're right."

The leader of the plainclothes men was making motions to move. "If you and your friends would just come with us, we have transport close by."

"Do we have any choice in the matter?"

"No, sir, none at all."

## CORDELIA

"You want me to what?"

"I'm afraid you're going to have to get into the crate, m'lady. We can't have you walking across the Boulogne fish dock in nothing but your underwear, now can we?"

"You could give me some fucking clothes."

Joe Conrad stared unhappily at her. "I've done the best I can for you, Lady Blakeney, all contrary to express orders, but this is how it's going to be. We're not messing around here. We're in the Empire now. There's

Zhaithan and Customs to contend with here, not to mention any number of prying eyes. So you can either be a good girl, or we chloroform you. What's it going to be?"

The crate stank of fish, herrings to be precise, but so, then, did absolutely everything else. Cordelia could see, however, that Joe Conrad wasn't messing around. He was handing her on to the next stage of this highly mysterious abduction. He might have treated her decently while she was aboard his ship, but now his only mission was to get rid of her, to get her ashore, along with all the other stuff he was running across the Channel: the machine parts, the drugs, the guns, the whiskey, the pornography, and the cigars. Cordelia knew that it would be a waste of time to resist, and the last thing she wanted was to be unconscious, and then come to, groggy and stupid, in a situation that was certain to require all of her wits about her. She allowed Reuben to cuff her hands, and then she stepped into the rough wooden crate that was uncomfortably close in both size and shape to a coffin. She lay down, and Conrad shackled her ankles. He winked before Reuben and Lars closed the lid on her. "It's been a real pleasure, m'lady. Just remember not to move or make a sound. It would be just as unfortunate for you if the wrong people opened the box as it would for us."

The lid closed, and Cordelia was left in darkness. She waited for what seemed to be an eternity before she felt herself being lifted and tilted. She was bumped a couple of times, and then carried at an angle. She could only suppose that she was being moved down the *Nancy Belle*'s narrow gangplank by bribed or otherwise fixed porters or longshoremen. Cordelia closed her eyes and did her utmost to think of nothing. The day, even with its wrenching shocks and dire revelations, had been manageable, but now night had fallen, she was in Mosul occupied territory, and the future really did not bear consideration.

The *Nancy Belle* had mingled with the Mosul herring fleet without hitch or incident, and none of the fishermen seemed to question that one ship could pull far ahead of the others, and then deliberately drop back so it was in the dense middle of the fleet with boats all around it. Maybe freebooters attached themselves to the fleet on such a regular basis that no one thought anything about it. Conrad had ordered Cordelia back to the chain locker when the fishing fleet had been sighted, but he had left the hatch open so she could peer out. She had seen a procession of strangely assorted craft drift past, as though they had been assembled from all over the Mosul empire. Ugly tug-like steamships sailed alongside narrow-beamed sailing boats with curved hulls and billowing triangular sails of a kind that Jesamine had only seen in picture books of the Mediterranean. Cordelia had seen the trim, squat fishing smacks that worked out of Gloucester and Boston, and the fishing villages on Long Island Sound, and these were nothing like this mismatched Mosul flotilla. The *Nancy Belle* had sailed into Boulogne just as the sun was setting behind sinister, windowless, waterfront buildings with belching smokestacks, and before it found a berth at the far end of what Conrad had called the fish dock, it passed two hulking, rust-streaked Mosul ironclads, and a Mamaluke trireme with unhappy galley slaves silhouetted in the oar ports. The warships were ugly, in need of paint, and of a crude and makeshift design in comparison to the sleek lines of Norse naval vessels like the *Ragnar,* the *Loki,* or the *Rob Roy*. Even before they docked, Cordelia did not need to be told that she had entered the domain of Hassan IX. In addition to fish, even the harbor was permeated with the aura of misery, fear, and oppression, and the tangible presence of evil.

Confined in the stink of her box, Cordelia was carried on a fairly level course for a few minutes, but then she was jerked upward and slammed down headfirst, hard enough to make her bite back a cry. After that, though, she remained still until she heard the sound of a steam engine firing up, and the box started to sway as though she was aboard a moving vehicle. On one, very minimal level, she breathed a sigh of relief. The cargo of the *Nancy Belle* had come through the port and its authorities without being detected. Doing her best to calculate time, Cordelia figured that the vehicle, most probably a truck of some kind, traveled for maybe fifteen minutes, huffing and puffing, before it came to a stop with a hissing escape of steam. Most of the time, it was on a paved roadway, with ruts and potholes, but for maybe the last hundred or so yards, the bed of the truck bucked and bounced, as if it was negotiating a back alley. Again she waited, and then her crate was lifted roughly, and bumped and bounced into some kind of building. The final jarring thud came when she was deposited on a floor. She heard voices, and then the lid was ripped off and Cordelia found herself looking at a brassy, overweight woman, with far too much makeup and a Teuton accent, who was pointing a double-barreled sawed-off shotgun at her. "Do one thing I don't like, sister, and I take your face off."

## RAPHAEL

"Take a seat."

Raphael considered the plain, hard-backed wooden chair for a moment before sitting down. "This has the feeling of an interrogation."

"I think, Major Vega, you are being a little paranoid."

"My Prime Minister has just been assassinated. I think I have a right to be paranoid."

"I'm sorry you feel that way."

"I'm sorry about the whole situation."

Sir Harry Palmer, the commander of the Metropolitan Constabulary Special Branch sat across the desk from Raphael. They were somewhere in the bowels of the Great Scottland Yard, a huge, redbrick pile, the architectural product of the gothic revival, that was the headquarters of combined law enforcement for the city of London. When the plainclothes men at the crime scene had asked Raphael and the others to come with them, this is where they had come. Palmer was a tall man, probably an athlete in his youth, but now, close to retirement age, his weight was running to comfortable excess. His gray hair was neatly trimmed, his formal suit was elegant and probably expensive, and he wore thick, wire-rimmed spectacles that gave him an especially penetrating stare. "Would you care to tell me all that you remember about the attack?"

"Why have we been separated?"

"You mean Majors Weaver, Jesamine, and yourself?"

"Jesamine is distraught. Argo and I should be with her."

"She has Commander Tennyson and a nurse with her."

Raphael looked around the room. Its only function had to be that of questioning suspects. It was bare except for a couple of posters on the walls, exhorting citizens to report crime, and a large mirror, bolted in place, that Raphael suspected might be two-way.

"That still doesn't explain why we've been split up."

"A terrible crime, with obvious international ramifications, has been committed in our city. We can't afford to leave any stone unturned, and I felt it was probably advisable to talk to each of you individually before you unconsciously formed some kind of mutual memory."

The desk between the two of them was empty apart from a short stack of orange-colored manila folders, and a very expensive fountain pen that Palmer had obviously brought in with him. Raphael was becoming increasingly angry and unhappy at the treatment he was receiving. "You mean before we could get together and fabricate a story?"

"I didn't say that."

"No?"

"You can't deny that when the four of you get together, you have some kind of collective consciousness. That's hardly a secret any longer." Sir Harry Palmer had a strange manner of speaking. His words came out in groups of three and four, with pauses in between that paid little or no account to the conventions of punctuation.

Raphael shook his head. "That's not quite how it works."

"No?"

"No."

"You will admit though, that the disappearance of Lady Blakeney does present something of a problem in present circumstances. Prime Minister Kennedy is shot, and simultaneously, one of your people goes missing."

"She's been missing all day. It would be a problem under any circumstances."

"I understand Lady Blakeney is especially vulnerable to what we might call the . . . ah . . . occult techniques . . . of Her Grand Eminence Jeakqual-Ahrach." Sir Harry used the words "occult techniques" with a clear distaste.

Raphael's face was set. "I wouldn't call Cordelia exactly vulnerable. Jeakqual-Ahrach seems to have a special grudge against her, but Cordelia gives as good as she gets."

"So you don't think she could be turned?"

"Turned?"

"She has vanished."

"I think we would have felt something if Jeakqual-Ahrach had taken over her mind."

"So there is some kind of thought transference?"

Again Raphael shook his head. "It really isn't like that."

Palmer changed direction. "You were all close to Prime Minister Kennedy?"

"I wasn't, and neither was Argo."

"But the women were?"

"We all knew Jesamine had started sleeping with Kennedy on the *Ragnar*."

"And Lady Blakeney?"

"She wasn't sleeping with him, but he was a friend of her mother's, by all accounts."

Palmer permitted himself a narrow smile. "He seems to have been a friend to many of the ladies."

Raphael regarded Palmer with bleak distaste. "I wouldn't know. I wasn't raised in Albany, I just came there to fight. All I know is that the man's dead, and should perhaps be given a break from cheap innuendo."

Sir Harry Palmer looked mildly contrite, but then shuffled the folders on the desk and opened the one he was seeking. He read for a moment and then stared at Raphael from behind the cold lenses of his spectacles. "You really haven't been in Albany very long, have you?"

"Less than a year."

"And before that you were part of the armed forces of the Mosul Empire."

"I was drafted into the Provincial Levies. I'm from occupied Hispania, and didn't have much choice in the matter."

"And you deserted right before the Battle of the Potomac?"

"I prefer the word defected. I escaped across the river and immediately saw action in the service of Albany. I think my loyalties are proven."

"And Major Weaver. He defected from occupied Virginia."

Raphael met Palmer's cold eyes. "So?"

"And Major Jesamine, she was the concubine of a Teuton colonel and she also defected?"

"To be exact, I helped Cordelia and Jesamine break out from a Zhaithan torture chamber where they had been confined by Jeakqual-Ahrach herself."

"So really, of the four of you, the only one native to Albany, and with no Mosul connections, is Lady Blakeney?"

Raphael looked long and hard at Sir Harry Palmer, and then leaned back in his chair. "Am I under arrest?"

Palmer shook his head. "No."

Raphael's lip curled and he rose to his feet. "Then fuck you, Sir Harry, I don't like your attitude and I'm out of here. Either get me a cab or the Albany ambassador."

As he stood looking down at the head of the Special Branch, Raphael felt a strange sensation, as though some faint, previously undetectable presence had slipped out of his mind. Previously he had been angry, but now he was furious. "Psychics?" He gestured to the mirror on the wall. "Are they on the other side of that thing trying to read me?"

"Please sit down, Major."

"Fuck it. I'm not one of yours. Get the Albany ambassador, or I'm starting an international incident."

Palmer remained icy calm. "I just want to know what you saw during the parade."

Raphael was heading for the door, half hoping that Palmer would stop him. Nothing would have pleased Raphael more than to break the suave English bastard's glasses. "I've already told you, I saw nothing. That's the problem. The carriage we were in was too far back. We heard the shots, and started running, but, by the time we got to the front of the parade it was all over. Jack Kennedy and Dawson were dead, and your man Branson was bleeding and in shock. I'd like someone to tell *me* what the fuck happened."

Palmer took Raphael total by surprise. "We can do better than that, Major Vega. We can show you."

"What are you talking about?"

"We have the moving pictures. We confiscated all the celluloid shot by *Biograph News,* and we're just waiting for it to be developed and dried."

## CORDELIA

Cordelia looked up at the barrel of the shotgun. She had come too far to be rendered hysterical by a fat, painted, Teuton-looking blonde in cheap, out-of-date, prostitute lingerie even if she did have a gun to her head, was calling her sister, and threatening to take her face off.

"I'm telling you. Do one single thing I don't like, and you're meat."

Cordelia regarded the whore coldly, aware that she, too, was in her underwear. "Believe me, my aim right now is to keep everyone just as calm and comfortable as they can be."

"Stand up."

Cordelia did her superior best to sound obliging but logical. "That's the one thing I can't do."

"Damn the Goddess, I told you to stand up."

"I can't stand up because my damned feet are shackled."

A second painted face came into Cordelia's field of vision. "The bitch is right, Hilde. How the fuck do you think she's going to stand up while she's all chained like a Mamaluke good time?"

The new arrival was a dark girl, as scantily dressed as the first, who might have looked a lot like Jesamine, had Jesamine put on weight, lost an eye, and acquired what looked like a knife scar on her left cheek. The blonde, who was seemingly called Hilde, backed off a half step, but still had the shotgun leveled. "I never did like this deal. We shoulda stuck to the booze and the pills."

"Someone needs either to unlock me, or at least help me stand."

The dark girl with the eyepatch glanced round. "Hey, Rotk, you got the keys to these things?"

Someone made wait-a-minute noises, and then Rotk was peering into the crate. Cordelia would have bet money that Rotk was a refugee from the Mosul infantry, who had either deserted, or wormed his way out of the ranks by some quasi-legal means, and taken to the life of a low-level

pimp and black marketeer like a duck to water. Rotk had a pencil mous-
tache and greased-back hair. He was dressed in an old-fashioned European suit; pinstriped and with broad shoulders. His nose was broken and
half his teeth were missing, but Cordelia was pleased to see that he was
holding a ring of assorted keys. He stooped down and examined the
shackles on Cordelia's ankles, selected a key, and unlocked first one and
then the other. He removed the chains and stood up. "Okay, girl. On
your feet and don't try nothing funny."

Cordelia gingerly stood up, with her hands still cuffed in front of
her, and took her first real look at the location to which she had been
brought. Her crate had been dumped in what appeared to be a windowless room—part office, part store room—a place of sepia shadows and
peeling wallpaper, lit by a pair of wheezing gas jets. Cordelia didn't have
to be told that it was the back room of what could only be one of the
cheapest knocking shops in the lands of Hassan IX. Jangling Mosul dance
music, drunken conversation, and forced girlish laughter could be clearly
heard from beyond a firmly closed door, and the air was an unattractive
cocktail of cheap perfume, cheaper tobacco, alcohol, military boots,
mildew, and the ever-present reek of fish. If the implausible turned out
to be true, and she really had been lifted to serve as a white slave in this
wretched hole, she would be running the place in two weeks, but she
continued to doubt that this was the case, because, although she was definitely in the back room of a whorehouse, it plainly doubled as a distribu-
tion point for cross-Channel smuggling, and the local black market.
Crates of scotch and aquavit were stacked up against one wall, and a table
was loaded down with boxes of cigars and jars of pills and other medicines. Cordelia realized that, in the luxury-deprived Mosul Empire, this
place was a veritable Ubu's Cave, too costly for Rotk to own in his own
right, and a clear indication that, wherever she was, it was a cell or branch
office of the mysterious Il Syndicato, and Rotk was the caretaker.

Deciding that, if she tried hard enough, she might bend the situation
to her will, she held up her manacled hands. "Are these coming off, too?"

Rotk shook his head. "Not possible, dearie. I'd be taking too much
of a chance."

"What can I do, handcuffed or not?"

The one-eyed girl, who Cordelia would later learn was called Zaza, surprised Cordelia by again intervening on her behalf. "Use what brains you have, Rotk. We gotta get some clothes on her real fast. If some drunken Zhaithan comes wandering in here, he's going to know there's something wrong here and start asking questions that can't be bought off with a bottle of scotch."

"She looks alright to me."

"And that only shows how fucking ignorant you are. Those knickers are straight out of London, we can't get nothing like that here."

"A Zhaithan wouldn't know that."

"You want to take a chance on that?"

"Who's the man here?"

Hilde sniffed. "Sometimes I wonder."

But Rotk had actually given in. He once more pulled out his keys and uncuffed Cordelia. "So get some fucking clothes on her, and look sharp about it." He covered his loss of face by picking up the crate that Cordelia had just vacated, and carrying it towards the door. "I'm going to dump this thing. Have her looking like all the rest of you by the time I get back."

As he lifted the crate, Rotk's suit-coat fell open, revealing a single shot pistol stuffed in his belt, an ancient flintlock, no less. The damned loser had one shot and that was that. On the other hand, he also sported a belt of four short throwing knives with which, Cordelia suspected, he might be quite skilled. The door closed behind him, and Hilde looked at Cordelia. "You going to behave yourself?"

"With drunken Zhaithan just a wall away? I'd be a fool if I didn't, now wouldn't I?" As if to remind her of their proximity, a roar of drunken singing came from elsewhere in the building.

*We marched 'em*
*We marched 'em*
*We marched 'em*
*To the end of the road*
*And at the end of the road stood Death*
*And we marched 'em*
*To the end of the road.*

Zaza was already rummaging through a trunk. "I don't have anything too fancy to give you. The best you can say about this stuff is that it's clean. You better hang on to your fancy skivvies, and put this over them." She held up a short lace slip that might have once been alluring but was now little more than a rag. Cordelia slipped it over her head and pulled it down. It was too large, but it hardly mattered in the context. Zaza handed her a black velvet choker with a cheap imitation cameo pinned to it. "This should help you look the part."

"I'm going to need some lipstick and stuff if I'm going to blend with you girls."

Zaza gestured to a makeup table and a dim, flyblown mirror. "Help yourself to what you can find. And don't be too ladylike about it, if you want to look like one of us."

"What makes you think I'm ladylike?"

"I can tell."

Zaza straightened up from the trunk, having found what she was looking for. "Here, you're going to need this when you leave here. It looks like shit, but it's warm and the nights are still cold." She held up a coat that was nothing more than a small-sized Mosul greatcoat, dyed black, and with some fancy buttons sewn on it.

"When I leave here?"

Zaza and Hilde exchanged glances. "You thought you'd been brought here to . . ." They both broke up, laughing hysterically. "You thought you'd been dragged across the water for a life of flatbacking and cock-sucking in this place?"

Cordelia stopped putting on the layers of thick bordello makeup and was frankly bewildered. "I . . ."

"You don't have a clue what's going on, do you?"

"No, I guess I don't."

"You hide it well."

"I suppose so."

"You really didn't know that this was just a stop on the line for you?"

"I know precisely nothing beyond what I've observed."

At that moment, Rotk returned, full of bluster, and made a massive show of sending the two women back to work. They shrugged, rolled their eyes, and left, but not before Zaza had winked her good eye knowingly at Cordelia. Having spent the day in a state of undress, Cordelia was happy to shrug into the warmth of the dyed greatcoat. Zaza was right. The best you could say about it was that it was clean. She turned to Rotk. "So?"

"I suppose you'll do."

Adopting a tone that implied she knew more than she did, Cordelia faced the pimp, hands planted squarely on her hips. "And how long will I have to remain here?"

Rotk avoided looking directly at her, turning instead and helping himself to a cigar from an open box of Caribbeans. "That's hard to say. They'll come for you when they come for you. These things don't exactly happen on a schedule."

"I suppose not."

Rotk sat back on the edge of the table as he lit his cigar. "There's one thing you've got to remember." He puffed on the cigar, and exhaled. "While you're here, you'll be pretending to be one of my regular girls, and although I'll do my best to keep the customers away from you, we got Zhaithan and Teuton officers coming in here who don't take no for an answer."

Was Rotk actually suggesting that Cordelia was supposed to work for her keep while she was in the house? "What are you trying to say?"

"I'm saying that, if a punter wants you to go upstairs with him, you'd be well advised to go, and no fuss. Fuss is something we need to avoid at all costs right now."

Cordelia carefully hid her distrust. "Flatbacking it like a regular jade to preserve my cover?"

"You're no blushing virgin, are you, girl?"

"I can hold my own when needed."

He flicked the ash from his cigar suggestively. "Then we understand each other?"

"It would seem so. Is that all?"

"There's one other thing."

"I thought there might be." Cordelia sighed and straddled a chair next to the table. "I think I need to sit down." She deliberated sat with her coat open and her legs spread. She almost smiled as Rotk's already small eyes turned beady as he looked at her casually spread thighs. Did he really think she was going to fuck him to make it through this stage of the still undisclosed game? "Why do I think this is something about you and me?"

Rotk smiled nastily. "I'm good to my girls. I take a lot of lip from them, and I probably don't beat them enough, but that's just my way. I just don't want you making any mistakes. I'm the man here, and . . ."

"And you expect a certain, how shall I put it? Tribute?"

"I'll just say that it behooves girls like you, the ones who pass through here, to be a bit nice to me. You'll come to realize that I can make the process a whole lot easier for you, and it's better you know that now than when it's too late. Can't say fairer than that, now, can I?"

"You can't say fairer than that, Rotk. You don't mind if I call you Rotk, do you?"

Rotk leaned across and put a hand on Cordelia's thigh. "You can call me what you like, darlin'. And now we're properly acquainted, why don't you show me a bit of what you're made of?" Cordelia noticed that Rotk bit his fingernails. She left the hand in place, but treated the pimp to a knowing look. "It's been a long day, Rotk. How about a drink, before I get down to any behooving?"

Without removing his hand, Rotk poured a stiff measure of raw scotch into a chipped china cup with an ugly floral pattern. He was just passing it to Cordelia when Hilde came through the door, and took in the scene between Cordelia and Rotk with the expression of one who had seen it too many times before. She halted, her lip curled, and she shook her head. "Forget it, Rotk. You try the same tired shit on every bitch they send through here. The order that she was to get to Paris untouched couldn't have been more fucking plain."

Rotk quickly took his hand off Cordelia's thigh, but she deftly seized the scotch before he could take that away, too. He began to protest to Hilde. "We were only fucking talking."

"Talking about how it was part of the deal for her to suck your cock." She glanced at Cordelia. "Am I right?"

"That seemed to be the way it was going."

"Well I just did you a big favor."

Rotk looked confused. "Favor? What the fuck are you talking about?"

"This lady has gotta be important, real important."

Rotk was at a total loss. "Important?"

"Because no less than Sera Falconetti herself has personally come to collect her."

"You're joshing me."

"There's a big, black, cherry-ass, gleaming petrol Benz parked out back in the alley, just like the high command came to visit, and Sera Falconetti herself is sitting in the back."

Cordelia didn't have the slightest clue who Sera Falconetti might be, but the sound of her name seemed enough to scare the shit out of Rotk. Hilde smiled vindictively. "Now aren't you glad you didn't fuck the lady?"

Cordelia downed the cup of scotch in a single burning gulp. In addition to not knowing who Sera Falconetti was, she was also puzzled by the mention of Paris. According to all the history that Cordelia had been taught, the city of Paris had been totally destroyed by the Mosul many years earlier.


## JESAMINE

Jesamine had always wanted to see moving pictures, but not like this and not these pictures. She sat between Argo and Jane Tennyson, on the hard folding chair, wanting to cover her eyes and hide her face, but having too much pride to do either. Acute and terrible instinct told her that these flickering, indistinct images of Jack Kennedy would be the ones to haunt her for the rest of her days, maybe more so than her real memories of the man himself, the one she held in her arms and around whose body she had so gloriously wrapped her legs. The room was much larger than the one in which she had been questioned by Windermere and Sir Harry Palmer, but just as bare and featureless. They were all there, sitting on folding chairs and watching in rapt silence, Argo and Raphael, Jane Tennyson, who seemed to have been delegated to look after her, Palmer and Windermere, and a number of men to whom no introductions had been made. A portable screen and a projector had been set up to run the *Biograph News* celluloid, and now the machine was whirring away, and the pictures were dancing on the white surface of the screen. The first shots were of the procession coming out of Jutland Square and moving down the wide street called Whitehall. Tiny black and white pipers marched past, and crowds silently cheered. A close-up of Jack in the back of an open carriage, smiling and waving, distinguished and debonair in an immaculate morning suit, almost wrung a plaintive groan from her. He seemed so alive and handsome, but they all knew what was coming and the knowledge was painfully grotesque. Tennyson leaned close to her and whispered, "Are you sure you want to do this?"

Jesamine stared fixedly at the screen. "I don't want to do it, but I have to."

The film of the parade ground on, moving to its inexorable climax, but even though Jesamine knew and feared the forgone conclusion, the terrible moment took her by surprise. She was looking at a medium shot of Jack and Governor Branson in the back of the carriage when Jack suddenly jerked, back and to the right, and it seemed, in the less than perfect focus, that a small piece of his scalp detached and flew away. She wanted to see what happened next, but the camera jumped elsewhere, suddenly showing four men in long overcoats pushing through the protective line of police that was keeping the crowd on the pavement, breaking out and running towards the lead carriage, pulling guns from under their coats. One of them fired, and the English Governor rocked in his seat, but the others didn't start shooting until they were close to the carriage. The puffs of smoke only appeared from the muzzles of their pistols when Norse horsemen were already breaking loose from the ordered ranks and charging towards them. Jesamine wanted to scream at the relived horror, but a fact suddenly struck her. She could not believe that she, of all people, was the only one to notice that all was not right with the sequence of events they were seeing.

"Wait!

Argo looked sharply at her. "What?"

"Wait a minute, stop the film!"

Tennyson attempted to be comforting. "Jesamine."

"I'm not having an emotional crisis. I saw something!"

"Are you okay?"

"Yes, I'm okay. I'm watching my lover being shot to death, and it hurts more than I can bear, but it doesn't make me stupid."

"What do you mean?"

"This film has to be chronological, right? I mean it hasn't been cut or spliced or anything?"

Windermere shook his head. "It's straight from the camera."

"Well, Jack was shot *before the assassins came out of the crowd.*"

"What?"

"Spool it back, or whatever you do, and look for yourself? You see Jack being hit the first time. I don't think the camera operator noticed, because he was distracted by those bastards coming out of the crowd. But when Jack was hit the first time, they were still back on the sidewalk pushing past the police, and their guns were still hidden. There had to be another gunman, a sniper on a building or something."

## CORDELIA

"A big, black, cherry-ass, gleaming petrol Benz" described the car perfectly. It stood in the alley with its engine running, smoke rolling from its exhaust pipe, looking quite as large and sleek and dangerous as the two men who stood on either side of it. They were burly and broad-shouldered, and dressed in identical leather coats. One hefted an old model Bergman, the one with the fat drum clip, while the other held a revolver down by his side. As Rotk let her out of the knocking shop's back door, the man with the machine gun called out to her by name in a heavy Frankish accent. "Lady Blakeney?"

Cordelia answered hesitantly. Things were moving with an all-too-alarming rapidity as she seemed to jump from fire to frying pan and back again. "Yes. I'm Cordelia Blakeney."

"Hurry please. Get in the car."

Cordelia did not argue or question. The man with the pistol opened the left rear door of the car for her, and she climbed in. A young woman had already installed herself in the left corner of the car's rear seat. "Cordelia Blakeney."

"That's me."

"I'm Sera Falconetti." She leaned forward, extended a gloved hand, and tapped on the glass partition that separated them from the driver and his gun-toting companion. "Drive on, Jacques. We need to be away from here."

Only jolting slightly on the ruts in the alley, the car smoothly accelerated, and Cordelia was off once more into the night, to a still-unexplained destination.

To say that Sera Falconetti was elegant was a severe understatement. Sera Falconetti had straight raven black hair that was worn long. Her skin was dead-white ivory, pale enough to be almost eerie in the dim interior of the car. Her black fur stole, her tailored leather coat (a superior version of the ones worn by the men), and her long satin skirt were perfect. The high double-laced boots with the stiletto heels and platform soles were out of date by London, and even New York standards, and, even back when they were in vogue, might have been considered a little slutty and overly provocative, but, except for this single error, she could pass for a carefully turned-out fashion plate, and Cordelia felt at a great disadvantage in her whorehouse hand-me-downs and garish makeup. Cordelia, however, was not going to allow herself to be placed in any subservient position by Falconetti's finery, her car, or her armed retainers. "Is anyone going to explain what I'm doing here?"

Falconetti folded her gloved hands. "I'm not insensitive to how you must be confused and mystified, and even very anxious after what's been happening to you."

Cordelia knew she had to keep anger and resentment in check for the moment. "That would be one way of putting it."

"I fear that, right now, for reasons that you'll understand later, I can't tell you much; more will be revealed to you when we reach Paris. Right now, the less you know the better. My associates and I have to protect ourselves should anything go wrong."

Cordelia made her expression as noncommittal as she could. "I can appreciate your care, but it hardly makes me any happier."

"This is one of those occasions when security takes precedence over happiness."

"But I'll hear all about it in Paris?"

"You certainly will, and if it's any consolation, I'm not an agent of Her Grand Eminence or the Zhaithan."

Cordelia glanced round the opulence of the car. "That had crossed my mind."

"I regret that's all I can tell you right now."

"You could maybe tell me about Paris. That would hardly be endangering anyone's safety. It comes as quite a surprise that it's there at all. I was always taught that it was leveled, as the pinnacle of the Mosul invasion of Western Europe."

"That's what you learned in Albany?"

"Our history teacher tried to drum into us how the Franks built the Clouseau Wall to keep the Mosul from attacking through the Lowlands, but, instead, they came through the supposedly impenetrable Forest of Arden, and up the Rhone from the south. That the last of the Frankish Grand Army made its stand at Amiens, and that was that, except, instead of occupying Paris, that huge bloody gun was hauled in so the Franks could be shown who was boss."

"The Great Paris Gun."

Cordelia nodded. "Right, the Great Paris Gun. The boys all liked that part. How the young Hassan held off and pounded the city with these huge shells for four straight days. They loved all the gruesome stuff about the poison gas, and the firestorm, and all the burned bodies. I must confess I really didn't pay a lot of attention back in those days."

"You had the luxury of being a girl?"

"I suppose."

"More than fifty thousand people are now living in Paris."

"In the ruins?"

"In the ruins and what's been made of them. Over the years, there's been a lot of burrowing and building. In the beginning, it was just a criminal hideout, but now you have refugees and outlaws from all over the Empire. Freethinkers and wandering Roma find sanctuary, most of the resistance groups use Paris as a bolt-hole and supply center, there's runaways, heretics, polyamory thought-criminals, denounced deviants, and the just-plain-on-the-lam."

"And the Mosul let all this exist?"

Falconetti shrugged. "Every so often, they mount some kind of offensive, although, in recent years, they have really only gone through the motions. They know it would be a murderous fight, cellar by cellar, sewer by sewer, and bunker by bunker, and, if they press the Parisians into any kind of last stand, we'll poison the Seine, and that would cause unthinkable chaos. Besides, both sides now clearly know the secret."

"The secret?"

"The secret is that the Mosul need Paris. They need it in the same way as they need Amsterdam, and they need Palermo and Naples. They need their cities of sin as an interface with the rest of the world. And Paris is the greatest of them, because it is also a city of terrible ghosts. They may have their Provincial Capital in Lyons, but Paris is the fountainhead of all of their corruption. It's the source of their forbidden fruit; it's where they get their luxury goods, and their modern medicines, and their exotic women."

Cordelia began to like the sound of Paris. If she were going to be kidnapped to a strange location, she could think of worse places. "And that's where we're going now?"

Sera Falconetti nodded. "With a single detour." She paused. "There is one other thing I believe I should tell you here and now, so you will be able to use this travel time to react and get over it before we get where we're going."

Cordelia looked at Falconetti warily. "What are you talking about?"

"News just came that your Albany Prime Minister has been assassinated."

"Jack Kennedy."

"I hate to be the one to tell you because I know you knew him, but Jack Kennedy is dead."

Irrationally, Cordelia thought of Jesamine, and specifically how she had once categorized her crush on Kennedy as "terminal."

## ARGO

"How are they reacting in Albany?"

Gideon Windermere looked uncomfortable. "From the telegrams we've received, the whole kingdom is in shock."

Argo was becoming angry. "This is going in every direction at once."

Raphael nodded. "He's right."

Argo numerated points on his fingers. "We have four dead assassins who could have been pros or fanatics, and what would seem to be another shooter was using a rifle from a window or rooftop, and he or she has gotten clean away."

Sir Harry Palmer looked coldly over his spectacles. "This fifth shooter is pure supposition."

Jesamine's counter-look was icy. "You saw the film the same as everyone else."

"Are we sure what we saw? It was only for an instant."

Jesamine was implacable. "I'm sure."

Argo ignored Palmer and continued. "One of the assassins was a swarthy sonofabitch with a fresh scar under his arm like a Zhaithan tattoo had just been removed. Another was a Nordic blonde who could have been one of Hassan's Teutons or possibly one of your home grown, polytheist Odin worshipers. The other two were nondescript fuckers who could have come from anywhere in Northern Europe. Their pockets were empty, their clothes were untraceable, and their weapons could have been bought in any underworld pub within a mile radius of where the assassination took place. Am I right so far?"

Palmer sighed and rolled his eyes. "Son, have you considered leaving all this to professionals?"

Argo came close to combative. He was very slightly drunk, and intended to be more so before the night ended. In the meantime, a poor boy from Virginia could take only so much. "Don't call me 'son.'"

Before Palmer could respond, Jesamine had jumped in. "If you're so fucking professional, how is it that your professionalism didn't extend to seeing any of this coming. Didn't your intelligence people have an inkling that a plot was being hatched?"

"This isn't a police state."

"But you're the police."

While the coroners, diplomats, and regular detectives did their work, cables flew between Oslo, London, and Albany. They had left Great Scottland Yard and sought sanctuary in a public house called The

Bow Street Runner for the restorative effects of beer, roast beef sandwiches, and scotch whiskey. Even in crisis, repairing to the pub when office discussions became either deadlocked or too heated for the participants' good seemed to be an English tradition, and it had Argo's full approval. On their way there, they had heard the shouting of leather-throated newsboys out on the street, as they sold the hot-from-the-press, special, late-afternoon editions of the three London evening newspapers, the *Star,* the *News* and the *Standard.*

"Read all about it! Horrible assassination! Jack Kennedy murdered!"

"Get yer special! Kennedy murdered! Read all about it!"

The Bow Street Runner was known as a coppers' pub, frequented by off-duty policemen and a few civilians with nothing bad on their consciences. Sir Harry Palmer's rank afforded him the use of a back room, a private telephone, and an aproned waiter to keep their refreshments coming. Also, their conversation would not be overheard, even by the rank and file of the Metropolitan Constabulary, some of whom were grouped around the piano in the saloon bar singing a mournful popular song that seemed to suit the prevailing mood of gloom.

> *Down in the valley*
> *Down by the river*
> *In the night I held you*
> *And I felt you shiver*
> *But now you left me*
> *And gone to the town*
> *And I have a notion*
> *In the river to drown.*

The gathering in the back room consisted of Argo, Raphael, Jesamine, Sir Harry Palmer, Gideon Windermere, Jane Tennyson, and the leader of the plainclothesmen who had brought Argo, Raphael, and Jesamine from Whitehall. His name had turned out to be Huntley and he held the rank of Superintendent. As an impasse had been reached between Palmer, Argo, and Jesamine, Windermere attempted to steer the discussion in a different direction. "There is also the matter of the autopsies."

This, however, only increased the ire of Sir Harry Palmer, who glared blackly at Windermere. "I thought we'd agreed not to talk about that?"

"I don't see how we can avoid it. We have a paranormal factor involved and these three are, if nothing else, paranormal combat veterans. They may also be targets. Let's not forget that one of their number is already missing."

Argo carefully put down his drink. "What paranormal factor? What else are we not being told?"

Now it was Palmer's turn to ignore Argo. "We can protect them."

At this, Jesamine snarled. "Like you protected Jack? Like you protected Cordelia? So far we've been really fucking secure. The leader of our delegation is dead and one of us is missing."

Argo looked coldly at Sir Harry. "It's time to cut the crap and start leveling with us, Sir Palmer."

Tennyson, who was, of course, Navy, and therefore not under Sir Harry Palmer's command, spoke up in support of Argo. "I don't see how we can guarantee their safety if we don't know what to expect."

Windermere looked tense. "That's the real problem. We don't have a clue what to expect."

"What's that supposed to mean?"

Windermere glanced at Palmer. "They have a right to know."

Raphael's voice was quietly dangerous. "We have a right to know what?"

Palmer threw up his hands. "So tell them, Windermere, but it's on your head."

"I'm very well aware of that."

"So what's the big revelation?"

"Aside from all four of the assassins being loaded to the gills on benodex, the coroner also reports that the brain of one of the assassins had already exploded before our lads shot him."

"That makes no sense."

"The benodex might indicate that the assassins on the street were a crazed and hallucinating diversion, providing a cover for the real killer, our possible sniper, if what we saw on the celluloid was what we surmise."

Argo was mystified. "And the exploding brain?"

Windermere shook his head. "I have no idea."

Raphael asked the obvious question. "Can too much benodex make your brain explode?"

Windermere shook his head. "It can make you feel like it is. But no, in actuality it isn't possible. I was hoping that you might have encountered something like it, and could tell me."

Both Argo and Raphael shook their heads, but Jesamine hesitated. Everyone at the table stared at her. "What?"

"It was something Cordelia said. After the battle, after Newbury Vale, she helped Slide interrogate a prisoner and, just as he started to spill his guts, his brain blew up."

"Blew up?"

"As in physically. As in the bastard's brain liquefied and flowed out of his eye sockets."

"No shit."

"Couldn't Slide have done it to him?"

Jesamine shook her head. "According to Cordelia, Slide said it was smart posthypnotics with an advanced destruct conjuration. Whatever that means."

"What the hell was Cordelia doing interrogating prisoners?"

"Slide apparently thought she might have a talent for it."

Raphael nodded. "I can buy that."

Jesamine ran her finger round the rim of her glass. "But I think she found she enjoyed it too much and it kind of spooked her. She was still kinda spooked when she told me about it one night on the *Ragnar*."

Argo spoke without thinking. Booze was starting to loosen his tongue. "One of the few nights the two of you were alone on the *Ragnar*?"

Jesamine shot Argo a murderous look. "Just shut the fuck up, Argo Weaver."

Argo felt bad. She and Kennedy had first become involved on the *Ragnar,* but it was too late to take back the quip. Sir Harry was shaking his head. "Do you people always go on like this?"

Raphael turned aggressively. "As a matter of fact we do. You have a problem with that, Sir Palmer?"

Windermere moved in quickly as Palmer began to redden. "Did Cordelia say anything else?"

Again Jesamine hesitated, looking to Raphael and Argo for some kind of support or council. "I'm not sure if I should say."

Argo shrugged. "We've just been lecturing these Norse folk about holding back information. I don't see how we can keep anything to ourselves now."

"The Zhaithan's brain blew out when he started to talk about the White Twins."

Argo groaned. "Damn it to hell."

"Why?"

"Because it moves Jeakqual-Ahrach way up on the list of suspects, even before we have a list of suspects."

Windermere looked surprised. "Wasn't she always?"

"Yeah, but, up to now it all seemed a bit terrestrial for her."

Sir Harry Palmer was looking mystified. "Would someone mind telling me who or what the White Twins are?"

Windermere signaled for a fresh round of drinks. "You have copies of a number of reports in your files. I believe you marked them "paranormal irrelevancy.""

All eyes turned to Sir Harry until the waiter arrived as a much-needed distraction. Argo reached for his fresh beer. "We need Slide. What the hell is he doing in Oslo?"

Windermere looked uncomfortable. "He's no longer in Oslo. His last message said he was leaving for Muscovy. He did, however, send you all a telegram."

He reached in his pocket and produced a folded sheet of coarse buff paper which he handed to Argo. Argo smoothed it flat and read silently.

*YS to 4 ++ Jack Kennedy has been assassinated in a thousand interlocking dimensions ++ Stop ++ He never escapes ++ Stop ++ If there is a goddess, she created these variable dimensions to*

*drive us crazy* ++ *Don't grieve* ++ *Stop* ++ *Act* ++ *Stop* ++
*Courage* ++ *Stop* ++ *Slide*

For an instant, Argo remembered a conversation with Slide, by a campfire, in what seemed like a different time, when they had first been on the run with the Rangers. As Slide had smoked and talked, Argo had assembled a vision of Slide as this dogged and relentless nonhuman desperado, fated to wander from dimension to dimension, and from reality to reality, waging a dark and personal war on the various incarnations of Hassan IX. Argo realized that he had always trusted Slide to turn up when he was needed. He still did. But the moment was both crucial and desperate, and this led Argo to the unpleasant conclusion that Slide was elsewhere because The Four were supposed to fly this one solo. But did Slide know that Cordelia was missing? That there might not be a Four? As time passed, and no word came from Cordelia, the assumption grew stronger that something had happened to her. It was some hours now since the assassination, and Cordelia must have heard what had happened, but she had not made contact. Slide was, usually and magickally, well aware of everything they did, and he had still not chosen to appear. Argo passed the note to Raphael, who read it and then gave it to Jesamine. She read the message in disbelief, and choked back a sob. "What the fuck is that supposed to mean?"

Argo took a deep breath. "It means the crucial word is "act." It means, before we do anything else, we have to find Cordelia."


## CORDELIA

She had sat in the corner of the big black automobile, and burst into multipurpose tears. If Sera Falconetti was to be believed, Jack Kennedy was dead, and she was looking at a highly dubious future. All through her sobs Falconetti had made no move and said nothing. She simply allowed Cordelia to cry out her shock, and only spoke after Cordelia had been sitting upright for a while, staring silently at the night world passing by outside the car. "Are you okay now?"

Cordelia nodded. "Yes. I'm okay."

On Cordelia's side of the car, the edge of the road was lined with evenly spaced tree stumps, perhaps poplars, like the pictures she had seen in schoolbooks when she was a child, but now hacked down almost level to the ground. They were motoring fast across flat country, head-lamps cutting through the blackness, and with almost no traffic to impede them, except an occasional wagon being dragged by a bony mule, or some beat-up rattletrap of a steamer. She noticed that, here and there, small knots of ragged men and women, and even a scattering of children, walked slowly and resignedly along the side of the road, as though there was a permanently drifting strata of homeless among the Franks. She glanced at Falconetti who could only shrug. "Migrant workers looking for the next job. The Empire has no economy."

"And what are those?"

By far the bulk of the traffic on the long and very straight road was made up of heavy and slow-moving tanker trucks, lumbering in both di-rections under wheezing steam-power, with the code IPP FK90 painted in large letters on their sides, and, once she was over her emotional vent-ing, Cordelia pointed out the next one to pass. Falconetti smiled wryly. "Slop tankers."

"What are slop tankers?"

"You really haven't been in the Empire before, have you?"

"Only occupied Virginia, when it was still occupied."

"The tankers are going to and from the big Boulogne slop plant, of-ficially known as Imperial Processing Plant FK90."

"And what's slop?"

"An idea thought up by the Mosul's Teuton allies to both feed the masses and humiliate the Franks. You must have noticed the stench of fish when you came into Boulogne."

"It was hard to miss."

"Well, the fish, along with all kinds of other stuff—offal, waste pro-tein, roots, spoiled grain, and, according to rumor, dead dogs and the odd human corpse—are fed into this huge grinder, boiled, and pounded until you have an unpleasant goo that is then dried or cooked into the var-ious colors, flavors, and grades of meat substitute that is issued to the general population as part of their subsistence ration."

"It sounds disgusting."

"Imagine how the Franks feel with their long history of cuisine." Falconetti broke off and stared ahead. "Best have your wits about you, we're coming up to a checkpoint."

Cordelia was suddenly alarmed. "A checkpoint? You mean Zhaithan?"

"Just Mosul regular army, and maybe a Ministry of Virtue agent. In this car, we should have no trouble."

Cordelia peered up the road ahead, and saw two military vehicles, light armored cars, pulled across the road, their presence dramatically marked by guttering flares and red oil lamps. All traffic was forced to halt and subject itself to inspection by the group of armed and uniformed soldiers who stood beside the machines. Cordelia might have viewed this roadblock as a cause for panic, but Falconetti seemed perfectly calm, so she waited to see what would happen next. The car's driver glanced back, and Falconetti nodded. He slowed the car as they approached the improvised barrier. A Teuton underofficer and two privates walked up to the car. Their carbines were slung over their shoulders and they showed no sign that they anticipated any sort of trouble.

"I don't have time to explain, but look abject. Like a totally intimidated prisoner."

Cordelia did as she was told and sank into her corner of the car, hunching her shoulders in a suitably cowed posture. The driver rolled down his window and talked to the soldier in a voice that was too low for Cordelia to hear. After a short conversation, the driver reached into a dashboard compartment, and handed the underofficer a file of papers. The underofficer inspected them, and his attitude noticeably changed. His heels came together and his spine straightened, until he was at de facto attention. The driver took back the papers, had another brief conversation with the underofficer and then rolled up the window, winking quickly at Falconetti. The car was waved through, and the soldiers manning the roadblock turned their attention to the next vehicle in line, an IPP FK90 slop tanker. When they were under way again, Cordelia straightened in her seat and looked at Sera Falconetti with a combination of admiration and curiosity. "How did you manage that? What was in those papers?"

"Jacques told the underofficer that we were on a special mission for Her Grand Eminence, and that the papers were letters of transit, personally signed by her, guaranteeing us the right to travel unhindered anywhere in the Empire."

Signed by Jeakqual-Ahrach? You told me you were not an agent of Her Grand Eminence or the Zhaithan. Those were your exact words."

Falconetti laughed. "And I'm not."

"But the papers . . ."

"Don't get paranoid, girl. The papers are forgeries, but coupled with the size and magnificence of the car, they are enough to impress any mere underofficer well beyond any thought of questioning them. Do you really think some noncom manning a roadblock in the middle of nowhere, who's never so much as seen a letter of transit signed by Jeakqual-Ahrach, is going to risk delaying us while he attempts to check via Mosul communications that refuse to work half the time?"

"It's starting to seem as though everything here runs on bluff or corruption, or it simply doesn't run at all."

"Bluff and corruption are two of our most effective weapons. Although don't be under any illusion. Jacques and Luc were ready and able to shoot our way through the roadblock if the need arose. Never underestimate the value of lethal force when all else fails." Falconetti produced a flask from a compartment of the car's seat arm. She took a sip and offered it to Cordelia. "Cognac?"

"Please."

"In reality the forgery was a damned good one, hand lettered on the right kind of parchment by a real artist. He even put a pinch of the paranormal on it; magicked the signature so it wavers and undulates when it's looked at closely. I couldn't imagine any bastard below the rank of colonel, in any of the Frankish Occupied Territories, having the balls to question it."

Cordelia was not only encouraged by Falconetti's confidence, but by the way she accepted the paranormal as part of life. It was refreshing after all those she had met who were so reluctant to face that it even existed. The big black car was once again racing through the night, almost alone on the open highway, and had it not been for the awful condition of the road surface that even bounced the Benz's luxurious suspension, Cordelia might have slept behind a haze of exhaustion and brandy. She was hardly able to think any longer and certainly did not want to talk. For a while her head whirled. Jack Kennedy, who had always been there, was suddenly gone. She would never see him again. Back in London, Jesamine must have been beside herself with grief. And her own state was no better, roaring through the night with plainly powerful strangers who she neither understood, nor trusted. Fortunately Falconetti was not turning out to be the kind who insisted on making conversation, and, for long periods, was quite as content as Cordelia to stare silently into the night as it wafted past the car. Thus Cordelia had time to wrestle down her fears until her mind was a melancholy blank, and she had been quite prepared to stay that way, except that the blue-white glow had showed on the horizon, like a strangely compacted false dawn, and Cordelia spoke for the first time in what seemed to have been hours. "Is that a city? Is that Paris?"

Falconetti shook her head. "No, that's no city, and it's certainly not Paris. That's our detour."

"I don't understand."

"Just be patient, Cordelia. You'll see for yourself soon enough."

They continued down the road for a few more minutes, and then Jacques and Falconetti exchanged glances. A turning was coming up on the right and Jacques slowed and spun the steering wheel. The ride was now really bumpy, over a scarcely paved country back road. They also seemed to be ascending a low wooded rise, and, all the time, moving closer to the unexplained luminescence. The car moved through trees, and Jacques cut the headlights, easing forward very carefully. Falconetti reached into a door pocket and produced a pair of shiny steel handcuffs, and indicated that Cordelia should take them. "It's highly unlikely that we'll be stopped again, but, if we do run into a patrol, they may check us out somewhat more carefully than they did at that routine roadblock. We are now in a highly restricted area, and it will be hard to talk our way out, no matter how flashy our letter of transit may look. It would be best if you put these on. It will make the story that you are our prisoner a great deal more plausible."

Cordelia took the cuffs, but simply held them with an expression of doubt and unwillingness. "Do I have to?"

Falconetti's face hardened. "It's not negotiable."

With a reluctant trepidation, Cordelia clipped the manacles loosely onto her wrists. The blacked-out car crested the rise and Cordelia could finally see the source of the illumination. Falconetti, Cordelia, and the two men stepped down from the automobile and stood looking. A vast expanse of the flat land below them was lit up by row after row of electrical floodlights. Two huge objects dominated the area, and Cordelia recognized both of them from schoolroom picture books. The perfectly equilateral Amiens Pyramid was so much larger than she had ever imagined it. The mighty earthwork reared into the night so its apex was just a dark shape against the sky, beyond the uppermost reach of the floodlights. The story of the Amiens Pyramid was known all over the world; how it marked the battlefield on which the Frankish Grand Army had been defeated by the Mosul, beaten into surrender by human wave after human wave, and then, after two days of unrelenting combat, the survivors had been systematically slaughtered until not a man, woman, boy, or horse had been left alive. Some estimates put the numbers of the dead on both sides as high as a quarter of a million, and they had all been buried together, Mosul and Frank alike, piled side by side, layer after layer, in a single huge pit. The story was that the pyramid had been shaped from the earth that had been excavated to create the vast mass grave, but it scarcely seemed possible. Looking up at the towering monument to war and death, Cordelia could only think that more dirt must have been added. Even the most gigantic grave could hardly have produced such a vast tonnage of building material.

On the far side of the pyramid stood the Paris Gun, the monstrous field piece, the crowning achievement of the Aschenbach Foundries in the Ruhr, with its twenty-four-inch barrel, the massive system of pistons that raised and lowered its elevation and absorbed its fearsome recoil, and the immense gun carriage that ran on steel wheels taller than a man, and double sets of railroad tracks. Again, the thing itself was much bigger than any picture had led her to believe. All those years ago, before Cordelia had even been born, it had fired on Paris for four ceaseless days and nights, raining down shells containing high explosives, poisoned gas, and incendiaries on the helpless population, until there was nothing left of the ancient city. The Paris Gun had, in fact, launched its barrage from a firing position some miles to the east, but, after the fall of the Franks, it had been hauled on specially laid tracks to its present position beside the Amiens Pyramid, as permanent monument to superior Mosul cruelty, and as a perpetual reminder of Frankish humiliation.

Something, however, was being done to the old and infamous memorial. Alterations or improvements were in progress. Much of the pyramid was cloaked in a spiderweb of scaffolding, with ladders and walkways, and, all around the base, excavations were being dug and concrete was being laid. It looked to Cordelia as though a circular perimeter track or outer road was under construction, with the pyramid at its exact geometric center, and, inside the circle, more pathways, or whatever, were being built. As far as Cordelia could tell, these would ultimately form an eight-pointed star, acres across, and she was well aware that the eight-pointed star was a powerfully protective configuration. Beyond the pyramid, the gun, and all of the work in progress, lines of long wooden huts had been constructed, and these were enclosed by high barbed-wire fences and guarded by watchtowers. Cordelia did not like the look of this part one bit. "What is that? A concentration camp?"

"It's the compound where they house the slave laborers."

Cordelia could feel panic edging up on her. "Why did you bring me to this place? You never intended to take me to Paris, did you? This is the end of the road, isn't it?"

Falconetti turned impatiently. "Get a grip, woman. Of course we're taking you to Paris. We've stopped here because it was part of our mission, and we also wanted, with your experience and sensitivity, to get your reactions to it."

"So why the handcuffs?"

"I already explained that."

Cordelia's resolve was falling away fast. She felt as though she was about to suffocate. "I want to get back in the car."

"What do you feel?"

"I feel I want to get back in the car. Now!"

She tried to turn and run, but Falconetti gripped her by the shoulders. Her tone was one of well-drilled command and control. "Get a hold of yourself, Cordelia. You are perfectly safe while you're with us. Just concentrate. It's vital to know as much as we can about what's going on here."

Cordelia took a deep breath and fought down the irrational panic. "Okay, okay."

"Concentrate."

She began breathing more normally. "I'm concentrating."

"And what do you feel?"

Cordelia shook her head. "I don't know. I mean, I already know there's a quarter of a million long-buried dead men under this place."

"Nothing more than that?"

At that moment, an invisible wave of raw evil swept over her like a toxic and threatening eddy. Cordelia stiffened with revulsion as it hit, and then gasped as it subsided. Falconetti gave her a moment and then looked at her questioningly. "Something?"

Cordelia nodded. "Definitely. Something powerful but half-formed. Something still under construction, like the place itself. I really think we should get out of here."

"There's nothing else?"

"Except that the whole setup smells of Jeakqual-Ahrach at her most grandiose."

"We have information that she's elsewhere."

Cordelia looked around uneasily. "Geography has never been one of her limitations."

As she spoke, a second wave of evil hit. The black bulk of the pyramid seemed to be pulling at her, wanting her to go to it. The great mass was changing its shape, extending and wrapping around her like the huge leather wing of some gargantuan mythic beast, blacker than the night behind it, and with a flickering, dark red tracery, like veins pulsing with contaminated ruby blood, and yet the beast was not mythic, it was fear metamorphosed, a creature somehow being created, maybe spawned was the better word, right there on the bloody historic battlefield. Cordelia backed away as the venomous and unwholesome vision threatened to enfold her. "We have to get out of here. We have to leave here right now."

Falconetti glanced urgently at Jacques. "Get the car started."

At the sound of her voice the malignance faded slightly, but it was then that she heard the voices, childish and chilling. *"Cordelia."*

*"Cordelia."*

*"We see you, Cordelia."*

*"She doesn't see you, Cordelia. She doesn't know you're there."*

*"But we see you."*

*"We know you're there."*

*"Shall we tell her, Cordelia?"*

*"Shall we tell her where you are?"*

Somewhere in dark of the vision she momentarily saw the two pale and tiny figures. Lit briefly by the ruby glow, the White Twins laughed, showing their sharp baby teeth. Cordelia raised her cuffed hands to her head and screamed. "The car! Get me into the car!"

# SEVEN

## CORDELIA

"Drink this."

Cordelia took a grateful pull on the flask of cognac and gasped. "Oh fuck. I'm sorry. Was I screaming?"

The black car was bumping down the hill as fast as Jacques could drive with headlights extinguished. Sera Falconetti cradled Cordelia's head in her lap. The handcuffs had been removed, but Cordelia couldn't recall it happening. She could hardly remember being half carried, half dragged back to the car. Jacques glanced back. "We'll be on the paved road in a couple of minutes. If there's no pursuit by then we can assume we're out of trouble."

Falconetti brushed Cordelia's hair out of her eyes. "You screamed loud enough to wake every guard in the camp."

"I couldn't help it. It wasn't the worst I've ever faced, but I've always had the others with me. It was more than I could handle on my own."

"Exactly what did you see?"

"Exactly, I don't know. It was like the pyramid changed into a living thing and tried to take hold of me."

"You mean for real or as part of some assault vision?"

Cordelia took a second hit of cognac. "I guess it was a hallucination or a grab from the Other Place. I mean, the pyramid didn't come alive, did it?"

"No, it didn't."

The brandy was making Cordelia feel considerably better, and, despite everything she had been through, more than a little sleepy. She leaned more comfortably against Sera Falconetti's thigh, but then the car lurched as Jacques spun it back onto the paved highway and she and Falconetti were tossed against each other. Again Jacques looked back. "There's nothing behind us. It seems like we got away clean, and you can safely assume we'll be in Paris inside of an hour."

Falconetti nodded. "Good." She turned back to Cordelia. "So you actually saw the White Twins?"

Cordelia sighed. She had not intended to talk about that. "I said that?"

"You were babbling about the bloodless little bastards."

"You know about the White Twins in Paris?"

"We've known about them since they were just the breeding program."

Now Falconetti had the better of Cordelia. What the hell was the "breeding program?" Cordelia was not about to betray her ignorance by asking. "I don't think they were there at the site. They seemed to be watching from a long distance."

"Anything else?"

Cordelia again made herself comfortable against Falconetti. "Yes. There was."

"What?"

"I got the impression that they had their own secrets and they might not be in full accord with their . . . mother."

Cordelia didn't know why she had used that particular word. It had simply presented itself, served right up from her subconscious, and totally apt.

## RAPHAEL

Madame de Wynter delivered a stern warning. "You should not really be present at all, so it's important that you remain completely out of sight. It is, by both tradition and necessity, an all-female ceremony."

Raphael looked at Argo, and then back to de Wynter. "We need to stay here for Jesamine, in case anything happens. We can't pretend that she hasn't been traumatized by the assassination."

De Wynter nodded. "We all realize that. All we ask is that you keep out of sight."

Raphael sighed. Both he and Argo were dog-tired and had also not expected to see Anastasia de Wynter quite so soon after the games in her turret room, if indeed they had been games. "We understand. We'll confine ourselves strictly to the shadows."

They were in the same ballroom at Deerpark where, just one night earlier, the loud band had played for the wildly dancing crowd. Little trace of the festivities remained aside from a number of large garbage hoppers awaiting collection at the end to the driveway where the cars had been parked. Even the floor in the ballroom had changed. The wooden dance floor had been taken up, revealing an expanse of highly polished white marble with a huge inscribed symbol, a red, eight-pointed star enclosed in a gold circle that was easily twenty feet in diameter. The star was geometrically formed, one square superimposed at an angle over another, and tall phallic candlesticks, with burning tallow candles, had been placed at each of the sixteen intersection points created by the figure. The room now had a magickal look, and, indeed, magick was about to be performed there, at the end of which, if de Wynter was to be believed, they would know what had happened to Cordelia, or, at the very least, where she was located.

To consult Anastasia de Wynter, so soon after the party, and so soon after what had occurred between her, Argo, and Raphael, had been a matter of last resort. The first idea, mooted after Sir Harry Palmer, Tennyson, and Huntley had left the Bow Street Runner, leaving the three of them alone with Gideon Windermere, had been that they should employ their own powers to find Cordelia. They would attempt to venture into the Other Place and use their four-way mutual rapport to search for any trace of her. At first, Jesamine had flatly refused. The idea of entering the Other Place in the wake of all that had happened filled her with extreme trepidation. She had relented after considerable argument only brought them to the inevitable conclusion that Raphael and Argo simply could not manage a wide-ranging occult search on their own, and, even after declaring herself reluctantly willing to make the attempt, Jesamine had raised another objection. If the three of them ventured into the Other Place, asymmetrical and already under stress, they could be easily spotted by anyone or anything keeping watch.

"Jeakqual-Ahrach and her Zhaithan will not only know where we are, but also that we're missing a member and are out looking for her."

"We might as well hang out a sign telling anyone who's interested that we're crippled and vulnerable."

"Precisely."

"That's if Jeakqual-Ahrach doesn't know already."

"That's if Jeakqual-Ahrach doesn't already have Cordelia."

At that point, Argo had rolled his eyes. "Oh shit."

"Right."

Raphael tried to reason his way to some positive solution. "Suppose we gave it a very limited try? . . ."

Jesamine had cut him off. "We tried functioning as a threesome in training. It never worked well without Cordelia being one of the three."

"So?"

At that point, Windermere had made his suggestion. "De Wynter."

"What about de Wynter?"

"Her Morgana girls don't have the same experience and training as you do. Also they tend to work by ritual, which is time-consuming, but they can be pretty damned effective."

"What could they do?"

"They might set up some kind of Other Place diversion, a cloak or smokescreen that could cover you while you looked for any trace of Cordelia."

Raphael had wanted to protest that they did not need Anastasia de

Wynter, but he could hardly sacrifice Cordelia to fear of embarrassment. "Whatever you say."

With this less-than-heartfelt assent, Windermere had gone to work. Telephone calls were placed, and Argo and Raphael had found themselves in a London taxi with Windermere and Jesamine following in his Armstrong roadster. De Wynter had also risen quickly to the occasion. More telephone calls had been placed, and while the night was still comparatively young, de Wynter announced that a quorum had been assembled. "I have eight of our most adept members on their way here. More would have been better, but these are all very experienced acolytes." It was only then that she had turned to Jesamine, and made plain the only drawback in what they were about to attempt. "This is a women's ritual."

"Meaning?"

"Meaning the men will not participate."

Jesamine suddenly understood. "No!"

"It has to be."

"I'm not going into the Other Place alone."

"You have no real choice."

Jesamine edged towards a whine. "Don't my feelings count for anything?"

De Wynter sighed impatiently. "My dear, you are now unfortunately paying the price of your success. First you were a child, then a whore, then a concubine, but now you are famous, and the famous go on regardless."

"But . . ."

The words were harsh but delivered with compassion. "We all mourn for Jack Kennedy. Our members have been sleeping with him for years."

Jesamine looked away, her face sullen. "I'm not one of your members."

De Wynter became brisk, indicating she was at the limit of her patience. "No . . . you're not. You are something else. You may be something new. All we can offer you is our total support."

Jesamine closed her eyes. "Yes. I know it has to be done. I'm entitled to ask 'why me,' aren't I?"

"You're entitled to ask, but no answer is ever guaranteed."

The eight women entered the former ballroom in a procession of pairs, preceded by a small girl swinging a copper censer, spreading skeins of pungent blue smoke that smelled of rose petals and opium. Four of the women wore yellow robes, four were dressed in blue, and each blue walked beside a yellow. Argo had half expected that Harriet Lime would be one of those de Wynter had contacted, since she had been among the last people to see Cordelia, but when he asked de Wynter about this, the only answer had been, "Harriet has a previous engagement."

Raphael and Argo moved to the end of the room that was farthest from the star in the circle and the sixteen flickering candles. They stood beside three squatting and blindfolded musicians—bodhran, guitar, and hipzither—whose music was an integral part of the ritual, but who were permitted to see nothing of what actually took place. The eight women moved silently to equidistant positions on the gold circle. Raphael had expected de Wynter to be part of the group, but, after donning the only scarlet robe in the room, she stood to one side. The robes all had deep voluminous cowls that hid the wearer's face, but when, at a softly spoken instruction from de Wynter, the guitarist stroked out a progression of minor chords, they pushed back the cowls revealing faces still concealed by elaborate masks. Gold, and silver, leather and feathers, complicated lace and embroidered fabrics, some were set with colored gems. Each mask was unique, but they all concealed identities, sublimated personalities, turning those round the circle into cloaked aliens or mythic beings, rather than human women.

The bodhran, beaten by the blindfolded drummer at the tempo of a slow march, joined the guitar. Now Jesamine entered the room. It might have been an illusion, but the perfume in the room seemed to become noticeably more musky and intense. Jesamine was dressed in a simple white shift of raw silk, and a lace veil that hung from a plaited chaplet of velvet cord. The hipzither came in, high-octaves above the other instruments, as though reaching for notes in the space between nebulae. Keeping time with the beat of the bodhran, Jesamine walked slowly around the circle and then turned, passing between the two women at the apex of the star, and proceeding to its center where she bowed and kneeled.

She settled back, upright on her heels, spine stiff, head held high, her face still veiled. The thud of the bodhran ceased, and time seemed to hang, waiting on a motionless tableau. Then the percussionist went to work again, faster and more urgently, and the guitar and hipzither spun stabbing and serpentine interchanges. A woman sang a perfectly pitched ululating note, and Raphael felt his body hair stand on end. Other voices joined the first, soaring even above the stringed instruments, but then, rehearsed and precise, all snapped to silence, and the women, as one, with a synchronized shrug of their shoulders, threw off their capes, and stood naked, but with each oiled and gleaming body heavily jeweled. Every woman wore a wide and opulently decorated belt secured with a clasp that was a larger replica of the rings worn by Anastasia de Wynter and Harriet Lime: the spider with its eight legs holding a semiprecious stone. The ties of the belts were wide and hung like narrow aprons. Heavy, intricate necklaces that also incorporated the spider design depended between their breasts. The spider motif was repeated in bracelets and anklets, and decorative bands around their thighs and upper arms.

For a moment Raphael saw it all as a lavish erotic vision, but then the singing resumed while the instruments forced an even faster rhythm. The women started to sway, but not the sinuous provocation of the cooch joint, the harem, even the dances at the Beltane fires. The dominant sexuality was constrained, and every move of every body, and every note of the wordless song, was focused on the generation of pure and pervasive energy. The movements of the eight were not in exact unison, but neither were they free and individual extemporizations. They all conformed to a definite and clearly preset theme, but each woman, in her own way, improvised within those limits. When they began to raise their arms, however, the move was fully coordinated, and that was the moment when Jesamine began to respond. Her head lolled back, her spine arched, and she was suddenly wracked with violent sobs. Raphael thought that he heard her cry out. "No! No!" But, over the singing and playing, he could not be sure. Then Jesamine ripped the veil from her face and tried to stand, but she staggered instead, and dropped again to her knees. She shuddered, convulsed, finally curling into a fetal position. Both Raphael and Argo started towards her. Something had gone terribly wrong. Maybe the energy created by the ritual was somehow at odds with the power that moved The Four, or maybe the ceremony itself was a total fraud. Raphael's overwhelming instinct was to get Jesamine out of there before any more harm could be done, and Argo, who was right beside him, seemed to share his resolve.

But before they were even close to the circle, de Wynter was in front of them, still in her red robe, but somehow larger and more powerful, blocking their way, and silently shaking her head, while the now-screaming music howled around her.

## JESAMINE

*The act of entering the Other Place was totally unlike the way it was with The Four. It was more akin to a painful birthing, a violent push from out of the womb of one reality into another dimension, tearing the actual membrane in the process. For the very first time, she realized how easy it was for them. The Four could slide into other materialities like effortless shadows. They all tended to forget just how much skill and talent they enjoyed, and in a strange comparison, how easily it had all come to them. Then she saw the Other Place into which she had been launched by the Morgana women's ceremony. She was totally surrounded by circles of gold that blazed like the sun, and filled her with a sense of comfort and protection such as she had never felt before. The pain of the entry had been replaced by perfect bliss, and she could have basked there all day except for the dark pillars and triangles of plainly toxic energy that reared in the middistance, reminding her that she had a mission. They stood like infinite cylinders of impenetrable evil with countless tiny points of darkness moving inside them, some rising, some falling, but all radiating a tangible misery. Jesamine did not want to go anywhere near the things that stretched back as far as she could perceive, but her trained instincts told her that it was the direction she would have to take if she was to find Cordelia.*

*She was still reluctant to move, but she found she had no choice in the matter. The instant she knew what direction to take, a golden path preceded her, a shining tunnel into the zone of darkness. She found she had no need to make any effort of her own, the energy was being supplied by the eight women in the perfumed room in London. All she had to do was think it or need it and they provided, the only thing they could not give her was a means to locate Cordelia. For this she needed to rely on her own resources. She had to define a way to recognize the mind-flare of Cordelia's power, and so far she had detected nothing. This was, of course, assuming that Cordelia was conscious, functioning, alive, and capable of a flare. This manifestation of the Other Place was so unlike anything that Jesamine had ever encountered before that she was less than certain she would recognize it even if it presented itself. She was both protected and concealed by the golden light around her, but she was also aware that she was looking through it, and the possibility had to be taken into account that she was perceiving everything as if through a distorting lens or an unaccustomed filter.*

*This moment of doubt and concern caused a side-slipping yaw in her basic paranormal equilibrium. Think it or need it and it will be supplied. Jesamine was being supported. She had help and she needed to trust that help. She blanked her mind of all concerns regarding how and what was happening to her, and how the present reality functioned.*

*"I simply have to find Cordelia."*

*In the vision of an instant, perhaps a nanosecond, she was beside a tranquil lake and a light wind breathed through stands of birch, and brought her the voice of Oonanchek. "The* Quodoshka *will be with you."*

*Again she made the mistake of questioning. Was his voice a prompted memory or was he somehow in contact with her? Which, in itself, was a pointless paradox, because she had no idea of how time might or might not function in this place, and the pointlessness for a moment sent her spinning sideways, until the golden light righted her and even, momentarily, took her to a warm place where her hands were bound with a scarlet cord, and the pale shape of a loping wolf was moving away into the golden distance.*

*"Wait!"*

*The golden wolf halted and turned. "You only have to follow."*

*The wolf had the voice of Jack Kennedy and Jesamine shuddered. The lake was gone and so was the light; she was plunging through a threatening purple cloud with bursts of black all round her, plunging headlong from a great height. Did the enemy already have her? Were the Zhaithan, or Jeakqual-Ahrach herself, or unknown evils from this reality already coming at her through her own memory?*

*"You only have to follow."*

*Again Jesamine slowed her thoughts and cleared her mind. She immediately heard the voice of Magachee. "It's the questions that make you fall. My darling Jesamine, stop looking down. Do not grieve. Simply act."*

*The wolf was again looking back at her, with knowing eyes. "We will make our own Quodoshka."*

*"I'm following you."*

*She was instantly in a new and very total realism. She and the wolf walked on the dirty, oil-slick waters of a befouled river. The banks were lined with blackened ruins, in which small children kept watch, some armed with muskets and crossbows and others manning catapults and ballistae. A low, flat-bottomed barge was drifting towards them, and, on the deck, near the vessel's blunt prow, Cordelia stood with a group of people. She looked tired and pale, wore tear-streaked brothel-clown makeup, and was wrapped in a disreputable black coat in which, under more normal circumstances, she would never have been caught dead. Could it be that easy? Had Jesamine really been brought to her missing companion with so little effort? The water around her heaved and boiled for a moment, and the golden wolf looked at her reproachfully. "Questions?"*

*"I'm sorry."*

*"Make contact. We are exposed here and cannot stay."*

*Jesamine projected. "Cordelia?"*

*On the boat, Cordelia twitched, but none of those around her gave any sign of having noticed. "Cordelia, it's me. I was sent to find you."*

*Jesamine could sense that Cordelia was tired and had to make an effort to direct her thoughts. "Jesamine. Is that really you?"*

*"I was sent to find you."*

*"Are the others here?"*

*"There's no time to explain. They are helping me. Where is this place? Where are you?"*

"This is Paris."

*"Paris?"*

"Don't ask."

*"Who are these people?"*

"Are you going back?"

*"I'm not really here."*

"Tell the others, and Windermere, that I am the prisoner of a woman called Sera Falconetti. And Jesamine . . ."

"*Yes.*"

"Please get me out of here."

## CORDELIA

"The first thing you have to remember, Lady Blakeney, is that the way of thinking here is probably very different from anything you're used to. In Paris, everything is relative and everything is variable. This is a den of thieves, heretics, aberrations; a place that shouldn't exist, and is therefore very different from those that have a more conventional raison d'être. On any given day we are the enemy of the Mosul, and yet, the same night, they may turn out to be our partners in crime."

Cordelia looked hard at the man who acted as though he was king. "So, if it suited you, you'd give me up to them?"

Damon Falconetti laughed, flashing a mouthful of gold teeth. Sera Falconetti's father had a deep booming laugh that echoed around the venerable stone walls of the room, and perfectly matched his bearlike physique. "Of course. In an instant. That hardly needs stating."

"It doesn't make me very comfortable."

"I'm sure you're well aware that your comfort is a very minor concern, and it certainly isn't why you were brought here."

"So why was I brought here? Someone seems to have gone to a great deal of trouble."

"You are here because you are an asset, and like other assets you can be bought, sold, traded, given in tribute, or bestowed as a gift in return for favors. You can also be held onto and preserved in the hope that you will attract other assets to you."

In fact, although Cordelia would never have admitted it, she was not, right at that moment, at all uncomfortable. She sipped her tiny cup of thick, sweet Ankara coffee and bit into another of the small, sticky honey and almond pastries, happy in her secret that the rest of The Four at least knew where she was. As far as she could see, Damon Falconetti lived in a manner that was piratical and untidy, but opulently lavish. Her guess was that the large chamber Damon Falconetti and his gang used as a banqueting hall and throne room had once been part of the old-time Parisian sewer system. Despite the tapestries and brocades, the satin pillows and velvet drapes, and the fine, if ill-assorted furniture, the sense was of a brigand's lack of permanence, and that Falconetti *père* and the men and women of his crew could have everything packed, cleared, and the stronghold vacated at a moment's notice, without so much as a backward glance, should the situation call for a rapid escape.

Damon Falconetti was apparently in a talkative mood, which made a refreshing change after all the silence and secrecy to which Cordelia had been subjected. He gestured to one of the henchmen gathered around him. "Take old Temps Perdu here." A small sinewy man with wrinkled leathery skin and a network of scars down the left side of his face grinned and raised a silent thumb to identify himself, then went back to the turkey leg he was gnawing on with intense concentration. "Old Temps had seen it all. He survived the uprising at Loudon, and then escaped the massacres that followed, only to find himself impressed into the 101st Provincials and shipped off to the African front to do battle with the Zulus under Cetshwayo, arriving right on time for the debacle at Mubende which turned out to be the worst Mosul defeat since they were routed at Volgograd by Joseph the Terrible."

Falconetti the father was drinking what Cordelia recognized as the finest de Richelieu cognac and paused to refill his antique balloon glass. "Now, Lady Blakeney, you might think, by this point, that Old Temps would be more than ready to jack it in and die, but oh no. Not him. *Mais non.*"

Old Temps Perdu shook his head. "Not me. *Mais non.*" He tossed the turkey bone to a waiting wolfhound, who seemed disappointed at the lack of meat left on it and treated him to a look of canine reproach as Damon Falconetti resumed his story. "Somehow he contrives to be one of just twenty who the Zulu take alive, and, moreover, he even manages to convince the officers of the Impi who captured him that he's nothing less than a Mosul master gunner, which greatly interests the commanding general, because he had just captured a field-full of Mosul cannon and, as anyone who's faced them is well aware, your Zulus may be deadly hand-to-hand killers, but they have something of a problem with artillery, and are pretty much unable to hit the side of a hill at two hundred feet with a muzzle-loading howitzer. More by luck and unmitigated gall than any skill, judgment, or calculation, Old Temps does manage to hit the side of a hill with a howitzer, and, instead of being impaled up the jacksie on a large and lethal stake like the rest of his comrades, such being the Zulu way of it, he is put in charge of a detachment of artillery."

Damon Falconetti extended the bottle of cognac towards Cordelia. She nodded and he filled her glass. Falconetti was dressed in the uniform coat of a ranking officer in an army that probably no longer existed, with a barrel chest full of decorations that she suspected he might well have awarded himself. Under the tunic, he cut a dash with a flowing dress shirt and leather riding pants with buckles down the outside of the leg. Cordelia sipped her brandy, because the story of Old Temps Perdu was not yet over. "So everything might have been well and good, and Perdu might have become a Zulu national hero with fucking statues of him all over Soweto, but he got a little too good at what he was doing and found himself running the guns on a Zulu trireme. The galley was sunk by Caribbean privateers and he found himself fished out of the drink and sold in the slave market in Marseilles, from which he managed to escape, and ultimately wound up here in Paris. Isn't that true, Perdu?"

Old Temps Perdu nodded and reached for the cognac. "Every word, boss, give or take?"

Cordelia smiled as though highly entertained. "And the moral of the story?"

"The moral, Lady Blakeney? The moral is that everything and anything, absolutely without exception, is capable of changing when the times demand it."

Cordelia observed that the senior Falconetti had called her "Lady Blakeney" three times, and seemed impressed by titles. She noted that for further use.

Although she had not slept, Cordelia felt considerably better than she had since she had so unwillingly been removed from the driveway at Deerpark. Since she arrived in Paris, she had been allowed to bathe, and

Sera Falconetti had lent her a change of clean clothes that actually fitted her, and then, dressed in a pair of snugly-fitting cotton pants and a loose silk shirt with flowing sleeves, she had been brought to Falconetti Sr., who had wined and dined her and treated her to his most amusing and informative discourses. She had hardly minded that some verged on the self-indulgent and long-winded. Paris was not as daunting as it had seemed when the big black Benz had stopped beside the dirty, mist-shrouded river in the very first light of a grim, gray dawn, and she had been transferred by Sera and her two male companions to the flat-bottomed barge that seemed to be the favored mode of transport in the ruined and partially flooded city.

As she had stood near the bow of the barge, cold, scared, and miserable, hunched in the old greatcoat that was a leftover from a Boulogne brothel, she had wondered if drowning herself in filthy, scum-covered water might be a better option than facing whatever horror presented itself next. Cordelia had been in tight spots before, but had never previously contemplated suicide. Later she would explain her near-terminal despair to herself as a result of being in multiple shock from the death of Jack Kennedy, her own kidnapping, and the frightening encounter with the White Twins beside the huge Amiens Pyramid. Not to mention the lingering effects of absinthe, chloroform, and benodex. Cordelia, however, was hard to keep down. The barge had floated between the blackened Parisian ruins, and she had found herself once again starting to take notice of her surroundings, if for no other reason than the city, although supposedly destroyed, was very much alive.

The first thing to present itself was what Cordelia called the writing on the wall. The blasted and soot-encrusted surfaces of the ruins that faced the river were daubed with complex layers of whitewashed graffiti. Cordelia could see words and slogans in a half dozen languages, and also texts and ideograms that were totally indecipherable, and probably invented or deliberately abstract. Representative art came in the form of monotone murals, often unfinished, and mostly vivid with violence or inventively pornographic, some crude but others executed with a high, if primitive, skill. As they moved deeper into the devastation, she started to see people. At first, it was children, which surprised Cordelia. She had not considered kids living in such a place, but on reflection it made sense. They were lean and dirty, ragged, and strangely silent. They stood or sat immobile, keeping watch on the river. Some, dressed in bits and pieces of ancient and discarded uniforms, cradled weapons like a juvenile guerrilla army: long-barreled muskets, crossbows, and single shot, flintlock pistols. One crew manned a primitive but effect catapult, capable of hurling quite large chucks of masonry, while two older boys leaned on the rude mounting of an antique three-inch brass cannon. The spectacle had been so eerie and menacing that Cordelia had turned to Sera and questioned her about it. "The children are the city guards, the watch on the Seine?"

Sera had shaken her head and shrugged. "Those are the *petits,* the little 'uns. The ones who've made it their mission to man the approaches. More kids come here than adults; all the runaways from all over the province and even farther. And they're one fuck of a lot harder to handle than the grownups, because the Zhaithan don't want the second and third generation subjects learning to read and write if they can help it. I guess that's one of the advantages of the gangs. If the kids attach themselves to a gang, they at least get some kind of education that stops them from turning feral."

"They're scary, so quiet and still."

"That's the mudlarks and river rats. They're the kind of predators who watch and wait. I mean, all *les enfants* are predators of one form or another, but most are more boisterous about it. The hardest thing with this lot is to stop them killing the Mosul agents when they come in to trade."

"What about us? Suppose they take a dislike to this boat?"

"They know enough not to fuck with me and mine."

"They still look scary."

Sera glanced up at the silent children once more. This time, she was not so dismissive. "I must admit that they have been looking a tad more scary of late. There are even rumors going around the city that the rejects from the breeding program were being dumped here to fuck with us."

"What?" The words breeding program had instantly snagged her interest.

"Supposedly the Zhaithan have been shipping them in and letting them go at the outskirts of the city. Seeing if they can make their way to the inhabited sections."

"What breeding program?"

Sera was surprised. "You never heard of the breeding program?"

"There are a lot of things I seem not to have heard of."

"That's something else we have to talk about later. Probably after my father has had his say."

Cordelia allowed herself to become just a little aloof and resentful. "I'll hold myself in readiness."

The exchange had, however, lifted Cordelia's spirits, and restored more of her hallmark resilience. While still reserving judgment, she accepted that all Sera had said tended to confirm she was more than just the helpless hostage. Indeed, by the time she had considered most of the implications, she was so well recovered that, when out of nowhere, she had heard Jesamine's unmistakable accent inside her head, she did not immediately break down in screaming horror.

*"Cordelia, it's me. I was sent to find you."*

The fleeting image of a golden wolf appeared for a moment, standing impossibly on the surface of the river. For an instant, Cordelia did reel, but she rapidly recovered, even remembering to focus hard and communicate without speaking or even moving her lips. "Jesamine. Is that really you?"

*"I was sent to find you."*

"Are the others here?"

*"There's no time to explain. They are helping me. Where is this place? Where are you?"*

"This is Paris."

*"Paris?"*

"Don't ask."

It wasn't until they were almost done that Sera Falconetti noticed something, but assumed that Cordelia was merely showing signs of wear and tear. "Are you okay?"

As the whisper of Jesamine departed, Cordelia put a modestly dramatic hand to her brow. "I suddenly felt a little faint. Today came with a sizeable helping of wear and tear."

In fact, Cordelia was feeling quite reinvigorated. Word of her location had been passed, and the others were free. They hadn't been kidnapped as well, and were seemingly addressing the problem. She was also fascinated by the vision of the golden wolf on the water. Maybe Jesamine had learned a thing or two while she'd been screwing around with the Ohio. What did they call things like the wolf? A *Quodoshka*?

Sera seemed to buy her charade of fragility and debilitation, and made her voice reassuringly concerned. "Don't worry, we'll be in the underworld in a moment, and not far from where we're going. When we get there, you'll be able to clean up and rest for a while."

Only minutes later the barge negotiated the slime-covered broken piles and fallen spans of a collapsed bridge, and turned against the current to pass through a broken arch into a dark and vaulted tunnel that must have also once been part of the Parisian sewer system. For a few minutes they were in semidarkness, only able to see little more than the silhouettes of each other, but very aware of splashings, scuttlings, murmurs, movements, all around them; but then they rounded a bend and into what had to be a main thoroughfare in this demolished outlaw city. A missing section of roof let in broad shafts of daylight, and other areas were lit by burning torches and braziers. The barge was floating through a continuous traffic of rowboats, dinghies, canoes, even circular coracles moving around and between more barges like the one they were on. Cordelia was surprised that so much travel was by water. Later she would learn that most of inhabited Paris was reached by boat, and that the operational sections of the city were the archipelago of tiny islands formed when, during the bombardment, the banks of the Seine had completely collapsed. Even after so many years, urban explorers and sewer-rat garbage prospectors would break into a previously sealed area, and find burned skeletons and even mummified bodies, undisturbed since the original Mosul firestorm.

A raised flagstone walkway, like a broad sidewalk, ran along one side of the water. Thronged with people, it offered all the fun of a ragged but energetic fair. An extensive and comprehensive flea market was in full swing, and Cordelia saw merchants conducting trade from behind booths and stalls, and even from blankets laid out on the flags. The fastest and most popular trade was in food and provisions, and, although standards of cleanliness and public health might not have measured up to London or Albany, customers lined up at the stalls of the bakers and butchers, the men and women selling relatively fresh produce, and even crowded round the vendors of decidedly dubious-looking canned goods. Food was not all that was on sale. An elderly man handed out dusty bottles of wine in exchange for what looked like goodly sums in coins and some kind of script. An armorer made deals on carefully restored swords and firearms. Racks of used clothing were pawed through and inspected for bargains, and still more tradesmen hawked tools, household goods, trinkets, while an apothecary presided over pills, potions, and powders in an array of bottles and jars. Wandering musicians, one playing an inevitable saccharine accordion, plus jugglers, a fire-eater, a man with a performing dog, another with a monkey, and a variety of low-level bawds and prostitutes moved through the more mundane buying and selling, offering their more exotic goods and services. Cordelia had to assume that a covert contingent of pickpockets was also working the multitude, while those who did not perform, fuck, or steal, wagered and gambled. During their short progress down the underground waterway, she noticed two crap games and a three-card, spot-the-lady table.

The barge approached a jetty that was guarded by a trio of armed and heavyset men. Ropes were thrown, and the vessel quickly secured. As soon as they stepped ashore, one of the guards informed Sera that she and Cordelia should make themselves presentable for her father. Stone side passages and a flight of medieval spiral stairs led to what turned out to be the Falconetti family's quarters, which proved luxurious in the extreme compared to what Cordelia had seen of the rest of the city. In most things, Sera had been as good as her word, but in the promise of resting for a while, she underestimated her father's impatience. Cordelia had barely been given time to wash off the streaked whorehouse makeup and scramble into a quick change of clothes before being brought to the lair of Falconetti senior.

By the time she had listened to all of Damon Falconetti's stories, plus an analysis of the Parisian gang structure, and how a long history of bloody family vendettas had only been brought to an end a few years earlier by a set of laboriously negotiated treaties, she was starting to feel the cognac weighing heavy on her eyelids. Maybe because she was tired, and also a little drunk, Cordelia made her first serious misstep. "So that was when Il Syndicato was formed?"

Falconetti's face darkened. The others in the room fell silent, and exchanged glances as he stared hard at Cordelia. "Il Syndicato?"

Cordelia was nervous and knew that it showed. "Did I say something wrong. I was only repeating what I heard."

"There is no such thing as Il Syndicato."

"I'm sorry."

"Do you understand that?"

"Yes, I do."

Falconetti repeated the words like a mantra. "There is no such thing as Il Syndicato."

"I can only apologize again."

"Repeat it for me."

"There is no such thing as Il Syndicato."

"It is an invention of the Norse newspapers. It sounds exciting and theatrical, but it is a fanciful fiction, and that's another way of saying it's bullshit. You'd do well to remember that."

"I will."

Then a slight twinkle wavered at the corner of Falconetti's eye. "That's not to say that there isn't a degree of organization."

"Oh course not. I could see that by the way I was brought here."

Old Temps Perdu actually smiled as Falconetti continued. "If some minimal accord had not been created, the gangs of Paris would be at each other's throats with axes and butcher knives like they were in the old days, planting nailbombs and creating royal fucking mayhem. We'd be decimating each other until there were so few of us, the fucking Mosul could walk in and clean out those that were left with half a regiment of raw recruits." A number of the henchmen nodded in agreement. "Damn right."

"I heard that the last time the Mosul came in here, you poisoned the Seine."

Now Falconetti actually smiled. "We threatened to poison the Seine.

That was enough for them. Plus, we made them aware just how much they needed us. Where else were they going to get their scotch, and their drugs, and the A-list whores?"

At the phrase, "A-list whores," one of the women in the background giggled. Falconetti glanced at her, but then turned back to Cordelia. "Once, of course, some kind of rough and ready common purpose, and sense of mutual interests had been established in Paris, it only made sense to put out feelers to the other centers where the Mosul don't have complete control. We'd be fools not to cooperate with the Lorenzo of Naples, or Van Cleef in Amsterdam, or form links with Palermo, and the one who likes to call himself The Sicilian. It has also, on occasion, been to our advantage for strangers and civilians to believe in such a thing as Il Syndicato, but there is no secret society with members spread across the Empire. So you see, Lady Blakeney, you really shouldn't come walking in here, talking of things you know nothing about."

Cordelia noticed that Falconetti was calling her "Lady Blakeney" again, and she took this as an indication that her faux pas had been forgiven. On the other hand, she could not fathom Falconetti's sudden anger, or even if it was real, or part of some devious charade. All she could do was bow her head and wait and see. "I'll try not to do such a thing again."

Falconetti seemed mollified, but then proceeded to take her completely by surprise. "I imagine you would like to know why you were brought to me?"

After waiting so long, and having been through so much, with no explanation so much as offered, the sudden blunt statement took Cordelia by surprise and she had to maintain tight control to not blurt the obvious reply. "Very much indeed."

Falconetti smiled. He seemed to relish keeping Cordelia off balance. "You're a very popular young woman, Lady Blakeney."

"That's flattering."

"Perhaps not in this instance. When it became known that you and your three companions were coming to England, a price was put on your head."

Cordelia was suddenly very cautious. "A price?"

"In fact, a number of interested parties made offers for the four of you, both dead and alive."

"I seem to still be alive."

"Indeed you are, but that is only because the more deadly offer was vetoed."

"I suppose I should be grateful for that."

"Perhaps not. The contract on your life and the lives of your companions was solicited by Zhaithan intelligence."

"I see."

"But it was vetoed by Her Grand Eminence Jeakqual-Ahrach."

"She wanted us alive?"

"She made it an inviolable edict."

Previously Cordelia had been nervous, but now she was terrified. "So after all the stories and cognac, you're going to hand me over to Jeakqual-Ahrach?"

Falconetti laughed and shook his head. "Even I am not that gratuitously cruel."

"You'd go against Her Grand Eminence?"

"That's the rules of trade. Her offer was more than matched by a party with whom I was far more comfortable doing business."

"And are you going to tell me who that might be?"

"I can do better than that." Damon Falconetti gestured to a short man with shaved eyebrows, an upper body covered in tattoos, and a broken nose with a steel spike through it, who stood by the entrance to the room, leaning casually, but definitely on guard."

"Ask the client to come in, Bonaparte."

Bonaparte nodded and gestured to somewhere beyond. Then, to Cordelia's stunned amazement, Harriet Lime walked into the room. She was wearing an extremely sexy and formfitting adaptation of a standard aviator's outfit, and seemed highly amused by Cordelia's reaction. "Well, Cordelia, my darling, I would seem to be the one who made the winning bid in the Falconetti auction."

For Cordelia, this was the final straw. Had she been the fainting type, she would have swooned dead away. As it was, her jaw dropped and she knew she must be babbling. "How can you be here? I left you in London. I left you at Deerpark."

"And rather rudely, I might add."

"But how can you physically be here. How did you get across the Channel and through Mosul territory?"

Harriet Lime replied as though the answer was obvious. "The Black Airship."

Cordelia didn't want to even speculate what the Black Airship might be. Instead, she half rose. "So am I rescued? Can you get me out of here? I need to get back to the others."

Harriet Lime gestured for her to sit. "You are perfectly safe here. The Falconettis and I have an understanding. All you have to do is relax and wait. The others are coming to you."

## ARGO

"Cordelia is in Paris and being held by Il Syndicato?"

"Unless what I went through was some bizarre hallucination."

"It makes no sense."

Windermere held up a hand. "In some respects, she's safer there than she might be here."

Raphael's expression was grim. "The fact that she's there clearly proves she wasn't being protected here."

Jesamine agreed. "And the same goes for the rest of us. There's been all this talk about security, and we've seen all these shows of force like the gun crew on the back of the damned train, but Jack is dead, Cordelia is in the hands of Frankish gangsters, and no one else seems to know or care what happens to the rest of us. We're stranded in Norse jurisdiction, and we don't have a clue what to do about it. If it wasn't for Cordelia, I'd say we should get on board the *Constellation* or any other ship bound for the Americas, and get the fuck back to Albany."

Raphael and Jesamine were ganging up on Windermere, and Argo was more than content to let it happen. The only problem was that, in their anger and confusion, they weren't listening to what Windermere had to say, and leaving him to ask the relevant questions. "What do you mean she may be safer there than she is here?"

This at least stopped them temporarily, and gave Windermere a chance to answer. "I think we're all agreed that the greatest threat to Cordelia, and the rest of you, is Jeakqual-Ahrach. Apart from a small handful of people, some of whom are in this room, the Norse have hardly heard about Jeakqual-Ahrach, and those who have hardly see her as a threat."

The room in question was a small sitting room on the ground floor of Deerpark, and in addition to Argo, Jesamine, Raphael, and Windermere, Anastasia de Wynter and a woman called Hortense made up the small private meeting that now followed the ritual. Argo could feel the anger that was building inside Raphael and Jesamine, if for no other reason than it completely matched his own. The greatest frustration was that, with Cordelia missing, they could no longer function as The Four, and they were all starting to see themselves as nothing more than moving targets. These perceptions were closely rivaled, however, by the strong sense that they were at the mercy of a Norse bureaucracy that had already allowed Jack Kennedy to be shot to death, and had little idea of the game that was being played, let alone the stakes that might be involved. Argo knew that it was hardly fair for them to be venting their discontent on Gideon Windermere, but he was, unfortunately, the only representative of the Norse security machine they had to hand. Argo was quite surprised at how calm the man remained as he attempted to explain the background of the latest developments.

"The situation of the Falconetti Family and the other gangs in Paris is complicated. They are an outlaw enclave deep inside the Mosul Empire. The popular wisdom is that the Falconetti, and the rest of Il Syndicato, will do absolutely anything for anyone for a price. What the popular wisdom overlooks is that, at the same time, they, even though they do constant business with the Mosul through smuggling and the black market, are also in a continuous guerrilla war with them."

De Wynter intervened on Windermere's behalf, appealing to their different memories of surviving under the Mosul. She sat deep in the room's most commanding leather armchair, with a Russe lamp beside her. "You've all learned the hard way how all these multiple levels of corruption exist in the occupied territories."

Windermere took a deep breath and resumed. "Let me give you an example. Richthofen, the head of aviation research for Aschenbach, has a standing offer to any pilot who will fly an Odin Mk 5 biplane over to Mosul territory. If Richthofen's technicians could back-engineer one of those babies, they could go into production, and have their own air power inside of six months. And the day the Mosul have air power will be the day when the NU finally goes to war. Falconetti could have organized the theft of an Odin by now. He more than has the resources. But he hasn't done it. Why not? Because he knows if the Mosul have aircraft, they can bomb him out of Paris anytime they want. It really isn't all about the money."

Jesamine frowned doubtfully. "There are those claiming that Il Syndicato put together Jack's assassination, so it couldn't be traced directly back to the Mosul and create an international incident."

Windermere sighed and nodded. "That's one of the theories going round. Of course, it doesn't account for the one whose brain melted; but, if they did, it wouldn't be the first time that they took a contract for the Mosul that would give the bastards plausible deniability."

"And these are the people who have Cordelia?"

Windermere was looking tired. "Personally I don't believe that the Falconetti Family arranged Jack Kennedy's death."

"No?"

"That's not to say that, if they knew the assassination was a done deal and unstoppable, they might not have come up with the weapons or the transport for a price. But to kill the Prime Minister of Albany in the heart of London? I don't think so. First they wouldn't go for it, and second they don't have the organization to see it through."

De Wynter again helped out. "Or melt one of the assassin's brains."

Jesamine was far from satisfied. "If Il Syndicato are happy to work for the Mosul, what's to stop this Falconetti handing Cordelia over to the Zhaithan if the price was right?"

Windermere shook his head. "I know for a fact he won't do that."

Jesamine didn't believe him. "What do you mean, you know? How can you know? I just made contact with Cordelia."

Raphael stared angrily at Windermere. "Are you telling us you knew up front that Falconetti was going to lift Cordelia?"

"Before you all arrived in Bristol, a report came in from one of our agents that a price had been offered for one or more of you."

"What?"

"We had a report that Falconetti had been approached by Zhaithan intelligence to kill or capture the four of you, but he turned it down."

"But they took her anyway."

"So it would seem."

"So if he's not turning her over to the Zhaithan, who did he lift her for?"

"I can't tell you that."

Jesamine was on her feet. "What do you mean you can't tell us? We're the ones potentially being fucked here."

Finally Windermere lost his temper. "I mean I can't tell you because I give my agents the same respect I give you, and I'm out on a fucking limb for you four already."

Jesamine snarled at Windermere. "You're the one that left her on her own the night she vanished."

Now Argo stood up, raising both hands. "Okay, everyone fucking hold it. This is getting us nowhere. What we need to do now is figure out how we rescue Cordelia. How we transport ourselves to Paris with enough intelligence and muscle to get her out of there."

## CORDELIA

Cordelia woke from a sleep that had not been totally dreamless, but in which the dreams had been pleasant and trivial, and not haunted by any wraiths either from her own subconscious, or sent from outside. This came as a considerable relief because it made it easier to handle the lurching instant of disorientation that came with waking in the dark, and having no idea where she was, or how she got there. Then she touched the fur of the bedcover, and it all came rushing back. How, exhausted and more than a little drunk, she had been helped by Sera Falconetti to the stone-walled bedchamber, and into the antique four-poster bed. What proved a little more difficult to grasp was the fact that someone seemed to be sliding into bed beside her, and that this might be what had woken her. The only response was to sit up, blinking, with a bleary demand. "What the fuck do you think you're doing?"

"Sssssh."

"What . . ."

"It's only me, Cordelia. Come to show you that there are no hard feelings."

A naked and definitely female body was moving close to her. "Harriet? Harriet Lime?"

"Who did you think it was?"

A hand was on her thigh and another stroked her shoulder and the back of her neck. Warm, perfumed breath was close to her face. It all felt very sexy and comforting, but Cordelia was too surprised and confused to respond, whether she wanted to or not. She blinked again, just about able to make out Harriet Lime's face, near to her own in the darkness. "I thought you might feel like finishing what we started at Deerpark. Now I own you, and you can't run away."

"You come to me like this, after you made a deal to have me kidnapped?"

"That was just politics, my darling. We had to get you out of London."

The hand stroking her thigh was very pleasant and comforting, and knew exactly what it was doing, but Cordelia was not quite ready to relax and enjoy it. "I really don't understand."

"Everything will be explained to you when Slide and the others get here."

"Slide is coming here?"

"Of course. And Argo and Raphael and Jesamine."

"I'm very confused."

Harriet Lime's voice was soothing, almost hypnotic. "Of course you are, my pet, but you're also tired and need to relax."

"Slide is coming here?"

"I just told you he was."

"When?"

"Very soon. In a day or so. No longer than that, and, until he does, we can make each other extremely happy."

In the previous thirty or so hours, Cordelia had been drunk, drugged, frightened, terrified, and then drunk again. Harriet Lime's hand was moving higher up her thigh. Cordelia let out a long surrendering sigh. She felt giddy and breathless, but in need of this soothing touch. Far worse things could be happening to her.

"Kiss me."

Their lips touched.

"Now kiss me again and I'll forgive you for the way you treated me before."

Cordelia kissed Harriet again, and her breathing quickened. "Oh, by the Goddess . . ."

Harriet Lime was gently stroking her breast. "By the Goddess indeed."

"There's something not right about this." But Cordelia reached for her anyway. She could feel athletic muscles under warm porcelain skin.

Harriet Lime positively purred. "Do you care?"

"Right now?"

"Right now."

"No."

## RAPHAEL

If Argo had not already managed to cool the brewing conflict between Jesamine and Windermere, the appearance of Garth would certainly have done it. Although Madame de Wynter's chauffeur/manservant/bodyguard entered the sitting room quietly and with due deference, his sheer size and appearance were enough to slow the rancor. "Madame?"

"Yes, Garth?"

"There is a reporter on the telephone."

"A reporter from where?"

"He says he is calling from the *News Chronicle*."

"He wants to speak to me?"

"He wants to speak to Major Jesamine. Seemingly the *Chronicle* wants to offer her money for what he kept referring to as her 'story.'"

Jesamine looked horrified and seemed about to choke, but de Wynter calmly gave Garth his instructions. "Tell the man from the *Chronicle* that the Major is not taking calls, and then take the telephone off its hook, please."

"Yes, madame."

"If anyone really needs to get us they can use the unlisted line."

"Yes, madame."

"And Garth . . ."

"Yes, madame."

"Have the early editions of the morning papers arrived?"

"They were delivered by cab a few minutes ago."

"When you've given the wretch from the *News Chronicle* his marching orders, bring them in, will you?"

"Yes, madame."

"And you'd better bring the good scotch. We may need it."

"Yes, madame."

Garth was gone for perhaps two minutes before he returned to the sitting room with a large tray on which was a neatly folded pile of most of the city's twelve morning papers, a cut glass whiskey decanter, and seven glasses. He set down the tray on a side table.

"You brought a glass for yourself?"

"Yes, madame."

Argo held up the cover of the *News Chronicle*. The headline blazed . . .

### KENNEDY GAL QUIZZED BY SPECIAL BRANCH

Jesamine gasped, and de Wynter shook her head. "It's worse than I imagined."

Argo glanced at Jesamine. "No wonder they wanted to buy your story."

Two pictures had been run side by side beneath the banner headline.

One was a formal portrait of Jack Kennedy that made him look distinguished, but a black border that indicated he was unmistakably dead. The other was a candid and lasciviously unflattering shot of Jesamine, obviously snapped by one of the mob of photographers on the Bristol pier. She was stumbling on her high heels, her uniform skirt had hiked up, exposing her long legs, and she was being pulled into the car by Jane Tennyson. The layout was arranged so Kennedy appeared to be posthumously staring at her legs. Argo read aloud. "The woman, known only as 'Major Jesamine,' but alleged to be the mistress of the Albany PM, was being kept under wraps by government officials even before the shooting."

Windermere leaned forward in his chair. "You Albany folk may get your second front if the *Morning Tribune* has its way." The headline on this paper was three huge letters and a question mark. . . .

## WAR?

Windermere read an excerpt. "Although no official statement has been made linking the Empire of Hassan to the killing, Khurshid Nawaz, the Mosul chargé d'affaires in London, is being held under house arrest as the massive investigation into the assassination of Albany Prime Minister John Kennedy moves beyond the dead assassins, and focuses on possible darker forces behind the scenes. Sir Harry Palmer, the commander of the Metropolitan Constabulary Special Branch, was quoted as saying, "Excellency Nawaz is only being held for his own protection . . . blah, blah, blah . . ."

Windermere stopped as Jesamine suddenly sobbed. She had found the *Morning Examiner*. That too had a one-word headline . . .

## CARNAGE!

Most of the page, however, was taken up by a huge grainy photograph of Jack Kennedy's corpse sprawled in the wreckage of the ruined carriage, legs twisted, arms outflung, just as Raphael remembered him, except the blood that covered his head and soaked his clothes was turned a horrible inky black by the monochrome print and cheap paper. Dawson's dead hand was in the very bottom of the frame. Raphael remembered how the policemen had pulled Argo and Jesamine off the photographer. He should have moved in and smashed the camera. Sir Harry Palmer's damned detectives had confiscated his and Argo's guns, but hadn't bothered to seize the exposed plate from the man's camera. Now the hideous image would be part of history forever. He definitely should have smashed the camera.

Jesamine was sitting stiffly, tears rolling down her face. De Wynter glanced at Garth. "Garth . . ."

"Yes, madame."

"You'd better pour the scotch."

"Yes, madame."

Jesamine spoke very softly. "We have to get out of this fucking country. We have to go. We have to get Cordelia and . . ."

"And?"

Jesamine shook her head. "I don't know. I don't really know. All I do know is that, if we stay here, the newspapers alone will make it impossible for us to go anywhere except into hiding, and that, I swear to the Goddess, is not why I fucking came here."

Raphael spoke for both himself and Argo. "It wasn't why any of us fucking came here."

Garth handed him a scotch. Raphael drank a little and shook his head. He had been trying to duck the thought, but it refused to be avoided. "It's happening again, isn't it."

Argo looked at Raphael doubtfully. Windermere was watching intently. "What are you saying?"

"A force is acting on us again."

"A force?"

"We're being moved to the Land of the Franks aren't we? It's all happening again."

Jesamine slowly turned her head in Raphael's direction. She had stopped crying. "I know what you mean. Like when we came together in the first place. We didn't have a choice, we were pulled like a fucking magnet."

"And it's happening again, except everything is pulling us to the south, to the Frankish Territories."

Argo still wasn't getting it. "How do you figure that? Okay, so Cordelia's in Paris and we have to get her out of there, but that's hardly any mystic pressure. Unless there's something I haven't heard about."

"There may be something none of us has heard about."

Windermere and de Wynter remained silent. Garth stood in the background. Raphael took a deep breath. "So much had been happening that I didn't think of it until just now, until Jesamine found Cordelia in Paris."

"What?"

"At the reception, at the Palace of Westminster, I met a Caribbean called Country Man."

Windermere nodded. "We know Country Man."

Raphael continued. "He said something was being built in the Frankish Territories. He talked about stonework and slave laborers. 'Big magick' he called it. 'Real big magick.' He thought it might be a power source, or some kind of weapon, and that the Ahrachs are behind it. I tried to get more out of him a little later, but he near as dammit blanked me."

"Country Man can be a tease. He's his own manipulator."

Jesamine looked at Windermere. "Did you know about this thing being built?"

Windermere met her gaze, but only after a brief hesitation. "We've had reports. There's definitely something going on in the Frankish countryside near Amiens."

Argo caught the hesitation. "Is it connected with Cordelia's kidnap, or the White Twins?"

This time Windermere met him head on. "It could be. We honestly don't know."

"Why didn't you tell us sooner?"

"I would imagine for the same reason Raphael didn't tell you about Country Man's story. There's been one fuck of lot going on to keep us distracted."

Surprisingly, Jesamine accepted this without question. "That's true enough."

Argo leaned back in his chair and held up his glass. Garth poured him a refill without a word. "Seems like the next line is 'so what the fuck do we do about all this?' "

Raphael nodded. "That also is the fucking truth."

Jesamine thought for a few moments and then began to offer a bitter summation. "As things stand, we make our way to the coast, we acquire a boat, we row or sail it across the English Channel, we infiltrate a heavily defended enemy coast, we hike however far it is to a ruined city, we find Cordelia, rescue her from well-organized gangsters, and then do the whole thing all over again in reverse. Which would put us back in the NU just in time for me to be questioned again by Sir Harry fucking Palmer as 'the Kennedy Gal.' Can anyone come up with something better than that?"

Windermere smiled. His first in a long time. "I think I can."

Jesamine regarded him coolly. "Then I would really like to hear about it."


## CORDELIA

Sera Falconetti found them intertwined, naked under the fur cover. "You two make a pretty picture."

Cordelia had been dozing in the pleasant aftermath of a long sleep and was not at all happy for the world to intrude so soon. "Make it all go away."

Sera sat down on the bed, wide awake and businesslike. "Sadly it won't."

Harriet Lime opened her eyes, took it all in, and immediately sat up. "Good morning." Without waiting for a response, she sprang quickly from the bed, naked, cold, and in a hurry. "I have to go to the privy."

She vanished into a rough-cut hole in the stone. Too ragged and irregular to hang a door, it was covered by a blanket. The blanket closed behind Lime, and, moments later, Cordelia and Sera head the sound of running water, splashes and gasps, then Lime's muffled voice. "This water is fucking freezing."

"What do you expect in Paris?" Sera glanced at Cordelia, and deliberately lowered her voice. "I see you picked a simple and efficient way to keep watch on Mme. Lime."

Was Cordelia being enlisted as an ally? "You think Mme. Lime needs watching?"

"Let's just say that she charms my father, but I try not to turn my back on her."

The splashing went on and on, as did the gasps. Cordelia frowned. "Does she do that every morning?"

Sera nodded. "She's very hygienic. I didn't know you . . . how shall I put it?"

Cordelia sighed. She felt better than she probably deserved. "There are men and there are women, my dear Sera."

"But women understand some tricks that really please."

"I think Mme. Lime has actually invented some that are totally original."

Sera nodded. "I know."

Cordelia was pulled up short. "Oh."

Sera smiled. "She can be very persuasive."

Before Sera could say more, Harriet Lime came back, wearing a floral silk robe of oriental cut, and Cordelia wondered from where she could have obtained such a thing. It was, after all, Cordelia's room. Or was it? Was Lime the guest, and she merely the chattel? Harriet Lime went to a large chest and began sorting out clothes, but Sera turned in her direction. "Harriet."

"What?"

"Don't you think, before we go any further, we should maybe fill in Cordelia on why she's really here?"

Lime turned. "Maybe we should." She came back to the bed, still in her floral robe, and sat on the other side from Sera. "This will be something of a confession."

Cordelia gestured somewhat peremptorily to Lime. "Pass me a shirt, before any confessions, darling. Sitting here in the nude makes me feel like the naked hostage."

Lime didn't look too happy but did as she was told. As she shrugged into her shirt, Cordelia looked to Sera. "Is there any chance of a drink?"

Sera seemed to think it was a little early to start drinking. "How about coffee?"

Cordelia negotiated. "How about both?"

Sera shouted. "Bonaparte, get in here."

The small but decidedly intimidating Bonaparte entered. "Problem?"

"No problem, but do you think you could scare up a pot of coffee and a bottle?"

"Shouldn't be too hard."

As he left on his mission, Sera and Lime looked at each other, unsure of who should start. Finally Sera bit the bullet. "You have to realize an issue needed to be forced with the Norse, and unfortunately you were the most efficient lever we could find."

Cordelia frowned at Lime. "What do you mean, an issue forced with the Norse? You're the damned Norse."

Lime paused. "Well . . . not exactly."

"What?"

"I'm Morgana's Web. Not the same thing."

Sera shrugged. "And I'm Il Syndicato, even if daddy's old school, and bellows that there's no such thing."

Cordelia closed her eyes. "Oh shit. This is turning complex, right?"

"You saw what's going on at Amiens."

"I saw the pyramid."

"And it was something?"

"It was something."

"It could be anything, right?"

"Right."

"It could be mass mind control."

Lime chimed in. "Or a paranormal deathray."

Sera nodded. "The Zhaithan are putting so much into it, it has to be something. And even the Knights of the Rhine have become involved."

She and Lime were double-teaming Cordelia. "The Norse had to be forced to take it seriously."

"So you kidnapped me?"

Sera made the qualified admission. "Betting that the others would follow."

"We wanted all four of you."

Cordelia shook her head in disbelief. "Did you have to be so bloody drastic?"

Lime was defensive. "Would you have come into enemy territory on the say-so of some girl you were making out with at an orgy?"

"You could have made more orthodox contact and talked to the Four of us."

"There was so little time. You were hemmed in by the whole social thing, plus ham-handed Norse security, and then you'd be off to Stockholm. We formulated the whole thing in advance."

Sera joined in again. "But then Jack Kennedy was shot."

Cordelia halted the conversation. "Wait a minute. You're not going to tell me that shooting Jack was another part of getting Norse attention?"

Lime looked away. "There's always that possibility."

Sera was more direct. "If you're asking if we had anything to do with it, the answer is no."

"So who did?"

Lime met Cordelia's stare with a firm and level gaze. "We don't know." She still seemed uncomfortable, however. "There's some even blaming it on Albany."

Cordelia turned and addressed herself to Sera. Her voice was brittle. "You should know that assassinating their own leaders is a game for nations who are not at war. In wartime it's too much of a luxury."

At that moment, Bonaparte returned with a battered and blackened coffeepot, some tin mugs, and an unlabeled bottle of booze. "There's another wireless message from the Tower Room."

"Has it been decoded?"

Bonaparte nodded. "It has."

"You want to read it?"

The man frowned at Sera, and gestured to Cordelia. "In front of her?"

"She's being put in the picture."

"Does daddy know that?"

"Just fucking read the message, Bonaparte."

"Whatever you say, Mme. Sera. It reads 'The jade figurine is secured.'"

Sera groaned. "I thought you said it had been decoded."

Bonaparte poured coffee and handed a warm tin mug to Cordelia. "Down to the cryptogram."

"But I don't remember all the cryptograms."

Bonaparte handed a mug to Harriet Lime. "It means that everything is fixed and that Windermere is bringing the other three tonight."

Windermere? The revelations were coming so thick and fast that she almost spilled hot coffee on herself. "Gideon is involved in all this?"

Lime smiled. "He's in all this up to his superior neck. As is Anastasia de Wynter, and the whole ES Section."

Cordelia looked to Sera for confirmation. "The others are coming tonight?"

"That's apparently the message."

Harriet Lime's laugh was not altogether pleasant. "Ironic isn't it, Cordelia? The last time you saw Gideon Windermere, you were running after him, and away from me, and now he's coming to both of us."

## ARGO

For some miles the road had been following the river through low, level countryside, with the sea on the horizon, duplicating its meandering curves, except where they were cut short by low bridges. The air smelled of brine, and the seabirds waded in the mudflats that flanked the river. The Shoreham by Sea Air Station had been visible for some time before they reached it. Argo had stared out of the window of the official ES Section automobile for some time, watching the aircraft landing and taking off, and observing the flapping windsock, and how the giant hangars that housed the dirigibles dwarfed even the control tower, and all of the other buildings. Every so often, he would glance back to see if the other car from ES Section was following them. Argo was in the lead car with Windermere, Bowden Spinrad, and an ES driver, while Jesamine and Raphael, along with Madame de Wynter and Garth, followed in the second. They drove along the perimeter of the airfield for a full five minutes before they came to the main entrance to the base. A sign over the gate proudly announced NORSE AIR FORCE—SHOREHAM BY SEA AIR STATION—"SHIELD OF THE BLUE YONDER"—ALL VEHICLES MUST HALT FOR INSPECTION. Lower down, beside the gate, a much smaller sign read AIR NORSE—COMMERCIAL AVIATION. Argo knew that Air Norse was their destination, and what they intended to do there was very close to the edge of both Norse and international illegality.

As Windermere had explained, back in the sitting room at Deerpark, as they had formulated their plans. "We'll be fine as long as we don't run into anyone who outranks me. What we're doing is totally without the sanction of higher authority, but no colonel or under is going to check on that. No one is going to call Sir Harry to see if he has given permission for a secret flight into enemy territory, if for no other reason than it would compromise all plausible deniability."

Despite all the reassurances, however, Argo could feel the tension building inside him as their two cars slowed to a stop at the checkpoint beside the guardhouse, and a NAF sergeant, wearing the brassard of the Regimental Police, approached the car, while two airmen with Bergmans over their shoulders stood off at distance, but watched with care. Windermere glanced at Argo and spoke in a fast low tone. "Let me do all the talking. Just sit there and look snotty in your Albany battledress with all the brass buttons."

"I'll do my best."

The sergeant looked in the driver's window, and saw Windermere. He came to attention and saluted. "I'll have to see your papers, sir. Standing orders in the current emergency."

Windermere nodded. He had put on a fairly well-groomed uniform, and generally done his best to look like a colonel. "No problem, Sergeant. I think you'll find they are in order."

He handed a pouch of papers to the driver who, in turn, passed them to the sergeant, who leafed through them. "The Air Norse hangar, sir?"

"That's right."

"Been a lot of comings and goings there in the last few days, sir."

Windermere was gently chiding. "Loose lips, Sergeant."

The sergeant stiffened. "Yes, sir. Sorry, sir."

He handed the papers back the driver, who returned them to Windermere. Then the sergeant saved a little face by making an elaborate show of having the airmen lift the barrier, and waving the two automobiles through. The driver then put his foot down, and they raced across the short manicured grass of the air station towards one of the big hangars that housed the dirigibles. It was the farthest from the gate, painted drab gray and with the legend AIR NORSE painted on the side and on the sloping roof. They passed close to a workhorse Odin biplane taxiing to a parking area, and sped by a Marlborough three-engined transport and one of the new Mjölnir Bombers, both being refueled by a NAF ground crew, who looked up from what they were doing as the two cars sped past. The activity reminded Argo that Shoreham by Sea would be in the very front line if the Norse and the Mosul ever fully went to war, and that the base had been on full alert ever since the Kennedy assassination. The hangar for which they were heading maintained the pretense of being that of a commercial air transport operation that leased space on the otherwise exclusively military base, but this fiction was compromised by the fully manned gun pit, and the brand new, rotating .50 caliber Locksley gun, so state of the art that it had not even been supplied to the Army of Albany lest a copy fall into Mosul hands. The guncrew were taking no chances. They brought the Locksley to bear so the multiple muzzles were pointing at the first car, and kept it trained on the new arrivals until they rolled to a stop, and the passengers began to alight. The airmen behind the gun plainly recognized both Windermere and de Wynter, and snapped off smart salutes. Out from the confines of the car, Argo found a stiff sea breeze was blowing. De Wynter was carrying a parasol and had difficulty hanging on to it. He frowned and turned to Windermere. "Will we be able to fly in this wind?"

"The met office says it will ease off after sunset."

"I sure hope so. A weather delay is the last thing we need."

An armed airman guarded the small door in the much vaster one that could let in or out the dirigible itself. Windermere let de Wynter and Jesamine through first and then ushered Argo inside.

"Now for the final surprises."

The matte black bulk of the Black Airship was more a looming and overwhelming shock than a mere surprise. It rested inside the enormous hangar, barely touching the ground, like a leviathan in its lair, but dull and featureless, almost a vast teardrop hole in space. It was by no means Argo's first close-up encounter with a dirigible, but to be so near to one in such a confined area could not help but fill him with a sense of awe and a feeling of being diminutive in comparison.

"Damn."

He was standing on his own staring up at it. At a distance, Raphael and Jesamine were with de Wynter, doing the same. Windermere turned and grinned. "It's something, isn't it?"

"That's the truth."

Windermere tried for a sense of perspective. "It's really not that big compared to the big civilian passenger liners that fly out of Croydon."

The Black Airship was all the perspective Argo needed. "It's big enough for me."

He could scarcely believe that, in a few hours, he would be riding in the belly of the floating monster, if the long gondola slung beneath could be considered a belly. He had accepted the Black Airship in theory when Windermere arranged its use to transport them to Paris, and avoid a lengthy and decided perilous trek through enemy territory. It had not seemed overly fanciful that Norse Military Intelligence should maintain an advanced dirigible with all the state of the art options to use on covert missions. He could accept, since the ruins of Paris were a hotbed of anti-Mosul resistance, that such a craft would make regular trips to city, and that the minimal three-man crew, a pilot who doubled as navigator, a flight engineer, and a gunner who also supervised the drops and pickups, were able to treat such a mission as routine. Even the fact that he himself was about to go on such a mission did not give him that much pause, after all the things he had done and seen in the preceding year. It was only there, inside the hangar, that the sheer momentous impossibility dropped its full weight on him. For a moment Argo's will buckled, and his legs felt weak under him, but then he adjusted. Life had been impossible for as long as he could remember, and he steeled himself with the reminder that there was actually no alternative. Windermere must have sensed what was happening to Argo, because he gently took him by the arm. "Stop being overwhelmed, and come and meet your support troops."

Argo had been so absorbed by his first sight of the Black Airship, that he had not paid too much attention to the half dozen men who sat in its shadow, hunkered down on supply crates in a way that indicated they were used to waiting. His eyes were now adjusting to the gloom of the hangar, and, for the first time, he was able to make out the forest green tunics with the characteristic two rows of buttons, the shoulder insignia of the half moon emblem, and the motto WE OWN THE NIGHT. "Rangers? I don't believe it."

Windermere smiled. "I said the surprises would be plural."

One of the Rangers rose to his feet. Argo immediately recognized the broad shoulders, bullet head, and bright blue eyes. "Steuben! When the fuck did you make sergeant?"

"I was wondering when you were going to see us."

A second Ranger was on his feet. Madden hadn't changed. He was still skinny and withdrawn, with blond hair and beard, and he still favored the black bandana wrapped around his head. "First Steuben makes sergeant and now Argo Weaver shows up a fucking major. That's the end of two beautiful friendships."

"How the hell did you get here? I don't understand."

The very last people in the world that Argo had expected to see were the Rangers who had been his protectors and mentors when he had first run away. He had been led to them by poor Bonnie Appleford. He looked at the men who were still seated. Penhaligon and Cartwright were there, the two farm boys, case-hardened by their trade, but the other two faces were new to Argo, and some that he might have expected to see were missing. Argo immediately became more cautious. "Jeb Hooker?"

A shadow passed over the Rangers' faces. "We lost the captain at Newbury Vale, on the bloody Western Ridge. A Teuton grenade did for him. Barnabas, too."

"I'm sorry."

"It's the way of soldiering. They weren't the only ones by a long shot."

"I still can't figure how you got here."

"Came over on the *Constellation* with Yancey Slide, didn't we?"

Madden's face suddenly became grim. "Our original mission was protecting the Prime Minister."

Steuben glared sourly at Windermere. "But they told us we'd be a violation of local law, and they had us in barracks with our guns racked, while their Viking ballerinas and ignorant fucking coppers were looking out for our man, and you've see where that fucking got him."

Resentment of the Norse seemed to be high among his former comrades-in-arms. Argo nodded. "I had some of that myself."

Windermere, on the other hand, was unwilling to be saddled with the responsibility for the assassination. "I thought we'd resolved all that, Sergeant?"

Steuben stiffened, not quite coming to attention. "Oh, we're professionals, Colonel. We'll do the job, we'll get you into Paris, and out again. No question there. We've got our orders, and that's all we need. It's just that the memory of Jack Kennedy doesn't rest so easy quite yet."

Argo intervened. "So what are your orders?"

"With the King now going straight to Stockholm and no public appearances . . ."

He quickly interrupted Steuben. "The King is coming? That's official?"

Steuben nodded. "Yes, Major. But not to London. Which leaves us more than ready to escort you all to Paris and pull Lady Blakeney out of the shit once again."

"So you're coming with us?"

"That would seem to be the plan, only . . ." Steuben hesitated.

"Only what?"

"Only we have a few stipulations, which we don't feel are unreasonable."

"Such as?"

Steuben looked round at the entire group that had arrived with Windermere. "We takes our orders from our own officer. I hope no one has a problem with that. And begging everyone else's pardon, you especially, Major Vega, but it would be best if Major Weaver was that officer. He's marched with us, and fought with us, and we pretty much have the measure of him. We know you have the rank, Colonel, but being under your command would be a bit too much like joining the Norse, and we're Albany, if you know what we mean."

Windermere nodded. "I know exactly what you mean."

Raphael agreed. "The rest of us will consult, but Major Weaver will command the expedition."

Steuben nodded. "However you want to work it." He grinned at Argo. "Don't you worry, Major. We'll all be taking real good care of you."

## CORDELIA

"Tell me more about this supposed breeding program. The one you mentioned in the car and then again on the barge while we were coming here."

Cordelia had been relieved to learn that nothing was expected of her, until the others showed up, and her only responsibility was to wait in comparative comfort with Sera Falconetti and Harriet Lime. This afforded her time to bring herself up to speed with all the ramifications of the game being played in Europe and especially the moves that Jeakqual-Ahrach appeared to be making in the Frankish territories. It also offered a pause in which she could make a further assessment of both Lime and Sera. The word was that the others would arrive sometime in the night, definitely before the dawn. When they did, matters could hardly avoid going into a higher gear, and the more she knew of those who would be around her, the better armed she felt. Harriet Lime seemed happy to confirm Cordelia's initial impression, from all the way back to Deerpark, that the woman liked to listen to herself talk and also show off how much she knew. Cordelia had gleaned all the distressing details that she had needed to hear about the murder of Jack Kennedy, and now she wanted to follow up on the remark that Sera had made, back on the water, just before Jesamine had contacted her.

"It's not all that 'supposed.' There's quite a solid body of information. The reports were coming in well before Hassan invaded the Americas. Just a piece here and another piece there, you understand?"

Cordelia nodded. "I understand."

"Just enough so those in charge back then recognized there was a puzzle. The young women of a entire Mamaluke village would be rounded up and marched away to an unknown destination. Then the same thing would happen in Hispania. A squad of Zhaithan would turn up at an infantry barracks and remove a number of healthy young men. That, too, would be repeated all over the Empire. The evidence started to mount."

At that point, Sera chipped in. "It was perhaps about a year or so ago that the stories changed. Rumors started to circulate about an ultra-secret facility on one of the Hellenic islands. Initially it was described as a prison, where maybe a hundred or more young women were confined. There was talk of strange fires in the night, and bodies floating in the sea, and of even stranger children."

Which, in turn, spurred Lime on to even more revelations. "Other odd characters were supposedly coming in from the East, seemingly as consultants, and also Teutons from the Knights of the Rhine. A volunteer actually went inside the place, but she only managed to get one incomplete message out before she was either turned or tortured. It was cryptic stuff: strange things growing in chemical vats. All over, the Zhaithan were suddenly very interested in the work that Dr. Mengele had done on the subject of twins, and even the experiments of the insane Moreau."

Cordelia frowned. She had heard of Moreau and his experiments. "I thought he had died years ago."

"He did, but the Zhaithan went to a lot of trouble to gain possession of his notes and records."

Cordelia did not quite understand. "I thought that Moreau did all his work on animals. Twisting their genetic makeup, making them more dexterous, giving them the power of speech and improved, long-term memory."

Sera nodded. "Moreau's aim was to create a subhuman superspecies that could take the place of human industrial workers."

"And what would happen to the human workers?"

Sera shrugged. "Moreau didn't seem to worry much about them."

Cordelia continued to question the Moreau connection. "But what would the Zhaithan want with a subhuman superspecies? The Empire has an exhaustible pool of slave labor."

"The thinking was that, if Moreau was could improve on animals, maybe his techniques could be used to somehow enhance human beings."

Lime added, "The Zhaithan wanted a superhuman species. Or, at least, a couple of superhumans they could bend to their will."

"You're saying that the White Twins are the product of Zhaithan genetic experiments and magick breeding?"

"That hasn't been discussed in Albany?"

"Of course, but only as wild speculation."

"After all the stories about a possible breeding program, a lot of people, especially adepts, Morgana operatives, and others, started to dream about the White Twins. The connection begged to be made."

Cordelia was not about to reveal that she was one of the "others" who had dreamed of the White Twins, or had a personal windwalking visitation from them, with Jeakqual-Ahrach acting like their damned mother. As she remembered the incident on the stern of the *Ragnar,* a brief image of the Twins appeared in her mind's eye. She would have considered it merely a memory, except that the White Twins were looking at Harriet Lime, and not at Cordelia, and directing their customary hostility at her. A thought suddenly struck Cordelia. "It would seem stupidly overconfident to create beings who were superior to you, without any real way of knowing how to control them. Isn't that what's known as hubris?"

Both Sera and Lime looked at Cordelia in surprise. The idea had clearly never occurred to them. Sera nodded. "She has a point."

Lime just looked uncomfortable and Cordelia wasn't sure why.

## JESAMINE

Jesamine was not ashamed to admit she was frightened. It might be ignorance and superstition, but she did not care, and, as the Black Airship lifted from the ground, she had gripped the arms of her seat so tightly she feared she might bend the frame. When Cordelia had flown on the NU98, it had crashed on her companion's very first voyage. Of course,

Jesamine had seen both airships and biplanes, either overhead or buzzing around, landing and taking off, but they were manned by fully fledged airmen who, by definition, had to be a little crazy, and even they mainly flew in daylight. Jesamine's first flight would be by night, and she was totally convinced that she was going to die. The seats in the long narrow gondola were arranged in pairs, and she found herself assigned next to Madden, who, now in his kit and fully armed, looked like a destructive force all by himself. He held a shotgun upright between his knees, and his broad military belt supported a sheathed, saw-edged Jones knife, and a small cache of Mills' bombs. A heavy revolver hung in a shoulder holster, while a bandolier of blue and copper shotgun shells were draped across his chest. The hilt of a second, smaller knife protruded from the top of one of his high hunter's boots, and his face was daubed with bootblack to stop his pale skin reflecting moonlight or skyshine. The pilot had told them that the sky would overcast, but Madden was taking no chances.

The pilot had also said that the cloud cover would help them drift across the Mosul defenses on the Frankish coast without incident. Although the Mosul had few actual antiaircraft units, some of their shore batteries could be elevated to shoot at anything in the air, and some even came equipped with searchlights that, if they fixed on the dirigible, could make it a sitting duck. It was important they cross the coast with the engines cut, running silent and invisible. To be even safer, a plan had been evolved whereby the airships would, after taking off from the base at Shoreham, first fly west and slightly north, staying over the English countryside. The first advantage of such a move was that it would confuse any possible Mosul agents who might be keeping a watch on the airfield. It would appear that their destination was somewhere in England. Once they had reached a suitable altitude, they would find a prevailing wind that would carry them back south and west. The crew would be using the airship's engines only to adjust course, and, according to the pilot's preflight briefing, they would drift over the Frankish coastline, unseen and undetected. It had all sounded incredibly complicated to Jesamine, but the airman claimed to have done the same thing any number of times before, and impressed on their passengers that they had no need to worry.

For Jesamine that was easier said than done, and when, after sunset, the Black Airship had been rolled out of its hangar, and freed from all but its fore and aft restraints by a large NAF ground crew, she had watched with something close to horror. Then they had all been expected to board the monster, and only massive pride stopped her from turning and running in panic, and she was extremely envious of de Wynter, and the boy called Spinrad, who were able to stay behind. Jesamine did not consider herself a coward, and she felt that, on numerous occasions, she had more than proved her courage. She was not afraid to face danger, and even the unknowns of the Other Place did not terrorize her like the thought of being helpless over thousands of feet of empty air, with nothing but a few bags of helium to hold her up. She knew she was probably being irrational, and revealing that, deep down, she was nothing more than a primitive peasant from the deserts of North Africa, but there was not a damned thing she could do about it.

She had started to feel a little foolish when the takeoff had not proved to be as traumatic as she had expected. The creakings and other noises from the airframe when the dirigible had been loosed from its moorings had not made her comfortable, and noise and vibration when the engines started had been worryingly ominous, but, after that, the craft had risen so effortlessly that Jesamine had assumed they were still on the ground. Without turning her head, and doing her utmost to keep a dry rasp of desperation out of her voice, she had asked Madden what the problem was. "I mean, how long does it take them to get this damned thing started?"

Madden allowed himself a slight smile. "Started, Major? We've been started for a good few minutes now. We gotta be a few thousand feet in the air."

Jesamine swallowed hard. "We're in the air?"

"Flying like a big fat blackbird."

"Oh."

"First time you ever did this?"

Jesamine nodded, knowing she had already given herself away. "Yes, first time."

"Me, too."

"What?"

"Never been in one of these contraptions before. Us Rangers usually walk where we're going."

He winked. "Gotta say, though, the whole thing does seem a bit unnatural." Madden patted the Jones knife and the grenades on his belt. "Even brought all my lucky charms along."

Jesamine was confused. "But how do you know so much about it."

Madden pointed to the tiny plastic window on his other side. "It's all going on out there. You can see the lights of tiny towns and everything. You want to change places with me and take a look?"

Jesamine quickly declined. "Not right now."

Madden had reassured her sufficiently that she felt it was safe to turn her head. She looked around the interior of the Black Airship's gondola to see if anyone else was suffering from maiden-flight jitters. Argo certainly was not. He was up beside the pilot and, along with Windermere, was poring over a map, the three men standing as dark silhouettes against the glow of the ship's instruments. Argo seemed to be taking his new leadership duties very seriously, and Jesamine had no problem with that. She had no desire to lead a team of Rangers on a mission into enemy territory. Cordelia might have taken exception, perhaps suggesting that the Rangers had only selected Argo to be their officer because he was a boy, and it was a boy's world, but Jesamine saw the sense in the decision. Argo had marched with these men, and they knew him. He was the only logical choice. She assumed that Raphael felt the same, although there was, at times, no telling what resentments the Hispanian might harbor. The other Rangers, who were also on their first flight, sat quietly with the infinite patience of really dangerous men. They were all loaded down with their personal weaponry, although none were quite as lethally equipped as Madden. She was familiar with the faces of four of them. They were the ones who, along with Argo and Yancey Slide, had pulled her, Jesamine, and Raphael out of the Zhaithan headquarters on the Potomac in the nick of time, and away from the clutches of Jeakqual-Ahrach. The other two were strangers named Graham and Peak, replacements who had transferred in from another unit after Newbury Vale.

In the front of the gondola, Argo, Windermere, and the pilot had concluded their business. The pilot raised his voice slightly to inform everyone else of their progress. "You'll all be pleased to hear that we now have a favorable wind, and in about a minute we'll be making a turn to get ourselves on our proper heading. After that, I'll be cutting the engines, and letting the wind carry us. By our best calculations, we should reach the Frankish coast in approximately twenty minutes."

The silence after the engines shut down was both overwhelming and eerie, and Steuben clearly felt the need to fill it with some kind of remark. "This fucking mission is already one to tell your grandchildren about, and we haven't even made the target yet."

Madden sighed. "This is how the next generation will go to war."

Graham looked round dourly. He nursed a telescope-sight long rifle, which denoted him as the marksman of the team. "It beats marching, don't it?"

Penhaligon frowned. "You may have to get back to me on that."

Cartwright nodded in agreement. "That's right. We ain't there yet."

Madden realized that this talk was hardly having a positive effect on Jesamine, and spoke quickly to distract her. "You really ought to take a look outside, Major."

"You think so?"

"I'll slide out and you can change seats with me."

Madden moved, but Jesamine hesitated, and he laughed. "The whole bag of tricks isn't going to tip over if you stand up. It isn't a row boat."

She managed a smile. "Right."

The exchange was made and Jesamine peered cautiously through the porthole. It was only seven or eight inches across, but what she saw beyond it took her breath away. They were above the clouds and, that high, the moon shone bright and pure white from a clear sky, illuminating a cloudscape of unparalleled majesty. Jesamine realized that only a handful of humanity had ever seen what she was now seeing, and, as she stared at the rolling vistas, like insubstantial mountains, or towering vaporous battlements, she imagined what it must look like from the outside, as the great black cigar-shape of the dirigible drifted silently among the clouds. She found that her attitude to flying had radically changed. She continued to stare and imagine until the pilot's voice broke in on her.

"This is the warning, people. Enemy coast ahead."

## RAPHAEL

After so much quiet, the Black Airship was suddenly alive with frantic activity. Seats were folded and stowed, and, on the order of the pilot, and under the direction of the airship's gunner, two wide sections of interior wall in the side of the gondola were slid back. The night air swirled in, and they saw that they were low over the ruins of Paris. The gunner hooked a lightweight .50 caliber to a mount beside what had now become an open door. The Black Airship was not a fighting vessel, but it carried enough firepower to deter marauders on the ground. The pilot was at the helm, calling off the altitude as they dropped into the city.

"Two hundred feet, dead slow, and coming in on the LZ."

From the air, it was easy to see how, years ago, the Mosul had hammered at Paris with their giant, long-range gun until there was next to nothing left of the city. The shapes of ugly shell craters were still visible. The blackened relics of once proud landmarks still reared as reminders of previous glory, surrounded by the heat-twisted frames, and skeletal remains, of dead and gutted buildings. The airship passed the misshapen supports of what had once been a stately dome, and then crossed the pitted expanse of a wide thoroughfare that was now choked with rank undergrowth. Peering into the gloom as the gunner and the Rangers prepared for the drop-off, Raphael could see big areas of black, featureless darkness that he was at a loss to explain. Then he realized that he was looking at water. The Mosul bombardment had smashed the banks of the River Seine, drowning areas of the city, and, in the long term, turning them into tracts of fetid swamp.

"One hundred and fifty feet, dead slow, and the LZ coming up."

It would have been easy to dismiss Paris as a dead city, a place of devastation and destruction, but there was evidence of humanity reestablishing itself. Burning fires showed themselves as multiple orange points of light under a pall of dirty smoke, and some sections even had crude electric lighting. Clearly a lot of outlaw ingenuity went into the survival of this vagabond community of rebels, criminals, and fugitives, but Raphael was still at a loss to understand how so much crime and dissent could persist right under the noses of the Mosul. He found it hard to buy Windermere's explanation that it was a combination of corruption, and a reluctance to take the kind of casualties involved in a full-scale clearing of the ruins. Okay, so the Mosul would have to fight their way into the very sewers, and from cellar to cellar, but he had never known the Mosul unwilling to waste the lives of the rank and file. As the airship continued its descent, he even saw small figures in the shadows. People looking up, grabbing hold of each other, and pointing. He could now see why the gunners first move was to mount the .50 caliber for full operation. In a city of thieves, someone might have the idea of taking the Black Airship for themselves.

"One hundred feet, and engines reversing. Ready yourselves for the drop."

Under the direction of the gunner, the Rangers deployed a folding winch and crane, and attached their packs to the hook. These would go down first, before the passengers themselves. With the crane in place, they opened up a section of the gondola's floor, lifted out the rope climbing net that was stored there, and rolled it to the door. The plan was that the airship should finally check its descent fifteen or twenty feet from the ground. The net would be dropped and the Rangers would climb down, followed by Argo, Jesamine, Raphael, and Windermere. This was the most dangerous part of the whole trip. The airship could all too easily be moved by any shifting ground-eddy, and the climbers on the net bounced around, clinging on for dear life. The worst case scenario was a sudden downdraft that could first crush those on the ropes and then wreck the ship itself. Raphael was not, however, unduly worried. With the possible exception of Windermere, they were all young and healthy, and even Windermere was taking his chances.

"Fifty feet, be ready to drop."

The winch rapidly lowered the packs. The net was thrown out and it reached to within a couple of feet of the ground. The Rangers braced to jump. The gunner was on the .50 caliber.

"That's as low as we're going. Everybody move out."

The Rangers jumped and were scrambling down the net. Argo followed. Raphael went after him, but turned as Jesamine climbed down, ready to help her if needed. Windermere's leg caused him some trouble, but he did his best to hide the disability. Raphael was about halfway to the ground when the ship suddenly shifted, and the net swayed. For a moment, Raphael, Jesamine, and Windermere were clinging on, if not for dear life, at least to avoid breaking an ankle or a collarbone in a heavy fall to the rubble below, but the Rangers quickly turned to steady the net for the others. Shaken but undeterred, the last three made it to the ground, and the Rangers grabbed their packs and scrambled away from the underside of the Black Airship. Again, the others followed, just in time to avoid hundreds of gallons of water, spilling fore and aft, as the dirigible let go of ballast, and began to rise. The small army of nine men and one woman stood and watched the craft vanishing quickly into the low overcast. When they could no longer see it, they still heard the sound of its departure. The engines cut in briefly, but then the ship returned to silent running and was gone altogether.

The Rangers looked to Argo for their next move, and he quickly responded, pointing into the night. "The pilot assured me that he was right on the LZ, and so making our way to the rendezvous point with Falconetti's people should be simple. Don't ask me how, but Windermere's people in ES Section have exchanged messages, and they are ready to make a deal for Cordelia."

Raphael supposed he should have been envious or something. He suspected that Jesamine had been looking at him for some sign of resentment that Argo had been selected to lead the mission rather than him. Raphael had never understood other people's need to lead. He had spent too long around military idiocy and military brutality to ever want to command anything or anyone. Argo, on the other hand, seemed to be taking to it like a duck to water. Raphael would have no complaint as long as Argo did not start putting on airs, or keeping too many need-to-know secrets. Raphael was already at something of a loss to understand how a deal could have been cut so fast with the people holding Cordelia, but this was not the time to start asking for clarification. Argo was already marshaling his troops, and the Rangers were gathering round him as he explained the next move. "We use that ruined dome as the first reference point. We walk a quarter of a mile in that direction, and we'll come to a fork in the trail. From there we see a signal fire on the right, and we go towards it. Any questions?"

The Rangers shook their heads.

"Madden?"

"Yo."

"Take the point."

Madden pointed with his shotgun. "That's the dome, right?"

Argo looked where he was pointing, at the dark outline of a misshapen framework. He nodded. "That's it."

"Okay, I got it."

The dome had plainly been used as a directional reference on many previous occasions, because a well-beaten path led in its direction from the Black Airship's regular drop-off point. Madden took a careful look around and started down the trail. Two Rangers fell in behind Madden, Argo took fourth place, with Raphael behind him. Jesamine and Windermere, who was limping a little, stayed near the end of the column, while Penhaligon brought up the rear. They spaced themselves, a couple of paces between each man, and, no sooner were they on the move, than they started hearing movements and rustlings in the scrub all around them, and even caught the odd sight of a small, quickly moving figure. After walking for a hundred yards, none of the ten were in any doubt that they had an invisible escort on either side of them, and Argo seemed to feel the need to reassure everyone. "Okay, people, we know they're out there, but take it easy. Don't on any account fire unless clearly threatened. We have no idea who's following us, or what kind of response the sound of gunfire might create in this place."

Steuben responded as though to reassure Argo. "Don't worry, Major. We're chill."

Raphael was completely surprised by how overgrown Paris was. He had expected a place of scorched earth and rubble, fallen masonry and broken walls, a sterile wasteland where all life had been eradicated by fire and toxins. Nothing in his imagination had prepared him for how nature had reasserted itself. On the ground, it was even clearer than it had been from the air that tenacious plant life was everywhere. Thick ivy and other climbing plants now covered many of the ruins, transforming them into great shapeless hummocks of green. Long rank grass now covered many open spaces, and thick stands of reeds had established themselves at the edges of the water. Dense scrub had taken over entire blocks, and even misshapen trees, random and nameless, had forced their way up to the light and air.

Up ahead, Madden had halted, and was signaling to Argo to come up the line and join him. Raphael could only assume that the point man had seen the fire that was the next reference point. Argo moved up the line, and, although it was probably against strict Ranger protocol, Raphael followed. They reached Madden, and he had indeed halted, because, as predicted, the trail had forked, and down on the right, the path widened out into what looked in the dark like a clearing, although an expanse of moss-covered cobblestones allowed it to retain some resemblance to an urban square or plaza. In the approximate center of it all, the predicted marker fire burned in a steel oil barrel, but a primary snag was immediately evident. People were in the square. They stood in small groups, some around the fire, others off in the shadows. Raphael could see a number of bottles being passed round. Off to one side, a number of children were eating something scarcely visible, but nebulously disgusting. Raphael, maybe irrationally, had not expected to encounter any people along their designated route, and Argo, when he spoke, sounded as though he had been under the same misapprehension. "If we're going to go on, I guess we have to face the natives."

Madden rested his shotgun on his shoulder. "How do you want to play it, Major Argo?"

Raphael was pleased that Argo did not try to act as though he was a real commander of Rangers. "How would you play it, Ranger Madden?

"Figure we should brazen it out. Close ranks, weapons down, but ready, and then just walk through. Quick march, going about our business, not stopping for anyone."

"When we reach the fire we're supposed to see some steps leading down to an old underground railway station."

"When we see them, we go straight for them. No hesitation."

Argo thought about this. "We have no reason to believe those people are armed."

Madden shrugged. "We also have no reason to believe they're not."

"Expect the unexpected?"

"You said it, Major."

By this time Steuben had moved up the line and was listening to the exchange. "So are we going to do it?"

Argo nodded. "Let's do it."

Steuben waved to the rest of the line to move up. When they were all together, they walked boldly towards the fire. The effect of a heavily armed crew, in full battledress, coming out of the darkness was instant and serious. The people round the fire may not have known who these ten new arrivals were, or where they came from, but they were taking no chances. A few stood their ground, but most backed away, and some even melted into the shadows, as though they had something to hide. A mangy one-eyed cat yowled as it scooted. Raphael could see that some of the loiterers were armed. Knives and old flintlocks were visible under the ragged clothes, carried on belts or thrust into boot-tops, but no one made a move. The people of Paris were probably aware of the havoc that could be wrought by advanced weapons. Only the children seemed unconcerned about the new arrivals, and went on eating as though nothing of interest to them was happening.

The pilot's instructions were once again correct. Beyond the square or plaza was a flight of stairs leading down from an undamaged piece of sidewalk. It had once been what was known as a Metro station. Raphael had heard that the underground railway had once been the pride of Paris. The ground level superstructure of the station had been entirely blown away, but the steps remained, clear and relatively intact. As they walked determinedly towards them, Raphael heard whispering from one of those in the square.

"From the Black Airship, we thinks."

"From the Black Airship, for sure."

The Rangers descended the steps more slowly than they had crossed the square, their guns now held at the ready as they went down into the darkness, except darkness was not what they found. A single gas flame illuminated what had once been the station platform, revealing a place that was scarcely recognizable as being of this Earth. Multiple layers of fringed white fungus, with odd pods and tendrils, had taken over just about every flat surface, and the effect, for Raphael at least, was like being inside a brain or a diseased intestine. He wondered if the fungus was some strange mutant legacy of the Paris Gun's poison gas shells, fully developed and growing beyond control. Water flowed where the rail tracks had once been, but its surface was a foot or so below the level of the platform. On one of the few visible sections of original wall, a stained and faded poster showed a smiling girl advertising a brand of Caribbean chocolate. Raphael could see Argo holding back distaste as he spoke to the Rangers. "Okay, so it looks weird, but the gaslight is the final marker. We go through the arch beneath it, along a section of smaller tunnel, and then we meet the men we've come to see."

The Rangers lowered their weapons. They didn't like being in the intestinal tunnel, but they were clearly relieved to have made it to their destination without incident. Or so they thought until the children appeared. They were pale and ragged, with wide watery eyes, as though they spent all of their time living underground with dark water and white fungus. They moved silently, and with an eerie purpose. They slipped out of the darkness of the tunnel, one at a time, and waited at the far end of the platform as their numbers grew to maybe two dozen. They had small weapons in their hands; knives, clubs, straight razors, and short lengths of metal pipe, all highly effective at close range. Jesamine voiced what everyone else was thinking.

"I don't like this one bit."

The pale children started to advance and Madden leveled his shotgun. "What do the rules of engagement say about shooting children, Major? Seems like we're being threatened here."

Steuben chimed in. His voice was grim and hollow. "Better look behind you, Major."

More children were coming down the steps that the party from the airship had just used. "They seem to have cut us off."

Raphael knew Argo was sweating the question of what to do. "I'm not about to slaughter children."

Madden had less compassion. "We gotta do something, boss. They don't look like they feel the same sympathy for us."

A small boy leading the creeping advance was baring his teeth at Madden in a grin that was pure infant insanity. At the same time, he made slow slashing gestures with a wicked length of broken glass with a makeshift handle fashioned from tape. Argo shook his head. "I really don't want to gun down a gang of kids, no matter how strange they look, but . . ." He took a deep breath and braced himself. "Steuben?"

"Major?"

"Fire a warning burst over their heads to see how they respond. But be ready to fire at will if they keep coming."

"Yes, sir."

Steuben raised his Bergman and clicked it to rapid fire, but as he raised the weapon, a tall, thin, and very familiar figure came out of same dark-of-the-tunnel that had spawned the children, gesturing for Steuben to hold his fire. "You'll rupture your fucking eardrums if you fire that thing in here."

Raphael, along with everyone else, couldn't believe his eyes. Steuben lowered the Bergman. "Slide? Yancey Slide?"

Yancey Slide was wearing a new duster coat, off-white and almost clean, with a velvet collar the old one never had. He advanced on the children and raised a hand, flashing small flickers of white fire from his fingers. The children halted. Their eyes grew even wider. He said something in an odd, unrecognizable dialect, at which they fled, silently scuttling back the way they had come. Argo took a step forward, an expression of disbelief still on his face. "Damn me. Am I glad to see you."

Slide gestured towards the archway under the gas flame. "Let's postpone the fond reunions, shall we? We're keeping the Falconetti Family waiting."

# EIGHT

## CORDELIA

Cordelia was in that place between sleep and waking where it was hard to tell drowsy thoughts from dreams, and neither the chair in which she sat nor the room she was in were wholly real. Cordelia, Lime, and Sera had drunk cognac, talked, and then talked more, and even called out for another bottle, while they awaited the arrival of the rest of The Four, but The Four had, so far, failed to materialize, and the talk had dwindled into long weary silences. Midnight came and went, as did two in the morning, and the three women found themselves slumped without brains, wit, or willpower. Sera was sound asleep, Cordelia was half asleep, while Lime seemed to have revived and was holding conversation with a materialization of Jeakqual-Ahrach, who was also seated, but in a throne-like dragon chair of her own materializing.

What?

The shock had Cordelia wide awake, and she discovered she had come in partway through a conversation in progress. Lime seemed anxious that either Cordelia or Sera might wake, but Jeakqual-Ahrach had no patience with her paranormal insecurities. *"You said you put them out. That should mean they are out, if you are as proficient as you claim to be."*

"I did put them out."

*"I seem to recall you boasting that it was easy. How did you put it? 'Once I've had the bitches to bed, they are always open to my manipulation?'"*

Lime defended herself; the pupil being unwillingly humbled by the martinet teacher. "It's true. They are always easy after I've had them to bed."

*"So why are you so anxious, Harriet Lime?"*

"I don't know the extent of the Blakeney woman's powers. She's gifted, and very highly trained."

Cordelia's thought was grim. You'd better believe that, bitch. She silently watched through her eyelashes, so busy eavesdropping that she had no time to feel the fury building inside her. She had known there was something less than right about Harriet Lime from the moment that she had met her.

*"You think I would trust you to neutralize Cordelia Blakeney on your own? I have her measure. I have her fully contained. She will know nothing of any of this."*

"And Falconetti?"

*"She is strong but wholly terrestrial. Should she wake, she would see you talking to yourself. You do have the experience to handle her."*

Angry as she was, Cordelia could not help feel herself filled with a suffusion of smug amusement. So Jeakqual-Ahrach thought she had Cordelia Blakeney contained did she? Except the containment was going the wrong way. Jeakqual-Ahrach had screwed up royally, and was seeing an illusion of an unconscious Cordelia, instead of knowing she was listening and watching. Cordelia moved an experimental hand, but neither Lime nor Jeakqual-Ahrach noticed. She could scarcely believe her own luck. Both Lime and Jeakqual-Ahrach were encapsulated and exposed, and without a clue what was happening to them. As Cordelia watched, Jeakqual-Ahrach leaned forward and looked hard at Lime. *"Do you have any other anxieties?"*

Lime shook her head. "No."

*"The other three are on their way?"*

"They should arrive at any time."

*"And the plan is for them to go to the pyramid?"*

"They will believe they are acting as spies or saboteurs."

Jeakqual-Ahrach seemed satisfied. *"That should allay any suspicions."*

"They don't know it yet, but that's how it will be presented to them."

*"The Zhaithan will take them at the pyramid."*

As the conversation continued, Cordelia stood up, but neither Lime nor Jeakqual-Ahrach noticed she had moved. Lime was confused by what Jeakqual-Ahrach had just said. "The Zhaithan will take them? I thought you would take them personally?"

Jeakqual-Ahrach looked away. *"I have procedures I must undergo before I vacate the Residence."*

Cordelia wondered what she meant by procedures, and why they should be more important than her being in at the capture of The Four? Harriet Lime appeared to be wondering the same thing. "But can the Zhaithan handle taking all four of them? The Albany Four have a lot of power when they're together."

*"The Twins will be there to negate their power."*

"The Twins will be there without you?"

*"That's one of the reasons why I trained you. I won't play mother to those little monsters, world without end."*

"But . . ."

*"You question me?"* Jeakqual-Ahrach's face darkened and flames rose from behind her chair.

Lime quickly shook her head. "No."

*"The Twins will shortly arrive at Marseilles on a special galley. They will then be brought to Amiens by road, under special escort. You will be kept informed. I need the Albany Four there by the time they arrive."*

Lime nodded. "I understand. It will be done."

Like Lime, Cordelia was surprised that Jeakqual-Ahrach was allowing the Twins to operate away from her, and also curious to know what exactly they did. They seemed powerful, but their capabilities were shrouded in mystery. What she was hearing only created a hundred more questions, but the visitation seemed to be ending, and Cordelia made a fast decision. She moved to the chair where Sera was sleeping and picked up Falconetti's leather coat. Cordelia patted the pockets, and felt the weight for which she'd been hoping. She took out the small lady's revolver, pointed it at the unknowing head of Harriet Lime, and waited. Cordelia knew she was taking a risk, but she believed the end product would be worth it. Lime and Jeakqual-Ahrach were performing some sort of parting ritual of elaborate and symbolic hand signals. When it was complete, the manifestation of Jeakqual-Ahrach faded to nothing, and Lime sagged back in her chair exhausted, and closed her eyes. It was maybe a minute before she opened them, and saw Cordelia, who relished Lime's intense surprise. She remembered Hilde, the whore in Boulogne, and the first words she had said to Cordelia. They seemed apt for the situation. "Do one thing I don't like, sister, and I take your face off."

Sera stirred. The disappearance of Jeakqual-Ahrach seemed to have lifted whatever was keeping her asleep and oblivious. She took in the scene, and sat bolt upright in her chair. "What the fuck is going on?"

"I just caught Mme. Lime here taking a personal psychic meeting with Her Grand Eminence, to whom she seems totally pledged and wholly in subservient thrall." Sera reached for her coat, but Cordelia indicated she need not bother. "This is your gun I'm holding."

"She was talking to Jeakqual-Ahrach?"

Cordelia nodded. "A full-blown, full-color, three-dimensional manifestation."

"Is such a thing possible?"

Cordelia laughed. "With Jeakqual-Ahrach? Infinitely possible."

Lime finally found her voice. "Of course it isn't possible. Lady Blakeney suddenly went out of her mind."

With the gun held firmly to Lime's head, Cordelia chanced a glance at Sera. "Do I look out of my mind?"

Sera shook her head. "Not noticeably."

"She was making the final arrangements to turn me over to the Zhaithan. We are to be taken by them when we go to the pyramid."

"Who said you were going to the pyramid?"

"Seemingly we are going to be persuaded. Are you in on this with her?"

"Of course not."

"And your father?"

"Our deal was made with Morgana's Web, with her as their representative."

Lime again protested. "This is pure craziness."

Cordelia looked back at Lime. "It's lame, Harriet, but I guess you were so sure of Her Grand Eminence's powers, you didn't think you'd need a cover story."

Lime looked desperately at Sera. "You believe her?"

"I tend to, especially as she has the gun."

"You're both insane."

Cordelia pressed home her advantage. "So, Sera, either you and I are insane, or Lime has been caught red-handed selling out not only The Four, but also Morgana's Web and Il Syndicato, and is now tap dancing for dear life."

Sera stood up and looked down at Lime. "I'm sorry, Harriet, but Cordelia is making more and more sense by the minute."

Lime snarled. "You're going to regret this."

Harriet Lime had said exactly the wrong thing. Sera Falconetti's face turned cold. "I am? What exactly am I going to regret, Harriet? Cordelia makes perfect sense, while you merely bluster, impugn my mental heath, and now you actually threaten me. Do you remember where you are, Harriet Lime? Or who you're fucking talking to?"

Cordelia knew she had won at the same time Harriet Lime knew she had lost. Lime cursed. "Damn the both of you."

Sera looked at her grimly. "And that really clinches it, Harriet. You gave up too fast." She turned to Cordelia. "What do you want to do with her?"

"Truthfully?"

"Of course."

"Hurt her until she confesses everything she knows."

"We have a quiet room for exactly that purpose."

"I rather thought you might."

Sera Falconetti raised her voice so as to be heard beyond the door. "Bonaparte, get in here."

## ARGO

"Are you the commander of this army, Gideon Windermere."

"No, Damon, I'm not."

The big man, the supposed boss of Paris, turned to Slide. "You?"

"You know I don't command anything."

Argo took a deep breath. "If anyone's in command, I am. The Rangers are under my orders."

Damon Falconetti motioned to Jesamine and Raphael. "And these are Lady Blakeney's other two partners?"

Raphael answered for both of them. "We are."

Now he regarded the Rangers. "I had only expected The Four. Not an Albany invasion force."

Steuben shrugged, refusing to be in any way impressed by Falconetti and his assembled henchmen. "We weren't doing anything so we thought we'd come along for the ride."

The tunnel from the Metro station had opened out into a flagstoned chamber, lit with more gas flames, and Falconetti's men had been waiting for them, a dozen or more hard-faced rogues, with scars and missing ears, tattoos and strange jewelry, looking grim and professionally intimidating. He could also see, however, that they were somewhat taken aback by the Rangers equally professional confidence and modern weapons. The initial contact had been tense, and in the first half minute, Argo had feared a fire fight might break out. The Rangers had not been expecting a reception committee, and the reception committee had not been expecting visitors with so much firepower. The Parisians had reacted with a combination of distrust and suspicion, and the Rangers had taken all this as hostility, and maybe the preamble to a shootout. Suddenly, fingers were on triggers, and thumbs on safety catches, and all hell was threatening to break loose until Slide, greeting a number of Falconetti's crew by name, shook hands, slapped shoulders, and managed to circulate the tension to a manageable level, and defuse the possibility of a lethal misunderstanding. "I thought we were here to deal, not to die."

Only then did Damon Falconetti come into the room, as though he had considered the possibility that trouble might break out, and absented himself until the threat was past. "You expect me to deal with you, Yancey Slide? You're not even human."

Slide lit a cheroot. "Something for which I am profoundly grateful."

Argo looked at Falconetti, and wished that he wasn't the one the Rangers had selected for command. When he smiled, the big man flashed a mouthful of gold teeth. The ample uniform coat over his barrel chest was covered in unrecognizable decorations, and a long-legged wolfhound followed at his heel. From the way his men deferred to him, Argo knew that Falconetti was the absolute ruler on his own turf, and he was glad that both Slide and Windermere had a prior relationship with him because Argo knew, once the pleasantries were out of the way, and they settled down to serious business, he had more questions than answers, and little confidence that he could in any way handle the big man on his own.

Falconetti looked Argo up and down. "I don't believe I caught your name."

Argo inclined his head in a very slight bow. "I'm sorry, I didn't give it. The name is Weaver, Argo Weaver."

Falconetti repeated Argo's name as though committing it to memory. "Major Argo Weaver of Albany."

"Of Albany and Virginia."

Falconetti grinned gold. "So welcome to my city, Major Argo Weaver of Albany and Virginia." He turned to include the Rangers in his gesture of greeting. "Welcome to you all. You've come a long way and you must all be hungry and thirsty." Falconetti gestured to a table against a side wall that was set with wine and beer, cheese, and cold cuts, and bread that looked crisp and fresh, but was a decidedly strange color. The Rangers saw the beer and wine, and moved towards it with a will, but Argo held up a hand. "Hold it. We have to stow the weapons before anyone starts drinking."

Falconetti was amused. "The Major looks out for the welfare of his men."

Argo knew he was being patronized, probably because of his youth. "Just recalling how alcohol and Bergman guns tend not to mix."

Falconetti was maybe aware that he was pushing Argo further than he was prepared to go. "Very wise. Your men can stack their hardware against that wall. Within reach, but not too easily seized in anger."

"I would expect your people to do the same."

"And indeed they will."

"Stack the heavy weapons against the opposite wall, boys."

Falconetti's men did as they were ordered, and Argo nodded to Steuben. "Have the men do as Mr. Falconetti has suggested."

"What about knives and sidearms, Major? Do we stash those, too?"

Argo looked at Falconetti. "Hold on to them I would think. Agreed?"

Falconetti happily assented. "Agreed. Some of mine would never give up their knives."

With the laying down of the weapons settled, everyone moved on to the food and drink, Argo included. He helped himself to a beer, assuming that this was an interlude for refreshment before the serious discussions about Cordelia and what was going to be done with her. Windermere, however, was in no mood to wait. Even as Argo was still swallowing his first, grateful mouthful, Windermere brought up the topic with Falconetti, loud enough for everyone to hear. "I think, Damon, before everyone gets too friendly, we should settle the matter of Lady Blakeney."

Falconetti stopped uncorking a wine bottle and looked at Windermere dourly. "What about Lady Blakeney?"

"A basic assurance that she's here, she's alive, and she's being well treated."

"Business before pleasure?"

"Always."

Falconetti looked disbelievingly at him. "Always, Gideon?"

Windermere smiled ruefully, obviously at some mutual piece of history. "Well, this time, at least."

Falconetti finished uncorking the wine, and drank straight from the bottle. "You want to know if she's alive and well? All I can say is that she was very alive and very well when last I saw her, which was yesterday, when I wined and dined her, and then fed her a most exceptional de Richelieu cognac. After that, I gave formal charge of her to Harriet Lime, strictly according to the terms of the contract, and they left."

"She's gone?"

Falconetti laughed and shook his head. "Of course not. She and Lime left for bed, not parts unknown. You think I would permit that? A contract is a powerful instrument, but it doesn't override basic common sense. In fact, Lady Blakeney, Mme. Lime, and my daughter are right now awaiting your arrival, or they should be. They recently sent word that they would be busy for a while, and join us as soon as they could."

Jesamine looked round in amazement. "We fly all the way across the sea in that damned Black Airship, and Cordelia's too fucking busy for us to rescue her?"

## CORDELIA

"We have a quiet room for exactly that purpose."

Sera had said the words like a flat statement of fact, and Cordelia had not known exactly what to expect. It turned out that the Falconetti Family maintained a compact, but well-equipped dungeon for the confinement and questioning of prisoners. After a long underground walk, Bonaparte unlocked a door in a damp stone passage with an imposing brass key. An eight-point star-in-the-circle had been daubed on the door in red paint, but no explanation of the symbol was offered. Located somewhere in the extensive and inexplicable Falconetti Family stronghold, the room had a stained wood floor, and the walls and ceiling were one continuous arch of dark, unbroken brick. It was too narrow to be a section of Metro tunnel, and Cordelia had to assume that it was yet another part of a sewer, now high and dry above the revised water level. The quiet room was lit by an electric vacuum globe that, once turned on, supplied a stark and remorseless light, and revealed a number of devices to which the unfortunate Harriet Lime might be attached while Sera and Cordelia, as Cordelia had put it, "hurt her until she confesses everything she knows." In addition, a wall rack was stocked with a very comprehensive selection of instruments with which the prisoner might be beaten or flogged, plus an array of modular straps, buckles, clasps, clamps, and rings that might be used for more ambitious and extensive infliction of discomfort. The choice was so wide that Cordelia found herself at a loss.

Bonaparte, who was now Lime's one-man escort, obviously realized this, and looked questioningly at Sera and Cordelia. "Do you want me to secure her?"

Sera nodded. "I think that's what we came here for."

"So where? Which one? The stocks? The chair?"

Sera deferred to Cordelia. "You choose."

Cordelia looked around the torture chamber. The room gave their voices a harshly ringing echo that, when combined with the harsh light, lent everything an edge of austere brutality. She was quite taken with a set of sturdy traditional stocks, but she thought it might be a little difficult for Lime to speak with her neck thrust into the merciless wooden collar, and also, when she did speak, Cordelia wanted to be looking her in the face. "You'd better put her on that cross thing. Let her look like a Jesu-cult martyr."

Bonaparte took Harriet Lime by the arm and steered her to the cross. It was constructed from a diagonal of weighty timber beams to which leather cuffs for wrists and ankles were affixed with stout screws, as was a belt that buckled around the victim's waist. Lime did not protest until Bonaparte started to cuff her left wrist. "I can't believe that you are doing this to me after I fucked both of you."

Cordelia's expression was bleak. "You should consider, my dear Harriet, how put out I am at having been fucked by someone who planned to betray me to Jeakqual-Ahrach."

Bonaparte attached Lime's other arm to the cross. Now Lime stared at Sera. "You shouldn't be allowing this. I haven't done anything to you."

"You've made use of Il Syndicato, and deceived us about your intended purpose. It has the potential to make us look foolish and inept. That alone would be enough to put your head in the vise over there. If this was my father's deal, he would be turning the screw until your skull cracked."

Bonaparte was now kneeling, securing Lime's left ankle to the cross. In a sudden burst of frustrated anger, she lashed out at him with her right foot, catching him in the chest and causing him to topple backward. He righted himself, out of reach of her thrashing leg, but, instead of doing anything, he simply sat and watched her struggling against the straps on her wrists. He only grabbed for her ankle again when she ran out of steam, hanging from her wrists, breathing heavily, with her blonde curls falling in her face. With a grip that compelled Lime to be still, he forced to her to submit to the restraints, while hissing between clenched teeth. "Try that again, missy, I'm going to have to put a hurt on you, over and above these ladies' plans."

Bonaparte secured the belt around Lime's waist, and synched it tight. He stood back and admired his handiwork, then he turned to Sera and Cordelia. "If you're going to want hot irons, I'll need time to get a fire going."

Sera glanced at Cordelia, who shook her head. "No hot irons."

Lime was, of course, fully dressed, and Cordelia decided to rectify that. "What you can do is strip her."

Bonaparte regarded the helpless Lime. "She really should have been stripped down before I secured her."

Cordelia shook her head. "It's more fun this way. It can be done slowly. Use your knife. Cut her dress off."

With the dexterity of a magician, Bonaparte caused a spring-loaded jackknife to appear in his hand. He advanced on Lime, who jerked against her straps. "Not the dress!"

"The dress is the least of your worries, girl."

Sera glanced at Cordelia. "I'm extremely glad she changed out of her chic aviatrix outfit."

Cordelia nodded. "The leather one? Oh yes, *très chic*."

"She and I are roughly the same size, so I decided it's mine when we finish with her."

Bonaparte slid the blade of his knife under the neckline of Lime's dress and slit the seam along the shoulder and sleeve. It fell away, exposing one of her breasts. Lime cursed him as he repeated the process on the other shoulder. "Bastard!"

Sera made a warning gesture. "Address your remarks to us please, Harriet. Bonaparte is only following orders."

"You think I'm going to talk, don't you?"

Cordelia smiled sweetly. "I'm certain you're going to talk, but feel free to hold out as long as you like. I will thoroughly enjoy the preliminaries."

Bonaparte had the blade under the hem of her dress and was ripping upwards. Now the dress was nothing more than strips of scarlet fabric hanging from the strap that bound her to the cross. With a second touch of the conjuror, he ripped these free, and Lime stood spread-eagled in her scanties and brassiere. Cordelia nodded to Bonaparte. "The undergarments also."

Two swift cuts, and Harriet Lime was exposed and naked. The rags of her former clothing lay on the floor in front of her. Cordelia turned to the implement rack. She took a pair of clamps that were attached by a short chain. She held them up for Sera to see. "What part of the body are these designed for?"

"The nipples."

Cordelia nodded. "Ah."

Next she picked up a short but deadly looking knout and swished it through the air. Harriet Lime whimpered and tugged at her cuffs, but then seemingly gave in to the inevitable and stood very still, taking deep, calming breaths. "Okay, let's deal. Stop this charade and I'll tell you everything."

Cordelia wasn't particularly interested. "I have a strong desire to hurt you anyway."

Bonaparte cleared his throat. "The real professionals always administer a first infliction before they even start to negotiate. It's supposed to dispel illusions, and get the subject's attention."

Sera glared. "Shut up, Bonaparte."

"Just trying to be helpful."

"You're not." She turned to Cordelia. "Which are you more interested in? Knowing what she knows, or causing her pain."

Cordelia flicked the whip and pouted. "I know it's probably childish and nasty, but I want to hear her screaming. I imagine what would have happened to me if she'd turned me over to Jeakqual-Ahrach and her Zhaithan. They'd have had me riding an electrode as they stripped the skin from my body one little piece at a time."

"Can't you let go of that?"

"Would you?"

Sera thought about this. "I guess not."

Lime used the discussion as the starting point for another chance to save herself. She tossed her head, to remove hair from her eyes. "You know you can't kill me, Cordelia."

"I know no such thing."

"Think about it. Jeakqual-Ahrach will be contacting me. If I'm dead, she can't do that, and you lose a vital source of information."

Sera took Lime's point. "You should hear her out."

Cordelia ran the plaited leather of the knout between her fingers. "Keep talking."

"The White Twins are arriving in Marseilles, and going to the pyramid."

"We already know that."

"But I'm the one who will know when and how they will come there."

Cordelia frowned. "You're saying that you'll totally sell out Jeakqual-Ahrach?"

Lime did her best to look helpless. It was not hard. "What other choice do I have?"

Cordelia continued to play with the knout. The temptation to lay it hard across Lime's thighs or breasts was very strong, part of a nasty aesthetic desire to watch her suffer. "I don't know, Sera. If we keep her alive, we'll have to watch her all the time."

"I've been with Jeakqual-Ahrach longer than anyone imagines. I know a great deal."

Cordelia scowled. "That only makes me even more inclined to take a whip to you."

"She turned me years ago. In Muscovy. No one ever suspected. I'm telling you, I have a lot of information. I'm valuable, dammit."

Cordelia flicked the whip. "But are you sufficiently humbled?"

"I'm sufficiently afraid."

"That, on its own, may not be enough."

"I even know about her rejuvenation techniques."

Suddenly she had both Sera's and Cordelia's attention. "Are those the procedures she was talking about?"

"That's right. She's really very old. She's the twin of her brother Quadaron-Ahrach, and she needs them more and more."

"Needs what more and more?"

"It's getting to be a longer and longer process. She spends all this time with these evil old men from the East, and there are rituals, and blood, and sacrifices, and then she goes into this long trance, while all these chemicals and potions are pumped into her veins through tubes. But when she comes out of it, she looks . . . well . . . young again."

"And she's having one of these done right now?"

Lime was puzzled. "How do you know that?"

Cordelia smiled nastily. "You forget I overheard your whole conversation with her manifestation."

"She needs her strength before this ritual with the pyramid and the White Twins. That's why you really need to keep me alive and intact, because there's more to it than anyone can imagine."

Cordelia knew there was a core of truth in this. "How much more?"

"She's attempting to mess with the basic fabric of dimensional reality."

"I don't understand."

"Neither do I, but I've overheard talk about stuff like the Dirichlet boundary conditions, and the Endpoint, and, most important, the manifold of something called the D-brane."

"The dee-brain?"

"No, D-brane."

"This is all nonsense."

"It really isn't."

"Are sure you're not just saying all this to save your pretty flesh?"

"No, I swear."

Cordelia was suddenly angry. Lime was making a fool of her. "I've listened long enough. Let's see where a little physical motivation takes us."

Cordelia swung the knout with precision, it cracked, and Lime sobbed. A livid welt appeared across her white skin, and more would have quickly joined the first had the door not suddenly opened, and an authoritative voice stopped Cordelia in full stroke.

"Easy, Cordelia. What Lime is saying may be more important than you know."

Cordelia spun round, unconsciously dropping the knout. "Slide? Is that really you?"

She wanted to run to him and hug him, but she knew this was irrational because no one ever hugged Yancey Slide. Instead she stood awkwardly. Sera, on the other hand, was staring in awe, the first time Cordelia had ever seen her even approach such a loss of control. "Are you really Yancey Slide?"

Slide pushed back his hat, and lit a cheroot with his fingertip. Cordelia suspected he was doing it to impress Sera Falconetti even further. He nodded. "Some of the time."

Lime apparently knew Slide. "Tell her, Slide, tell her. Tell Cordelia that I'm telling the truth."

Slide nodded. "She unfortunately is telling the truth. What little she knows of it."

"You understand any of this D-brane stuff?"

"I'm afraid I do."

## RAPHAEL

To call it a war council was no exaggeration, and the primary subject of debate, to which everyone kept returning, was who should go to war and when. Although Falconetti would never allow the name to be used, he had insisted the meeting should be convened according to the model of what Il Syndicato called a "sit-down," in which representatives of all interested factions were present, and able to have their say. Raphael found this an oddly egalitarian process for an organization that was basically a hierarchy of brute power. It was thus that those seated round the big circular table in the hall of the Falconetti stronghold came to include Damon Falconetti, his daughter Sera, Old Temps Perdu, and Bonaparte, representing the various levels of the Family; The Four representing themselves; Slide and Windermere, who seemed to share a less well-defined common interest in total war on Jeakqual-Ahrach, and Madden and Steuben on behalf of Albany and the Rangers. A dancer called Hyacinth was also present, who, although she worked for Falconetti, was also the local operative for Morgana's Web, and had been drafted to replace the disgraced Harriet Lime. A first look around the round table had caused Raphael to whisper to Argo. "If the Mosul set off a bomb in this room . . ."

Argo had shaken his head. "Don't even joke about it."

At the start of the meeting, The Four had been given time to catch up and get over their indignation that the kidnapping of Cordelia had been a ruse, connived in no small part by Windermere, to lure all of them to Paris in order to confront the problem of what to do about the Amiens Pyramid, and whatever plans Jeakqual-Ahrach might have for it. Raphael had obviously not been at all happy to have been so manipulated, but, in the bigger picture, he saw how they might be of much more use there than either in London, or even back in Albany, and resigned himself to that which he could do nothing about. Somehow it had been deemed that The Four's current battle was right there, in among the Franks, and a warrior, even an occult warrior, had no choice but to go where he was sent. He knew that resentment would come later, and much of what wasn't directed at Harriet Lime would hit Gideon Windermere, and even Slide. He could glean some satisfaction that Lime, who had played them all with crucial duplicity, was currently kneeling naked in the Falconetti dungeon, locked in a set of old-fashioned stocks, "contemplating her errors." Although Slide had stopped Cordelia from torturing Lime, save for a mere couple of lashes, Cordelia insisted that she should at least be humiliatingly confined until they decided what to do with her.

The Rangers did some token complaining about how their orders had been to come to Paris to extract Cordelia, but had said nothing about fighting any pyramid. Steuben had done the talking while Madden, chair tilted back, one boot up on the edge of the table, nodded occasionally, murmured "right," and worked on the edge of his Ranger-issue Jones knife with a small whetstone. They were, however, very easily convinced. The Rangers would never complain too long at the prospect of a fight. After that, some outlaw legalities relating to Cordelia's situation were resolved. It was agreed that the contract was voided, and that Cordelia was no longer anybody's property, and was once again her own woman, but Falconetti would retain the payment that had been made to him thus far. That was the price of Morgana's Web not noticing the traitor in their midst.

With the more mundane business addressed, the talk turned to Jeakqual-Ahrach and the Amiens Pyramid. Falconetti took the initial position that it was really none of his concern. He and his associates ran a moneymaking operation. They were not in the world-saving business. The Four, Slide, the Rangers, and Windermere could do what they liked about her Grand Eminence and the Zhaithan. He would not interfere, even though their action could well stir up a hornet's nest among the Mosul, which could be traced back to their ruined city, and easily provoke reprisals. He would contribute that much to the common cause. Having stated where he stood, Falconetti lounged back in his chair, put his boots squarely on the table and ordered wine. From that point on, he expected the rest to convince him otherwise. The obvious weakness of Damon Falconetti's position was that he totally lacked the support of his daughter, who recognized that even the narrowest interpretation of Il Syndicato's interests would plainly be jeopardized if Jeakqual-Ahrach turned the Amiens Pyramid into some kind of paranormal weapon. Raphael found Sera Falconetti fascinating, and, while she talked, he couldn't help staring at her. One time she caught him, and he quickly looked away, embarrassed. It was hardly appropriate to become moonstruck as Sera made the case for Falconetti involvement to her father.

"The winds of war have shifted. Whether we like it or not, Paris has become a focus of resistance. We cannot hang back and let others do our fighting for us. Falconettis aren't raised to be spectators."

Falconetti drank his wine from a pewter tankard and waved away her appeals to his better, or more heroic nature. "Paris has only become the focus of all this because outsiders have made it the focus. The Norse and Albany, and Slide here, wherever he might come from, want to drag me into their war."

"The Norse or Albany aren't dragging you into anything. You think Albany declared it wasn't their war when the Mosul landed at Savannah?"

Falconetti belched. "I seem to recall that Albany took its sweet time to get mobilized. So long, in fact, that Virginia fell, and they did nothing about it."

Cordelia became irate. "That's a damned lie."

Argo had to say something. "Actually it's not. We had a saying, even a song, back in Virginia after the invasion. It was, "Why Doesn't Albany Come?""

Cordelia glared at Argo. She seemed about to say something but changed her mind, deferring instead to Sera who continued. "Irrespective of who did what back when, it was Jeakqual-Ahrach who brought this on all of us, and we need to respond accordingly."

At this point, Slide rose in his seat. Raphael knew Slide was powerful, but he had never seen him gather his power like this before. Damon Falconetti removed his feet from the table, took a quick drink, then put down the tankard, as Slide slowly scanned each face in turn. "This argument rapidly becomes redundant in the light of the new information Cordelia's forced from the woman Lime. Jeakqual-Ahrach's plans for the Amiens Pyramid are far more perilous than we ever imagined. She is about to attempt a planned disruption of dimensional reality, and, should she even come close to her intention, Paris, in its present form, and all of you along with it, will simply cease to exist."

Falconetti swallowed hard and almost choked. "What do you mean, cease to exist? You mean we will all die?"

"You have to have lived to die. When I say 'cease to exist,' I mean like you never were. Like there never had been a Damon Falconetti."

Jesamine raised a tentative hand, like a pupil who wanted the attention of an intimidating teacher. "I don't understand all this dimensional reality. I know there's here, and I know that there's the Other Place, but in all my training we were taught that was it, give or take."

"You and your companions have made jumps to a handful of very specific extremes to encounter what you term magick, or the paranormal. In between those extremes are an infinite number of other possibilities and alternatives."

Jesamine shook her head. "I really don't understand."

Madden looked up from his knife. "For what it's worth, I don't either."

Windermere added reluctantly. "I find it hard to conceive just how it all works."

Raphael would have happily added his expression of bafflement, but Slide retreated under the brim of his hat. "Human minds really aren't designed to conceive of how it works."

Cordelia sniffed. "That sounds inhumanly snotty."

"Maybe, my dear, but it's the unfortunate truth. I have moved, mostly at random, through thousands of dimensions, and I know what I've seen is only a tiny fraction of all the possibilities."

"Are you saying that every time a choice is made, or that there are a number of possible options, a new reality is created in which each one happens?"

"That's one theory. I've seen realities where man never evolved on this planet, and others where humanity had mutated all the way beyond the physical and was running on pure magick."

Old Temps Perdu was sucking on a pipe. "You ever see one where the monkeys took over, like in those Zulu comic papers?"

Slide shook his head. "I never did, but I have every confidence there's one out there somewhere. Maybe one or maybe a few hundred million."

Argo was frowning. "So how can Jeakqual-Ahrach make use of all this if, as you claim, she's unable to understand it?"

Slide puffed on his cheroot for a moment. His face was grim. "That's what makes her so fucking dangerous, and why she has to be stopped. She has absolutely no clue what she's really doing."

"But she's doing it anyway?"

Slide nodded. "She's doing it anyway."

"But what is she doing?"

"As far as I can figure it, she's looking to use the pyramid to smash through into another dimension. In the Other Place, you have only seen the distant extremes, the dimensions of the Dark Things and the Mothmen. There are other, closer realities, only fractionally different from this one. I suspect that she wants to break in where the Mosul Empire exists, but is in much better shape."

"And what happens then?"

"She takes control of this other reality, without being hampered by either Hassan or her brother. For her, the battle in the Americas—or anywhere else, for that matter—has become functionally irrelevant."

Madden was thinking hard. "But isn't she going to meet herself coming back, so to speak?"

"I imagine she either plans to co-opt or dispose of her Other Self."

Falconetti was frowning. "And what about this reality right here?"

"It ceases."

"Just like that?"

Slide nodded. "Out like a light."

"Really?"

Slide shrugged. "Again it's a theory, but losing all this may well be the very least of the sustained damage if she does what she intends and ruptures the D-brane manifold. It could rewrite the boundary conditions, and that could be the end, quite literally, of everything. Endpoint, or one version of it."

Cordelia sighed. "Damn, Slide, are we into all the D-brane business again?"

"I'm afraid we are."

"Can't you make it more simple?"

"It's as though a goldfish believes he can rule the world if he just breaks the glass of his bowl and escapes."

Sera asked the obvious question. "Can Jeakqual-Ahrach really be that stupid?"

"It's one of the side effects of being a tyrant, and it frequently brings about their downfall. She has a great many people around her telling her what she wants to hear, rather than what she needs to hear. Plus, she lives in that place where magick meets mathematics, which makes her vulnerable to all kinds of nonsense. She has somehow been led to believe that there's a means to rupture the interdimensional membranes and come through intact."

"And is there?"

"I've never heard of one. Quite the reverse. The best thinking is that a single rip on any interdimensional membrane could reproduce itself infinitely, and there goes the current universe."

Raphael's head was starting to ache from trying to grasp multiple infinities. Round the circle at the table, others were showing symptoms of the same. He noticed, however, that Falconetti seemed to be easing away from his original position. Even if what Slide was telling them was impossible to fully grasp, it was having its effect. Falconetti was now leaning forward on his elbows, paying rapt attention. "So, whichever way you slice it, she has to be stopped right now."

"She has to be stopped on any level you look at it."

Instead of trying to understand, Steuben went for monosyllabic practicality. "How?"

"That's right, how?"

Slide stared hard at Falconetti. "Does that mean you're in, Damon?"

"It doesn't mean I'm in and it doesn't mean I'm out. It means that I want to know what's going to be involved right here on the ground."

Sera rounded angrily on her father. "Damn it, just give me the use of some men, so I don't go to this thing on my own."

Old Temps Perdu laughed. "I'll fucking go on my own tab. I fancies blowing me up a pyramid."

Falconetti's face darkened. "You seek to shame me, daughter?"

Sera didn't waver. "If that's what it takes."

Falconetti slapped his hand down on the table, hard enough to make his tankard jump. "Damn it to hell, Sera. I taught you too well, didn't I?" He looked all round the gathering. "Okay, I'm in. The Falconetti Family will take the fight to Her Grand Eminence, and let's hope there's a chance for looting. But like the Ranger Sergeant already so succinctly asked, how do we do this?"

## ARGO

Old Temps Perdu's smile was pleasantly evil. "Start thinking with your brains and not your assholes, lads. We don't have to construct a bomb. The best bomb we could come up with is already right there."

"The Paris Gun?"

"What else? A cannon, no matter how big, is just a huge great bomb-casing with one end left open. We pack it with explosives, and seal the muzzle well enough, it'll rip a big enough hole in that earthworks to put a stop to whatever weirdness the Mosul bitch has planned."

Old Temps Perdu seemed to be as adept at blowing up artillery as firing it, and he was setting Steuben to thinking. "It'd need one fuck of a lot of explosive."

"Doesn't have to be fancy. Nitrates and fuel oil; crude shit. Not a problem."

"You can get that?"

Perdu nodded. "What did I say, lad? Not a problem."

"Penhaligon's our boy for the explosions."

"Then bring him in, young Sergeant. Bring him in."

The war council had broken up into separate working parties. Argo knew that he should be with the rest of The Four, Sera, and Hyacinth, discussing the interception of the White Twins, but he found himself fascinated by Old Perdu's instantly conceived ideas. The old man had an enviable talent for planning sabotage.

Slide had turned the table over to Windermere when it came to the time for practicalities, and the atmosphere had chilled considerably. The Four considered Windermere and ES Section duplicitous in the extreme, and that was hard to shake. What he had to say, however, made eminent good sense, and they found themselves warming to him, despite their reservations. As Windermere had broken it down, Jeakqual-Ahrach and her Zhaithan were basically creating an energy exchange. According to the most recent reports, both to Il Syndicato and Morgana's Web, small black spheres being were placed by slave laborers all over the sloping sides of the original dirt pyramid in irregular but predetermined patterns. These spheres were made of the same Other Place material as Dark Things, and, like the mini Dark Things that had attacked Dunbar's headquarters during the Battle of Newbury Vale, they were about the same size as wicket balls, but they had somehow been rendered inert and seemingly harmless enough for humans to handle. The consensual theory, as Windermere told it, was that the spheres would be energized at the commencement of some kind of power buildup. Since the White

Twins were being specially sent to the pyramid, they had to be a part, maybe even the culmination of this process.

Windermere had put it very clearly. "The object is clearly to prevent this power buildup ever getting started, and, as I see it, our attack has to be twofold. On one hand, we need to do as much physical damage to the outer structure of the pyramid as possible, while on the other, we have to kill or capture the White Twins. We also have to remain alert, if Harriet Lime is to be believed, to any Zhaithan plan to grab The Four. I think I now have to open the meeting to any and all suggestions as to just how these ends should be achieved, and how we find the resources to achieve them."

Old Temps Perdu had again laughed. "Well, you came to the right place, Mr. Windermere. You're talking mayhem, and there's plenty of talent, even genius, for mayhem here in Paris." He had then launched into his impromptu plan to destroy the pyramid, but, while most were listening to Perdu, Cordelia asked a question of those who remained. "Has anyone considered that the Twins might be killed as the culmination of this power buildup? Or the deaths of The Four might be part of Jeakqual-Ahrach's plan? I mean, the Zhaithan have always been damned keen on human sacrifice as a means of power generation. Hundreds were hanged before the Battle of the Potomac. I was there, and I saw it happen."

Raphael backed up Cordelia. "We were all there. We all saw it. They were trying to create what they called the primordial warrior frenzy."

Slide nodded. "Death-moment energy release is their scientific name for it."

"And if the plan is to kill the Twins, do they necessarily know about it?"

But before anyone could consider what Cordelia was saying, Penhaligon entered the hall. The normally imperturbable Ranger looked concerned and a little bemused. "What the fuck was that?"

Madden and Steuben looked at him blankly. "What the fuck was what?"

"You didn't feel it?"

"Feel what?"

"Get the fuck outta here. The whole fucking building shook, and all the lights went on and off."

"Not in here they didn't."

Argo, catching the odd exchange, looked round to see if anyone at the table had felt anything. It seemed not, but then he saw Jesamine, who was as pale as a ghost, and holding on to the table for support.

## JESAMINE

*The sheets of white light blinded her, and she couldn't see the shower of black spinning triangles until they were right on top of her, but somehow Jesamine knew that the edges of the things, although two dimensional, were razor sharp, and she dodged desperately, twisting and ducking. Then the triangles were gone and she found herself in a grid of blue intersecting lines, also in a triangular formation. The two voices, when they came, were painfully overamplified, and horribly distorted. At first, Jesamine had thought it was a psychic attack, but, when she was able to make out what the voices were saying, she decided that it was an attempt at communication, but generated by someone or something with a great deal of power, but no idea how to control it.*

*At first the voices were so intense in their frantic childish anguish that they threatened Jesamine's brain. "We met the wolf."*

*"We met the wolf and he told us."*

*"We met the wolf and he told us to find you."*

*Jesamine steeled herself. She had to stop reeling and take some sort of control of the situation. "Easy, easy, tune it down a whole bit."*

*The white light diminished in intensity, and the voices became more manageable. "We met the she-wolf who told us to come and find you."*

*"Are you who I think you are?"*

*"We are who we are."*

*Jesamine's forced calm was turning the white light a softer blue. "Okay, I'm glad we established that."*

*"The wolf told us to find you."*

*"Why didn't she send you to find Cordelia."*

*"Cordelia has red hair."*

*"Cordelia doesn't like us."*

*"Why doesn't she like you."*

*"We hate her."*

*"We were taught to hate her."*

Jesamine could hardly believe what she was experiencing. The White Twins were apparently communicating with her. *"But why have you come to me?"*

*"Cordelia with the red hair."*

*"Cordelia with the red hair said our mother will kill us."*

*"Cordelia with the red hair said our mother will kill us at the pyramid."*

Jesamine, despite her initial shock was now listening intently. *"Is your mother with you?"*

*"No."*

*"No, she sleeps."*

*"She sleeps the sleep that makes her young."*

*"So how can she kill you?"*

*"Zhaithan say it, too."*

*"Zhaithan say we die."*

*"Zhaithan say we die, but they don't know we hear them."*

*"Cordelia with the red hair and Zhaithan said our mother will kill us at the pyramid."*

*"Our mother will kill us at the pyramid."*

Jesamine suddenly felt the Twins' fear. They were monsters, but they were afraid. *"So don't go to the pyramid."*

*"They make us go."*

*"Zhaithan put us on a boat, and they make us go."*

*"Help us?"*

*"Please help us."*

## ARGO

Old Temps Perdu looked up with a concern that did not suit his battered face with its leather skin and network of scars. "The honey-colored one?"

"Jesamine."

"Right, Jesamine. Is she okay?"

"She'll be fine. Cordelia and Sera are taking care of her."

"And she really received a communication from the White Twins?"

Argo spread his hands. "So it would seem."

"And they're turning on Jeakqual-Ahrach?"

"That's what she said, although it could be a ruse."

Perdu nodded. "You gotta look out for ruses." He turned back to the charts and diagrams in front of him. "Seems to me the first thing we gotta do is move the damned cannon a whole lot closer to the pyramid. It's out beyond that perimeter circle right now. We gotta move it right hard up to the pyramid."

Argo, Madden, Penhaligon, and Steuben all looked where Perdu was pointing. Steuben again asked the question. "How the hell are we going to do that? It's a hundred yards or more, and the damn thing's gotta weigh beaucoup tons."

Perdu tapped the chart impatiently. "It's on rails isn't it?"

Argo objected. "But it's been there for decades. It has to be rusted solid."

"Wrong, young Major. Dead wrong. In the old days, it stood right up by the pyramid. That's why the tracks go there. It must have been moved out when the Zhaithan started their hell-work. Which means it must have been oiled, and greased, and made mobile."

"We still have to roll it back."

"Maybe we'll get lucky and find the locomotive, or whatever it was that moved it the first time, still there and still working."

"And if it's not?"

"There's a whole camp of slave laborers, isn't there? So they can do a bit of laboring for us. We just remind them that once a slave always a slave, until we say different."

"And what if the Mosul say different?"

Perdu's eyes took on an unpleasant gleam. "The Mosul ain't gonna say nothing, because, when we move the cannon, they'll all be fucking dead. Ain't that right, Ranger Madden?"

Madden's eyes had the same gleam. "That's right, Old Temps, they'll all be fucking dead."

At this juncture, Bonaparte came into the room, and he was in a hurry. "A message just came through to Hyacinth from a Morgana agent in the labor camp by the pyramid."

"What's it say?"

"That there was some kind of test of the work that's been done on one side of the pyramid. Seemingly the Teuton engineers who are working for the Zhaithan tried to fire up one section of the black spheres."

"And?"

"And there was suddenly all this white sheet lightning and the whole fucking pyramid vanished for a full fifteen seconds. Then it came back again with all the black spheres fused out."

Penhaligon looked vindicated. "That must have been what caused the tremor I felt."

Bonaparte continued. "Seems like it wasn't the desired effect because the Zhaithan went crazy and there's been a bunch of executions."

Old Temps sighed. "Whatever it means to them, it's telling us that we gotta get our shit packed and make our move."

## CORDELIA

"You think the weirdness at the pyramid and the Twins breaking in on you were connected?"

Jesamine nodded. "It would be a hell of a coincidence if they weren't."

Cordelia, Jesamine, and Sera walked down one of the dark and seemingly endless passages that led to Falconetti's "quiet room." As Sera was unlocking the door to the torture chamber, Jesamine looked curiously at the eight-pointed star daubed on it. "Does that have some kind of purpose?"

Sera shrugged. "As far as I know, it's always been there. Maybe it's supposed to ward off demons."

Cordelia grinned. "It didn't keep Slide out."

"Perhaps he's another kind of demon. It was probably Noire who had it put there. She was my father's most effective interrogator when I was a kid." Sera pushed open the heavy door. "She used to have this saying that she told to her subjects before she went to work on them. 'The shortest way to heaven is through hell.' She said it gave them something to contemplate through their suffering."

Inside, Harriet Lime was still locked in the stocks. Cordelia walked around her, amused by her helplessness and obvious humiliation. "And what have you been contemplating, Harriet?"

"Damn you, Cordelia."

"Damn me? You've changed your tune. It wasn't long ago that you were groveling to protect your lily-white skin from the thrashing of a lifetime."

"If I've been contemplating anything, it's what I'll have done to you when the positions become reversed."

"You think you'll get me in the stocks?"

"I have far more unpleasant ideas. You do know that ultimately you can't win, don't you?"

Cordelia snorted in harsh amusement. "You'll have to excuse me if I find that statement less than plausible coming from someone in your situation."

Sera drew back the bolts that secured the stocks and then swung up the top half of the device, freeing Lime's neck and wrists. Lime gingerly straightened up, wincing as she moved cramped muscles. "How do you know I haven't already alerted Jeakqual-Ahrach to what you're all planning?"

"You haven't. I would have known about it." Cordelia was bluffing, but with such supreme confidence that it seemed to work, and Lime's face clouded as if she believed her. Sera thrust an orange-colored bundle at Lime. "Put this on. It's clean."

Lime shook the bundle open to reveal a one-piece orange overall, with a large letter "P" on both front and back, and held it up with an expression of extreme distaste. "This is what Zhaithan political prisoners wear."

"It'll make it harder for you to try and run. Approach the enemy wearing that, and the average Mosul grunt will shoot you out of hand before you've had the chance to say a word."

Lime reluctantly started to pull on the overall. "What about shoes?"

"We'll find you some shoes."

She shook her head as she buttoned the buttons. "You really won't get away with this. Her Grand Eminence is miles ahead of you."

"I'd shut up if I were you, Harriet. The only thing that's stopping me doing my worst to you is that everyone is so busy mobilizing to stop this thing at the pyramid, and Her Grand Eminence's absurd attempt to break into another reality."

Jesamine added, "Our mobilization is all that's saving your sorry ass."

## RAPHAEL

The sun was setting as the barges approached the point on the river, towards the eastern outskirts of the ruined city, where the vehicles were assembled with which the small force would make their journey to Amiens and the pyramid. Some of those around Raphael had slept, but the majority had spent the day in frantic preparation for the attack, and he was amazed just how much had been achieved in such little time. It made sense that Damon Falconetti could muster a crew of armed men and women in a matter of hours, but the speedy location of explosives, heavy weapons, fuel, and ammunition, even Mosul uniforms and vehicles, and some strange concoction of quick-drying cement that Old Temps Perdu had demanded, indicated that the Falconetti Family had resources that were far more extensive than Raphael had ever imagined, and Il Syndicato were much more than the "degenerates and cutthroats" he had thought them to be before he had arrived in Paris. He was also surprised and impressed at the intelligence, ingenuity, and capacity for improvisation that had been demonstrated all over the Falconetti stronghold once the bit was between the Family's teeth. Plans were formulated, details checked, weaknesses were discovered and corrected, and the needed materials obtained. As the barge Raphael was on floated past the last major outcrop of tall ruins, armed but silent children had stared down at him, and he could not shake the eerie feeling that Paris was being left in their care while the grown-ups went to war.

He remembered how his last battle had started, and how very different it had been. At Newbury Vale, the fight had been joined in the bright light of morning, with flags and banners, wild optimism, the thunder of hooves, and artillery pounding the enemy positions with shot and shell. This assault on the Mosul was diametrically different. They would be driving secretly into the night, relying on stealth, silence, and total surprise. A hundred things, unseen and unknown, could go wrong, and, instead of optimism, the mood was one of grim determination. About the only one who was viewing the attack with any obvious relish was Old Temps Perdu, who made no attempt to hide the fact that he hardly gave a rat's ass about the defeat of Jeakqual-Ahrach, or even saving reality and the world. He was going to Amiens for just one reason—to create the biggest bang of his long career in explosives, and this made him happier than the proverbial widow on her wedding night. The only others who seemed to grimly relish the prospect of the coming fight were the half-dozen Rangers, who seemed relieved to be back in harness, and ready to melt into the night to, as they put it, "ply their trade."

The luxury of observation ended abruptly the moment that he stepped off the barge. The army might be very small and highly ragtag, but it was saddling up and moving out, and doing it with dour efficiency. Once Damon Falconetti had committed to the cause, he had made manpower his first priority. Only a small force could be moved out of Paris, and Falconetti had gone to every length to see that it was made up of the best soldiers and centurions from his own ranks, plus the top guns of other Parisian gangs and outlaw bands who owed him fealty, plus the best contract freelancers. The force traveled light and was quick to sort out the transports to which they had been assigned. The war party from Paris would go to Amiens in convoy. A motorcade of cars and trucks that would, everyone hoped, descend on the unsuspecting Mosul, Zhaithan, and Teutons sometime around dawn, and without the slightest warning. The Four had been divided for the journey to the pyramid. Raphael had argued against it but had eventually been overridden. The obvious difficulty was that Cordelia had to stay with Lime, since Lime would be the one to hear and tell when the White Twins were coming, even if she supplied the information under physical duress. This made Cordelia a crucial part of the unit that would kill or capture the Twins, but to have the rest of The Four with her would make them nothing more than a nonfunctional appendage. None of them particularly wanted to go into the Other Place so close to the Amiens Pyramid after Cordelia had described what had happened when she had been near it. They all hoped that the attack and the seizing of the Twins would be a strictly terrestrial operation, and it had therefore been decided that they should split up, distributing their individual talents where they were most needed, and, they hoped, also manage to maintain at least rudimentary four-way, psychic communication. If they were called on to go paranormal, they would try to move to a prearranged meeting place.

Cordelia and Jesamine, with a handcuffed Harriet Lime in tow, were to travel in the immaculate Benz, along with Sera, her driver Jacques, and Madden as an extra armed bodyguard. They would be the lead vehicle and pathfinder for the others. Sera's Benz created such a convincing impression of Mosul brass on urgent nocturnal business, that, should they encounter a routine checkpoint, the Mosul giving the order to stop would be more nervous of higher authority than fearful of armed guerrillas. The Benz was to travel a few minutes ahead of the rest of the motorcade. If they ran into a problem on the road, the plan was elegantly simple. No showing of forged papers or any other kind of deception. They would simply kill the soldiers at the roadblock as quickly and efficiently as possible, before any alarm could be raised, and proceed on, leaving the road clear for the rest of the convoy, that would remain close together in one body, except for the truck carrying Old Temps's explosives, and that would follow at a quite considerable distance, with one car of volunteer gunmen driving behind it to protect the rear. Raphael would be riding with the main force that would attack the Mosul camp, and free the slave laborers, either to escape and cause a huge chaotic diversion, or to move the Paris Gun, if so needed. Argo, on the other hand, was going with Old Perdu's crew, that included Penhaligon, whose objective was to blow up the gun and wreck the pyramid.

As Raphael swung up into the liberated Mosul truck that was to carry them, and settled himself between Cartwright and Bonaparte, Jesamine's voice spoke in his head. *"Raphael?"*

The psychic linkage was being tested. He did his best to respond without being obvious to those beside him in the truck. "Jesamine?"

*"Are you hearing me?"*

"Without a problem."

*"Cordelia?"*

*"I'm in."*

*"Argo?"*

*"Loud and clear."*

Jesamine sounded satisfied. *"We're moving out in the Benz right now. Let's hope it stays loud and clear."*

## JESAMINE

The interior of Sera's black Benz contained more passengers than was strictly comfortable. Jacques drove and Madden sat beside him with a shotgun across his lap. Madden still wore his Ranger uniform, although Sera had expressed some concern. "Isn't it a little obvious?"

Madden hadn't seemed worried. "By the time they see me, they'll be as good as dead. And anyway, Jesamine and the others are doing the same." He had been totally unwilling to change into anything more anonymous. "If they catch me, they're going to hang me anyway, and I'd rather be hung as a Ranger than a spy."

Sera, accustomed to being obeyed with little or no question by the Falconetti rank and file, seemed distinctly irked by Madden's attitude, but Jesamine and Cordelia found it comforting. It was good to have a familiar psychopath in the car with them, as they led the drive into danger, and they were especially glad he was there when the oil lamps and red flares of the first Mosul checkpoint were spotted. Madden had turned in his seat and grinned at the two of them, crowded in the back with Sera and Lime. "You ladies should check the silencers on your pistols. We don't want any noise right now."

Jesamine already had the silencer screwed firmly onto the muzzle of her revolver. She steeled herself. To hesitate would be fatal. She remembered what Madden had told her earlier. "Aim and shoot, without thinking of them as men. They are targets, merely in the way." He had also laughed and added, "But don't worry too much about having to do any killing. Jacques and I should have it all under control."

Jacques had started to slow the car. He glanced back. "Looks like a routine roadblock, with just three of them manning it. A couple of soldiers and an Agent from the Ministry of Virtue."

Madden put aside his shotgun, and held his silenced revolver down beside the door. Cordelia glared at Harriet Lime, whom she seemed to have made her personal responsibility. "If you're tempted to try something, first remember how that orange suit is a shoot-to-kill signal to every ignorant Mosul with a loaded gun."

Lime sat very still with her cuffed hands in front of her. She said nothing, which angered Cordelia. "Do you understand what I just said?"

Lime finally nodded. "Yes, I understand."

"And if they don't kill you, I will."

Jacques stopped the car a little short of the roadblock and waited. It was nothing more than an antique armored steamer pulled across the road as a barrier that any approaching vehicle would need to drive around. The two soldiers approached the car on foot, one leading, and the other a few paces behind. The one farthest from them had unslung his rifle, but the closer one had not even bothered. His eyes were screwed up against the glare of the Benz's powerful headlights. Madden signed to Jacques that he would dispatch the two soldiers while Jacques should concentrate on the Agent by the steamer. Jacques indicated this was fine by him. In a single, easy movement, Madden was out of the car, down on the surface of the road, firing around the door. His pistol made a quiet *pifft,* and the first Mosul staggered backward as a heavy caliber slug hit him in the chest. The second one had not fully grasped that anything was wrong before the second *pifft,* and he, too, was shot. Jacques had to negotiate the Benz's steering wheel, and was maybe a second behind Madden. Two silenced shots came in rapid succession, and the Agent from the Ministry of Virtue went down.

Madden and Jacques moved forward, checking that the fallen Mosul were in fact dead, and when satisfied that no one was shamming, they picked up each body in turn and dumped them in the weeds and long grass at the side of the road. With the bodies out of the way, they turned their attention to the steamer. Madden, for once, had no answer, and he looked to Jacques. "You know how to drive one of these things? I don't have a clue."

Jacques shook his head. "I can give it a try, but . . ."

Inside the car, Sera cursed. "Fucking men!"

She opened the passenger door and stepped from the car. "At least one of us knows what to do."

She swung up into the driving seat of the steamer, valved off excess steam, and then heaved on the heavy gearshift, and put it in reverse. The machine lurched backward off the road, and Sera, who was wearing the leather flight suit that had previously been Lime's, jumped clear as the wheezing bulk started to upend itself in a ditch. She walked back to the car, wiping grease from her hands. "You know, those poor bastards' only means of communication was a couple of signal rockets in the steamer. No one will know they're dead until someone comes to relieve them."

As she got back in the car, she smiled at Madden, perhaps as a token apology for her earlier ill temper. "Nice work, Ranger Madden. Very clean."

Madden winked. "Wait until we hit the Mosul for real, Miss Falconetti. You'll see some real clean wet-work."


## ARGO

The truck in which Argo was traveling came upon the Benz, another car, and three trucks parked under the cover of a grove of trees. The pyramid loomed so large that anyone could be forgiven for thinking they were right on top of it, until Old Temps Perdu reminded them just how big the Amiens Pyramid really was. "We're still a good half mile away, maybe more."

He climbed down from the truck and made known the next phase of his plan to the group from the other vehicles. "While you wait for the others to catch up, I'm going ahead right now. I need to look at the gun before all hell breaks loose." He indicated Argo. "I'll try to keep in touch via the young major's mumbo-jumbo, but if that doesn't work, the truck with the explosives needs to keep its engine running, and head straight for the gun as soon as the first attack starts. It's vital you all re-member that."

Sera Falconetti, who was de facto leader of those who had so far ar-rived, nodded. "No problem, Old Temps, it will be done."

"I don't want to be at the fucking gun and lacking the wherewithal to blow it all to hell."

"Don't fret, old man. I'm telling you it will be done."

Apparently satisfied, Old Temps climbed back onto the running board of the truck and leaned in to speak to the driver. "Okay, real easy and lights off."

In the back of the truck, Argo, the Ranger Penhaligon, and nine of Falconetti's best arsonists and cat burglars rode in silence as they rolled quietly forward, headlights off, blind in the darkness, until Old Temps decided that they had gone as far as they safely could along the main road to the Mosul labor camp. "Take her off the road and stash her behind those bushes yonder. It won't be no hiding place come daylight, but, come daylight, it won't matter."

As the driver eased the truck forward, doing as instructed. Argo, Penhaligon, and the others grabbed their kit and weapons, swung down to the road, and gathered round Old Temps. He turned immediately to Penhaligon. "You think you can take us up to the gun on foot, Ranger?"

"Easy. Just follow the ditches and hedgerows for as long as we can; then a brisk sprint at the end."

"If we're seen, we risk the whole attack."

Penhaligon looked surprised that the warning even needed to be given. "The bastards will never know what hit them."

The eleven men on the Paris Gun detail started off into the darkness. Argo cleared his mind, concentrating completely on one moment at a time. He was not thinking what might happen in the future, and he was especially not thinking about the pyramid. Even at a distance, the thing was emitting waves of black anxiety, and he did not want to open up to it, unless absolutely forced. He focused solely on the simple stuff, like where he was putting his feet, and keeping in sight of the man in front of him; in Argo's case, a shifty-eyed Falconetti thief called Lapin. Penhaligon led them from one piece of natural cover to another, stopping, ducking down, and then moving in bursts of fast and silent motion, along a dry ditch, around the perimeter wire and the floodlights of the labor camp, in and out of the shadows of what seemed to be unused outbuildings, and piles of construction materials. The whole Mosul site proved relatively unguarded, as though those in command believed no one would have the crazy audacity to stage any kind of attack.

The group finally found themselves sheltering in the shadows between stacks of timber that looked like railroad ties, with the pyramid looming over them, and the Paris Gun a scant hundred and fifty paces away. Like the pyramid itself, the Paris Gun was so big that it confounded all ideas of relative size. Argo's first impression was that it seemed shorter and more squat than he remembered from pictures, with much of the lower part of the barrel concealed by the thick cylindrical levers that absorbed the recoil, and it was not until Penhaligon made what he had called his "brisk sprint," and a human being was in the picture, that Argo finally realized just how huge the thing really was.

Before Penhaligon made his run, he carefully laid the groundwork for himself, and those who would follow. He gathered the other men around him, and pointed. "You see the guard tower on the near corner of the slave camp?"

They all nodded, and Penhaligon continued. "The guard on it seems to be the only one interested in this area. He now and again shines a light over here to take a look, but it's several minutes between inspections. Plenty of time to make it over, and, once we're beside the gun, he can't see us. I'm going over on my own first to check for bad news we don't know about, then the rest of you should come across in threes. Just keep one firm eye on that tower monkey, and, if he looks like he's swinging his light your way, hit the deck and freeze."

Penhaligon waited until the light was just gone from the area he had to cross, and took off running, low and cautious. Halfway across something must have spooked him, because he dropped like a flat shadow, and waited, but then he was up again, and, in a matter of seconds, beside the gun and beckoning for the others to follow. The first group, Argo among them, waited long minutes until the light came again, but, when it was gone, they managed to cross the open space in one uninterrupted, desperate dash. The second group also made it across without incident, but the third, that was four in number, dropped and froze halfway across, as the light unexpectedly turned in their direction. They would never know whether the guard had half-noticed something, or if he was just looking on a whim, but he failed to spot their prone figures, and they, too, reached the gun unscathed. When Old Temps had all his chickens safely home, he turned his attention to the gun itself, running his hands over one of the great steel wheels, and talking to himself in a voice that verged on awe. "This fucker is unique. Maybe the only work of art to ever come out of the Ruhr."

Penhaligon had looked at him with a puzzled expression. "You sound like you don't want to blow it up."

"Oh, I want to blow it up, my boy. Make no mistake about that." He looked sharply at Argo. "Weaver."

"Yes."

"Can you do the whammy, and let your ladies know we're in place."

"I can try."

"Then try."

Argo knew this would be required of him, but he was also dreading it. He opened his mind, and, as he had feared, the pyramid forced its way in like an invisible wind, filling his head with a clashing plague of venom-filled wordless chatter. All he could do was soundlessly shout above it. "Cordelia! Jesamine!"

The voices that came back were faint and distorted, but they were there. *"Argo, we hear you."*

"Inform everyone that the team on the gun is in place."

*"We'll do that."*

He must have shown sign of the strain, because Perdu was looking at him with concern. "Trouble?"

Argo shook his head, and stared at the pyramid. "No trouble. But that fucking thing is alive."


### RAPHAEL

To call it a hill was an exaggeration, the slight rise was nothing more than a mild roll in the otherwise flat countryside, but it gave them a slightly elevated view of most of the Mosul slave labor camp, and also afforded them a hidden vantage point. Steuben had made it clear to all around him that one of the most prized Ranger skills was making the terrain work for you, rather than against you. Steuben, Falconetti, Slide, and Windermere lay flat on their stomachs on the damp grass, watching and waiting, looking for the weaknesses in and around the camp and construction site while the main body of their force waited some yards back, crouched and ready for the order to go. Raphael's first surprise was at how quiet it all was. The Amiens Pyramid project did not work a night-shift, which seemed odd. When he had been an unwilling recruit in the Mosul Provincial Levies, there had been much barrack-room talk about the labor camps, and, for most of the young conscripts, it had been a choice of forced labor or the army, and they told stories of slaves being worked to death in twelve-hour shifts, twenty-four hours a day. On the other hand, to be assigned to guard a labor camp was the desired miracle that would save them from near-certain death in combat in the Americas.

Falconetti seemed quite as amazed as Raphael, although for slightly different reasons. He gestured to the two rows of workers' huts enclosed in the electrically lit rectangle of barbed wired, with a watchtower on each corner, and the guards' barracks and other buildings beyond. "It all looks so easy. The damned place is hardly guarded."

Slide nodded. "A prison is always easy to take. The concentration is always on the business of keeping in, not keeping out."

Falconetti shook his head. "I don't get it. They have the big secret, but without enough guns to protect it."

Slide smiled. "That's because they believe their secret is still a secret, and that no one would attack what looks, from the outside, to be nothing more than the needless renovation of an unpleasant monument."

A voice called in Raphael's head, distorted and somewhat dizzying from the interference of the pyramid. *"Raphael. It's Cordelia."*

"I hear you, although not well."

*"Argo has made contact. Perdu's team is in place, and ready for the explosives truck to come to them."*

"And what about the White Twins?"

*"Lime has heard nothing yet."*

"You believe her?"

*"I think so. She knows she'll be killed if she fucks with us."* She paused as though distracted. *"What?"*

Raphael was confused. "Cordelia?"

*"Raphael, wait . . ."*

"What?"

Only the noise of the pyramid remained in his head, and Raphael glanced in the approximate direction of where Cordelia, Jesamine, and the others in that team were waiting for the supposed arrival of the White Twins. To his dismay, he saw headlights on the road. He nudged Slide, who looked in the same direction. "That can't be one of our cars or trucks, driving so close to the camp with full headlights."

"If it is, the driver's a damned fool."

Falconetti snarled angrily. "I didn't recruit any damned fools."

"So what the fuck is it?"

Slide shook his head. "Beats me."

"Could it be the Twins arriving unannounced?"

"I sure hope not."

## JESAMINE

"What the fuck is that?"

"It's a fucking car. And coming this way."

"Is it the Twins?"

"It had better not be."

Jesamine, Cordelia, and Sera all rounded on Harriet Lime. "If you've fucked us, you die."

Lime knew they weren't bluffing and her response was pure desperation. "I swear, I heard nothing."

Sera looked urgently up the road. "Maybe it's just a normal piece of late-night camp traffic."

They now had their own roadblock in place. The Benz was parked across the road, ready to halt all incoming vehicles, and it was too late to clear it before the strange car was upon them. Madden and Jacques readied their weapons, but Cordelia was shaking her head. "This can't turn into a firefight. If we start shooting now, the whole damn camp will be alerted. The element of surprise will be lost for the other groups."

Madden did not seem concerned. He slung his shotgun over his shoulder, drew his side arm, and began screwing on the silencer again. "So we stop them and hold them, whoever they are. We just have to be quiet about it."

Jesamine drew her own pistol, and also replaced the silencer. Meanwhile Sera beckoned to the men who had joined them to reinforce the roadblock that was designed to stop the Twins. "You guys in the uniforms. Get in position."

A number of the newcomers were dressed in Zhaithan and Mosul army uniforms. The idea was to deal with any occurrence like the one they now apparently faced. The roadblock would look, at first glance, like a genuine Mosul emergency, and that should be enough to bring any official vehicle to an unsuspecting stop. They moved quickly into place, taking up positions beside the Benz, doing their best to look like enemy soldiers in the middle of a long and tedious nighttime guard duty, while the others melted away to crouch, weapons drawn, in the shadows at the side of the road.

The still unidentified car slowed and came to a halt, and finally Jesamine could see more than just the headlights. She lay prone beside Cordelia and Lime. Cordelia had her pistol to Lime's head, and she whispered tensely, "Not a sound."

The car proved to be a small two-seater, a Teuton copy of the Armstrong roadster that Windermere drove in London. The car stood for a moment, with the men in the Mosul uniforms watching it carefully with their carbines leveled, then both doors opened and two men climbed angrily out. One was overweight, with a shaved head, and wearing the uniform of a colonel in the Teuton Engineers. The other was thin and angular and affected a monocle in his right eye. He had a seriously receding chin and seemed to be a major in the same regiment. The colonel was the more incensed of the two, and instantly demanded to know why he and his companion had been stopped. "What the fuck is this all about?"

One of Falconetti's men, wearing a fake Zhaithan uniform, took a step forward. "State your names, ranks, and what business you have here."

The demand only increased the colonel's indignation. "I'm Colonel Helmut Phaall of the 4th Engineers, you idiot. Don't you know me? And this is Major Vogel. We're stationed here, damn it. Working on the damned pyramid for you people. And after the recent fuck-ups, you have a lot of gall bothering us like this."

Jesamine let out a gasp. "Phaall?"

The phony Zhaithan continued with his questions. "And where are you coming from?"

"From Rotk's whorehouse in Boulogne, as if it's any of your business."

Cordelia, realizing what was happening, quickly put a hand on Jesamine's arm, but Jesamine ignored her, and, throwing all caution to the winds, stood up and stepped into the aura of the headlights. "I though you'd died at the Potomac, but I guess that was just wishful thinking."

Phaall looked at her in amazement. "What the . . . Jesamine?"

"Yes, Jesamine."

"How did you escape the retreat? And what are you doing in that ridiculous uniform?"

"Right now I'm remembering how you fucked me, how you beat me for no reason except your own amusement, and how you made me suck your drunken flaccid cock, and dance for you, and touch myself, and take it up my ass, and how you loaned me to your friends, you motherpenis. You used to think you owned me, but guess what? It's fucking payback time."

Phaall seemed incapable of grasping what was taking place. He began to bluster furiously. "Put that gun away, you stupid girl. Do you have any idea what will happen to you if you shoot me? They really should have caned you harder in that Cadiz whorehouse where I found you."

Jesamine pulled the trigger on her silenced pistol. The *pifft* seemed a less-than-fitting end for Phaall, who still appeared unable to believe what was happening, even when the bullet hit him in the chest. She shot him a second time just to make sure, and, even before Phaall fell, she pivoted gracefully and put a third shot into Vogel's head, as he watched the drama open-mouthed. "You picked the wrong bloody night to go whoring with the colonel, boy."

Sera came out of the darkness and looked down at the two bodies. "I guess that was one way to solve the problem." She looked round at her men, who also seemed unsure of what they had just witnessed. "Okay, stop your gawking. You've all seen revenge before. Get the two stiffs and their car off the road and out of sight."

But no sooner had her orders been carried out than a new crisis fell on them. Cordelia and Harriet Lime had just emerged from cover when Lime suddenly doubled over, choking and gasping. She fell to her knees, clutching her stomach with her cuffed hands. Cordelia's first response was to raise her pistol. "If you're faking this, I swear I really will kill you."

Lime, however, continued to gurgle and gasp. Her entire body started twitching, but she forced out a few words. "The Twins . . . The Twins, I can't . . . control it."

At the same time, a red signal flare arced into the air.

## RAPHAEL

Falconetti fired the signal flare, and, at the same time, standing or kneeling, Graham and the other sharpshooters that Falconetti had called forward, took aim with their long rifles and began picking off the sentries on the watchtowers at the four corners of the slave compound, and the foot soldiers patrolling the perimeter. Down on the road, truck engines were grinding to life, and, in a matter of minutes, the first vehicle had smashed through the main gates of the camp. Two Mosul ran out from the guard shack beside the gate, but were brought down. More trucks and cars were coming up behind. The lead vehicle made a wide, reckless turn, swaying and rolling on its suspension, and then deliberately smashed into what looked like a Mosul barracks hut. Armed men poured from the back, shooting as soon as they hit the ground.

On the low ridge, Falconetti turned and roared to his men. "Okay, let's go! Let's hit them!"

Thirty men rose from the grass as one and started running. Raphael was between Steuben and Slide, slightly behind Falconetti, who was leading the charge. The unreality of combat had him in its grip, the dry-mouthed combination of fear and exultation. The sound of small arms fire was all round him, the rattle of musketry, the bark of heavy caliber pistols, and the rhythmic chop of Bergman guns on automatic. The camp's floodlights went out, but it hardly mattered. A gray dawn was appearing in the eastern sky. Half-dressed Mosul stumbled from the huts, fumbling with their carbines and muskets, bemused, and, in most cases, were meat before they even knew for sure they were under attack. A handful of Mosul soldiers had the presence of mind to stay in their hut, trying to defend themselves from within, but then a grenade exploded, and the hut was matchwood. Two uniformed Zhaithan, black field capes flapping, ran for a car, but were shot down before they could make good their escape. Another tried to get away on horseback, past the camp's gallows, where a dozen corpses were hanging, but was unseated by a bullet, leaving the riderless mount to panic through the fighting. Four men came out of a bathhouse, naked, clutching towels and underwear, and were slaughtered as they tried to cover themselves.

Falconetti's group reached the fence that surrounded the slave laborers' compound. A number of the men carried wire cutters, and swiftly ripped a path. Raphael climbed through the gap in the barbed wire, right behind Slide, who had his strange, matching pistols drawn, one in each hand. He found himself amid the smell of unwashed fear, helping to rip open the locked doors to the slave laborers' huts, as Falconetti shouted to the dazed prisoners in their ragged and dirty overalls. "Come on! Out, out, get out of there! Don't you fuckers know when you're being set free?"

One prisoner called out, "Food, did you bring food?"

Falconetti's laugh verged on maniacal. "Food? Find your own food. We're delivering liberty and fraternity!"

## CORDELIA

The battle was being joined all round them, but the women at the roadblock had more important problems. Harriet Lime lay on the hard road, close to the Benz, and the blood left behind by Phaall and Vogel. Her face contorted, her legs made involuntary kicking motions, her hands clawed spasmodically at the air, and, all the time, she maintained a meaningless, wordless babble. She had scraped her skin in a number of places, and two of her usually immaculate fingernails were broken.

"The . . . the . . . the . . . the . . ."

"I don't think she's faking this."

"The . . . the . . . the . . . the . . ."

Cordelia knelt down beside the uncontrollably shaking Lime, while Jesamine and Cordelia looked on. "What? What are you trying to say?"

"The . . . the . . . the Twins . . ."

"What about the Twins?"

"The . . . Twins . . . they . . ."

Cordelia was rapidly losing patience. Her nature was not to play nurse in the middle of a firefight. "Yes, the Twins. I get it. They what?"

"They . . . they . . ." The paroxysms abruptly stopped, and she spoke, face blank as an automaton, talking with the voices of The White Twins. *"We want to talk."*

"You are talking."

*"We want to talk to red-haired Cordelia."*

"You are talking to Cordelia."

Sera looked at Jesamine. "Holy shit. Harriet's channeling them."

*"We are sorry."*

"Why are you sorry?"

*"We are sorry, red-haired Cordelia."*

"But why are you sorry?"

*"We were trained to hate you."*

*"We were trained by our mother to hate you."*

*"But now we hate mother."*

*"But now we hate mother because she intends to kill us."*

"You just learned that?"

*"We just learned that."*

*"Help us?"*

*"Please help us."*

Cordelia looked round at Sera and Jesamine with the obvious silent question. They both nodded. They would go along. Cordelia asked, "How do we know we can trust you?"

A request for assurance did not seem to be part of the Twins' world. *"We trust you."*

*"Help us?"*

*"Please help us."*

"Where are you?"

*"We travel."*

*"We travel by road."*

Sera was becoming frustrated at the slowness of it all. "Do they have to say everything twice?"

The Twins somehow heard her. *"We say everything twice because there are two of us."*

Cordelia ignored the exchange. "Do you know where we are?"

*"Yes."*

"Are you close to us?"

*"Yes."*

"Are you among Zhaithan?"

*"Yes."*

Explosions were coming from the camp, and Sera looked round anxiously. "This is like a fucking séance."

Jesamine watched the channeled exchange between Cordelia and the Twins intently. "They don't seem to have any real sense of place or time."

Sera shook her head. "And they're supposed to be superior to us?"

"We don't know what else they may have a sense of."

Cordelia kept focused on the twins. "I can't help you if the Zhaithan try to hurt me. The Zhaithan will want to hurt me."

*"We will not let the Zhaithan hurt you."*

*"We tried to stop the Zhaithan hurting your friend Kennedy."*

*"We couldn't help it that there was only one."*

"This makes no sense."

*"We will not let the Zhaithan hurt you if you help us."*

## ARGO

By bleeding off the hydraulic fluid from the big steel recoil cylinders, Old Temps Perdu had been able to lower the elevation of the Paris Gun so the massive barrel, with its twenty-four-inch bore, was almost parallel with the ground. So far everything was going as Old Temps had predicted. The gun had been oiled and greased, and returned to some approximation of working order. "Not that I'd like to fire the thing. It ain't been that well restored, but we can give thanks that the wheels ain't rusted solid."

With the barrel now at its lowest incline, it would be far easier to load the explosive into the massive two feet of gaping muzzle. While the other men kept watch with weapons at the ready, Old Temps, with Penhaligon at his side, had inspected the gun in the most thoroughgoing detail, and seemed pleased that everything, so far, was fitting in with his plan of destruction. After lowering the barrel, he had locked down the breech, and declared himself ready to start loading the explosives. The only real problem seemed to be the move of a hundred or so feet that would bring it hard up by the pyramid. He seemed oblivious to the fact that a raging firefight was being fought out just a few hundred yards away from them. When asked about this, Old Temps had laughed. "Hell, I thought we'd be doing it all under fire. This is a piece of cake. Now where are those fucking explosives?"

Lapin pointed. "There they are. The truck with the red cross on the side."

Everyone stopped what they were doing and watched as the olive green, former Mosul army truck steamed its way through the confusion of running, shooting men, bouncing towards them, with the driver apparently working on the principle that the shortest distance between two points was a straight line, no matter what got in the way.

"Just pray he don't catch a stray bullet. Always been the big question. Do you make your ammunition trucks real visible, or real indistinguishable?"

"The Mosul don't seem to be trying to stop it."

In fact, most of the Mosul that Argo could see were doing their best to get out of the way of the speeding truck, doubtless afraid that it would come to a sudden stop and disgorge yet another wagonload of remorseless gunmen with blazing revolvers and roaring shotguns. For an instant, Argo caught sight of Yancey Slide in the middle of the mêlée, calmly firing his otherworldly pistols at any target that presented itself.

Argo knew that Raphael was probably somewhere nearby. It was somehow reassuring to know that, although separated, they were all part of the same struggle.

Old Perdu, meanwhile, anxiously fingered the scars on his face. "I think the Mosul have their hands more than full with our boys, but there's a whole lot of hot metal flying about out there. You never fucking know."

The truck was now through the worst of the fighting, and coming straight at them. Perdu looked round at his men. "Let's not waste time, lads. The moment the truck comes to a stop, get it unloaded and start pushing the stuff into the barrel of the gun. All except Calq and Riffi, you two get that cement I had made up, find water and start mixing it."

The truck halted and the men went to work under the supervision of Penhaligon. The explosives were packed in dozens of small, one-gallon casks that were easily rolled down the barrel of the gun. Perdu watched for long enough to satisfy himself that all was well, then he turned to Argo. "You think you can get word to Falconetti?"

Argo nodded. "It worked before. Unless something's happened to Raphael."

"So pass the word to get all the slave laborers over here pronto, and bring all the ropes they can get their hands on. I don't see no locomotive, so we'll have to move this monster the hard way."

### JESAMINE

Jesamine was not happy. "So basically we're in the hands of the White Twins. We've agreed to help them, but the whole thing could be a Jeakqual-Ahrach trap that we've just walked into it."

Cordelia looked bleakly at her. "I don't like it either, but what did you expect me to do."

"If we only knew when they were coming."

The noise from the firefight had become more spasmodic, and short lulls even occurred in the fighting. Jesamine could only hope that it meant that their people had overrun the Mosul opposition and were now mopping up pockets of resistance. It had been some time since they had heard anything from either Argo or Raphael, and, in their position, out on the road to the camp, they had no idea how the fray might really be going. The dawn was turning dark to day and, according to the rough timetable that had been set for the operation, Old Temps Perdu should be getting the gun ready to destroy, or at least damage, the pyramid.

Madden joined Jesamine, Cordelia, and Sera. He seemed completely unaffected by the general tension. "The waiting's the worst. That's what the old-timers say."

Jesamine laughed despite herself. "Doesn't anything get to you, Madden?"

The Ranger shrugged. "I figure if I can't kill it, it probably can't kill me, and vice versa, so all I gotta to be is faster."

"I'm not sure I quite follow you."

"What I'm saying is that you don't have to worry about any crew of Zhaithan coming down this road. They'll be no problem for me and these here Falconetti boys."

Jesamine sighed. "This part of the fight may be more than just a matter of speed and firepower."

Madden looked away. "I know what you mean, Major, and if you and Lady Blakeney just cover me and the boys from that witchy shit, we'll do the rest."

Jesamine smiled. Again, despite herself, she was starting to find Madden oddly adorable, but before she could decide just how much she liked him, Argo's voice was in her head, painful with the distortion from the pyramid. *"Perdu needs all the slave laborers to the gun, with all the rope that can be found."*

The message was plainly intended for Raphael to pass to Falconetti or Slide, but they had no way to avoid all Four hearing it. Jesamine glanced at Cordelia. She had plainly experienced the same pain. Sera, on the other hand, was just plain curious. "What was that?"

"Just Argo for Raphael. They're ready to move the gun. Not our problem."

Madden seemed a little wistful that he was not part of the action at the Paris Gun, but then he looked up the road and pointed. "But here comes our problem, I think."

## RAPHAEL

A Mosul infantryman appeared in front of Raphael, lunging with a bayonet. Almost without thinking, Raphael feinted sideways, away from the blade, and shot the man. He had forgotten how easy it was to kill in the heat of battle. A detached part of him observed, in the graphic instant before the blood spurted, and the Mosul fell, that the man looked sallow and undernourished, and his uniform was dirty and threadbare. Two more Mosul were right behind the first. They were part of a raggedly organized wedge that was attempting a breakout under the command of two Teuton officers. It wasn't clear if they had an objective, or if they were just trying to get away from the attackers' overwhelming ferocity and superior weapons. Raphael retreated a couple of paces, recocking his double-action pistol to fire again, but was blinded by noise and pain that took over his mind, and brought with it the urgent voice of Argo.

*"Perdu needs all the slave laborers to the gun, with all the rope that can be found."*

The communication could not have come at a worse moment. Raphael could see nothing but white light, but he knew Mosul bayonets were coming at him.

*"Raphael? Can you hear me?"*

"I hear you. I understand. But stop."

Argo left Raphael's mind, and he could see again. He heard two fast shots from behind him and, to his surprise, two unfortunate soldiers lay dead in front of him, and the Mosul wedge had changed direction, and was seeking escape another way. He turned and found an impassive Slide, with a smoking pistol in each hand, and a cheroot in the corner of his mouth. "I thought I was dead there."

"Bad time for communication?"

Raphael nodded, catching his breath. "My thought exactly."

"Argo?"

"Right."

"What did he have to say?"

Raphael snapped back to the task at hand. "Perdu needs all the manpower he can get to move the gun, and he needs rope."

Slide nodded. "I'm on it."

He was already shouting and waving to Falconetti. "We need to start wrangling those slaves to the gun. Perdu wants it moved."

## CORDELIA

The armored car was of a type that Cordelia had never seen before, low with wide, fat heavy tires, and a narrow slit for a windshield. Its reinforced sides were painted a dull slate-gray, without sign or insignia. The machine looked powerful, but it was traveling much more slowly than Cordelia would have expected, and swerving from side to side as though the driver were drunk or incapacitated.

"If it doesn't stop, it's going to wreck my Benz." Sera, who had been standing with Cordelia by the Benz, started to back away, but Cordelia waved her back.

"Help me move Lime, she may be a traitorous bitch, but even she doesn't deserve to go under the wheels. Also we may need her again."

Jesamine also moved to help. She and Sera took Lime's trembling arms, Cordelia took her legs, and they half carried, half dragged her residually twitching form to the side of the road. Madden looked quickly round. "You need help?"

Cordelia shook her head. "Deploy the men. We have no idea what to expect from this thing."

Madden and Jacques spread the gunmen into a half circle. Although some still wore enemy uniforms, no deception was intended. They were simply ready to shoot down anything that might emerge from any of the doors of the armored car. Cordelia watched as the car began to slow. At least it was not going to try to smash its way through the roadblock, which would thwart all plans so far formulated, but whoever was driving it still did not seem in anything like total control. The armored car was slowing, but not enough to bring it to a stop before it reached the Benz. It rolled for the final few feet, before nosing into Sera's automobile, hard enough to leave a dent in the previously immaculate paneling before finally halting.

For long, anticlimactic seconds, absolutely nothing happened. No sound came from the armored car except the idling engine, and no doors opened. Madden looked at Cordelia, who could only shrug. She had no better idea of what to do next than he did. Then Harriet Lime jerked and the voice of the Twins spoke through her.

*"We can't get out."*

*"We can't open the door and we can't get out."*

Madden approached the armored car, shotgun leveled, ready for anything. "Want me to try the door?"

Cordelia nodded. "But be very, very careful. This really could be a trap."

Gingerly, Madden advanced on what he assumed was the driver's side door. Jacques and another gunman covered him from a few paces back. What passed for a window was only another narrow slit, so there was no way to see in, but a functional-looking lever looked like an exterior door handle. Shifting his shotgun to one hand, he tentatively gripped the handle. "I sure as shit hope this isn't wired to a bomb. It would be an embarrassing way to go out." He eased it down a tad, half expecting it to be locked or otherwise secured. "Of course, if it is booby trapped, we won't know a fucking thing about it."

The handle yielded to pressure, and Madden tossed caution to the winds and pushed it all the way down, but then leaped back like a cat as the door swung open, and a corpse in a blood-soaked Zhaithan tunic toppled out and flopped on the road, adding more blood to what was already there. Satisfied that the corpse was dead, Madden paid it no more mind. Tersely gesturing for his backup to move into second position, and protecting himself with training and long experience, Madden pushed his shotgun in the open door, before peering inside. "Holy fuck!"

Madden withdrew from the car and took a step back. "I think you better come and look at all this, Lady Blakeney."

Cordelia did as he asked without question. Madden pointed to the corpse on the ground. "You ever seen anything like that? It's as though the inside of his head exploded."

Cordelia had, of course, seen something exactly like it, but that wasn't the moment to admit it. She had seen the corpse of Borat Omar, the night after Newbury Vale, after she and Slide had interrogated him, and his head had also exploded. The same fluid still seeped from the mouth and ears, and drained from the hollows where the eyes had once been.

"There's four more like that inside. They make quite a stench."

"And the Twins?"

Madden took another step back, and indicated the door, as though making an introduction. First the girl and then the boy scrambled from inside the armored car. The White Twins moved like infants, unsteady and unsure, but, at the same time, totally self-possessed. The early morning light tended to lend an air of unreality, and they looked just like the image that Jeakqual-Ahrach had conjured on the stern of the *Ragnar* in the middle of the Northern Ocean; a white-faced boy and an equally pallid girl, intense three-year-olds, identical, and possibly albino, with fine, doll-like hair, those huge, unnerving eyes, and pointed, porcelain teeth. When Cordelia had seen them in the vision, their tiny Zhaithan cowls had been black. Now, on the road near Amiens, they would have been white, except the fabric was splashed with blood like butchers' aprons. They first inspected the dead driver, and then they raised their damp, pale blue eyes to Cordelia. On the *Ragnar,* they had radiated a malign hatred, but this had been replaced by sinister trust.

*"They wouldn't let us out."*

*"They wouldn't let us out. So we made their head's go goopy."*

Cordelia took a step back and whispered under her breath. "So it's you that do the sophisticated mindfuck."

Cordelia sensed Sera beside her even before she whispered. "What's the sophisticated mindfuck?"

"It's a term that Slide once used for what we see here."

*"Please take us away from here."*

*"Please take us away from here."*

The Twins were now staring intently at Cordelia, but she was still able to sense the gun in Sera's hand, and how she was imperceptibly raising it. She dropped a fast hand to Sera's wrist. "Think of daisies and butterflies, something nice, and very quickly. They may be able to read your intentions."

"We have to . . ."

"No, we don't. I gave them my word and I intend to keep it." She glanced down at the corpse on the road. "If for no other reason than I don't want to end up like him."

"So what are you going to do?"

Before Cordelia could answer, Harriet Lime had risen to her feet. She moved like a zombie, trembling, and apparently attempting to speak. The Twins heads snapped round faster than Madden could raise his shotgun. *"Mother!"*

Lime's lips moved, but the voice was that of Jeakqual-Ahrach. *"I do not suffer deceit gladly, or accept betrayal as pragmatism."*

Madden was fast, but the Twins were faster. His shotgun blast struck Harriet Lime in the chest, but blood and brains were already gushing from her eyes. All three, though, were too late. The voice and power of Jeakqual-Ahrach was already in Cordelia's head."

*"I DO NOT SUFFER DECEIT GLADLY!"*


## ARGO

"On the count of three . . ."

Every man or woman who wasn't directly engaging the Mosul had streamed across the construction site, a ragtag horde, ready to move the Great Paris Gun. Some had come willingly and others had been threatened at gunpoint. Some saw the destruction of the gun as an act of historic revenge, others were only there because the whips of the labor camp overseers, who Falconetti had bribed or threatened to the cause, were at their backs. Ropes had been found and ropes had been brought, and they had been attached to every part of the gun carriage, first by Perdu's crew, and then by increasing numbers of willing hands. Human muscle wasn't the only power being put to use. A half dozen cars and trucks had been secured to the Paris Gun, and their motors and traction would also be employed to overcome the huge artillery piece's monstrous inertia. When all the ropes were in place, Argo could imagine how, from the air, it must look like some giant spider had attached its web to the lower areas of the gun.

"One, two, three . . . now heave!"

The explosives were packed inside the barrel, and Calq and Riffi were riding the muzzle, putting the finishing touches to the cement plug. All else was ready. The gun just had to move. No one wanted to believe that they had come so far, and done so much, only to be defeated by the leviathan's incalculable weight. Calq and Riffi paused as the massed horde prepared to take the strain, looking anxiously down at the men who levered with wooden planks, struggling to turn the immense steel wheels. A mass groan went up, ropes stretched, overseers yelled curses, muscles strained, engines howled, wheels spun in the dirt, feet scrabbled to find purchase, but the gun did not move. It remained motionless in the face of all the concerted effort. A tow chain snapped, and one of the trucks that had brought them from Paris jumped forward, out of control, until its driver was able to brake. Men straightened and looked round. Even with so many of them, the gun remained immobile.

Old Temps climbed up on the gun carriage. "Okay, let's try it again. One, two, three . . . heave!"

Some sporadic firing continued around the slave laborers' compound. A squad of Zhaithan had holed up in one of the empty huts, and seemed prepared to shoot it out with the Parisians until the bitter end, but, for the most part, the battle was over. It might be said that the small army from Paris had won the day, but, if the Paris Gun could not be brought to the pyramid, and all the strange new modifications destroyed, no victory could be claimed. Men and women squared their shoulders, spat on their hands and, on Perdu's command, tried again. They grunted and strained, and for a moment, they almost felt an illusion of the gun moving, but it didn't.

Old Temps was shouting, refusing to give up. "Third time! Third time! Don't give up! One, two, three . . . heave!"

Argo closed his eyes and pulled. A man near him was chanting. "Come on, come on, come on."

Another was rhythmically grunting. "Move you bastard. Move you bastard."

And just as defeat seemed inevitable, a loud clank was followed by an extended metallic groan, and the bastard moved. The Paris Gun gave up its inertia and lurched forward. Some had been leaning so hard into the ropes that they fell when the gun moved. It seemed to take on a life of its own and started gathering speed. Workers and gunmen were running, pulling, cheering, more fell over as they tried to keep up. The gun was rolling straight at the pyramid and would only stop when it plowed into the dirt at its base, and Old Temps Perdu would test his theories of demolition physics.

Argo was hauling and cheering, just like all those around him, but then a terrible voice invaded his head, blotting out everything.

*"I DO NOT SUFFER DECEIT GLADLY!"*

## THE FOUR

*"I DO NOT SUFFER DECEIT GLADLY!"*

*The Four found themselves facing Jeakqual-Ahrach in a place of Jeakqual-Ahrach's creating: a towering peak of black volcanic rock somewhere in a vision of hell, above the inevitable fires of Ignir and Aksura burning below like the lava seas of some primeval planet. The Four had been spread out on the earthly battlefield, but now they were grouped together in this sulphurous place over which Jeakqual-Ahrach, with a crown of blood-gold roses, presided from a diamond throne that shimmered with rainbows of refraction that cut like razor-edged, infinite swords, and slashed through what remained of The Four's power as it was wafted from them by foul and ripping winds that cried with the moans of a million heretics. The Four were trained in the combat space of the Other Place, but this was something else. Everywhere they looked, they were inside a total construct of their archenemy.*

*"Did you really think you could negate all my efforts and bring me low while I was in the Sleep of Youth?"*

*The Four did not believe an answer was required. Mothmen rolled in distant turbulence and batwing things rode the high currents of the enclosing vortex. The manifestations of Jeakqual-Ahrach's towering rage were all-encompassing and wholly inventive. The Four were clearly intended to marvel and become awed before they finally suffered whatever fate she intended should befall them.*

*"You think you turned my children against me, but did you ask yourselves how long they would remain turned?"*

*The Four did not believe an answer was required to that question either, but seemingly the White Twins did. Out of nowhere, they appeared in a pool of pure*

*light between Jeakqual-Ahrach and The Four, and the blades of the diamond
throne could not penetrate the bright aura around them.*

"We have turned against you, mother."

"We have turned against you, mother, because you meant to hurt us."

"We have turned against you, mother, because you meant to kill us."

Jeakqual-Ahrach looked past the Twins, concentrating on The Four. "Would
you care to watch while I strip the overweening infants of their power?"

Cordelia pulled out of the fear and awe. She knew that was what Jeakqual-
Ahrach wanted, and thus she would fight it. "Do we have a choice?"

"Recovered some of your former insolence, Cordelia Blakeney? The aristocrat
who can joke in the face of death and worse? Will you play your part to the end?"

"I merely asked if we had a choice."

Jeakqual-Ahrach's whole construct pulsed crimson as Cordelia goaded her,
and this gave the White Twins the instant they sought. A line of light extended
from the Twins to Jeakqual-Ahrach, and also back to The Four, and then on behind them. Cordelia knew what she had to do. She had to shift The Four into combat mode. Maybe this was Jeakqual-Ahrach's construct, but that was no reason to
forget their training. "Behind me, people. Just as always."

Jeakqual-Ahrach laughed. "There's no place to hide in organization."

Argo, Jesamine, and Raphael moved to their accustomed positions. The Twins
line of light was spreading horizontally. The little monsters were up to something.
Their light was beginning to crush the volcanic rock. The role of The Four was to
keep Jeakqual-Ahrach angry and distracted, and Cordelia had a knack for this.
"Will you look at this place? The woman is insane."

Jeakqual-Ahrach snarled. "You think me insane?"

"This is what she'd do to another dimension."

Red flame screamed around them and Cordelia used it as cover to ask a question of Raphael. "Do you have the backdoor?"

"I do."

"What's happening behind us?"

"The path goes back to a logical horizon, and then to infinity, and, wait a
minute, something's coming down it."

"What?"

"White children."

"What?"

"I think the Twins must have summoned them. They are like the Twins, only incomplete and imperfect."

Cordelia projected, "Like the ones in Paris."

The Boy Twin gazed back at The Four. "They are our brothers and sisters. The ones who came before us, and were not right. The ones she cast away."

Cordelia projected again. "The breeding program."

Raphael shushed her. "There are hundreds of them. The path of light has become a bridge."

Hundreds of pale-faced children, some resembling the White Twins, but others twisted and deformed, swarmed over the bridge. A number of toy bears, ducks, pandas, parrots, other animals, moved with them, perhaps fragments of bad memory used as disguises. They were all coming for Jeakqual-Ahrach, but they would pass through The Four before they reached her.

Raphael warned, "They will pass through us. Let them do that. Don't resist."

Finally Jeakqual-Ahrach noticed what was happening. "The rejects dare to approach ME?"

The horde of white children continued to come ahead.

"Go back to the sewers to which I consigned you."

The white children kept on coming.

"Go back!"

The white children and the toys kept on coming.

"Stop!"

Jeakqual-Ahrach's anger erupted to such a pitch that it threatened her own construct. The flow of children faltered, but then moved on again remorselessly. Venomous waves of flame and fury crashed around the diamond throne, as Jeakqual-Ahrach screamed.

"STOP!"

The distant Mothmen moved in protectively, but the Girl Twin raised a hand and the Mothmen halted. The Four experienced the unnerving sensation of having the procession of white children pass through and around them. Small, seething minds brushed against theirs with a touch like bitter feathers. They surged around the White Twins and closed on Jeakqual-Ahrach. For the very first time in their experience, fear suffused the woman's aura.

"Keep away from me, you misbegotten little fiends."

But the white children simply surged around her, crawling up onto her diamond throne. Fear was disintegrating the whole construct as they engulfed her, drowning her, even muffling her screams.

"No! No! No! No! No! No! No! No! No! No!"

The last image that The Four retained was that of Jeakqual-Ahrach's left arm in a long velvet glove, rings on the fabric fingers, reaching up and clawing for salvation that was not ever going to materialize, and then being pulled down to vanish into the surging sea of terrible, magickal infants.

## ARGO

Argo had no idea how he had returned to the terrestrial world from Jeakqual-Ahrach's collapsing construct. Maybe, as it failed, with no creator to control it, the thing had simply let him go. All he knew was that he was on the ground, on his knees, disoriented, and with his head painfully spinning, not far from where the Great Paris Gun had crashed into the base of the pyramid, slewed sideways off its rails, and wound up canted over to one side, with its wheels spinning, and with avalanches of dirt sliding down beside it from the sloping south face of the pyramid. It was the first time that Argo had been close enough to see the way the surfaces of the massive geometric figure were being progressively covered by a mosaic pattern of the mysterious black spheres and how the overall design was forming into one huge unreadable ideogram on each surface, from an alphabet so alien to him that it might have been from another planet.

Argo, however, found he had no time to dwell on the disposition of the gun, the meaning or purpose of the patterns, and certainly not what had just befallen him in the private realm of Jeakqual-Ahrach. He'd hardly had time to recover his earthly balance when he saw Penhaligon running towards him, waving his arms, and generally acting wholly out of character for the combat-scarred Ranger. "Major Argo, we gotta run, we gotta get the fuck out of here."

Argo didn't immediately react. He stood bemused. "What are you talking about?"

Penhaligon was shaking his head, and even attempting to pull Argo along with him. "When the gun hit the pyramid, some weird shit came out of there like an evil wind. We all felt it, but Old Temps went fucking crazy."

Argo wondered what his own physicality had been doing when the gun hit the pyramid. "What do you mean, fucking crazy?"

"He starts saying he doesn't trust the electric detonators, and then he tells everyone that they should get out of there, because he's going to blow up the gun by hand. And blow himself up along with it. He says it's a fitting end, riding the back of the biggest bomb ever made by man. He starts talking this lunatic shit about it's his bomb, and he don't want to be around when they build a bigger one."

"He means it?"

"I left him sitting astride the barrel of the gun with an old flintlock pistol rigged to the fuse, and him saying that we should fuck off because he wasn't going to wait too long."

Argo wasn't about to let Old Temps blow himself up. Penhaligon might think Perdu had gone insane, but Argo knew it had to be the pyramid getting to him. "I've got to talk to him."

Penhaligon was shaking his head like a maniac. The pyramid was also getting to him. "There's no talking to Perdu, Major. He just rubs at those scars on his face and goes right on with what he's doing. And I figure he's about finished doing it by now. So, begging your pardon, Major, but you can do what you like, because I'm out of here."

Argo took a last look at the gun half buried in the pyramid, and the small figure of Old Temps Perdu squatting above the breech, and he allowed himself to be persuaded. He and Penhaligon ran maybe twenty paces and then, behind them, and at a distance, they heard Old Temps Perdu give a last triumphant shout. "Fuck you all, you bastards. You should all hope to live so long!"

Argo and the Ranger hit the ground as one. They lay flat and covered their heads with their arms.

No two accounts of the actual explosion at the Pyramid of Amiens were ever the same. Some described how the barrel of the Great Paris Gun had blown up like a balloon before it burst, but Argo had always thought this was hallucination, or pure tall-tale embroidery. Others talked about a blossoming fireball that had risen from the pyramid, hanging momentarily in the air like a second sun before collapsing into a falling pillar of roiling black smoke that was immediately followed by a monumental blast and shock wave that was all that Old Temps Perdu could ever have desired. Argo found the second version of the story a great deal more plausible, especially when told by those at a safe distance. Those like him and Penhaligon, though, who been relatively close to Perdu's last exit, had really no story to tell. They had simply lain in fear, wishing they could will themselves deeper into the protective ground, as heat swept over them, the shock tossed their helpless bodies clear into the air, and then, moments later, huge chunks of hot metal from the gun screamed down from above and smashed into the ground all round them.

## CORDELIA

After the explosion, Cordelia had lain prone, not even daring to move as the hail of debris crashed down. She did not want so much as to open her eyes. She could all too easily imagine red hot jagged iron from the exploded gun slamming into her body. When, at last, she gingerly turned her head and looked, the first thing she saw was Yancey Slide holding out a hand to help her to her feet. Smoke still billowed, and small but mainly harmless particles of debris were still dropping with a patter like falling rain, but the worst was over and she had survived. She gripped Slide's gloved hand and allowed him to pull her to her feet. His unholy brace of pistols was holstered, so she could assume that the firefight was over.

"Do you have any idea how I got here?"

Slide stared down at her from under the brim of his hat. "What do you mean?"

Cordelia slowly turned, taking in a landscape of near-total ruin and devastation. The gun was in pieces, with its shrapnel spread over a couple of acres, and half the pyramid was gone. The flat terrain of the construction site was littered with the very pieces of iron that she had so feared. A huge crater had been gouged out of the nearest side of the pyramid by the explosion, and the pointed apex had collapsed into it. Even as she watched, the process of collapse was still continuing. Tons of dirt and rock were shifting, sliding, and falling away, and made her think of the slow organic death throes of some huge living thing. Although dwarfed by the ruin of the pyramid, the whole of the area presented a grim spectacle of havoc. She saw overturned vehicles, destroyed fences, and barrack huts on fire. At first, she thought the entire field was littered with bodies, but then some previously prone figures began rising to their feet, and she realized that, like her, they had been protecting themselves against the explosion, but now thought it was safe to stand. When the survivors were up, however, many remained who actually were dead or dying, and by far the majority were Mosul and Zhaithan. The numbers of the dead were nothing in comparison to what she had seen in the aftermath of Newbury Vale, but they were enough to give her pause, and cause her to forget her own confusion.

"Damn."

"Damn indeed. Old Perdu sure made an exit."

"He died in the explosion?"

"Quite deliberately."

Cordelia was quiet for a moment. She looked around the field one more time and then turned back to Slide. She had survived, but she wasn't sure how. "I still don't know how I got here."

A flake of ash landed on the sleeve of Slide's duster, and he brushed it off. "Where do you think you should be?"

Cordelia wasn't sure. "The last thing I recall was being out on the road, and we had just met the White Twins for real, after they had rather unpleasantly eliminated their Zhaithan escort."

"The sophisticated mindfuck?"

Cordelia looked bleakly at Slide. "You already know this story?"

"Some of it."

"You know that Lime channeled Jeakqual-Ahrach, and we were suddenly grabbed up, and all Four of us were taken to her idea of hell?"

"And that Lime was killed by the Twins, and Jeakqual-Ahrach was overwhelmed by the children from her breeding program."

"You've already talked to the others?"

Slide shook his head. "No."

"How do you know all this?"

"I have some fairly unique sources."

"And is Jeakqual-Ahrach dead?"

"Who knows for sure? If she's not physically dead, her powers will be crippled for a very long time, and the failure of this project, and the breeding program, and whatever else she might have had going that we don't know about, is going to create a political firestorm for the Zhaithan, all over the Empire. As to how you got here, I guess you just all fell out of the construct together."

"And the Twins? What about the Twins?"

Slide's face became grave. "I have seen the Twins."

Cordelia didn't like his look. "What's that supposed to mean?"

Slide turned and started walking. "Follow me."

Slide walked swiftly and Cordelia had to trot to keep up. She spotted Argo up ahead; he seemed to be staring at something on the ground. She hurried to him, happy to see him alive and unharmed, but when he looked up at her, and she saw the expression on his face, she stopped. "What?"

Argo pointed to what was on the ground. Cordelia looked down and saw that a blackened piece of the Paris Gun had crashed down, making a small smoking crater, and inside it, she could see a ghastly confusion of bloody organs, tiny white limbs, tattered rags, and the unharmed head of the Girl Twin.

Cordelia shook her head. "Shit . . . no."

"It must have come down right smack on top of them. It crushed them and all of their secrets along with them."

"Do Jesamine and Raphael know about this?"

Argo turned away. "No, but they're coming now." He pointed to where the other two of The Four were making their way across the litter of destruction. They already looked in shock at what they were seeing, and when they joined Argo, Cordelia, and Slide, a long silence ensued that was finally broken by Jesamine. "We never found out what they really were, or how they were created."

"Or how they did what they did."

"Or what they meant about trying to save Jack Kennedy."

Raphael seemed the least affected by the death of the Twins. "I guess if the remains could somehow be taken to London, Windermere's ES Section could maybe do an autopsy."

Jesamine looked at him in surprise. "You really think they'd learn anything?"

"No, but . . ."

Jesamine became more aggressive. "Or do you want the Norse figuring out how to breed White Twins of their own?"

Raphael backed off. "I was just thinking about science. I mean, they had to die anyway."

Jesamine blinked. "What?"

Raphael was confused. "I said they had to die anyway."

"But they saved us from Jeakqual-Ahrach. They changed sides, and came over to the good guys. Why the fuck would you want to kill them after that?"

Raphael looked to Slide for support. "But that was always the plan wasn't it? They may have turned on Jeakqual-Ahrach, but they could just as easily turn on us. They weren't human, they were maybe superior to us, and they had too much power. Hell, they got into our dreams."

Argo joined in. "Not very different from us, really."

Raphael was at a loss. "Tell them, Yancey. The Twins could never have been allowed to survive."

Slide shook his head. "I'm keeping out of this."

For once, Cordelia could see both sides of the argument. The White Twins would have been incredibly dangerous even as friends, but to make that a reason to exterminate them was nothing short of Zhaithan thinking. The best thing she could do was to end the debate. The Twins were dead. It was academic. "I think they should be buried right away. Get the poor little bastards off the ground and into it. Right here, in an unmarked grave."

Slide adjusted his hat. "But some may not want to touch them."

Jesamine frowned. "What's that supposed to mean?"

But Slide didn't answer. He was staring off into the distance. Over by the still-burning barracks, Sera Falconetti's black Benz, with a fresh dent in the door, was steering its way through the wreckage. As soon as the car came to a halt, a white-faced Sera Falconetti jumped from it. "What happened? You, Jesamine, the Twins, you all vanished from the car, right into thin air. I thought I'd lost my mind, and even Madden turned pale."

Cordelia shook her head. "I think Jeakqual-Ahrach may be the only one to explain that, and she is now in no position to do so."


## JESAMINE

Damon Falconetti thrust a foaming bottle of Frankish champagne into Jesamine's hands. "Drink deep, girl. It's looted from the Teuton officers' quarters, and you shot two of those bastards."

Jesamine wasn't quite sure how to react to that, but she knew it was well intended so, as instructed, she drank deep and her nose filled with bubbles. Bottles were being passed, and for the moment, the White Twins had been forgotten, as the victory over a hated conqueror was being celebrated. Damon Falconetti was drunk and waxing grandiose for the future. "This, my beautiful Major, is only the start. Today, the people of Paris, and all of you who fought this fight, have started what could turn into a full-scale Frankish uprising. Who knows?" He made a sweeping gesture to the east, south, and west. "There's the whole stinking Mosul Empire out there, rotting from within and ready to fall. Hispania and the cities of Italia and the Hellenes, and the Transylvanians, then all the way down into Africa; they could all follow. Who knows where it all might end? You ever dream of returning to Africa, beautiful Major Jesamine?"

Jesamine did not think too much about returning to Africa, but earlier there had been much discussion of returning somewhere. Everyone was well aware that they could not linger. As soon as word spread, the Mosul would be coming in force to see what had happened to their gun and their pyramid. The Parisians were going back to Paris, and Jesamine had assumed that the Rangers and The Four would go with them, to live the outlaw life until they could somehow be extracted, but then Gideon Windermere had informed them that the Black Airship was on its way to bring out the Rangers, The Four, Yancey Slide, and himself. The dirigible was taking the more dangerous and direct daylight course from Shoreham by Sea, and would not be long in coming. On hearing this, Jesamine had become adamant. She was not going back to London. As far as she was concerned, London was the city that had killed Jack Kennedy, and she would join the Falconettis, if they would have her, before she returned there. The rest of The Four could do what the hell they liked, but she was staying put. She had expected her resolve would be met with an argument, if only from Cordelia, but Cordelia had said nothing. It seemed that her infatuation with both the city and Gideon Windermere had cooled to nothing after her kidnap, and all the duplicity that had surrounded it. In fact, the only response her outburst had received was extreme amusement on the part of Windermere.

"Oh my dear, London is the last place you are going. The fallout from this expedition will be monumental and it would be better if you were someplace else. Also the Crom fundamentalists hold you suspect in the assassination, and claim you killed Jack to force the NU into war with the Mosul. The conspiracy theories are flying and you'd best be away from them, too."

Slide sighed. "Whenever poor Jack is killed, it's never resolved."

Jesamine pretended that she hadn't heard him. "But we can't fly across the Northern Ocean in an airship, can we, even the Black Airship?"

Slide now smiled. "We have the good fortune that, right now, the ironclad *HMS Constellation* is steaming through the Straits of Dover to make a rendezvous with the Black Airship in the English Channel. The *Constellation* is even dropping a few shells on Boulogne and the Mosul shore defenses, just to add to the confusion. We will be set down on the ship, and it will take us home."

Jesamine did not quite think of Albany as home, but it was the best news she had received in a long time. She must have a leave-of-absence coming from The Four, and her honorary position in the Rangers, and that meant she could journey into the interior, back to the protection of the Ohio, to hide in the warmth of their lodges, and lick her wounds.

After Slide's announcement, nothing remained to do except to say boisterous good-byes and emotional farewells to the various members of the Falconetti Family as they made ready to pull out. Then they had heard the sound of engines, and everyone turned. The Black Airship was coming in low, and under power. The huge phallic cigar flew majestically right above the broken ruins of the pyramid, and it was a breath-stopping vision that Jesamine knew she would never forget. Yancey Slide noticed her awe and smiled. "You've learned to enjoy flying, haven't you, Major Jesamine?"

Jesamine nodded. "When you get up high it somehow seems very different."

Slide winked. "And the higher you get, the more different it looks. Believe me."